DAYS OF DEATH AND DARKNESS

DAYS OF THE APOCALYPSE, # 4

MARK E. FISHER

Extraordinary Tales

Publishing

DAYS OF DEATH AND DARKNESS (DAYS OF THE APOCALYPSE, #4), BY MARK E. FISHER

Extraordinary Tales Publishing, LLC
@ExtraordinaryTalesPublishing.biz
First Extraordinary Tales, LLC edition October 2023
Copyright © 2023 by Mark E. Fisher

Print Book ISBN: 978-1-950235-19-3
eBook ISBN: 978-1-950235-20-9

Cover art purchased from 123rf.com
Cover design and eBook formatting by Booknook.biz
Editing by Deirdre Lockhart of Brilliant Cut Editing
Fonts from fontbundles.com

To learn where to buy this book or for more information about this and the author's other books visit: MarkFisherAuthor.com

Library of Congress Cataloging-in-Publication Data:
Fisher, Mark E.
Days of Death and Darkness (Days of the Apocalypse, #4) / Mark E. Fisher 1st ed.

Printed in the United States of America

CONTENTS

CAST OF CHARACTERS

THE PRINCIPALS

* Brianna—Now sixteen-years-old, she was orphaned when a bear killed her parents shortly after the vanishing. Caleb and Tanya have made her their adopted daughter.
* Caleb Turner—Brother to Dylan and Chelsea and a Minneapolis native, Caleb recently married Tanya Baranov. They now reside in Shetek State Park in southern Minnesota.
* Chelsea Turner—Sister to Dylan and Caleb, she's the daughter of Adam Turner, head of the Ministry of Truth. Chelsea is stuck with Fabio Caruso and Enzo Rivera on the island of Palma de Mallorca, Spain, waiting for engine parts for their trawler.
* Dylan Turner—Brother to Chelsea and Caleb, Dylan is a member of the Nazarene Friends, a group fighting the Antichrist. He's in love with Margot Durand.
* Margot Durand—A Belgian woman whom God directed to paint visions of the future. After the Nazarene Friends freed her from a death camp, Margot joined Dylan and her rescuers at the Kronberg Mountain resort.
* Tanya Baranov—A Chicago resident and granddaughter of the previously raptured Uri Baranov, a famous author. She is now married to Caleb.

THE NAZARENE FRIENDS

* Pasqual Berger—Founder of the Nazarene Friends, some call him their pastor.
* Danielle DuBois—Rescued from Marseille, she's now a good friend of Victor.
* Jakob and Emma Huber—A Swiss farm couple joining the Nazarene Friends at the Kronberg Mountain resort.
* René LeClerc—A former spy, René is the unofficial leader of the Nazarene Friends.
* Victor Marceau—The group's tech wizard and guitar player.

THE UNITUM IMPERIUM

* Adam Turner—Former CEO and founder of Turner Enterprises, he's father to Caleb, Dylan, and Chelsea. He heads the Ministry of Truth, below whom is the feared Central Security Agency its Truth Squads.
* Davato—The Antichrist and ruler of the Unitum Imperium, also called the Imperator, the man of lawlessness, the son of destruction, and the beast. He is part of an unholy trinity, including Satan and the Prophet.
* Gaston Soucy—Head of the Ministry of Charity.
* General Eric Hofmann—Head of the Ministry of Peace and Supreme Commander of all Unitum Imperium forces.
* Grady Wilson—A Jew from New York City who served on the Raleigh-Burke class destroyer, the USS *Avenger*, Chaim (Cam) Weinberg assumed the identity of Grady Wilson, Chaim's deceased lieutenant. He's now Davato's personal secretary.
* Jack Anderson—Governor of Australasia.
* Sebastien Rey, the Prophet—Green-eyed false prophet sent to corrupt the message of God, part of the unholy trinity of Satan.
* Umberto Gómez Rodriguez—Governor of South America.

THE ISRAELIS

* Amos Bernstein—Leader of the Jericho Faction, a group of Jewish rebels fighting the Unitum Imperium.
* Ariel Geller, aka Big Matza—Head of a large Israeli black-market operation helping refugees escape Unitum Imperium tyranny.
* Baruch Abramovich—Leader of the Great Assembly, a group of 144,000 men chosen by God to bring the message of Christ to all who would believe during the Tribulation. Dylan, Margot, and Chelsea once released him from a Unitum Imperium prison. He is bringing refugees to Sela, a biblical rock city in Jordan.
* David Benjamin—Jewish friend of Baruch Abramovich and self-appointed head of Baruch's security.
* Menachem, aka Falafel—A new, inexperienced runner for Ariel.
* Noah Blum, aka Kishke—A twenty-one-year-old runner for Ariel.
* Yitzhak, aka Latke—One of Ariel's runners.

THE FREEZER TRAWLER

* Enzo Rivera—An Italian Christian who's taking passage with Chelsea on the *Am Albahr*.
* Fabio Caruso—Untrustworthy Jewish sea captain of the *Am Albahr*, a freezer trawler out of Haifa, Israel.

THE AMERICANS

Camp David

* William Cole—President of the United States, residing at Camp David after Chinese nukes destroyed the Washington DC.

Cheyenne Mountain Space Force, Colorado

* Lena Chang—A Christian first lieutenant, an airplane mechanic, and close friend of Daniel Price.
* Chase Cooper—A Christian first lieutenant, airplane mechanic, and electrician.
* Daniel Price—A major, a pilot, and the leader of the Cheyenne Mountain Christians.
* Frank Scott—The atheist colonel in charge of Cheyenne Mountain, who opposes the Christians under his command.
* Amber Bright—A Christian first lieutenant and airplane pilot.
* Robert Williams—A Christian first lieutenant with radar and airplane weaponry experience.
* Sam Smith—A Christian second lieutenant with training on airplane weaponry.

Currie, Minnesota

* Henry Adams—A preacher at the church in Currie, Minnesota.
* Jack and Linda May Manson—Members of the Currie church.

Custer, South Dakota

* Marty and Ella Eastwood—Friends of Caleb, Tanya, Andy, and Brianna and members of the Custer church.

PREFACE

The signs of the end mount daily, and darkness, like some raging, black inferno, spreads across the country and the world at an accelerating pace. The prophets predicted it all, and mankind—through its sinful, unrepentant thoughts, words, and deeds—fairly begs for judgment.

The zeal to advance godless ideologies across the globe has unleashed a spirit of anarchy, chaos, and lawlessness, hurtling cultures toward a breaking point.

The rights of criminals now supersede those of victims.

The media, corrupt in every respect, either looks the other way or celebrates and promotes every kind of evil.

Mass shootings occur almost weekly. And they never learn it's not the gun that kills its victims but the spiritual darkness possessing the shooter that pulls the trigger.

Either churches abandon the Bible and the Gospel, embracing social justice; woke ideology; a message of health, wealth, and prosperity; and the teachings of an atheistic culture (2 Peter 2:1–3; Jude 1–4). Or they bury their heads in Scripture, and, like the proverbial frog, they ignore the danger boiling up around them.

Public schools now suppress the rights of parents while encouraging sexual immorality. They distort the nation's past, teaching students to despise their heritage and hate their country. In league with the medical establishment, they promote gender confusion, gender-altering therapy, and genital-mutilation surgery for children too young to understand the ramifications.

Governments at all levels have become lawless, tirelessly working to ensure the murder of the unborn, stirring the fires of racial unrest, promoting immorality, embracing godless ideologies, suppressing peoples' rights, and advancing totalitarian agendas. Whatever is good and right and honorable—nearly every government now works against such things.

All have turned their backs on God, denying he exists, spurning his teachings, rejecting his commandments and his every wish for humanity (Psalm 14:2–3). They have purged any mention of his name from all public discourse. And they mock all who believe in the Son whom God sent to save them (2 Peter 3:3).

Man-made events are converging, lining up with biblical prophecy so fast, it's hard to keep up:

* The push for consolidated power and one-world government ruled by elites.
* The beginnings of a digital currency, allowing governments to track and control a person's every movement so they can dictate what we can and cannot buy and sell.
* The suppression of any voice that dares pit truth against falsehood.
* The elimination of borders, and the destruction of America, a country nowhere found in the biblical end-times prophecies.

It's as if the world is a dry savannah and a consuming fire rages unchecked toward the horizon.

It's as if Satan has run rampant, seeking to devour all whose faith is not firmly grounded in Christ (1 Peter 5:8).

It's as if Isaiah 5:18 & 20 (NLT) was written for the age in which we live:

> What sorrow for those who drag their sins behind them
> with ropes made of lies, who drag wickedness behind
> them like a cart! . . . What sorrow for those who say that

evil is good and good is evil, that dark is light and light is
dark, that bitter is sweet and sweet is bitter.

Indeed! Woe to those who promote the teachings of demons, the
twisted ideologies of today's culture inspired by the Prince of Darkness
himself (1 Timothy 4:1). Can God's judgment on the world not be far
off?

Across the planet, brutal tyrants oppress their peoples and wage war
against hapless neighbors.

The preceding events are mostly man-made. And God, being
omniscient and knowing what's to come, predicted them through his
prophets.

But it's not man, alone, who's authoring the signs of the end. God
himself has foreshadowed what's to come by sending plague and famine
and by increasing the number and severity of earthquakes.

It all completes what Jesus warned us about in Matthew 24:6–8
(HCSB):

> You are going to hear of wars and rumors of wars. See
> that you are not alarmed, because these things must take
> place, but the end is not yet. For nation will rise up against
> nation, and kingdom against kingdom. There will be
> famines and earthquakes in various places. All these
> events are the beginning of birth pains.

The world has flipped upside down, and everywhere we turn, the
stage is set for the end, leading us closer to the Rapture, the rule of the
Antichrist, and God's judgment on a sinful world.

Meanwhile, Jesus watches and waits for the moment he can take his
people home. We hear this in 1 Corinthians 15:51–52 and in 1
Thessalonians 4:16–18 (NLT), below:

> For the Lord himself will come down from heaven with

a commanding shout, with the voice of the archangel, and with the trumpet call of God. First, the believers who have died will rise from their graves. Then, together with them, we who are still alive and remain on the earth will be caught up in the clouds to meet the Lord in the air. Then we will be with the Lord forever. So encourage each other with these words.

Thus, after heeding the signs of the times, this author decided it was time to tell the biblical story surrounding the end, updating it for the troubled age in which we live.

In Revelation 21:8 (NLT), the apostle John begins a warning with one word, here italicized: "But *cowards* . . . their fate is in the fiery lake of burning sulfur. This is the second death." If by "cowards", John includes Christians who are too afraid to speak truth against the Satan-inspired evil ideologies and madness now infecting our world or who shrink from warning others, in love, about the judgment to come, then we should tremble, fall down on our knees, and find motivation to act.

Those who understand what's coming should also take heed from Ezekiel 33:6 (HCSB):

But if the watchman sees the enemy coming and doesn't sound the alarm to warn the people, he is responsible for their captivity. They will die in their sins, but I will hold the watchman responsible for their deaths.

Throughout this series, I have tried to be one of the watchmen on the wall, staying true, as much as is humanly possible in a work of fiction, to the biblical prophecies from the books of Revelation, Matthew, Ezekiel, Daniel, Joel, and others. My hope is that this might inspire Christians to warn others, but also to bring the reader comfort and certainty. For Scripture assures us that all whose names are written in the Book of Life will escape the final wrath to come (Revelation 3:10; 1 Thessalonians 9:10). God will not punish those who are his own for the sins of those who reject and despise him.

They say the Tribulation casts its shadow before it. That dark cloud surely falls upon our world today. Though we might have to live through some troubling times of persecution, chaos, and anarchy before the Rapture, we can only pray that such times are brief.

But for those who embrace the doctrines of demons, who spurn the King of Kings and Lord of Lords, Jesus gives this warning in Matthew 24:21–22 (HCSB):

> "For at that time there will be a great tribulation, the kind that hasn't taken place from the beginning of the world until now and never will again! Unless those days were limited, no one would survive. But those days will be limited because of the elect."

During the Tribulation, there will be time to join the elect, yet how the latecomer will regret such a tardy decision!

For those who persist in rebelling against God, let Jesus's words and these books be a warning, a call to repentance, and a possible lifeline of escape.

We are all temporal, earthly beings, destined for the dust. At the same time, we are immortal creatures, headed for either eternal bliss or eternal destruction. And someday, one of two events will occur:

We will die.

Or the end times will come crashing down upon us.

So take heed. No one wants to live through the seven terrible years of the Tribulation.

Instead, take refuge in the Son God sent to lead us into the best of all possible worlds, a blessed kingdom where God will love his people, they will love him, and he will live with them forever.

Mark E. Fisher
Rochester, Minnesota
June 2023

NEWSLETTER INVITATION #1

Subscribe to Mark's Newsletter.

Keep abreast of new releases & book news.

The shadow of the Tribulation already darkens our world. Know what's to come, stay true to the faith, and seek refuge in Christ.

Subscribe to Mark's newsletter and receive two free gifts:

1. 10 Reasons Why the End Times Could Come Tomorrow.
2. How the Green Agenda Prepares the Way for Earth Worship and the Antichrist.

Go to: www.MarkFisherAuthor.com/newsletter

THE FIFTH YEAR

~

DARKNESS
AND
DEMONS

Revelation 8:13 (HCSB): *I looked again and heard an eagle flying high overhead, crying out in a loud voice, "Woe! Woe! Woe to those who live on the earth, because of the remaining trumpet blasts that the three angels are about to sound!"*

CHAPTER 1
CHELSEA

Daniel 12:1b (HCSB): *There will be a time of distress such as never has occurred since nations came into being until that time. But at that time all your people who are found written in the book will escape.*

Palma de Mallorca, Spain – August, Year 5

The world is ending, and here I sit at the end of this lonely breakwater, atop a piece of someone's dock washed up by the tsunami, gripped by doubt, fear, and guilt.

Above me, this anemic excuse of a sun sheds a cold, pale light on my shivering legs. Below me, waves pound the rocks and shoot up spray. Further out, imprisoned in a raft of rotting kelp, the bloated carcasses of tuna and porpoises bob in the waves. Did the lava bombardments get them? Poor creatures, they didn't know what hit them.

A bit closer, a gull dives for fish. But oh, the wretched bird! She's losing her feathers! I hope she finds something to eat. I wonder where the others have gone. Is anything left of her flock?

She's like me, that gull, frightened and alone, separated from the only family she's ever known, struggling to survive in a world gone mad.

Here at the end of time, I remember how it used to be, and I struggle with despair. Maybe she does too.

I lay back on the wood, hoping to catch a few rays on my sun-starved face, out here at the end of my secret jetty, my refuge at the end of all things. But the late-August wind chills my bare feet soaked with spray. As if that weren't enough, the Ruger LCP Max at my belt pokes my side. Yes, I have to wear that thing everywhere I go now.

After Fabio gave me back my pistol, he gave another one to Enzo. I've never fired mine, but once I waved it, and the ruffians who thought they had easy prey grew pale and fled.

Everywhere in the city, gunshots now echo from the alleys, and corpses lie rotting in the streets. It never used to be that way. Here on the island and even on the continent—we discovered this from our solar phones—order is breaking down. Because of that, the Unitum Imperium has relented. They now allow anyone to buy a weapon.

In the market, I looked for a new blouse—my fraying garment has holes—but they've got nothing decent a girl could wear. In their makeshift stalls, the fish mongers complain of poor catches, the olives are shrunken and bitter, and the bread is dear. And buying a twenty-liter jug of untainted water—you can't believe what it now costs. Only the wine is plentiful. On market day, I see hunger, fear, and suspicion on every face. The people are desperate.

A time traveler from ten years past would never recognize this world.

The planet has flipped upside down, and here I am, worrying about a decent blouse. Is that being selfish or what?

Most days, with nothing to do but wait, I look back on all that's happened since the vanishing and attempt to process it. Was it God, not my stupid choices, who spared me? Am I really part of some divine plan to thwart the Antichrist?

A better, wiser person would have listened when people like my brother Dylan warned me about what was going to happen.

But no, at the first opportunity, when Davato smothered me with his charm and dangled his earthly prizes before me, like a dog before a hunk of meat, I lunged. How easily he dragged me into his world! And how deep and chilling did his evil worm its way into my soul! Even now, I shudder at how close I came to losing myself in the darkness.

No one can comprehend the depths of the evil I witnessed.

Grady and Father faced the same temptations, the same promises of wealth, status, and power, and they surrendered. I fear for them. Once you take the mark of the beast, there is no turning back.

I am convinced that everyone is born with some profound, innate longing for something greater than themselves. For me, I tried filling the vacuum with one cause after another, each promising to change the world for the better. But they were only traps to capture my mind, enslaving me to a series of false ideologies that, in the end, embraced every kind of immorality. In the end, all they got me was Davato.

In New Babylon, I saw it all.

And because ideologies like theirs are based on lies, their practitioners cannot tolerate even the slightest hint of dissent. Even before the vanishing, the elites were guiding us toward totalitarianism and one-world rule. Davato and the Dragon do not want individuals deciding anything for themselves. They and their kind always want central authority, elites whose minds they own telling everyone what to do. And most of the people? They're sheep. They'll sell their eternal futures for earthly bread, security, and "fitting in".

And where do you think that takes you?

To the New Babylon shooting galleries, of course, where people wait in line to fire rifles and pistols at Christian heretics.

And finally, inevitably, it leads to CSA agents and Truth Squads breaking down doors in the dead of night to rip Christians and Jews from their beds before sending them to the death camps and the guillotines. If I'd stayed, that's where I'd be now.

Back before the vanishing, some people thought the craziness was political. But now I see it for what it always was—deeply spiritual. Good versus evil. Right versus wrong. Everything that happened before V-Day was simply preparation for the Antichrist. Davato, the League of Abaddon, and all whose unwitting spirits were captured by every evil ideology—they were behind it all.

My, how I wax philosophical! Has Davato done this to me?

But how they sucked me in! How they led me to work against what God wanted for mankind!

5

I pray every day now, asking forgiveness for my part in what I did. Good grief, I was the personal secretary to the Antichrist, the son of destruction, the one we call the beast.

And yet, somehow, I escaped even Davato. And my father, head of the Ministry of Truth and the Central Security Agency, who told me either I must take the mark of the beast or he would disown me. How he'd changed! Both he and Grady.

And so, one night, after we returned to Davato's second headquarters in Jerusalem, I fled.

What followed nearly destroyed me—endless wandering as a homeless beggar in Tel Aviv. Dirty, desperate, starving, and having lost any privilege I'd ever been born with, I begged for food, slept in parks and alleys, and hid from every uniformed officer and police siren. A garbage bag carried everything I owned. Imagine it, if you can—Chelsea Turner, a bag lady.

It changed me. It left my soul raw and bleeding. It stripped me of all I once was. Maybe that's why I still experience these spells of depression. I was never good at being poor and desperate. What a wretch I was! What a wretch I still am!

If Ariel Geller hadn't rescued me and bought my passage on a trawler to Italy, I don't know what would have become of me.

But then, in the middle of the Mediterranean, my world changed forever—but all for the good. When the three angels flew overhead, how could I not believe Jesus had sent them? They shouted a message not only for the entire world, but for me, personally, one that plunged deep into my soul. How could I not be moved? How could I not realize that, yes, Jesus was real and those heavenly, light-filled beings were his messengers—of either eternal doom or heavenly bliss.

And so I became a Christian.

But Fabio Caruso was our captain, and shortly after that, he revealed his true intentions. Afterward, we escaped the lightning storms, the eruption of Mount Etna to the north and its flaming lava balls, plunging and hissing into the sea, barely missing us. All along Sicily's coast, quaint villages burst into flame. High upon the pine-covered ridges conflagrations roared.

But once again, I was spared, and we sailed to Tangier where Fabio planned his treacherous liaison. If he'd had his way, I'd now be a sex slave in an Arab harem.

Fabio is not to be trusted. And yet, beneath that faithless, wavering surface, I sense a flicker of light struggling to break into the darkness. It's the same for all of us, I guess. Even so, I can't let him fool me again. From moment to moment, I'm not sure he knows his own mind.

But God foiled a promising future as a harem concubine, and we fled Tangier port with a CSA patrol boat close behind.

You know the rest—the asteroid and the resulting tsunami we barely escaped. How casually we speak of such things now, as if any of it were normal. Of course, the tsunami capsized our pursuers and washed Altin, the Albanian, overboard. Altin was never good for Fabio, always feeding the worst in him. I don't miss his absence. Now, as the gangsters say, he swims with the fishes.

So here I am, stranded on the island of Palma off the coast of Spain. Everything, everywhere is breaking down, and the harbormaster keeps promising that the parts to fix our engine will come soon. Only a few months, he said at first. Then a few more months, he promised. And now? Who knows?

How I long to rejoin Dylan, the only family I have left. I have little hope for Caleb. He couldn't have survived when multiple Chinese warheads struck Chicago. All of us were close, and as the world ends, who else should I be with besides Dylan?

Once we fix the trawler, I'll join Bettino at the family villa in Italy. Father has long since abandoned the place, so it's safe. Surely, Bettino knows where my brother is hiding.

But I've read the Book, and I know how it ends. Any hope I put in this life is foolishness. My hope now lies in God's promises of the world to come.

So this, now, dear Jesus, is what I pray—

If I have any part left to play in your divine plan, show it to me and lead me to it.

And if it be your will, let me again join Dylan wherever he's hiding out. Let me make amends with the brother I ignored, abandoned, and too often rejected.

Then, at least, when the end comes, we can face it together.

CHAPTER 2
MORGOTH

Ephesians 6:12 (HCSB): *For our battle is not against flesh and blood, but against the rulers, against the authorities, against the world powers of this darkness, against the spiritual forces of evil in the heavens.*

Currie, Minnesota – August, Year 5

Stomping its feet, shaking its head, and whinnying, Caleb's horse stopped before the barricade on Mill Street. Tonight, even his horse knew something was horribly amiss. They'd just arrived, and all the town was in the street behind makeshift barriers, holding shotguns, rifles, and pistols. Their expressions told him they were steeled for a fight.

In the middle of the street, a pile of logs and empty tables testified to an abandoned bonfire and a late-night picnic that was no longer going to happen.

"What's going on?" he asked Henry Adams, the Currie church pastor.

"About an hour ago, a man staggered in from Marshall. Yesterday, the squaddies attacked their church and killed or captured most everyone. He's been walking all day, and he said the squaddie army was right behind, heading our way."

Caleb sucked in breath. "How many?"

"Good question." His rifle pointing at the ground, Jack Manson stepped beside Henry. "The man passed out shortly after arriving. Before that, he didn't tell us much. But he did say they had a demon with them."

"A demon?" A chill ran down Caleb's spine.

"Yes."

Her face twisted with worry, Tanya came up beside him. "What

9

should we do?"

"Join them in the fight." Caleb shook his M16. "Stand beside them."

A smiling Brianna slapped her Glock 19 in its holster. "I'm ready."

Caleb turned to her. "Young lady, this could get ugly. People will get shot. Are you ready for that?"

"Yes." She held his gaze. "I am."

"Can we ask this guy some questions?" Caleb asked Henry.

"If he's awake. He was wounded and in pretty bad shape."

Then Andy stepped forward. "Last we knew, there were only a few UI goons in Pipestone. Ask him if they came from Sioux Falls. They might be regular CSA. That would be a problem."

Nodding, Caleb followed the pastor to an enclosed staircase beside a secondhand shop. They climbed creaking stairs to a bedroom where a thin-faced man lay on the bed with eyes closed. A bloodstained bandage wrapped his shoulder, and an elderly woman knelt beside him.

"I got some soup in him, and he's sleeping," whispered his white-haired caretaker. "Why don't you come back—?"

But the man opened his eyes, saw his visitors, and waved her away. "It's okay. I'm awake."

"This is Caleb," said Henry. "If you're up to it, we'd like to ask you some questions."

"Sure. Go ahead."

"The men who attacked you," said Caleb, "do you know where they came from? Did they wear uniforms?"

"Yeah. Green-and-white uniforms, and they came from Sioux Falls. They're going town to town, taking prisoners of everyone without the mark who won't worship the beast. Even though it's now legal, they wanted to confiscate our weapons. Maybe because we were Christians. I heard what they demanded from a distance before things got bad."

"How many?"

"Hard to say. Maybe fifty."

"A small army." Henry drew a hand through his hair. "Were they on foot?"

"Yeah, on foot."

10

"Do you know how many prisoners they took?" asked Caleb.

"Maybe twenty. Everyone who was left." Then his glance swept the room, side to side. "It was the demon that was our undoing. We couldn't stand against it."

The color seemed to drain from Henry's face. "W–what?"

"Yeah, it gets inside your head, and you freeze. I wasn't where the action was until late, but I saw what happened to the others. They couldn't fight, couldn't flee, couldn't do anything. They just stood there and let themselves get shot."

No one spoke. Caleb exchanged worried glances with Henry and the woman.

Then the wounded man tried to sit higher and winced. "When I saw what happened to my friends, I hid around the corner. I didn't fight. It was no use." He bunched the coverlet in a fist. "I don't know how many they killed. Men I've come to know well. Women too. When they were done, there wasn't much left of Marshall."

"Are all of those squaddies heading this way?" asked Henry.

"A few left to march the prisoners back to Sioux Falls." The man began to shake, and tears streamed down his face. "But the rest . . . they're on their way here. They'll be here soon."

"That's enough," said the old woman. "He needs more soup and rest."

"Right." Caleb patted the covers over the man's knee. "Thank you."

Back in the street, Henry and Caleb told the others what they'd found.

"So there could be forty or so squaddies on their way?" asked Andy.

"Yeah." Caleb scanned the main street. The townsfolk had pushed dead cars across the road and propped logs beneath the undercarriages, with sandbags filling the gaps. The barricade faced west, blocking the route of anyone coming from Marshall. Torches on the perimeter lit the scene.

Above, the moon shed a wan shade of yellow. Faint pinpricks of stars poked through a smothering black sheet.

"Jack," said Caleb, "what if you put all those torches beyond the barricade so we could see who was coming but they didn't have a clear

11

view of us?"

"Good suggestion. We'll do it." He hurried to move them.

Moments later, the fifteen men, twenty women, and six youth of Currie hunkered down behind their makeshift barricade in the dark.

But the horses would be in the line of fire, and Caleb motioned to Brianna. "Can you help me move the horses down the street, away from the fighting?"

"Sure thing, boss." She saluted, and they each led two mounts to the town's east side, hooves clopping noisily over broken asphalt.

On tonight's trip from Shetek State Park, they had left the wagon at the cabin, each riding their own mount. At the far end of Mill Street, Caleb tied the horses to a fence behind a house. He stroked a mare's nose and turned to his adopted daughter. "This should keep them safe while we—"

A feeling of dread, like the point of a knife, sliced into him. It was as if some nameless black terror, some dark spirit from the underworld, had arrived—here, now, down the street—and it stabbed icy needles into his soul. He'd felt it before. He knew what it was.

In the distance, someone screamed, and pattering feet raced toward them.

"W—what was that?" Brianna turned wide, frightened eyes toward him.

"Morgoth!" Caleb gripped his rifle and headed toward it. "Stay here."

Rifle shots cracked the air and echoed between buildings.

As he ran, terror solidified, darkened, and thickened around him. An invisible force dragged at his feet, trying to cement them and plant them, unmoving, on the asphalt. He'd felt this before, back in Chicago, under dark trees at night.

As his glance swept the street ahead, he saw that others had already succumbed to the demon's will. Half the villagers were frozen where they stood, unable to raise their weapons, unable to flee.

Up and down the street, the booming of rifles bounced off the buildings. One after another, the CSA agents were mowing down those the demon had paralyzed.

12

"Nooooo!" He raced past one body after another, men and women and youths he'd eaten with, sang with, and worshiped with. If only they had looked to the Son of God and called to him . . .

Andy was ahead, crouched behind an overturned table. He was firing at men in green-and-white uniforms who had already captured the town's own barricade. Blood streamed down his right side.

Caleb knelt and joined his friend behind the table. "You've been hit!"

"I'm okay. There are too many." Andy's eyes were wild. He raised his rifle over the table, rested it against his good shoulder, fired, and ducked. "It's hopeless."

Tanya was hunkered down beside him. "He's bleeding, and we need to get him out of here." Pain narrowed her eyes, and she shook her head. "Caleb, Henry's dead. So is Jack. So is Linda May. We can't fight them."

Squaddies occupied the barricade thirty yards to the west. The remaining townsfolk had fallen back, and some were trying to fight. They must have remembered what Caleb had told them. They, at least, had trusted in the name of Jesus.

"Go to Brianna." He waved them east. "The horses are at the end of the street."

"What are you going to do?" Tanya's brows were wrinkled with worry.

"Confront it." He waved again, and, after a moment's hesitation, they departed.

A half dozen men and women bearing rifles and pistols fled past him, joining Tanya and Andy. Caleb now stood alone between the enemy, ahead, and the fleeing townsfolk, behind.

The shooting stopped. With each breath, the air thickened and darkened. It was as if a hole in the world of light had been ripped open, and the underworld was seeping through. Up at the barricade, even the CSA men fled to both sides as a formless creature of shadows stepped through.

It was Morgoth.

A shudder began in Caleb's shoulders and rippled down his spine. Yet he stood his ground.

13

The light from the torches dimmed. The air grew colder. And the demon approached.

The hairs on his head tingled and itched. A chill, as of a sudden cold dew, fell upon his forehead.

You cannot run, Caleb Turner. Its words came, not through the air, but formed inside his head. *You are a weak, cowardly vessel, and you belong to me.*

Shivering, he shook his head. But the creature kept coming, and the darkness increased. All around him, as if he had entered an endless black tunnel, the light dimmed.

That's right, Caleb Turner. You belong to the Dragon, and you cannot escape.

His right foot seemed to have merged with the asphalt roadway, and it wouldn't budge.

Open your mind to all the Dragon has to offer, and you will be free.

His hands became ingots of lead, and he struggled to lift them. His feet were anvils, sinking into the street. The night swirled and spun and deepened around him.

Resist and you will die. Accept and join with me and the—

But no! It was an illusion! It was Satan's deception, carried through an underworld demon.

"No!" One arm broke free, and he raised a hand and pointed a finger. "In the name of Jesus, Lord of Lords, King of Kings, and the holy God of Creation, I banish you into the night!"

The darkness wavered. The torches brightened. The shadowy creature began melting at the edges. The light breeze that was sweeping the street pulled thin fingers of smoke from the thing, and it began losing shape. He could see right through it. Then it vanished.

But no sooner had the demon departed than the CSA poured over the barricade.

"Run!" shouted Andy, now fifty yards to the east. "We've got to get out of here!"

Caleb turned and ran. Shots followed, sparking and chipping asphalt off the street around him. Ahead were the survivors of Currie—four men, three women, and two youths. Too many fallen. Too few alive.

At the end of the street, Brianna waited with the horses, and Tanya helped Andy into the saddle.

They started off at a gallop.

Two hundred yards later, Caleb glanced behind. But there was no pursuit, and he breathed easier. When they were well away from town, they stopped so Tanya could wrap Andy's shirt around his wound.

"We'll go east for a mile or so to throw them off," said Caleb, "then go north, cross-country, and return to the park."

He frowned at the blood-soaked shirt wrapping Andy's shoulder. Sweat dripped off his friend's pale forehead. "Are you okay?"

"I'm okay," he whispered.

"No, he's not," said Tanya. "We need to get that bullet out and get him to bed."

"Right." Caleb faced the road ahead, shadowy and dark under a pale-yellow moon. With the squaddies' attack and the end of the Currie church, everything had changed.

As soon as Andy recovered, they must renew their search for someplace safe.

They would go west.

To the Sanctuary.

CHAPTER 3
THE COLOSSEUM

Revelation 17:3b–6 (NLT): . . . *I saw a woman sitting on a scarlet beast that had seven heads and ten horns, and blasphemies against God were written all over it. The woman wore purple and scarlet clothing and beautiful jewelry made of gold and precious gems and pearls. In her hand she held a gold goblet full of obscenities and the impurities of her immorality. A mysterious name was written on her forehead: "Babylon the Great, Mother of All Prostitutes and Obscenities in the World." I could see that she was drunk—drunk with the blood of God's holy people who were witnesses for Jesus. I stared at her in complete amazement.*

New Babylon, Iraq – August, Year 5

Grady Wilson shifted higher in his seat as the crowd below roared and stamped their feet. He sat beside the Imperator and his inner staff in seats perched atop a wall twenty meters above the arena. The sun had died over the horizon, and the ghost of an orange moon crept into a sky robbed of too many stars.

"Welcome to the third week of the Babylon Games!" boomed the announcer's excited voice. "Watch as our illustrious Minister of Truth lights the torches."

Wearing the green-and-white formal dress uniform of the Central Security Agency, with its ponderous high cap, epaulets on both shoulders, and medals dangling from his chest, Adam Turner strode to the arena's center with torch in hand. Circling the arena's vast perimeter were perhaps fifty metal poles, atop which were chained fifty Christians. Tar coated their bodies, and gags wrapped their mouths.

"Light them! Light them! Light them!" chanted the throng, their feet stomping, shaking the bleachers.

Grady sympathized with the frenzy that had taken hold of the people. He, too, felt their bloodlust, their desire for revenge. Someone must be held responsible for all that had happened, and these Christians would do.

Turner bowed, acknowledging the crowd's desire. He raised his torch high, pointed it north, then south, east, and west. He dipped it to the sand and jumped back. Fizzing, smoking lines of sulfurous powder burned outward in fifty directions, racing toward the edges. When they reached the poles, flames leaped up the tar and engulfed the unfortunates held fast above. Beneath the fire, the victims squirmed and writhed.

Fifty human torches now lit the arena.

The crowd clapped and stamped its feet. The burning human flesh only further inflamed their bloodlust.

At first, Grady joined in the clapping. But soon, his hands refused the order to come together. Something about the bubbling flesh and the squirming bodies beneath that smoking tar brought a hand to his mouth. Now he struggled to keep his gorge down.

"Quite a sight, is it not?" asked a beaming Davato beside him.

"Y–yes, my lord."

"But now watch."

From the top of the poles, revealed now as hollow metal cylinders, rockets shot skyward, showering the slumping bodies with hundreds of sparks. High above the Colosseum, the rockets exploded. The crowd oohed and aahed and clapped again as a multicolored, booming light display burst into the night. Following the rockets, dozens of missiles exited the cylinders in quick succession, each a different color.

For ten minutes, the fireworks and the giant Roman candles continued.

Meanwhile, Adam Turner had left the sand and climbed to a seat beside Davato, opposite Grady.

"You have outdone yourself, Turner." Davato slapped a hand on his knee. "That was quite an opening."

17

"Yes, but now watch as we recreate Daniel and the lions' den as it really happened."

As the Roman candles fizzled out, CSA soldiers in Roman garb led another fifty men, women, and youths to the far end of the arena floor. Dressed only in tunics, the Christians blinked and stared at the crowds.

The Colosseum was a vast oval one hundred fifty by one hundred meters, with bleachers rising seventy meters in height. It held perhaps forty thousand seats, all filled with stamping, shouting, bloodthirsty spectators.

"Release the lions!" they cried. "Release the tigers!"

At the amphitheater's other end, five doors opened, and thirty carnivorous beasts—lions, tigers, and panthers—entered the arena. At first, they wandered over the sand, prowling, looking this way and that, perhaps unsure of where they were, why they were here.

One beast pawed at the remains of a Christian dripping down from his asphalt pole.

Then two tigers spotted the Christians huddling for protection. Slowly, the beasts crept toward them.

"We've been starving them for days." Turner leaned toward Davato and Grady. "They will be hungry."

Davato grinned, feasted his eyes on the scene, and nodded.

One of the cats sprung. Claws raked over a man standing erect. Teeth closed on his shoulder, and the victim crumpled. As the other cats discovered the prey, they, too, leaped.

The crowd yelled encouragement and applauded.

Up and down the aisles, youths now hawked beer, wurst with mustard, and hamburgers. Other vendors brought marijuana and opium cigarettes, syringes of heroin or methamphetamine, bottles of whiskey or vodka.

Grady perused the stands.

Some spectators were already slumped in their seats. Others were so high, they were jumping up and down, urging the animals to more bloodshed. A few got so carried away they engaged in fistfights with neighbors. Colosseum security men descended on these for eviction.

Down in the arena, some Christians tried to run, but the cats chased them down. Soon, all the carnivores were feasting on prey, tearing meat from arms and legs, organs from torsos. Even before they'd finished, the animals rose and stalked the remaining Christians.

"Why don't you give them a knife or something?" asked Grady. "To make it more interesting."

"We did that last week but lost too many beasts," said Turner. "Until we bring more animals from Africa, we don't want to deplete our stock."

Nodding, Grady turned back to the scene.

After the last Christian had been mauled to death, trainers with whips herded the animals back to chutes leading to cages. Slaves removed the body parts, raked the blood off the sand, and prepared for the next event.

A rhinoceros chase followed, with a dozen Jews fleeing two armored, rampaging beasts. But unarmed men and women against such huge enraged creatures was no contest.

Next, seventy Jews and Christians were given swords, placed on a makeshift mountain, and forced to fight a handful of trained gladiators. Again, the battle was short. The Christians either didn't fight at all or gave too weak a defense. The gladiators made quick work of the killing.

With each victim murdered, the crowd's bloodlust only increased. It was as if they drew energy from the carnage, the gore, the sight of their enemies—Christians and Jews—being slaughtered without mercy. The bloodier, the gorier, the more agonizing the death, the louder came their shouts of encouragement.

Grady's original excitement now changed to a horrified, stunned amazement. It was the same every time he came. At first, he felt the desire for revenge, and the Christians and Jews below would do. If there was an Enemy in Heaven who had sent the plague, earthquakes, asteroids, erupting volcanoes, and darkened sun—then the victims below were the Enemy's proxies, and some part of his mind told him it was just and right. They were responsible. They deserved to die.

But as the blood and gore mounted, his enthusiasm always waned, replaced by an uneasy shifting in his seat, a churning in his stomach. And he wished he were elsewhere.

19

Two more events followed. Gladiators against the Christians. Lions, tigers, and leopards against the Jews. When it was over, the arena sands had become red mud, soaked with the blood of the martyrs.

Then Davato took the microphone, thanked everyone for coming, and reminded them to take home a free bottle of whiskey, brandy, vodka, or a pack of marijuana or heroin cigarettes on their way out.

Later, as Grady stood in his room overlooking the Temple of Davato—formerly the Temple of Gaia—he felt as empty as the half dozen whiskey bottles filling his garbage can.

The deaths of the Christians today only reminded him of the God they worshiped, of the angels who'd flown overhead bringing their warning of eternal doom. He remembered the flight of the eagle and its dire pronouncements. And the earthquakes, the asteroids, the volcanoes, the darkened sun and moon.

What great power had sent those supernatural warnings? What had wreaked such terrible judgments upon the earth? It could only be the Christian God. How could Grady not now acknowledge that God was real?

And that knowledge brought tremors to his fingers and sweat to his forehead.

He stared at the mark on his right hand. What if he hadn't taken it? What if he'd gone with Chelsea and escaped to some faraway place where people's joy wasn't fed by mindless slaughter in the arena?

But no. What was done was done. There was no going back, was there?

He went to the cupboard, opened a new whiskey bottle, and poured a full glass. After downing it in one gulp, he poured another.

Why was he feeling this way? He was an important assistant to the most powerful man in the world, at the pinnacle of power. His salary was beyond anything he'd ever dreamed of. He could have any woman, anytime, anywhere. His cupboard was stocked with the best whiskey. While so many were starving, his belly was always full. The Unitum Imperium provided more amusements than he could ever partake. His every carnal and earthly desire was fulfilled.

And yet, he was empty, drained, deeply unhappy, and fighting a profound loneliness.

He took another swig of whiskey and dropped his head into his hands.

CHAPTER 4
THE RAID

Kronberg Mountain, Switzerland – August, Year 5

The world was ending, and everywhere, it seemed, was chaos, madness, and opposition. Despite this, Margot's return had restored Dylan's faith.

But he feared for Chelsea, and for her sake, he must start a new journey. He held onto a thin strand of hope that his sister might have escaped, that she was still alive, and that, somehow, she would make her way to the family villa in Tuscany. He also feared for Bettino, who was no longer answering his phone.

Beyond the open window in their Kronberg Mountain hideout, a hawk, oblivious of his troubles, cried and circled.

But he'd neglected to go to God in prayer, and he feared to start his trek south with so many unforgiven sins. He got down on his knees. "Dear Jesus, I have been such a fool. I have taken life. We have all taken lives. We thought it necessary, but if it was not, please forgive us—all of us. And me? I have, at times, doubted and turned away from you. I have not held fast to my faith in you as I should. Forgive this poor soul, for I am only a weak vessel of mortal flesh. Make the Holy Spirit strong in me, strong against the many trials to come. And help my sister find her way to Tuscany where I must now go. In Jesus's name, I pray."

He sat up from the bed, stuffed a last change of clothes into his rucksack, and lifted the pack. He had full clips for his Glock 17. Pasqual would drive him to Appenzell and drop him off. There he would find an abandoned car and drive south to Bettino.

Bettino was his only hope of ever seeing Chelsea again.

He loved his sister and brother, and somehow, against all odds, he would bring them together again. He belonged to the family of God and to Christ, yes, but what was left to him, here, now—in this world, at least—was family. Those that he loved: Chelsea and Caleb.

He wouldn't give up on them.

At least now he had Margot. And for that he was grateful.

Did he love them more than his Savior?

Oh, dear Jesus, please forgive me if I have sinned. But I do love them and want to save them.

Throwing the pack over his shoulder, he descended the stairs.

But no sooner had he entered the common room to say goodbye than René held up a hand. "Dylan, I know you've been planning this for some time, but I'm asking if you can delay your trip. We need your help."

Feeling as if the air were leaking out of him, he put hands on hips, and his gaze settled on Pasqual and Victor as well as Jakob Huber who had joined their group. Their eyes told him something was up. "What kind of help?"

"Our supplies are critically low. In another week, we'll be eating shoe leather."

"What do you need me for?"

"We're almost out of flour, oil, salt, meat—everything. The woods are nearly hunted out, and we're running low on ammunition. I want your help to raid the central CSA storehouse in Kaufbeuren that we've been watching. They've got everything we need and more. This operation only involves three of us—you, me, and Pasqual."

Dylan frowned and rubbed his brow. "Didn't we decide Kaufbeuren was too heavily guarded? A lot of troops are stationed there."

"Oui, but when I was gone for two days last week, I hired on as a mechanic in their maintenance shed at night with their skeleton staff. A hefty bribe, and the foreman didn't ask to see my mark. While there, I discovered when the distribution truck leaves the lot and when it goes to the central storehouse. At the warehouse, they fill the truck then send it out to resupply all the region's local stations. Victor's hacking also tells us that most of the CSA guards will be on parade at the Kaufbeuren airbase for Gaston Soucy, the Minister of Charity. He'll be visiting this week from New Babylon."

Sighing, Dylan set down his backpack. "What's your plan?"

"I'm hoping to avoid bloodshed, so here's what we'll do. You and I will hijack the truck, take the drivers' places, go to the headquarters where they keep the goods, and steal their entire load. Pasqual will wait with another truck I've obtained to which we'll transfer everything before leaving the city. The booth guards and the warehouse are expecting only two drivers, so we mustn't disappoint them. I need you, Dylan, as your German is excellent. Victor is too short, and Jakob doesn't fit the bill as a CSA guard."

Pasqual shook his head. "This is crazy, René."

"It's insane," added Dylan.

René rubbed his chin. "It's bold, for sure. But if it works, we'll be stocked for the next six months, possibly a year."

"When do you want to do this?" Dylan's plans for traveling to the villa were fast disappearing.

"Tomorrow morning."

"In broad daylight?" He gasped.

"Oui. But if anything goes wrong, we'll have this—much of the guard station will be at the parade." René shrugged. "This really is our best option."

Dylan drew a hand through his hair. "This is the craziest plan you've ever come up with. But okay, if you need me, I'll go."

"Good." His eye sockets appearing less deep and dark, a smiling René laid a hand on Dylan's shoulder.

"But after this mission, I *must* go to the villa and find out what happened to Bettino."

"Agreed."

* * *

LATER THAT AFTERNOON, THREE OF them drove René's new truck to Kaufbeuren, Germany. Just before eighteen hundred hours, they checked into a pension in the dark. They drove past the maintenance shed and parking lot where the CSA kept their inventory of vehicles. René pointed

24

out the guard booth through which drivers entering and leaving the lot must pass, showing their badges and work orders before being allowed through the gate.

The next morning at eight, while Pasqual drove the new truck to a spot a kilometer distant from the CSA headquarters, Dylan followed René to an alley behind a door leading into the maintenance building. They hid out of sight behind a dumpster.

"Every morning before signing in, the drivers go in for coffee." René checked his watch. "They'll leave the shed around eight thirty. Any minute now."

"When does the guard booth change shifts?" asked Dylan.

"No worries there. They do that at six in the morning."

Moments later, the shed door banged shut, their signal that the drivers had left the building. René nodded, and with pistols drawn, they crept out of the alley and snuck up behind the two drivers in green-and-white CSA uniforms. On René's signal, they stuck their guns into the backs of the men ahead.

"Hands up and don't reach for your weapons," said René. "Or you're dead."

But the man in front of René refused to listen. When his hand dropped to the pistol at his belt, René whopped his gun barrel against the man's skull with a loud crack.

The man staggered, slumped to the ground, then rose, drunkenly, to his knees.

Before he could rise again, René removed the man's pistol, and Dylan followed his lead. Then they led their prisoners back to the alley behind the dumpster, where they took the work orders and ordered the men to remove their uniforms. After zip-tying their hands and feet, they gagged them.

The CSA uniform Dylan tried on was a bit big, and René's was somewhat small. But they would do.

Before leaving the alley, they pinned on the badges Victor had created for them. Then René looked down on the hapless guards, dressed only in their underwear, and smiled. "Lucky for you, meine Herren, it's a warm morning. We'll be back."

Trying to still his racing heart, Dylan followed René toward the guard booth. When they were a few meters away, one guard, an older, shorter, balding man, left the booth and approached.

As planned, Dylan smiled at the younger one standing inside the booth's open doorway.

"You two must be new," said the older man to René. "Always someone new. Let's see your work order." He reached out a hand.

As the younger one lit a cigarette, René nodded to Dylan, who passed along their papers. But as the man examined them, René and Dylan drew their pistols. "Hands up, and don't touch those guns," said René.

"What the—?" The younger man in the booth dropped his cigarette, and his hands shot skyward.

But beside Dylan, the older man hesitated. René waved his gun and shook his head, and slowly, the man raised his hands.

They confiscated the guards' guns then tied their prisoners' hands behind their backs. Smiling, René lifted a full pack of cigarettes from the younger one's front pocket then pushed the button inside the booth and opened the gate. They led the men past rows of CSA vehicles to a van with the CSA's typically opaque windows. There, they gagged their prisoners, tied their hands and feet together with zip ties, and fastened them both to the steering wheel.

After returning to the alley, they led the other two prisoners back inside the lot and tied them up inside a second black van.

Then they found the truck René identified as the one used for deliveries. They left the lot, closed the gate, and, with René behind the wheel, drove toward the regional storehouse.

"It's nine-oh-five, and we're only slightly behind schedule." The ex-spy reached for a cigarette, lit it, and smiled. Dylan marveled at the number of times he'd seen René's uncharacteristic smile in the last twenty-four hours. "By now, all but a skeleton crew should be at the parade grounds."

The drive to the warehouse took only ten minutes. René followed the road behind the warehouse building then backed the truck to the loading dock.

Dylan wiped sweat from his brow. Would René's plan actually work?

As they left the vehicle, two solemn-faced guards manned the dock, rifles draped across their shoulders. One of them approached. "What happened to Schwartz and Johan?"

"Ordered to the parade ground," answered René.

"Of course. I should check your work order." The guard reached out a hand, and Dylan passed him the authorization to fill the truck.

The man made his inspection, gave a cursory glance at their badges, and handed back the papers. Then he returned to a watchful position on the dock.

Two others, younger, muscled, and barely nineteen, opened the sliding door and began pulling hand trucks, one after another, down the ramp into the truck bed. Like the maintenance workers, they wore the khaki uniforms of hired day laborers, not the CSA.

As the boxes entered the truck, Dylan and René stacked them: wooden chests with ammunition. Boxes of food, canned and dried. Cold chests with vegetables and fruits. A box labeled Pistols and Ammunition. Another marked Electronics. Nothing but the best for the UI elites.

"I'd rather be here," said a blond-haired youth with a pockmarked face, "than standing at attention on the parade ground all morning."

"Me too," said Dylan.

"You're new, aren't you?" With a clinking of metal, the black-haired youth set his hand truck upright. "Where'd they transfer you from?"

"Mainz," answered Dylan, as instructed by René. Then he turned away to avoid further questions.

When the truck was full, René yanked the door closed and clicked the locking bolts shut. "Now we'd better start on our rounds."

The two youths nodded, and as they ambled back through the warehouse door, one of the guards answered a call on his cell phone.

As René headed for the driver's side, Dylan walked beside him.

"Wait!" shouted the guard from the dock. "Stop where you are!"

The other man unslung his rifle, and René said under his breath, "Eyes forward and keep walking. When I reach the door, run to your side and get in."

Footsteps pounded down the concrete steps. "Step away from that vehicle, now!"

"Run!" René's hand was on the driver's side door. But as he reached for the handle, a rifle shot split the air.

Something tore into Dylan's shoulder and spun him around. More shots exploded from behind.

Metal screeched, and a gouge ripped into the truck's hood.

He staggered around the vehicle's front. He was now out of range.

Breathing fast, he yanked open the passenger door.

He slumped into the seat, but the view out the window was spinning. Something had stung his shoulder. He stared at a bloody hand.

The engine was running. René rammed his foot to the accelerator, and the truck jerked away from the loading area.

"You're hit!" Beside him, René's brows crinkled with worry.

Pain shot through Dylan. His back slammed against the seat back.

"Take off your shirt, if you can, and press it against the wound."

Wincing, Dylan nodded and did as ordered.

As the vehicle roared away for the rendezvous with the other truck, Dylan rammed a fist against his knee.

This wound would take weeks to heal. His trip to Tuscany and Bettino would have to wait.

CHAPTER 5
SUSPICION RETURNS

Joel 2:10–11 (HCSB): *The earth quakes before them; the sky shakes. The sun and moon grow dark, and the stars cease their shining.*

Palma de Mallorca, Spain – August, Year 5

A faded orb of sun struggled to shed a dim light, while the moon shone a pale reflection of its former self. Too late, the days banished the nights. Too soon, the nights blackened the skies and streets. Thus fell a shadow of gloom over the survivors of Mallorca.

In what passed for daylight, Chelsea and Enzo left the ship on their mission to buy whatever was available at the Tuesday market. The island's lone Truth Squad was derelict, corrupt, and so often drunk in their quarters, Chelsea had little fear they'd discover two Christians without the mark.

As they strolled, she marveled how most of the parked cars lay rusted and abandoned. Blackened bodies still slumped inside front seats. Even in the alleys and empty storefronts, corpses and the gnawed bones of the forgotten dead reminded her of the carnage the first seven seals had inflicted on the city. Few vehicles drove the streets now, and few people walked the sidewalks.

Enzo pointed to a store entrance piled with the desiccated skin and fur of dead rats. "During the worst of the plague, they say the rodents swarmed like cockroaches across Mallorca. No one could avoid the fleas. No one understands why the rats multiplied in such numbers or why they died off so quickly. The Black Death and the following famine took almost seventy percent of the population. It was much worse here than anywhere else."

Chelsea shuddered. "Even in the Clal Center in Jerusalem, the rats brought their fleas. I came down with the plague, but since Davato had antibiotics for his staff, I recovered."

"I, too, bought antibiotics on the black market, or I might look like one of those unfortunates lying there." He pointed to a blackened corpse sitting upright behind a dirty car window. "Every statement coming from the government said they didn't work, but that was a lie."

"I'm just glad that part of it is over."

"The CSA is still afraid of the island. And the Truth Squad here is so inept, they haven't even installed the digital payments and credits system."

"That's good. 'Cause we still have plenty of cash."

They turned a corner and entered what passed for the central market. Everyone here took cash. But the number of booths were few, and the produce substandard. The oranges were small and wilted. The almonds and olive oil were dear. Only the fish mongers and vintners had plenty to sell. And the wine was reasonably priced.

Chelsea haggled for the prices she could get and filled their bags.

When they'd finished, an old man with a sun-dried face and raggedy clothes approached with an outstretched hand. "Ten euros, signorina, for my family?"

She handed him a bill, and they moved on.

Then a young woman called out from behind, also begging. Chelsea gave her a few euros, and they started out again.

But when more than a dozen beggars left the alleyways and followed, Enzo shot a glance behind. "You'd better stop, or we might have a riot on our hands."

She nodded, and they picked up the pace.

The docks came into view, and she turned to her companion. "Did you speak with Fabio today? Did he meet with the harbormaster this morning?"

"Yes, and I was keeping the news from you."

"What news?" She stopped him with a hand on his arm. "What aren't you telling me?"

"It isn't good, and I didn't want to spoil your morning. We won't receive the engine parts until December."

Her free hand slid from his sleeve to the top of her head. "*December!* We're stuck here for another four months?"

"I'm afraid so. And I fear what I'll find when I return to Bergamo in December. I'd rather arrive in summer than in winter."

They crossed the Avinguda de Gabriel Roca, found the ship's berth, and stepped aboard the *Am Albahr*. After dropping their purchases in the galley, they parted.

But as Chelsea returned to the deck, the television blared from above, and she climbed the ladder to the wheelhouse. When she opened the glass door, the captain's back was to her, and the television volume was up. Even after she shut the door, he didn't turn around.

A number filled the screen—one million euros flashing in red, then yellow, then back to red.

Then came an announcer's breathless voice. "That's right, folks. One million euros is yours. And all you have to do is turn in one of those Christians or Jews who have been plotting with the Enemy against our divine Imperator. For some time, they've worked for the destruction of the Unitum Imperium, and they need to be rounded up and dealt with. And you, good citizens of the Imperium, when you turn them in, you have the opportunity to receive a handsome reward. Just call the number on the screen, and wherever you live, an agent will respond." The flashing euro figure shrank to a sidebar on the right while the screen showed the announcer on the left, now standing in a business suit on a sun-drenched beach, his arms open wide.

When Fabio took pen in hand and wrote down the number, Chelsea gasped.

"Yes, my friends, when you turn in an enemy of the state, you get one million euros for each of them, and this vacation paradise could be yours. Not only that, we will throw in this extra gift: If you have ever committed a minor offense against the Imperium, our divine Imperator, in his extreme generosity and beneficence, will give you a pardon for your transgressions. So don't delay. Call the number today. Join the ranks of

31

the privileged few living in tropical retreats like this." He spread his arms wide, taking in a vast sun-drenched beach. But how, Chelsea wondered, had they ever found such a sun? "Or take your newfound wealth wherever you want to go. Now, let's listen to a testimony from one happy couple who have already taken up this . . ."

As a smiling middle-aged man and woman in shorts and flowered shirts stood barefooted before palm trees and a sunny beach house, Chelsea slipped through the door, down the ladder, and back to her room.

No decision Fabio had ever made could be trusted. Surely, he'd do nothing here in Palma. But when they landed in Italy?

Well, she had her gun, didn't she?

CHAPTER 6
THE SEPARATION

John 15:18 (NLT): *"If the world hates you, remember that it hated me first. The world would love you as one of its own if you belonged to it, but you are no longer part of the world. I chose you to come out of the world, so it hates you."*

Cheyenne Mountain, Colorado – August, Year 5

To the humming of fluorescent ceiling lights, Major Daniel Price set down his empty coffee cup and took a deep breath. He wasn't going to tell his friends about the dream. Not yet. But it was more than a dream, wasn't it? It was a vision, with an angel, and a vital message for everyone in this deep mountain complex who believed in Jesus as Lord. No, he'd tell them later, after the meeting. Today, too much was happening of too much importance. Glancing at his watch, he realized he was late.

He pushed his chair from the table and left the break room. Following the underground corridors, he wended his way past the Command Operations Center, now defunct, to the expansive conference room. Swallowing, he pushed through the door.

The Christians, twelve men and women, sat on one side. Numbering the same, the others—they were calling them the others now, weren't they?—sat opposite. A scowling Colonel Scott occupied the center. The room wasn't big enough to hold the missing eight Christians or the missing thirty who opposed the King of Kings and Lord of Lords.

As Daniel had requested, everyone on his side of the table wore their sidearms. This ensured that the colonel couldn't force his will on the dissenters. Naturally, the colonel's people would come armed.

He found a seat between Lieutenants Chase Cooper and Lena Chang. Even though the United States was no longer a functioning entity, everyone still wore their Space Force uniforms. But that was the issue today, wasn't it? Whose uniform, if any, were they going to wear? And where would they wear it?

"I'm glad you decided to join us this morning, Dan." Colonel Scott waved him to a seat, and Daniel ignored the breach of protocol. "If we're all here, I've asked Lieutenant Walter to read the issues under discussion. Lieutenant?"

Diminutive Walter glanced over his wire-rim glasses, smoothed the few strands of hair on his nearly bald head, then buried a too-small nose in the paper before him. "Under discussion are items one through four. Item one: The Sanctuary has exhausted its supply of food and medicine, and with no supplies being shipped from the current government for the last five years and none expected, we face imminent starvation."

A chorus of grunts from the colonel's side followed.

"Two: After the nuclear destruction of Denver and Colorado Springs and the radiation poisoning of Peterson Space Force Base and its environs, the Unitum Imperium has abandoned its Colorado facilities." Walter glanced around the table before continuing.

"Three: The governor of North America, now the lawful ruler of this country, has given this complex an order to abandon Cheyenne Mountain. We are to proceed, forthwith, to join a Unitum Imperium command center at the former Cannon Air Force Base in New Mexico."

Walter raised an accusing glance at the Christian side of the table before again lowering eyes to his document.

"Finally, item number four: Those of us here at Cheyenne Mountain are split into two factions. Those who remain loyal to the country's chain of command have pledged to obey the lawful order from their commander in chief and accept their new assignment, whereas those who now follow a religion in opposition to the Imperator have decided to break ranks with their fellows, disobey orders, and go their own way."

As Walter adjusted his glasses and laid down his paper, Colonel Scott cleared his throat. "Well, Dan, that about says it all, don't you think?"

"No, Frank, it doesn't even come close." Since the colonel decided to skip protocol and not use Daniel's rank, Daniel returned the favor. "You forgot to mention that, in order to join the Unitum Imperium's air force—if there's anything left of it in New Mexico—we would be forced to take the mark of the beast."

Gasps erupted from Scott's side, and the colonel slammed a palm down on the table. "I've told you never to use that term in my presence, *Dan!*"

"And I've told you—*Frank!*—that those beside me will never take the mark." Dan breathed in, trying to calm the whirlpool boiling inside him. When next he spoke, he lowered his voice. "This is a matter of life and death, Colonel—spiritual life and death. Long ago, this government abandoned us. Until now, we've had little contact with them. And from what I've seen, it's evil. This man Davato is, without doubt, the Antichrist, the beast, the man of lawlessness. And all who follow him do so to their eternal destruction. Y'all need to follow Jesus, who is both God and man, the only Savior who can lead you through the terrible days ahead and into a future of eternal life, not death."

A seething Colonel Scott gripped the table edge and glared. "I reject your mythical Jesus and your fairy tales—*Dan!*—and I'll ask you again: When we leave here in two days and abandon this facility, will you come to your senses, join us, and take the mark?"

Daniel crossed his arms. "We will not!"

Frowning, Scott nodded. "Then it appears we have a mutiny on our hands. So . . . if you and yours willfully refuse to follow orders, I hereby strip each and every one of you of your ranks. As of this moment, you are all dishonorably discharged. I order you to vacate this base by"—he checked his watch—"thirteen hundred hours. And none of you will be allowed to leave this base wearing the uniform you have just dishonored. I will have guards escort you from the premises."

"That's unnecessary," said Daniel. "We will leave of our own accord."

"Regardless, we will oversee your departure." The colonel stood, and those on his side of the table joined him. "This meeting is over."

In a strained silence, Daniel motioned for his people to wait as the colonel's men, women, and nonbinaries filed out of the room. When they were alone again, he turned to Lieutenant Lena Chang. "Is everyone packed and ready to go?"

She nodded. "We have ammunition for our sidearms and rifles, civilian clothing for summer and winter, what medical supplies we could scrounge, a few tents, and survival gear. We have extra packs with food and water. We're ready."

"Good. I suggest we return to our bunks to retrieve our things in groups of three, just in case the colonel tries to force someone to change their mind."

Beside him, Chase scratched his beard. "But where will we go? Do you have a destination in mind?"

"No." Daniel laid a hand on his friend's shoulder. "But trust me. I have faith that God will lead us to a place of safety, wherever that might be."

Standing, he walked to the table's opposite side and faced those who'd sided with Christ. "Y'all are honest and brave men and women, and, like me, you have chosen Jesus over the Antichrist. I don't know what lies ahead of us. But I am greatly honored to stand with you and face whatever trials might come our way."

He raised a hand to his forehead, and, with moisture building at the corners of his eyes, he saluted.

CHAPTER 7
RECOVERY

Kronberg Mountain, Switzerland – September, Year 5

Margot pushed through the door into Dylan's room with a tray bearing a ham and cheese omelet, a slice of buttered toast, and a cup of tea. "How is my patient today?"

Dylan sat up in bed and smiled. "Better, especially when my favorite nurse brings me breakfast. The fever is gone and look—" He pulled his arm out of the sling, swiveled it, and reached for the tray. "I'm cured."

Margot frowned. "Eat and we'll see."

"You're a hard taskmistress, Margot Durand."

She let him take the tray from her. While he ate, she opened the window to let in the cool fall air. "You've been recovering for six weeks, and if your fever is gone, we should get you out of bed."

"We?" He shot her a quizzical look.

"Of course. You're not going anywhere without me. And a few trees with leaves are beginning to change color. It might do us both good to take a stroll."

She sat in the chair beside the bed and regarded her charge. When they'd brought him back from the Kaufbeuren affair, he'd been covered with blood, and his pulse was weak. Fortunately, medical supplies were among those they'd stolen from the CSA, including saline IV bags, needles, and antibiotics. She and Danielle looked up what was required and gave him several units of whole blood. Fortunately, Pasqual had the same blood type.

When questioned about the affair, René described his frantic effort to stop Dylan's bleeding after they left the warehouse, leaving Pasqual to transfer equipment to the new truck. Somehow, they escaped the area before the CSA cordoned off the town.

In the weeks that followed, Dylan struggled with a fever that wracked his body.

Time and prayer had saved him and dispelled her fears. As he ate his last bite of omelet and handed her the tray, she leaned down and planted a kiss on his forehead.

He reached for her head, brought her lips to his, and kissed her back.

"I guess that means you're better." She laid the tray on the nightstand. "Are you up for a walk?"

"Of course!"

She helped him out of bed. At first, he was wobbly, leaning on her to keep his balance as they descended creaky wooden steps.

Down in the common room, Pasqual rose from an easy chair. "It's good to see you up and about." He extended a hand, and they shook.

René approached and slapped him on his good shoulder. "I second that thought. We were worried about you. I had always thought that one day I'd be the one laid up with a gunshot wound, not you. I once had a dream I would die by a bullet, and I wondered how I have escaped until now. It's haunted me ever since."

"No, René." Margot shook her head. "Don't say such things."

"It's true. But not today." He took another drag on his cigarette. "Dylan, my friend, you look almost as good as new."

"In a few days, I will be," he responded.

Again, Margot frowned. "Maybe in a week." Then she turned to Pasqual. "Were you able to get the art supplies I requested on your last trip?"

"I did. They're in the downstairs closet."

"Thanks."

Dylan faced her. "Another vision?"

"Yes." She hadn't painted a vision for over a year, but these last days, the urge to take brush in hand had been building.

They left by the front door and stepped onto the porch where Dylan insisted they must go into the yard. With his hand on her shoulder, they walked the path through the trees, half now bearing leaves of gold or ruby red. Breathing deeply, she rejoiced at the cool air.

Above, not a cloud filled the sky. The sun struggled to shed a weak glow on the path ahead.

He stopped, let go of her, looked to the heavens, and put both hands behind his head. "I need to leave for Tuscany as soon as possible."

"When you're well."

"That will be in a few days. You'll see."

"You really think Chelsea will go to the villa?"

"I do. And I'm worried about Bettino."

"Let me go with you."

One hand moved to probe his healing wound. "I don't know, Margot. This might be something I have to do alone."

She shrugged. "Your legs are shaking. We should get you back to bed. And I need to start painting."

Then she helped him back up the porch and to his room.

Later, she set up the easel, placed the palette on the nightstand, picked up the brush, and began. When she'd painted the commandant in the camp, none of the Spirit had come upon her. But today, the urge to paint returned as strong as it always had, driving her on. An invisible force guided her hand, filling her with a passion to put to canvas a vision only now forming in her mind.

The moment she started, she knew that this painting, like the last one she did over a year ago, was deeply personal. She stopped, took a step back, and shuddered. It involved both her and Dylan, and now dread crept over her. Wrapping her arms about her chest, she closed her eyes. "Dear Lord Jesus, forgive me if I hesitate. But today I fear to see the future."

Yet the desire to paint welled up with such power, it overwhelmed her fears. She touched brush to palette, brought it to canvas, and began.

The picture that emerged was of her and Dylan in a basement. Chains wrapped their legs. On the wall, a faded poster showed the Imperator, the Prophet, and the Dragon. But when she painted what was etched on her wrist, her heart nearly stopped.

She lurched back from the easel and gasped. She hadn't painted it on Dylan's wrist yet but knew that this, too, was next.

How could such a thing be? How could it happen? For what she'd drawn in thin black lines on her right wrist was—

The mark of the beast.

CHAPTER 8
REBELLION

Ezekiel 32:7–8 (HCSB): *When I snuff you out, I will cover the heavens and darken their stars. I will cover the sun with a cloud, and the moon will not give its light. I will darken all the shining lights in the heavens over you and will bring darkness on your land. This is the declaration of the Lord GOD.*

Camp David, Maryland – September, Year 5

On a pleasantly cool September morning, outdoors and under the trees, William Cole, governor of the Province of North America, finished breakfast with his guests. If only the sun had shone as it used to, the morning's repast would have been perfect. But the sickly pallid light seeping through the nearly leafless trees was a big downer. It only reminded him something was terribly amiss in the world. An outdoor breakfast was merely one of the woodsy amenities he used to woo visitors to his Catoctin Mountain retreat. Such niceties often helped loosen attitudes. And for today's meeting, he needed all the help he could get.

The world depended on the outcome.

His potential coconspirators had arrived yesterday evening by helicopter from Camp David Airfield in Catoctin Mountain Park, Maryland. Looking like a reincarnated Fidel Castro in green military fatigues, big-bearded Umberto Gómez Rodriguez, governor of South America, flew in from Brazil. Appearing in a casual suit, no tie, and dress jeans, full-bellied Jack Anderson, governor of Australasia, flew in from Australia.

After breakfast, Cole led them down the tree-lined walkway to his office in Laurel Lodge where comfortable easy chairs awaited. It was early, but he offered them brandy, whiskey, or beer. Also available was fresh, untainted water from a Pennsylvania well. Rodriguez declined, but Anderson took a beer. For himself, Cole ordered a brandy from an aide who served from the wet bar on the counter and a small refrigerator.

To date, their communications had been written and hand delivered by trusted personnel. But he knew both men, knew how they chafed under Davato's rule. Earlier, he'd hinted at the purpose of today's meeting, and he'd sensed interest, but also resistance. The only way to get them to agree was a face-to-face meeting. That they'd acquiesced to coming here, knowing the risk, was encouraging.

"Well, Cole." Anderson set down his beer and sank back in the chair. "Explain what this is about."

Cole took a deep breath. After what he was about to say, what would be the reactions of the two leaders sitting across from him? Everything depended on that. He gripped the arms of the chair, tried to slow his breathing, and began. "The man in charge of the Unitum Imperium is insane. He has to go."

Anderson reacted with a fist smashing down on the chair's arm. "I agree."

But Rodriguez narrowed his eyes. Then, slowly, oh so slowly, he nodded.

Cole breathed out his relief. Both were good signs. He continued. "Davato is not a god. I don't know what that stunt in Temple Square was all about, but he didn't rise from the dead. It was surely a well-crafted illusion. And this man calling himself the Prophet, well . . . Sebastien Rey is behind everything Davato does. Both of them have a stranglehold on our provinces—our money, commerce, military, and laws. They've filled our lands and halls of government with Truth Squads, CSA goons, and spies. Davato convinced me to go against China over the Taiwan invasion—what a disaster that was! I was stupid enough to fall for his advice." He spread his hands wide. "Now look where I am. Look where you are."

"All true, Cole." Apparently changing his mind, Rodriguez glanced around for the missing aide then rose and poured himself a shot of whiskey. He downed one, refilled it, downed another, then returned to his seat with a third. "But what can anyone do?"

"You're right," added Anderson. "Australia, Japan, and the Pacific Island nations have been reduced to second-class—no, third-class— entities. Europe gets everything—phones, food, equipment. And what does Australasia get? More control. More spies. More laws over which we have no say. And if you believe in bad luck, everything that's happened to us—earthquakes, asteroids, lightning, fires, plague, famine—it all happened since he came to power. He's a jinx."

"So I repeat my question." Rodriguez smoothed his beard. "What can anyone do about it?"

Cole pressed his hands together and leaned forward. "Assassinate them both!"

Anderson scrunched his brows together, reached for his beer, and took a long draught.

A frowning Rodriguez clutched his third shot and shook his head. "Bold, Cole. And dangerous. So now tell us why you called us here. If that's your plan, why don't you do it yourself? Why involve us?"

"Ah, that *is* the question, isn't it?" Cole smiled. "Well, I had planned to do it myself but was stymied. Several times, I asked for a private meeting with the Imperator. First, I wanted to make a few requests to better the North American situation and give him an opportunity to improve our lot. If he refused to help, then I would use the meeting to scout the situation and come up with an assassination plan. But—" He shook his head and gritted his teeth. "But he declined to meet."

"Declined?" Rodriguez's eyes opened wide. "He wouldn't even hear your petitions?"

"No. And that's when I decided on this course of action. He won't meet with me alone, but if the three of us request a meeting, he's sure to agree. So here's the plan: In November, Davato is calling a conference in New Babylon where all the governors will attend. Before the general meeting, we three will see him privately. At the meeting, I, myself, will bring a pistol and do the deed."

43

As the mantel clock clicked, both men stared at their host.

"You really think this is possible?" Anderson's beer glass clattered onto the side table, and he scowled. "How will you get a weapon past security?"

"With a plastic handgun created specially to avoid detection."

"What about the Prophet?" asked Rodriguez. "You want them both there, don't you?"

"Rey will also be present, and I will shoot them both. We'll create bogus requests, some of which Sebastien Rey will want to answer. We'll give them a preliminary list that will flatter and suck in both Davato and his so-called Prophet."

"It might work." Anderson rubbed his chin. "But even if you do the deed, what will happen afterward? His goons will arrest us and charge us with murder."

"In the halls outside the meeting room, there will be a security contingent answerable only to me. They agree with my vision. They'll intercept any attempt by the CSA to arrest us. Weeks before that, we'll gradually bring in personnel, in secret. Their task will be to take over key functions of the UI army leadership. You'd be surprised how concentrated their lines of control are."

Anderson waved a hand. "A security presence like that will invite scrutiny. Someone is sure to suspect something."

"We will identify them as aides. They, too, will have untraceable weapons, and the room in which we'll meet is only a short walk from the main conference room where, this time, we'll be allowed to bring whomever we like."

"How do you know all this?" asked Rodriguez.

"My new ambassador, Helen Schmidt, poked around, found a reliable source, and relayed the information."

"This is risky, Cole," said Anderson. "Too many people will know about it. Someone could snitch. We need something to incent those involved, something beyond loyalty."

"Maybe a tripling of salary and promotions for all?"

"Perhaps. But it's still a big risk." Rodriguez sat back again, rubbing his beard. "What happens when Davato is out of the way?"

"That's the best part." Cole grinned. "That very day, we'll seize control of the government. We'll make a worldwide announcement dissolving the Unitum Imperium and throwing out our overlords. Each of us will rule our territories as we see fit. All power and authority will return to me and to you! And when we announce to the rest of the governors that they will soon be solely in charge of their own provinces, I think everyone will back us up."

The two men exchanged glances, and then smiles brightened their faces.

"I'm in." Anderson slapped his knee. "Australia and the Pacific deserve better than what we're getting from this arrogant dictator."

"As am I." Rodriguez leaned forward in his chair. "To rule all of South America as it should be ruled—ah, that would be grand, indeed!"

"Then let us shake on it." Cole stood and reached across the desk, and they finalized their agreement.

That afternoon, the two governors boarded a helicopter for a flight back to Camp David Airfield where private jets would ferry them home.

Shortly after their departure, Cole met with the security leaders who would accompany him in November. At that meeting, he offered them the world, and they accepted his offer with eagerness.

That night, he went to bed, satisfied that, after all his careful planning, nothing could stop the impending demise of Sebastien Rey and Davato, this Imperator who fancied himself a god.

CHAPTER 9
ARIEL GELLER

Tel Aviv, Israel – September, Year 5

The brakes squeaked as Ariel stopped in front of an apartment on Kiryat Shmona Street in Tel Aviv's Holon district. He crossed the walk to a first-floor flat with cracked walls and pulled blinds. Was there anywhere nowadays without cracks in the walls?

He'd never met the man about whom he'd heard so much, and now he would finally hear him speak. Through intermediaries, both men had agreed to meet this afternoon on business, but this morning, Ariel wanted to hear, as a mere spectator, what the fuss was all about.

A tall, thin, tawny-haired man met him at the door. "David Benjamin," he said, extending a hand, "and welcome."

Ariel shook the hand, nodded, and entered a crowded room bearing nearly forty folding chairs, every one occupied. Barely had he sat on the side when a man with curly black hair, thick eyebrows, and a wide nose entered from an adjacent room.

"My name is Baruch Abramovich," he began, "and I'm here today to convince you that time is running out, that the choice you make today is for all eternity. And I pray with all my soul that your hearts will be open to what I have to say. Because of the attention these gatherings engender, our meeting must be brief. Note that we are only using this location today."

As Ariel glanced around the audience, he guessed that most were unconverted Jews with a few Gentiles mixed in. Present were mostly men but also a few women.

"How can anyone deny," continued Baruch, "that God has brought

46

his wrath down upon the world? He has sent war, famine, plague, asteroids, earthquakes, and storms of lightning. He has blackened the sun, moon, and stars, poisoned streams and lakes, and turned an ocean into blood. He has allowed the Antichrist, the man of lawlessness, also called the beast, to impose his rule upon us. And now, for those who have not turned their hearts to the Son he sent to earth to save us—oh, my friends!—the worst is yet to come. Untold woes will soon be visited upon those whose hearts are not sealed with the Messiah."

He took a deep breath before continuing. "Yes, my friends, the Messiah came to earth over two thousand years ago, and we of the Jewish people did not know him. If not for the forgiveness he offers, we should clothe ourselves in sackcloth and ashes and mourn. Jesus of Nazareth *is* the Christ, the Messiah that our ancestors waited for, and when he came to us so long ago, to our shame, we did not recognize him. This I believe with all my heart."

By the expressions in the room, Baruch's first words had hooked his audience. He'd even piqued Ariel's interest.

"If you do not already belong to him, here is what you must do to be spared the coming pain and judgment: Repent of your sins, believe in Jesus with all your heart, and follow him. Do that, and he will admit you into the family of God. Then you will become a child of God. Ignore that advice, and, here on earth and for all eternity, you will face unimaginable pain and suffering."

Baruch paused, sending a troubled glance over his audience, landing for a moment on Ariel.

And with that simple gesture, Ariel squirmed in his seat. Was it true? Would he endure an eternity of suffering if he rejected this man's advice?

"For those of us who are Jews, proud of our traditions, I say this: It is not by following the law that we are saved. It is not through endless efforts at complying with hundreds of rules—most of them man-made— that make us right with God. No, my friends. Just as Abraham found favor with God, it is our faith in God's promises that saves us. It is through giving our hearts and minds and souls to the Son the Father sent us that saves us. For that is God's greatest promise—that salvation comes only through belief in Jesus Christ, our Lord."

Again, Ariel shifted in his seat. Many times had he heard this message. But hearing it today, from this man, whose conviction seemed etched deep on his soul, drilled the words deep into his consciousness. His sister had become a Christian, and for her belief, Davato had murdered her and her entire family, including Ariel's beloved niece, Tiki. Since then, he'd spent his life working against the Antichrist, disrupting his rule, providing aid and comfort to Jews and Christians alike, anyone Davato targeted.

"So today, that is my simple message." Baruch straightened to his full height. "Today, you stand at the brink of eternity. Your choice is to repent of your sins, believe in Jesus, and follow him into eternal life. Do that, and you will be spared most of the suffering about to rain down upon those who do not belong to God. We are living in the end times, and no one can promise you a pain-free life. But believe me when I say that your lot will be far, far better as a Christian. Awaiting you in the life to come is a Jesus who loves you and who wants you to be with him. He is a personal Jesus, and he eagerly expects and desires that you enter into his eternal family."

He glanced around the room.

"Your other choice is to follow the beast. Do that, and here on earth, you will soon experience pain and suffering beyond imagining. And when you die, you will burn forever in the lake of eternal fire, experiencing conscious, unending suffering. I pray: Do not take that path!"

The words hit Ariel like a bullet in the gut. The man had a way and a manner of speaking that was genuine. He was a true holy man, and Ariel felt unworthy to be in his presence.

Baruch wrapped up his talk by inviting each person to speak with one of four individuals in back wearing white armbands and waiting to tell them about the next steps.

Ariel stood and headed for the exit. But before he opened the door, a hand landed on his shoulder, and he whirled.

"You must be Ariel Geller." Baruch stood before him.

"I am, and that was quite a talk you gave."

"We were to meet later, but now that you're here, perhaps we could

48

depart together and meet now. If that works for you?"

"I can do that. But I drove."

"David Benjamin has a car waiting for me. My helpers can wrap things up here. You can follow us."

* * *

IN A BASEMENT APARTMENT IN Ramat Gan, Ariel sank into an easy chair with Baruch and David Benjamin sitting opposite.

His host offered coffee, and Ariel accepted a glass of espresso. When both were settled, Baruch began. "Long have I been waiting to meet the man who has helped so many of us. I cannot convey the depth of my thanks to you, Ariel, for all you have done."

Ariel shifted in his seat. "Whatever I can do to oppose Davato, I do. He murdered the only family I had."

"Ah, yes, I was told of your loss and of your vendetta. He is truly the man of lawlessness."

"He is, and I have spent the last years doing all I can to thwart him."

"I was told you have not yet converted. Is that true?"

Ariel coughed and nodded.

"Did my message today resonate with you?"

"I have to say, Baruch, that it did."

"And have you come to a decision?" Baruch's eyes widened and brightened.

"I–I—" Ariel looked away. The man had spoken of eternity, of a loving Jesus, whom Baruch believed was the true Messiah, the one his people had long awaited but then rejected. Long had Ariel struggled with this question, and here, today, this Baruch was forcing him to make up his mind. "You believe that this Jesus was always the true Messiah? It's a difficult thing to wrap one's mind around."

"For those of us brought up by rabbis, with the Torah and all its laws, that is so."

Ariel closed his eyes. Was it true? Was Jesus the only way to Heaven? Was he truly on the path to escape the horrors Baruch insisted were coming? "I–I do . . . believe."

The instant he said the words, some unexplained force, some invisible burst of energy, shot through him. He raised a glance to his host.

"Yes, Baruch." His voice was stronger now, filled with conviction. "I do believe in Jesus as the Son of God, as the Messiah you say he is. It's been a long time coming for me, but yes, I do believe."

"And do you repent of your sins?"

Of sins, Ariel had more than enough. But if Jesus could absolve him, he would turn a new leaf. "I do." He slammed a fist on a knee. "And I want to become a Christian."

Baruch rose from his chair, crossed the gap, and hugged him. "Then welcome, my friend into the family of God. Today, the angels are rejoicing in Heaven."

David, too, rose from his seat and congratulated him.

Before they talked business, Baruch handed him a pocket copy of the New Testament that spoke of the life of Jesus and the teachings of his apostles. "Read this and study it. You will be amazed."

As Ariel took the book, David Benjamin received news that everyone had departed the meeting site safely, the chairs were loaded into a truck, and the apartment was vacated.

"But now, Ariel, let us talk business." Baruch shifted in his seat. "Are you aware that the Jewish black market working with Rabbi Ehud Efron only prefers to help other Jews? And unfortunately, the rabbi also supports the violence of the Jericho Faction."

"Yes, I am aware of him and his organization. Sometimes, I, too, supply the Jericho Faction. Anyone who opposes Davato."

Nodding, Baruch then spoke of his need for safe houses in which to place new converts awaiting passage to a place he called the Refuge. He also needed supplies.

Ariel grinned. "My friend, I have a number of such safe houses, many more than Rabbi Efron, and I will put as many of them at your disposal as you need. I will also stock them with food from my warehouses. But what is this Refuge you speak of?"

"A place in the south where God has promised us safety from the trials to come. It is yours whenever you are ready to go there."

"Safe from the Antichrist's armies? From his CSA and his Truth

Squads?"

"Yes, Ariel. When the time comes, every convert and Jew who can make it will find safety there. I will take you there when you are ready to go."

Ariel's heart surged. He'd often wondered what his end game would be. Even as God's wrath descended on the planet, Davato's grip on the world was tightening. If Baruch had a safe location, protected by the hand of God—well, it was more than Ariel could hope for. "Someday, I will take you up on that offer."

"We also have need of transport vehicles that can pass through checkpoints, and—"

"Of those, I have more than enough. I will share them with you. And drivers. And routes that bypass most of the checkpoints."

"And food, Ariel? Once we get to the Refuge, we have no need of food, for there, God will provide. But for those still in their homes in the cities and villages and on the road—"

"Again, I can supply all you need."

David Benjamin was beaming. "This is a match made in Heaven."

When they'd worked out details and Ariel was ready to leave, they shook hands, and he headed for the door.

But Baruch stopped him. "Before you go, I have one more piece of advice for a new Christian."

Ariel turned back, his brows twisted in a question. "What's that?"

"I sense that, before now, you were driven by a deep desire for revenge for what Davato has done to your family. Is that not so?"

Startled by the man's insight, Ariel hesitated then nodded.

"Then my advice is to work not from hate against the man of lawlessness, but to work instead from love for those you can help."

Ariel swallowed. It went to the heart of what he'd done these past years, didn't it? And now this holy man, this Baruch Abramovich, was telling him to be driven by love, not hate. The man's words rang true. "I will, Baruch Abramovich. From this day forward, I will work from love. And thank you."

Once more, they shook hands, and Ariel departed.

CHAPTER 10
DEPARTURE

Joel 2:28–31 (NLT): *"Then, after doing all those things, I will pour out my Spirit upon all people. Your sons and daughters will prophesy. Your old men will dream dreams, and your young men will see visions. In those days I will pour out my Spirit even on servants—men and women alike. And I will cause wonders in the heavens and on the earth—blood and fire and columns of smoke. The sun will become dark, and the moon will turn blood red before that great and terrible day of the LORD arrives."*

Shetek State Park, Minnesota – September, Year 5

Sweating, his heart pounding, his eyes wide, Caleb woke from the vision and sat up. The dream was so clear. He could still see a mountain valley with a few log cabins, a garden, a pasture and horses, and a small gathering in a square. Was this the Sanctuary? Whatever he saw, it was real. It existed. And it was somewhere out West, with blue-green mountains rising on all sides.

Was it a vision from God? Or just a wishful figment of his imagination?

From the cookstove at the cabin's far end came the sizzle of meat in the frying pan.

He shook his head and dropped his feet to the floor. For now, he'd keep the vision to himself. And besides, Andy wasn't a man to believe in visions.

Andy's wound had healed, and today, they were leaving. For days, they'd gathered everything they needed for the trip—bales of dried grass and oats for the horses, easily packed and cooked food, weapons and ammunition, water jugs, tents, firewood, sleeping bags, coats, and backpacks. And, of course, a barrel of beer for Andy.

On their few trips back to Currie, they'd found an empty town. The handful of survivors from the squaddie attack had fled, leaving them free to loot every house and apartment for what they needed. But Caleb feared the squaddies would return, and they made their visits brief.

Last night, before a bilious yellow moon, they'd piled everything in the wagon bed, ready to go.

Now, the others were at the table, eating breakfast. He dressed and joined them.

"How far do you think we'll get today?" Andy lifted a forkful of venison to his lips.

"I'm hoping to make Lake Wilson." Caleb took a plate from Tanya— bread, venison, and potatoes and onions fried in lard. "With the horses, we can do at least thirty miles a day."

"If they last," added Tanya.

"Yeah, if they last. They've lost weight. The lack of proper feed is taking its toll. Let's hope they get us to Sioux Falls. That's a ninety-mile trip."

"They'll make it." Brianna raised worried eyes. "They can't die."

"They're weak." Tanya laid a hand on her shoulder. "It'll be a hard trip for them."

"Why Sioux Falls?" asked Andy.

"Without the horses, we're in trouble." Caleb brought another spoonful to his mouth. "Let's just say: I'm hoping we'll find alternative transportation in the city."

* * *

UNDER A STRUGGLING, PALLID SUN, two rode the horses while the other two and Nika, their black-and-white miniature Australian shepherd, sat in the wagon. Their route led them south to I-90 then west. In the fields on all sides, green stalks already poked through blackened husks of burnt grass. Cracks filled with weeds broke the concrete. Abandoned, rusted cars, probably driven by the vanished, and cars disabled by the EMP attack occasionally blocked the way. On the first day, after the sun had

53

set in midafternoon, they traveled a few more miles under what was left of the moon then found an abandoned house in which to sleep.

Three times, they met other travelers. Twice, they encountered men and women on foot, locals scrounging for food, but when they saw Caleb's group approaching, they fled into the fields.

But on the second day, their view of distant strangers left him troubled. They'd barely hid the wagon and horses in a barn and entered another vacant house when out on I-90, a dozen CSA agents riding horses led a line of prisoners west, men and women and youths linked with chains and dragging their feet.

"They're taking them to the death camp," whispered Andy from a dark downstairs window.

"Are we headed that way?" Brianna's face twisted with worry.

"Not necessarily." Caleb scratched his beard. "But the quicker we finish our business in Sioux Falls and leave the city behind, the better."

On the third day, only twenty miles from Sioux Falls, they camped beside a stream well away from the highway. To conserve water, they let the horses drink from the stream.

But that was a monumental mistake. By morning, every one of them lay cold and unmoving.

"No, no!" Brianna fell to her knees before Betsy, her hands gripping the horse's head. "She was such a good animal. Why did they have to die?" She buried her head in her hands and wept.

"They were weak before we started." Andy laid a hand on her shoulder. "We knew they weren't going to last the journey."

Andy's words only made her weep all the more. Tanya tried consoling her, but her attachment to the animals went deep.

"Now what are we going to do?" Andy put hands on hips and regarded the wagon piled high with supplies.

Trying to control his own grief, Caleb tore his glance from the horses. For three years, they'd served him well. But they lived in the time of the end, and death waited everywhere for the unwary. The stream was a fatal mistake. They needed to be more careful.

Andy shook his head. "How are we going to carry all this stuff?"

Caleb made a mental inventory of their equipment and climbed up into the wagon bed. He pushed three bales of moldy hay to the ground, feed that, in any event, wouldn't have taken the animals far. When he also dumped the beer barrel off the edge, Andy's pained grimace followed as it rolled, sloshing and wobbling, across the yard. Then Caleb hopped down and wiped his hands on his pants. "We're about twenty miles from the city. The four of us can pull the wagon until we get to Sioux Falls. Then let's see what we can come up with."

Thus did they pull the wagon until, late in the afternoon of the fourth day, I-90 took them to the intersection of I-229, another broken, weed-infested stretch of concrete. As they neared the crossroads, they passed occasional businesses, defunct and dark beside the highway.

"I've been here before." Caleb looked down the empty exit ramp. "For miles south of here on I-229, there isn't much." He pulled out his solar phone. "I've got a signal!"

He tapped the icon for his search engine and typed in "bicycle shops". Looking up from his query, he smiled. "What if we each had a bicycle with a trailer? We could haul everything we needed. A child carrier could also carry Nika. That would get us to the Black Hills."

"Great idea!" said Tanya.

"A bicycle?" Brianna scrunched her face. "I've never ridden a bicycle."

"You'll learn." Andy slapped her shoulder. "It's fun. And, Caleb, that's a great idea."

"There's a big bike shop only a few miles south off I-229. Let's find a place to stop and hide the wagon."

As they headed south, a handful of isolated farms bordered the deserted highway. At the first place they tried, a farmer, his wife, and three sons barred their way with rifles, and they quickly backtracked.

But at the second house, the former owners' moldering corpses in the yard testified to an abandoned farmstead. They stored the wagon in a corrugated metal outbuilding, and Tanya made supper in the kitchen.

After they'd eaten, Caleb went to the picture window. Shadows from the setting sun were already spreading across a dried-up lawn. He turned back to his companions. "We should find this bike shop tonight, in the dark. It's only a few miles south of here. Who knows what we'll encounter in the city? Better at night than in the day."

They tied Nika to the wagon seat in the outbuilding then each took a backpack and a pistol. The adults also brought their rifles and some candles. After Nika quit barking her displeasure at being tied up, they started out on foot, walking in the ditch beside I-229.

"Those with rifles," said Andy, "set them for semiautomatic fire. Who knows what we'll encounter? But please, Brianna—be careful where you point that thing."

She nodded then lowered her pistol.

But as they traveled south beside the main road, a glow appeared in the southeastern sky, growing brighter as they walked.

"What's that?" asked Tanya.

It was the death camp, and it must be the source of power for the cell tower Caleb was using. But Brianna didn't need to know that. "Not our concern. The bike shop is only another half a mile from here, so let's—"

"Look behind you!" Andy pointed, and Caleb whirled.

The silhouettes of men on horses appeared on the highway to the north, heading their way. They were pulling what appeared to be a wagon packed with people. CSA agents with prisoners?

Caleb searched for a place to hide. But the fields were bare, without trees, and the volunteer crops didn't give enough cover. Fifty yards ahead was a highway overpass.

"Up there!" he shouted. "On the overpass."

They ran to the slope, clambered up, then hid behind the concrete parapet.

Five minutes later, the clopping of horses' hooves and the grinding of wagon wheels crossed beneath them, heading south. After they passed, Caleb peeked over the southern edge, and what he couldn't see before was now visible.

On the brightly lit horizon, dozens of guard towers poked the sky. Searchlights scanned the perimeter. Barely visible fences stretched around hundreds of low buildings. A single chimney trailed smoke to the east.

"The death camp!" Brianna slapped hands over her mouth.

"Yes, but we're not going near it." Caleb brought up the map on his phone. "The bike shop is only a quarter mile to the west then south. We're close. We can even take the road we're on."

By a dim quarter moon, they followed the overpass road west into a neighborhood of dark houses and cracked, weed-filled streets littered with burnt or abandoned cars. But as soon as they turned south, two men with shotguns appeared from behind a garage and blocked their way.

"You folks must pay the toll to pass through," said a brown-bearded man.

Caleb lifted his M16, and the others raised their weapons.

"We're just passing through." Andy waved his AR-15. "We want no trouble here."

"Everyone pays the toll," said the shorter, skinnier man. "A bit of food will do. What you got?"

"We have no food with us. We're just out for an evening stroll." Caleb cocked his weapon. The others did the same. "Now step aside."

A woman's voice called from one of the houses. "Harlan, get out of there! It's not worth it."

"Never you mind, woman," answered the brown-bearded man. Then he faced the travelers. "Now it don't have to be much, just something to respect our sov'renty over this here piece of street."

"All this here ex-marine has for you"—Andy took a step closer and raised his rifle—"is a gutful of lead. Let us pass, and no one needs to get hurt."

A shot rang out, and concrete sparked off the street beside the bearded man. His eyes wide, the man jumped back.

"Brianna!" Andy's glance speared her. "Careful with that firearm!" Then he waved his weapon at the men. "Hard to control, that gal. Now if you don't want to be lying dead on the street—get out of the way!"

Visibly shaken, the men exchanged glances then hurried into a house where a lantern now shone from the window.

The group hurried on. When they were safely past the threat, Andy whirled on Brianna. "What were you doing? You could have got us all killed."

"I–I'm sorry. I guess I pressed too hard on the trigger." She dropped her gaze. "I didn't mean to shoot."

"Well . . ." Caleb laid a hand on her shoulder. "Don't let it happen again. But it certainly scared them off."

Laughter broke the tension.

Moments later, the bike shop appeared around the corner. But its windows were broken, its door hung askew, and behind a yawning entrance waited a dark interior.

CHAPTER 11
ESCAPE FROM SIOUX FALLS

Sioux Falls, South Dakota – September, Year 5

Caleb lit one of their candles and poked his head inside the shop. Andy and Tanya also lit candles, and they examined what the place had to offer. Some of the bikes were missing, and near the counter, the cash register was open and empty. Otherwise, the looters hadn't found much to take.

"We need touring bikes with wider tires, not road bikes," said Caleb. "The highways aren't in the best shape, and sometimes we'll be off-road. The touring bikes also carry more gear."

Toward the back, they found rows of fully assembled bicycles the shop must've rented out. After everyone chose something that fit them, Caleb examined stacks of bike trailers still in cardboard boxes. "Here's a brand that carries the most weight and sits low but needs assembly."

Brianna frowned. "But it's only got a single wheel. How are we going to carry Nika in one of those?"

"We aren't." Caleb moved to a box with a child carrier. "We'll put her in this. It'll hold Nika and some extra gear beside her."

With the candles burning, they assembled three heavy-duty bike trailers and one child trailer then attached them to the rental bikes. They also pilfered water bottles, bike repair tools, extra tires, headlights with functioning batteries, and saddlebags for everyone. Then they walked the bikes and trailers out to the street.

"We can't go back the way we came." Caleb pulled out his phone and brought up the map. "We can take this street west to I-229 and then north."

"Wait a minute." Brianna was standing beside her bike with an attached trailer. "I don't know how to ride."

"We'll teach you." Tanya stood beside Brianna's bike and held it. "Jump on and start pedaling. I'll keep you from falling."

Brianna hopped onto the seat, gripped the handlebars, and pedaled. As Tanya ran beside her, holding on, a smiling Brianna kept the bike upright. But a few seconds after Tanya let go, she lost her balance. Tanya tried to grab her, but she was already on the pavement. She stood, gave the bike an ugly look, then brushed gravel from her hands and knees.

"We'll go to the end of the block and back a few times," said Tanya. "You'll catch on."

Brianna shot her an even uglier look but hopped back onto the seat.

For the next half hour, Tanya worked with the girl until Brianna was able to ride to the end and back, alone and without falling. The last trip was a bit wobbly, but when she dropped one leg to the pavement, straddled the crossbars, and kept the bike from crashing to the ground, everyone clapped.

"See?" said Andy. "Wasn't that fun?"

A beaming Brianna nodded. "The Black Hills here we come!"

As Caleb led them east, he glanced back often to make sure Brianna was keeping up. When the street met I-229, there was no exit, so they crossed a field. Then they walked their bikes down a gully and climbed the slope onto the southbound highway.

At the top, Brianna gazed south. The camp was closer, its lights brighter, and a shift in the wind brought the odor of burnt flesh and bone.

"Come on." Caleb waved. "Let's get back to the farmhouse. We've got to make time tonight."

With Caleb in the lead, they headed north. Brianna and Tanya were right behind, and Andy brought up the rear. But they hadn't gone a mile when Andy called out. "A group on horses in the other lane is following us."

Caleb shot a glance back. Lit by lights from the death camp, a half dozen mounted men were heading north in the northbound lane. "I don't think they've seen us, but let's pick up the pace. If they see us, we'll have to outrun them."

"Outrun th–them?" Brianna's voice trembled.

He pedaled faster and looked back. Everyone was keeping up, even Brianna.

Moments later, Andy cried out. "They've seen us!"

Again, Caleb looked back. Perhaps a half mile behind, the horses had crossed the median and were galloping toward them. "We can outrun them. The horses will tire before we do." The road was flat, and he ratcheted up the speed.

But a quarter mile later, the horses were gaining ground, closing half the distance, and Brianna had fallen behind. Waving Tanya and Andy ahead, he slowed beside the girl.

"You can do this," he said. "Just pedal faster, and the horses will tire before we do."

"Easy for you to say." She frowned and took her glance off the road. But the moment she did, she lost her balance. The front tire wobbled and tipped sideways, and she went down.

Caleb dismounted, helped her up, and she examined her scuffed palms. They started again. But now the horses were only a hundred yards behind.

"Come on!" he urged. "We've got to go faster. If they catch us, they'll send us to the camp."

Brianna took one look behind her, grimaced, and began pumping her legs.

Surprised by her burst of speed, he raced to catch up. The others were a quarter mile ahead. But Brianna now seemed energized, and both she and Caleb were gaining.

Another glance back convinced him the horses were indeed tiring. They'd lost all the ground they'd gained after Brianna's fall, and now the bicycles were pulling away.

After another mile, the horses had fallen back even further.

"We're beating them!" Brianna came even with Andy and Tanya. "The bikes are winning!"

Only a few yards ahead, Tanya looked back. "Good job, girl!"

"Thanks. I'm catching on, aren't I?"

"At the next turnaround," said Caleb, "we should cross to the northbound lane. By the time we get to the farmhouse, let's hope we're out of sight of whoever is following us."

"Probably some kind of CSA patrol," added Andy.

"Probably."

In another twenty minutes, their pursuers had dropped from view, and they crossed to the northbound lane. A moment later, the farmhouse appeared on their right.

"Quick!" he said. "Into the outbuilding and out of sight."

They walked the bicycles into the garage where an excited Nika wagged her tail in greeting. They closed the door. Then, from a dirty, cobweb-covered window, Caleb watched and waited.

Ten minutes later, horses appeared on the highway. He held his breath as they continued north in the southbound lane. "They're going on! They didn't see us!"

"Great!" Andy came up beside him, looking out. "Now what?"

"I'd like to start west tonight and get past the city before daybreak. But first, we need to transfer our gear and supplies to the carriers and the saddlebags."

"But if we head north," said Tanya, "what if we run into that patrol?"

Caleb scratched his beard. "Our other option is to wait until tomorrow night, and I'd rather get out of here now. Once we make the turn west on I-90, maybe we'll lose them."

Deciding what to keep and what to leave was difficult. By the time the bike trailers and the saddlebags were loaded and Nika was strapped in the child carrier, two hours had passed.

They left the shed, crept back onto I-229, and pedaled the short distance north until they reached the I-90 intersection and headed west.

Caleb kept looking back, but the CSA must have either given up the search or taken a different route.

The bike's odometer told him when they'd covered the nine miles to the Buffalo Ridge Ghost Town west of the city. A bit further and they pulled off the road, crossed a field, and bedded down in a shelter belt.

Hidden by trees, they camped in the dark.

Caleb unrolled his sleeping bag and glanced toward the others in the dark. "From here, it's three hundred and forty miles to the Black Hills and, hopefully, the Sanctuary. If we do thirty-five miles a day, we should arrive in ten days, well before cold weather sets in."

"Ten days, huh?" said Brianna. "I can do this."

"You can," said Andy. "And we're proud of you for learning how to ride so fast."

But as they were settling in, Caleb glanced toward the highway. "Look there."

Everyone stood from their sleeping bags. From out on I-90, heading west, came the clopping hooves of a CSA horse patrol, shining a searchlight on the road.

"I thought they'd not come this far," said Caleb. "Guess I was wrong."

"Let's hope they don't follow us tomorrow," whispered Andy in the dark. "I've no wish to end up in that camp. We need to pray to the Lord to keep them away. For surely, it is he who has helped us so far."

And that simple statement, coming from a friend who rarely spoke of spiritual things, buoyed Caleb, and he smiled. "They are ruled by the underworld, the realm of darkness, and the Dragon, the one who controls Davato. And Jesus, Lord of Lords, King of Kings, the one who sits in Heaven at the Father's right hand, is stronger and greater than the ones who follow us. Thank you, Andy, for reminding us."

Then he knelt and prayed to the Savior, asking him to thwart and mislead those the Adversary had sent against them.

After he'd finished, he was content. He crawled into his sleeping bag and slept.

CHAPTER 12
A TRIP DELAYED

Joel 2:1b–2a (NLT): *Let everyone tremble in fear because the day of the* LORD *is upon us. It is a day of darkness and gloom, a day of thick clouds and deep blackness.*

From Appenzell, Switzerland, to Tuscany, Italy – October, Year 5

As the dim yellow globe touched the mountains and ended the day, Dylan left the van for an Appenzell side street and began his journey. With Pasqual still in the van, he glanced up and down the cobbled lane. No lights in the windows. No one about. Only lengthening shadows and a line of abandoned vehicles.

He approached a black Mercedes and tried the door. Locked.

The next vehicle was a white VW sedan with busted windows and leaves filling the seat. But it was all-electric and wouldn't do. All electric cars were trackable. The CSA could take over the controls whenever they liked. Only UI-manned stations could charge them. And their range was shorter, especially in winter.

Passing this, he stopped at a blue Opal sedan. It was occupied, but the driver was long dead, probably a plague victim. A woman's desiccated corpse sat upright in the driver's seat, her long blonde hair falling over black, shriveled flesh, her jaw hanging open as if ready to complain should anyone try to steal her car.

He tried the door, and it opened. Inside, the key was still in the ignition. Only the desperate would trouble to steal a vehicle occupied by her corpse.

"Sorry, ma'am, but I need your car." Grimacing, he grabbed the body, yanked it onto the sidewalk, and brushed pieces of dried, blackened flesh off the seat.

When he tried the key, the engine emitted a weak groan then fell silent.

Pasqual left the van and came up. "Battery?"

"Probably. And it will need gas."

They pulled the van beside it, poured some gas into the tank, and attached jumper cables. They waited a bit for the battery to charge. After a half dozen tries, the motor started, sputtered, and then roared.

Pasqual filled the tank from cans they'd brought, and Dylan deposited his gear in the passenger seat.

He shook his friend's hand, slipped behind the wheel, and rolled down the window. "I have a feeling this may take some time. If Bettino isn't there, if something happened to him—well . . . I don't know what I'll do." He gripped the wheel and stared straight ahead. Without Bettino, how would he ever contact Chelsea?

Pasqual patted his shoulder. "Let us know what you find. Now take care, my friend. Travel these days is perilous."

Dylan nodded, and, as a sliver of dark moon rose in a night devoid of too many stars, he pulled away from the curb.

* * *

THE TRIP TO THE VILLA SHOULD have taken seven hours at most, but it took two days. In Switzerland, gangs again blocked intersections, demanding payment for passage. In Italy, the Autostrade had been cleared of pileups, but again he had to bypass broken asphalt and crevasses. Near Milan, he was forced to detour around spots in the A50 where quakes had opened huge gaps in the highway. Everywhere in the villages, youths patrolled the streets with knives, tire irons, and axes. Where was the peace Davato had promised?

On the way, Dylan couldn't help but think about Margot's last painting. How could they both end up as Unitum Imperium prisoners with the mark of the beast? He would never, ever agree to such a thing. He shuddered. No, it cannot, will not happen. But if they were never captured, such a thing could never occur. They must take care never to

65

be captured.

In early afternoon, he turned on the radio to hear a Unitum Imperium announcer gushing praise for the upcoming World Economic Forum meeting in New Babylon:

The wealth that New Babylon has created for its followers has catapulted ten companies to control 85 percent of the world's commerce. Three CEOs at the top of that list account for 60 percent of that business, and this afternoon they are arriving in New Babylon to join the others at the World Economic Forum being chaired by the Imperator. One cannot help but be awed by the wealth and power represented by the fleet of jets landing at New Babylon's International Airport today.

Sam Wainwright arrived first. By gobbling up most of his competitors, he has made PetroSol into the world's main provider of wind, solar, minerals, pharmaceutical and petroleum products.

The second arrival is Bill Gray, the Australian tycoon and CEO of Daintree. The planet now orders 70 percent of all merchandise from Daintree's online company, delivered to our doors via trucks and drones from a vast, worldwide network of warehouses.

Jason Howard is third on our list. He's just been appointed the CEO of Worldnet, replacing the company's former CEO, Adam Turner, who now heads the Ministry of Truth. Mr. Howard recently moved the company's headquarters to Hyderabad, India, from Rome. Worldnet maintains the planet's premier search engine and gives us nearly all our software, computers, microchips, and security systems.

Yes, the world stands in awe of these men, celebrates their success, their wealth, and what they have done for—

Dylan shut off the radio in disgust. Even before the vanishing, those same woke companies and many more endorsed the kind of immorality and evil that Davato and the Prophet now promoted—LGBTQ, abortion, gender confusion and transformation, universalism in religion, and the toxic division of races. They championed the climate change agenda and all the totalitarian solutions to "fix" the supposed problem. In the COVID-19 and climate lockdowns when the government shuttered the mom-and-pop businesses but allowed only the behemoths to stay open, they grew even larger. They were instrumental in suppressing every voice that spoke truth against the lies destroying the culture.

Long before the vanishing, they were already in lockstep with the Antichrist's agenda.

* * *

ABOUT AN HOUR BEFORE SUNSET, he turned into the drive leading up to the family villa. But the tall cypresses were barren, stripped of green. And the unharvested grapes clinging to the vines were small and sickly.

He parked in the lot below the hill, grabbed his bag, and checked the garage where Bettino's green Fiat was still parked. The second stall was empty, and he drove the Opal inside. With his bag in hand, he shut the door.

After his father had left with Davato for Jerusalem and New Babylon, the villa would be abandoned to Bettino's care. He had no worries that Adam Turner would ever return.

But as Dylan hiked up to the villa, no lights shone in the windows, and his heart beat faster. When he tried the second-floor door leading to the living room, it opened into a dark, musty interior. He flicked the switch, but the electricity was off.

"Bettino?" he called but received no answer.

He switched on his phone light and began a search, calling out several times for the caretaker. All that returned to him was silence.

Checking each room, he found desk and cabinet drawers pulled out and flipped upside down, their contents spewed across the carpets. Paintings were missing from walls. Everywhere was evidence of looting.

He examined the second floor, the third, and then the ground floor. In every room, looters had come, taken what they wanted, and departed.

In the basement, he opened the breaker box and turned on the electricity someone had shut off.

But as he pushed through the door into the kitchen, the smell of death and decay smacked him in the face, and he backed up, his heart beating fast. When he reentered, he slapped a hand over his mouth and gasped.

Lying face down, riddled with bullet holes, and covered with dried blood was Bettino's shriveled corpse.

"Oh no." He slumped to his knees. "Not you. Not this dear, sweet old man."

He wiped a tear from his cheek, stood, and staggered out the door into the hall.

But he hadn't taken ten steps before he reentered the kitchen and, holding his nose, checked the caretaker's pockets. When he found Bettino's phone, he raced for the fresh air of the hall. The phone was dead, but he retrieved the charger from Bettino's bedside table. He waited for it to receive enough juice to operate then searched the history for a message from Chelsea.

But there was nothing. She never called him.

Was she still alive? If so, why hadn't she contacted Bettino?

He slumped onto the bed and held his head in his hands. For long minutes, the villa's silence crept into his soul. What should he do?

Some sixth sense still told him she was alive, and he couldn't give up.

What about the bishop's place? Maybe Emilio Gallo knew something.

A short drive to the villa next door only increased his concern, for there, too, the place was dark and abandoned. It was now after sunset, but the electricity was on. Flicking on lights as he went, he searched every room but encountered no sign that anyone had been here recently.

The bishop's place, too, was deserted.

Here was another mystery: What had happened to the bishop? Had the Truth Squads taken him?

But after driving all day, Dylan was hungry and exhausted. In the kitchen, the water from the family well was safe, and he found penne pasta and tomato sauce. The bishop's refrigerator, still humming, yielded sausage and peppers. As he sat down with a bottle of Emilio Gallo's wine, for the first time that day, he relaxed. And he formulated a plan.

Tonight, he would sleep in one of Emilio's bedrooms. Tomorrow, he would return to the family villa and bury Bettino among the grapevines. Then he would go to the entrances leading to the family villa and Emilio's place and set up the two trigger devices Victor had prepared for him. If a car entered either drive, the pocket receivers he would carry with him at all times would sound an alarm. That would alert him if the squaddies were on their way.

He would clean a few rooms in which to live. Then he would wait.

Chelsea was alive. He felt it. He knew it. She must have left Davato and was now on the run. But for some reason, she couldn't call anyone. Or she'd lost everyone's numbers. He knew Chelsea, and with no other options, her next step would be to come here, in person. And when she arrived, he would be here to lead her to Kronberg Mountain.

How long he'd have to wait, he didn't know.

But wait he would.

CHAPTER 13
THE BLACK HILLS

Across the South Dakota Plains – October, Year 5

To the hum and bounce of bike tires over uneven concrete, Caleb, Tanya, Andy, and Brianna pedaled west across the South Dakota plains, making good time.

Green stalks poked everywhere through the blackened husks left from the May fires and the lightning storms. This was farm country, and V-Day had taken much of the populace, leaving behind abandoned farmhouses where the group spent their nights. Most places had their own wells where the water was untainted and safe to drink.

Brianna not only kept pace, she soon out-pedaled them all, often riding far ahead and egging the others on. In the bike carrier behind Tanya, Nika mostly slept.

When they passed the Missouri River and entered a sparsely populated dry country, they ate up the miles. Caleb now expected to beat his original estimate of ten days. Endless signs for Wall Drug measured the distance—Wall Drug, with its singing cowboys, five-cent coffee, and Western gear for sale. Probably empty and abandoned now.

When they left Sioux Falls, they also left behind all cell service. Caleb checked periodically, but he'd lost contact with Dylan.

The fifth day, despite the pallid sun, was warm and humid, and dust devils swirled across the fields.

Toward evening on the sixth and seventh days, when no farmhouses appeared near the road, they pitched tents and slept in the open.

On the morning of the eighth day, despite the wounded orb that passed for a sun, it was still warm. Shortly after they started, the barren red cliffs of the Badlands rose on both sides of the highway.

Then, at midday, a storm hit.

The sky darkened, the wind picked up, and a massive dust cloud obliterated the horizon. From earth to heaven, the black monster roiled and churned and ate up everything in its path.

Caleb pulled off the road into a field and ran to his trailer. "We've got to get under shelter before that thing hits."

Brianna straddled her bike with hands on top of her head and stared at the oncoming storm. "I've never seen anything like it."

"Nor I," added Andy. "Only in pictures from the 1930s dust bowls."

"Stop gawking and help with the tents!" ordered Tanya.

Inside the cloud, lightning flashed, and thunder rumbled. As Caleb frantically pounded in stakes, the angry roar grew louder, closer.

The first cold winds whipped past just as they tied tarps over their bikes and finished raising one tent for Caleb and Andy and another for Tanya and Brianna.

As the nylon whooshed and flapped wildly, Caleb crawled in after Andy. He zipped shut the front flap and breathed deeply.

Day became night, the wind screamed, and a hurricane of dust whipped around them. The tent poles lifted off the ground and rammed the earth. A continuous hail of sand pelted the walls. Dust and sand seeped through cracks, until, even inside the tent, Caleb was breathing dust, tasting dust, and wiping dust from his eyes.

The storm was an angry beast, and it roared and fought against all who dared traverse its path. The hours passed, and he tried to sleep. But the flapping and whooshing of tent walls and the nearby lightning strikes kept him awake.

As the day wore on, the temperature plummeted, and he pulled a sweater, gloves, and a stocking cap from his backpack.

In a lull, Nika's whine came from the women's tent, followed by Brianna's soothing words. He called to them, and they assured him they were okay.

In this way, they hunkered down until late afternoon when the winds died and the storm passed.

Gritty and dirty, he emerged from his nylon cocoon and brushed himself off. Everywhere he turned, inches of dust and sand covered the fields. He took a few steps onto the highway. Two to six inches of dust and sand coated the road.

Andy stood beside him, regarding I-90. "If we have to slog through that, it'll be slow going from now on."

Caleb nodded. "We're maybe a hundred and thirty miles from the hills. We can walk the bikes if we have to. But now it will take forever."

"Do you have a destination in mind?"

"Maybe Hill City or Custer. There, we can ask around. If the Sanctuary is nearby, someone is certain to know about it." He raised his glance to the sun, now a dim orange bulb in a darkened sky. A few white flakes drifted down, and when he stuck out a hand, he brought it back cold and wet.

It was snowing.

"I hope you're right." Andy grabbed a snowflake on its way down and stared at it. "Because winter is coming."

* * *

WITH THEM WALKING THEIR BIKES, the trip to Custer took far longer than planned. Past the Badlands, the road cleared, and again they rode, making up some time. Though the snow ended, the cold did not. Well before Rapid City, they headed south on a back road to avoid unwanted encounters with strangers.

The country there was parched and barren, made more so by the drought. On the fourteenth night, they found an abandoned farmhouse where they slept and replenished their supplies.

On the fifteenth day out from Sioux Falls, their route met SD-79, and they headed west through brown rolling hills, sleeping that night in another abandoned house.

The next morning, they entered forests of pine, their needles leached brown. Here the land was devoid of ranches and farms. Where US-16A turned west, they entered Custer State Park and began climbing a winding, tortuous route—at least for bicycles. For miles, they cycled through the charred remains of a forest populated by nothing but fallen and blackened trunks.

Further on, they neared a pocket of green pines and the Grace Coolidge Campgrounds with several campers. Nearest the road, sitting on a picnic table beside an RV and a fire, sat an older couple.

Caleb parked his bike on the highway. The others followed.

A white-haired elderly man yanked a revolver from his belt, and a woman left the fire and hid behind him.

Raising his hands, Caleb approached. "We mean no harm. We only want to ask a question."

"Then speak your piece and begone." The old man waved his pistol.

"Can you tell me if the Sanctuary is nearby? We've been riding since Sioux Falls. That's our destination."

A laugh escaped the woman, who stepped from behind the man. "The Sanctuary? Hah! How many times haven't we heard that, Elroy?"

The man lowered his weapon and grinned. "I'm sorry to disappoint you folks, but you're not the first to ask about such a place. There's nothing like that around here, or we'd go there ourselves."

"Have you heard any rumors about where it might be?" asked Tanya.

"It's in Colorado." The man sheathed his revolver. "Or Wyoming. Or Montana. Or Utah. Take your pick."

"It don't exist," said the woman.

Caleb nodded and faced the others.

"What do we do now?" asked Andy.

"We need to stop somewhere before winter," said Tanya. "It's barely above freezing."

"We'll go on to Custer." Now that he wasn't riding, Caleb wrapped his arms about his torso to ward off the chill. "We'll ask there. Somebody must have heard something. Maybe there we can find a place to stay."

* * *

THE RIDE TO CUSTER TOOK ONLY a few hours, but the place was a ghost of its former self, with rusted, abandoned cars and vacant buildings lining Mt. Rushmore Road down the center. They parked their bikes outside the single remaining restaurant—The Black Hills Burger and Bun Company—beside two thin, mangy horses tied to a flagpole still flying the colors of the United States of America.

When Caleb started for the door, Tanya laid a hand on his shoulder. "Is it safe? What if there are CSA inside? We don't have the marks."

He patted the Glock in the holster at his hip. "I don't care. If this place serves food, I'm ready to eat in a real restaurant. And I doubt the CSA would get far in Custer, South Dakota."

"Maybe they have beer?" added Andy. "I'm with you. Let's go in."

With Brianna leading Nika on her leash, they entered. Two couples at tables raised worried glances. Sitting beside his white-haired companion, a middle-aged man with a full black beard frowned, pulled a pistol from his hip, and smacked it down on the table.

From the back came a man wearing a black goatee and bearing a shotgun. A young, attractive woman with a ponytail entered from the side, carrying a pistol. "What do you want?" asked the proprietor. "We want no trouble here."

"Nor do we." Caleb pointed to the two tables with the burgers and fries on the customers' plates and the glasses of beer. "What will you take for four meals like the ones you've given these folks? It's been years since I've had a good meal in a restaurant."

"Well." Though the woman didn't lower her gun, the man holstered his weapon and scratched his beard. "Some of us around here still take cash, and the going rate for strangers is fifty dollars for exactly what those folks are having. That's the only thing on the menu now—burgers, fries, and beer. Cattle are scarce, and we use buffalo meat when we can get it. But they're dying off too. The horses, the buffalo, every living thing— they're all dying."

The man closed his eyes and shook his head. "That's the way of things, isn't it? Everywhere you turn—death and the end of all things. Nothing anyone can do but live through it. And trust in God. And Jesus. And the life to come."

While the woman holstered her gun and nodded, the man raised his head. "We make our own bread and beer, but nothing's growing as it should. Not the wheat. Not the barley. Not the hops. If you've got a gun and ammo to trade, we'd sure appreciate it. Otherwise, cash will do."

74

"Sorry, we can't part with our guns, but we *can* pay cash." Caleb swallowed. He had a wad of bills stuck inside his pack, money he hadn't used in years. Still, two hundred dollars for a meal was a bit much. "Give us four plates and—" He squinted at Brianna. "Yes, and four beers."

The man's smile followed Brianna's. "Do you know how long it's been since we've had a paying customer? Coming right up." While he left for the back, the woman found a nearby table, her gaze never leaving the newcomers.

As Caleb and his group sat, the man with the full beard beside them sheathed his pistol. "You folks passing through?"

"We're headed for the Sanctuary," answered Caleb. "But we're thinking of staying here for the winter."

"The Sanctuary, huh?" His white-haired companion shook her head. "You're not the first person to ask about that."

Marty nodded. "We've heard folks say it's in Cheyenne Mountain near Colorado Springs."

Tanya's face lit up, and Caleb's heart leaped. "That's the best news I've heard since we left Sioux Falls."

"Mind you, we've heard that more than once, but who knows? They say nukes hit the Denver area, but I don't know about Colorado Springs."

"We heard Denver got it. But nothing about Colorado Springs."

"Name's Marty Eastwood." He reached a hand across the gap. "And this here's my wife, Ella."

After Caleb introduced everyone, Marty asked where they'd come from, and Caleb told him most of their story, starting with their departure from the North Shore, leaving out some parts, including the demon. He finished with a question. "Have you had any trouble with the CSA and the Truth Squads around here?"

Marty frowned and patted the pistol on his hip. "Those green-and-white scum came here twice. They wanted our guns. They said to take down the Stars and Stripes. And they told us to worship this Davato fellow. But we're Christians now, and we know who he is, don't we, Vernon?" He waved to the young couple at the far table, and the man tipped his black cowboy hat in acknowledgment.

"The first time, there was a gun battle. We lost a man, but we took out every one of them. The second time, four goons left with their tails between their legs with one killed and another wounded. We also lost another man in that fight."

Caleb laid his palms on the scarred wooden table. "Good to know."

"We don't like killing," said Ella Eastwood. "The Bible's clear on that. But our men did what they had to do. I'm glad you're churchgoing folks. If you're still here Sunday, you're welcome to come to our little church that meets on North Sixth Street."

"We'd like that," answered Tanya. "But we need somewhere to stay for the winter. Do you know of a place?"

"There's a number of empty houses in Custer," answered Marty. "Most of them are abandoned. V-Day, you know. And the plague. And starvation. And the fighting. Most of those who stayed have turned to the Lord. The ones who didn't—they've gone to Hill City or Rapid City. We've seen what's going on—the quakes, the lightning, the volcanic ash—and we know what's happening. This is the end times, and we have to make our hearts right with God."

Caleb thanked them both as the owner brought them plates of hamburgers, fries, and mugs of beer, the first restaurant meal he'd eaten in years. The proprietor also set down a bowl for Nika. "I'm throwing in this here for your dog. Ours up and died last year. I'll also give you two bags of dog food I've got no use for."

Again, he thanked the man as Nika gobbled up the food.

Afterward, they followed Marty and Ella Eastwood to an abandoned house on the edge of town, a place with its own fresh water well.

And there, they settled down for the winter.

CHAPTER 14
THE CONFERENCE OF GOVERNORS

Daniel 7:23–25a (NLT): *Then he said to me, "This fourth beast is the fourth world power that will rule the earth. It will be different from all the others. It will devour the whole world, trampling and crushing everything in its path. Its ten horns are ten kings who will rule that empire. Then another king will arise, different from the other ten, who will subdue three of them. He will defy the Most High and oppress the holy people of the Most High. . . ."*

New Babylon, Iraq – November, Year 5

Even before William Cole entered the grand reception room in New Babylon's World Casino, he was sweating. They'd allowed him to pass through the first level of security unmolested. They never found the plastic gun hidden inside his jacket. And their machines never squawked about the special coating hiding the magazine's six bullets. Even so, he couldn't stop his heart's wild beating or the sweat pouring off his forehead.

Trying to convey an air of confidence, he strolled through the assembly of governors and aides, probably a hundred men, women, and nonbinaries, who'd crossed the world to attend today's conference. The only countries not represented were China—devastated, starving, and near collapse after the US EMP and nuke response—and Russia, whose military and governmental institutions had been obliterated in what some were calling the Battle of Gog and Magog. Reports from Russia indicated some activity in the east beyond the Urals, but no one knew if anyone was in charge. Most of the Islamic countries had also been rubbed out of existence and were not present.

Cole still didn't understand what went on during that battle. Someone was surely hiding what really happened. Davato's and the Prophet's explanations were nonsense.

Appearing from a crowd of other representatives came black-bearded Umberto Gómez Rodriguez, governor of South America. "No problems, signor?"

"None at all. Everything's according to plan." When Rodriguez cocked his head, Cole wiped the sweat from his brow. Was his discomfiture showing?

The two men passed Cole's fifteen-man security contingent, disguised as aides. All were equipped with hidden guns. Each man was assigned a CSA target, ready to neutralize Davato's men after Cole had done the deed and given the signal. Umberto's security contingent was similarly equipped and ready as was Anderson's. In addition, at least forty others claiming to be trade and business representatives dealing with the UI army brass had arrived last week with hidden weapons. They were standing by to take out any uncooperative military leaders.

In the room's center, one of the nonbinary aides, dressed as a woman, but clearly once a man, bumped him, spilling some of her—his?—coffee onto Cole's black suit. She was a horror to behold, but she apologized and tried to brush off the spill. Cole waved her away. "It's all right. It doesn't show." Pulling a handkerchief from his pocket, he dabbed at the liquid then continued. What a time for something like this to happen.

Across the room, big-bellied Jack Anderson, governor of Australasia, waited at the entrance to a small hallway. Beside him stood a bald man dressed in a suit emblazoned with the six-sided Davato patch—one of the Imperator's lower functionaries. Anderson said nothing but simply joined the two as the aide checked their IDs then led them down the hall.

At the meeting room's door, a fat, busty, unsmiling CSA woman with a scar on her right cheek and her hair tortured into a tight bun checked their badges again. She ushered them into the meeting room and left.

On the far side of a round table holding eight chairs sat a grinning, green-eyed Sebastien Rey. Beside the Prophet, Davato rose and walked toward them with an open hand.

What unbelievable luck. Only Davato, the Prophet, and the three coconspirators were present. Cole didn't know what he'd have done if there'd been security people to deal with. His plan was proceeding better than he could have hoped.

"Welcome, gentlemen." Davato smiled and shook each of their hands. Then he pointed to seats near the door.

Was this the moment?

Still feeling the strength of the Imperator's grip, Cole swallowed.

Should he shoot these two now while Davato stood and Sebastien Rey sat across the table?

While the security people were outside?

Before a lot of annoying conversation?

His right hand reached inside his jacket and slipped into the pocket where waited the thin plastic pistol, created by a 3D printer with a 9mm barrel, a weapon designed to end the lives of these two monsters.

His fingers groped, seeking for the item, but—

The gun was missing!

The pocket was empty!

It had been there when he entered the building, of that he was certain.

"Something wrong, Cole?" Davato's grin told him all he needed to know. Was it the nonbinary who'd bumped into him as he crossed the reception room floor? Had the woman/man picked his pocket?

"N–no. Everything's fine."

But as Rodriguez's and Anderson's worried glances found him, everyone in the room knew everything was *not* fine, something here was terribly, horribly amiss.

Cole feared what would happen next.

Would security people now burst through the door and haul them away?

"Please sit." The Prophet, wearing a grin so wide it could split a face, waved them to seats opposite. "I am dying—no pun intended—to hear your questions."

Cole's heart raced out of control, and he was light-headed. Still, somehow he found a seat. Beside him, his coconspirators, startled expressions marring their faces, plopped into chairs.

"Please." Now sitting, Davato raised an open hand. "Ask away."

The conversation that followed was stilted, awkward. The three men ran through their list of prepared complaints.

They weren't getting enough of just about everything. Food. Solar phones. Fuel. Cole couched his requests in the niceties of diplomacy speak. Everywhere, there were too many CSA goons, Truth Squads, and spies. The governors didn't have enough control over their own provinces to properly carry out their responsibilities. Unitum Imperium troops were stationed everywhere, and they felt like occupied countries.

The men's complaints to Sebastien Rey were different. His commercials encouraging people to turn in their neighbors caused distrust and discord. They made people suspicious of everyone else. With the promise of big rewards, neighbors suspected innocent neighbors and friends of being a Christian or a Jew. Anderson had a list of cases where former officials of his previous government, men and women he was certain had nothing to do with Christianity or Judaism, had been taken away in the middle of the night, never to be seen again.

To those complaints, the Prophet's only response was, "Who of us knows what rebellious thoughts run through our neighbors' heads? Do you?"

The conversation dragged on, each man trying to recover from the failed assassination, each stumbling to say the same thing in different ways.

But Cole and his coconspirators were clearly rattled.

Rodriguez kept looking behind him, as though he expected someone to burst through the door at any moment.

Anderson kept glancing sideways at Cole, as if to ask, "What have you done to us?" And he tripped over his words.

When they'd finished, Davato again crossed the room, shook each of their hands, smiled as if nothing were amiss, and said that both he and the Prophet would look into each and every "suggestion" they'd heard.

The Imperator knocked on the door, and three aides, not one, ushered them back to the reception room.

* * *

IN THE VAST RECEPTION AREA, COCKTAILS swung from every hand as governors and aides carried on the buzz of conversation. Davato and Sebastien Rey took a separate path from the three conspirators, disappearing through a door at the far end, no doubt entering the main conference room.

A burly CSA man appeared at Cole's side. "From here on, I will be your escort." His arms bulged with muscles, his neck sported a devil's-head tattoo, and a mop of red hair fell down over one eye.

Cole was in no position to argue. He looked around for his own security men, but they were missing—all of them.

Beside him, CSA men had also found Anderson and Rodriguez. Anderson's forehead was twisted into a look of stark terror as he, too, searched for his missing aides.

Cole's new CSA companion escorted him through the milling governors, some of whom now stared at the three men with obvious alarm. Or was it disgust?

The conference room was designed to impress attendees with how small, insignificant, and helpless were its occupants, and Cole started for a chair as far from the front as possible. But the CSA man shook his head, laid a crushing grip on Cole's shoulder, and guided him to the front. There, he was pushed into a seat closest to Davato at the table's head. Opposite him was a grinning Sebastien Rey. His glance found Rodriguez and Anderson seated to his left.

Cole turned around. There stood his burly CSA friend, winking, smiling, and waving a finger that said, "No, you don't."

The governors occupied the front seats. Each had been allowed only five aides for the core meeting, and these sat in chairs behind their master, mistress, or whatever sex the person claimed that day.

When the room had settled, Davato looked down from his seat

perched above the assembled, appearing like some kind of god. "Men, women, and nonbinaries—welcome to this conference of governors, those to whom I entrusted power, gave honor, and upon whom I have showered endless boons. But before we begin, we have some unpleasant business to attend to."

He paused, and when he spoke next, his speech carried an air of power, authority, and menace. "Unfortunately, some among us did *not* listen to the warnings I gave when they signed onto this venture. Indeed, three of our number demanded more than what they received. Far more. Three have even plotted against the Unitum Imperium and their Imperator."

The silence of the grave seeped into every corner of the room. Not a whisper was heard. Not a pen was dropped. Not a head turned away.

Cole's heart now raced so fast, he feared it would burst. He gripped the seat's arms so hard, his knuckles ached. His gaze, fixed on Davato not ten feet away, filled with bursting spots.

"Now you might ask: Who are these men who dared rebel against their benefactor, the divine Imperator who gave them everything, who will lead the world into the next century? I'll tell you who they are." Davato stood and extended his arm. He pointed straight at Cole. Then his finger moved to Rodriguez. Then to Anderson.

"Yes, they are the governors of North and South America and the governor of Australasia." He lowered his arm and stared at Cole. "So what should we do with them? What punishment is appropriate? A public display is out of the question. We cannot make them martyrs or give the public an idea that men of such exalted, trusted positions would plan what they have planned. Their punishment must occur here, in this room, in the next few minutes. And whatever happens here, must, of course, never, ever leave here. But your Imperator, your leader who has risen from the grave, who has been given divine power, does know what to do with them."

With those words came a sound behind Cole that chilled his blood and pricked his spine.

Three metal slides clicked in three pistols.

Sending three bullets into three metal chambers.

He whirled, and the burly man smiled, laid one hand on Cole's head, and jerked it back to the front. The force of the turn was so sharp, Cole felt something in his neck crack, and he wanted to scream.

Davato's attention now drilled into his would-be assassins. His visage twisted, his eyes turned black, and a cloud passed over his face.

Silence, deep and long, stole through the room, and Cole feared he was going to pass out.

His gaze was drawn irresistibly to the Imperator. Then the lights dimmed. The people vanished. And the room swirled with restless shadows. He was staring not at a man, but at a demon, a prince of earthly demons. Instead of a conference table, what filled his vision were wavering tongues of dark fire, trembling and licking and caressing a towering figure from a world not of this one. Even as it mesmerized him, it sent his heart racing. It locked his hands into fists so tight, his knuckles were like to burst. For he knew with certainty that this was the end.

Davato's hands shot together in a loud clap, and Cole jumped.

It was the signal, of course. For a split second, Cole's ears registered a pistol shot, and something slammed into the back of his head.

Then he was falling, spinning and turning, dropping headlong through an endless shaft of deep darkness and twisting black fire.

Some sixth sense told him that the God of the Universe had allowed this, that at the end of this tunnel waited the Prince of Darkness, the one Davato called the Dragon, and that before he was thrown into the lake of eternal fire, the Dragon would deal with Cole however he wished.

He opened his mouth to scream. But he had no breath in him.

CHAPTER 15
VISITORS

In the Tuscan Countryside, Italy – November, Year 5

I t was the last day of November, and Dylan Turner had been in Tuscany for a month. He was settled in, dividing his time between the family place and the bishop's. In each villa, he'd left a note for Chelsea in obscure language, hinting that it was indeed he and that she should check the other villa.

In the family villa, the utilities were paid automatically from Father's accounts. It must have been the same for the bishop's.

In case the squaddies came to visit, he decided to clean and keep the lights on in only three rooms in each villa: the kitchen, a bedroom he claimed for his own, and a small den where he relaxed at night with a book and a glass of wine or two. Emilio had a vast collection of books, and now those—and his Bible—became Dylan's only companions.

He called Pasqual and René, told them what he'd found, and said he was going to wait for Chelsea no matter how long it took. Then, one day, he received a call from Caleb.

"We're in Custer, South Dakota, now," Caleb had said. "But today, I'm traveling with a group that's scouting for nearby CSA agents. For now, I have a cell signal. But when we return, I'll lose it again." Before they hung up, Dylan told him about Bettino's death and his plans to wait for Chelsea. They agreed to stay in touch if Caleb ever had a signal again. And that was the last he heard from his brother.

But the weeks passed, and as the lonely quiet of the empty villas seeped into his soul, Dylan's resolve to remain in Tuscany weakened. He missed Kronberg Mountain, Margot, and the others.

During the day, he sometimes walked the hills, hiking up through the dried-up grape vines, over the hilltop, and through woods now barren of leaf. But the dim and darkened sun cast a pall over the days. And the languid, pasty moon, struggling to shine in a blackened sky, pulled a blanket of gloom over the nights. And he wondered when the next trumpet judgment would fall upon the earth.

Then, in the afternoon of the fifth week, his pocket alarm pierced the air with a squeal. He was in the den on the second floor of the family villa, and he rushed to the window. Coming down the drive was one of the black vans the Unitum Imperium was so fond of driving.

His heart pounding, he raced to the third-floor master bedroom where he kept a bag packed with everything important in case he had to flee: a change of clothes, emergency food rations, a bottle of water, a pistol and ammunition, and some hard cash. Scooping this up, he ran to the room's tiled balcony opening onto the hillside. He closed the balcony's glass door. He stepped onto the top of the railing. Leaning across, he grabbed the rope ladder he'd positioned there. Trying not to look down three stories to the concrete patio below, he placed one foot on a rung and swung out onto empty space. Once the ladder stopped swaying, he climbed onto the roof.

When he'd decided on this plan earlier, he'd used a ladder from the basement to access the roof where he nailed the rope ladder securely between the clay tiles, ready for a time like today.

As he gripped the half-pipe roof tiles and pulled the rope ladder up behind him, men's muffled voices came from below. They were already on the third floor, in the master bedroom he claimed as his own. He shuffled back a few feet so they couldn't see him from the balcony, but one of the tiles smashed against another. Did they hear it?

Trying to still his racing heart, he listened. The glass door opened, and feet scuffled onto the balcony.

"People have been living here," came a man's voice, deep and gravelly.

"Sì, and recently," came another, younger voice. "Lights on in this room. And a rumpled bed."

Dylan leaned back further. Was he far enough away that they couldn't see him or his coiled rope ladder?

"Let's check the rest of the house. If they're not here now, we'll come back."

"Sì. They're probably Christians without the mark."

Then came the sounds of feet crossing the tiles, the door shutting, and silence.

For the next forty minutes, he waited for the piercing alarm telling him their vehicle had driven past Victor's sensor. Then he climbed back down the rope ladder to his room.

Now what should he do? They knew someone lived here, and they would return. Should he move to Bishop Gallio's place and wait there? But he'd left notes in both places hinting to Chelsea that he might be in either villa. Could the squaddies decipher his veiled descriptions? What should he do?

Tonight, he would sleep at the bishop's. He still felt Chelsea would come here first, and his desire to stay hadn't diminished. Yet the risk of discovery had grown.

From now on, he must be twice as vigilant.

CHAPTER 16
FABIO'S PLAN

On the Western Italian Coast – December, Year 5

Even though the sun struggled to eke out a dim glow by day and the moon illumined a dull yellow sea by night, Chelsea rejoiced. For the last five days, the freezer trawler had chugged northeast across the Mediterranean toward Italy without incident. Wearing a sweater and windbreaker, she stood in the bow, watching for land in the fading light, letting the sea spray wet her face as the ship slapped through the waves. Any time now, the captain expected to sight the western Italian coast. Fabio had finally received his engine parts, and she counted the days until she could see Dylan again.

How long had it been? Was it over three years ago in the Paris restaurant that they'd last met? She couldn't remember. About seven years ago, she, Dylan, Caleb, and Mother had visited the Cinque Terra on holiday without Father, busy as usual with business. Once an isolated fishing village on Italy's rugged western coast, centuries-old Vernazza and its four cousin villages were known for quaintness and tourism. But who, now, in these troubled times, visited anywhere for pleasure? Unless it was to New Babylon, the decadent whore city of the Unitum Imperium devoted to hedonism and Christian bloodshed.

Fabio insisted that the Vernazza harbor was out of the way and small enough it might escape the notice of the Truth Squads and CSA.

A dark line appeared on the horizon, and Chelsea squinted, trying to make it out. Yes! It was the cliffs of the Italian Riviera. As the ship pulled closer, Fabio tooted the horn from the wheelhouse in celebration, and Enzo came out of his cabin to join her.

The coastline grew larger, a black mass barely lit by the setting sun. It would be dark within the hour.

"It is good, is it not, Chelsea, to be going home?" Enzo leaned against the rail as the ship approached the harbor.

"It is." Like sunshine after a chill breeze, relief washed over her. She arched her back, let the air out of her lungs, and briefly closed her eyes. "I don't expect anyone to be at my family's villa except the caretaker. But he will know how to get in touch with my brother."

Enzo zipped up his jacket and laid a hand on her shoulder. "When we land, I want to get as far from Fabio Caruso as quickly as possible. I don't trust the man."

She nodded. "Nor do I. Especially after what I saw in the pilothouse back on Mallorca. On the one hand, he takes us where we want to go. On the other, he writes down a number promising a big reward for turning in Christians."

When the trawler rounded the harbor's jetty in the dying light, she could barely make out a handful of fishing boats anchored beyond. Fabio slowed the engine and pulled beside the wharf, and she and Enzo threw out the buoys before the vessel bumped the concrete.

The engine quieted, and Fabio climbed down the ladder to join them. "Well, my friends, we are here. Just as I promised, no?"

"Yes, Fabio." Enzo turned his face away. "And this is where we part."

"Ah, but we must take rooms tonight in a hotel. I checked, and the next train to La Spezia and beyond doesn't leave until morning."

Enzo stared at him, and Chelsea frowned. Was that true?

"Cheer up, my friends." Fabio smiled, but Chelsea didn't feel like returning it. "Tonight, using my black-market credit cards, we will eat in a restaurant and sleep in a hotel bed, and tomorrow, you will be on your way. If you will gather your things and wait for me on deck, I will secure the ship and join you."

They did as he asked. A half hour later, Fabio had locked the wheelhouse, padlocked the hatches, and secured the ship. She watched as he hid the keys in a secret compartment under the winches on the aft deck. "I don't know if I'll ever be back here." For once, his voice carried a note of wistfulness. "Still, she's been a good ship, and I don't want anything to happen to her."

Then they strolled past the Santa Margherita Church and down an alley where they found an empty pensione with rooms for each. When the hotelier asked to see their marks, Fabio presented a wad of cash, the proprietor gave a knowing nod and, slamming shut the hotel register, waved them upstairs. They took showers, dropped their bags, and met again in the lobby where Fabio seemed especially jubilant.

They crossed the Piazza Marconi to a trattoria where a beaming proprietor waved them to an outside table under an awning. Again, after the man asked to see their marks, Fabio's bribe brought a wave of a hand and a whispered, "Good enough, *signorine e signori.*"

Though it was cool, Fabio insisted they sit outside, and she'd brought her sweater. In the lane beyond, it was now pitch-dark, and the group hid their wrists from passersby while a waiter took their orders.

As they waited for food, Fabio pulled out the phones he'd taken from them earlier in the trip. "Forgive me for holding onto them, but these belong to you." He handed them over, and Chelsea thanked him for his attempt at repentance. In Palma, he'd already given them weapons.

After the ship's monotonous diet, she savored the *antipasti frutti di mare*, mixed "fruits of the sea", and deep-fried anchovies. Having emptied two bottles of wine, they started on a third. She downed a plate of spaghetti with pesto, the special. By the time they'd finished dessert—flan, of course—her head was spinning, and her belly was full.

She sat in the open air beside her traveling companions, relishing the best meal she'd had in years.

Fabio sank back in his chair and cleared his throat. "I understand, Enzo, that you plan to leave us tomorrow?"

"That's right. We are parting company."

"Of course. Of course. But how are you to avoid the Truth Squads? They will surely patrol the trains, no?"

"You are right. It's a five-hour hike from here to La Spezia. There, I will commandeer a vehicle and drive only back roads to my destination."

"That might work." He rubbed his chin. "What about you, Chelsea

Turner? How will you get where you are going?"

"My family's villa is near Florence. It's not far. I will join Enzo on his hike, and then I, too, will find an abandoned car and drive the rest of the way."

"But do you not know there has been resistance from the Florentine locals and that the Unitum Imperium has set up checkpoints on every highway leading into and around the city? Until they crush the rebels, they will check every vehicle. This I have discovered."

She gripped the wine glass tighter. If he was right, then the risk of discovery was high. Leave it to Fabio to present a serious complication.

"But I have a request for you, Chelsea, one that means a great deal to me, and one that might also prevent you from being discovered. I hope you will agree."

"What?" She frowned.

"I have lost my shipmate and cannot continue my business." He lowered his gaze to the empty plates. "So I must abandon the *Am Albahr* here in the harbor. Ever since Tel Aviv, I have been in constant danger, and now I feel a deep need for security and safety. I am sick of running from one threat or another, no? Always hiding from the Unitum Imperium. The one thing I fear above all else is to let the government brand me with their mark. This I will not do. So now you can see the reason behind an important decision I have made." He raised his glance and gazed into her eyes. And what did she see there but tears welling up?

"Yes, my friends, I want to become a Christian." He wiped the moisture from his face and held her gaze.

Chelsea gasped. This was the last thing she expected.

Beside her, Enzo gaped. Then he faced Chelsea and shook his head.

Did she believe Fabio? He seemed sincere. He'd actually shed tears. Real tears. "So what do you want from me?"

"Take me with you to your villa and then to this place of safety where your brother is hiding."

She sat back in the chair, and her jaw dropped. "N–no, Fabio. I can't promise that. That is not my decision to make."

"How then, am I to become a Christian if you reject me?"

"I–I don't know."

"But I do have something of value to offer, a foolproof plan to take you as far as you want while avoiding the Truth Squads and the CSA men. I discovered this only tonight. It is something I will do for you if you will take me with you."

Now her heart sped up. Was he serious? Did he really have such a plan? "What is this plan?"

"While you were taking showers, I went to the ground floor, looking for a towel as my room had none. As I passed one of the rooms, a man in a CSA uniform departed with a bag in his hand. I hid my wrist, as I always do. But by his hurried manner, it appeared to me he was heading somewhere in too much of a rush and was checking out. He left the door to his room open, and peeking inside, I saw clothes he'd forgotten on the bed. Curious, I entered. And what do you think I found? On the bed, still in its hanger, was a CSA uniform. This uniform and some ID cards declaring the man's authority I have now secured."

"So you have a CSA uniform? So what?" Where was he going with this?

"Do you not see the possibilities?" He smiled. "What if I wear this man's uniform and escort you as my prisoner? And what if I take a pen and outline this mark of the beast on my wrist? No one will know it's not real. No one would then question my authority. I have the man's digital passes. They never check the encoded photo. I will become Ferro Bellini, CSA agent, and then you and I can go anywhere we want. You could take me to Florence and then to wherever your brother and his friends are staying where I could become a Christian."

Her mouth opened further, and she cocked her head. Could it work? Maybe. But was he sincere? He'd written down the number to call to turn in Christians for a reward. Was he just trying to find out where Dylan and the others were so he could turn in the lot of them?

As the waiter came and Fabio paid the bill with his black-market card, her head swirled.

Should she accept his offer and go with him? On the journey, she could further gauge his sincerity. If he could escort her safely past

Florence and its checkpoints, it might be worth the risk. She could always ditch him before they made the last turn.

"Well, Chelsea Turner, what do you say?" Smiling even wider, he opened his hands. "Can you think of a better way to travel without fear of discovery?"

"No." Shivers skittered up her spine, and Enzo was still shaking his head, back and forth.

"Then what is your decision? Will you accept my offer?"

She swallowed and gritted her teeth. Perhaps it was the wine. Or the knowledge that the CSA had surrounded Florence with checkpoints. But she surprised even herself with what she said next.

"Yes, Fabio, I accept your offer."

Fabio then turned to Enzo. "If I'm to escort Chelsea from here, you might as well join us tomorrow as far as La Spezia and skip the hike, no?"

Grimacing, Enzo rubbed his forehead. Finally, as though it pained him, he lowered his hand and nodded.

CHAPTER 17
THE FIFTH TRUMPET

Revelation 9:1–2 (NLT): *Then the fifth angel blew his trumpet, and I saw a star that had fallen to earth from the sky, and he was given the key to the shaft of the bottomless pit. When he opened it, smoke poured out as though from a huge furnace, and the sunlight and air turned dark from the smoke.*

2 Peter 2:4 (NLT): *For God did not spare even the angels who sinned. He threw them into hell, in gloomy pits of darkness, where they are being held until the day of judgment.*

Into the Abyss – December, Year 5

High in the atmosphere, far above the earth, flew the angel. In his hands, he held the fifth trumpet, carrying the terrible decree of the fifth judgment. Putting the golden instrument to his lips, he blew.

Beside him, a globe of blinding light formed. It hurtled downward toward its target, a spot in the desert not far from New Babylon, a city above which the spirits of demons already hovered.

The sphere of light dove into the sand, melted, and collapsed a hole. It sucked everything behind it and formed a glassy tunnel, diving deep toward the planet's center.

The angel flew down after it.

But at the border between the physical and spiritual worlds, the light dimmed and then vanished. Before him now, a massive iron door blocked the entry of all who came from the world above.

The angel took the key and turned it over in his hands. Forged at the beginning of time, never once had it been used. Shuddering at what it represented, he stepped forward and shoved it into the lock. The hinges creaked, and, for the first time in its long history, the iron door opened.

Beyond loomed the prince of the bottomless pit, beautiful beyond description, surrounded by a halo of shimmering darkness. Once called Lucifer, once the greatest and most honored of angels, his names were now Abaddon, the Dragon, and the Prince of Darkness.

On all sides, barely visible through a curtain of black, churning mist, dark flames leaped from rock crevices, and black lava bubbled from flaming rivers.

Lucifer stood to his full height, and both angels held each other's gazes—the once mighty and favored Lucifer cloaked in swirling shadows and the trumpet bearer bordered by golden, heavenly light.

"The Lord of Hosts is taking command of your pets," said the trumpet bearer. "Then they will descend upon all you have called your own."

A sneer marred Lucifer's features. As if batting at flies, he brushed away the other's words. "The Enemy will not win. Nothing is foreordained. I do not believe in his Book."

"Believe what you will, but everything declared in his Word has come to pass, just as it was foretold. And so will the prophecies to come. Once, I believed in you. Once, I followed you. But you forgot from whence you came and to whom you owed your allegiance. Now, your doom is certain."

A storm cloud crossed Lucifer's forehead, and darkness gathered deeper around him. "Take your lies and begone, minion! I will hear no more."

The trumpet bearer narrowed his gaze on the one he once called friend. Then he whirled and flew from the chasm.

Behind him boiled a cloud of smoke, thick and dark and churning. Within that toxic mist came the roar of millions of tiny wings from millions of demon locusts.

They erupted out of the shaft. They flew high into the air and spread out across the world.

Adorning each human head was a tiny crown. Carved upon each tiny visage was the mockery of a human face. Filling each tiny mouth were sharp incisors, like those of lions. Wrapping each tiny chest was a suit of iron. Flowing down upon each tiny breastplate was a woman's hair. And the buzzing of their wings—soon to become the most feared sound on earth—announced their approach.

But what everyone who saw them dreaded most, what inflicted anguish for hours on end, bringing a pain that didn't kill but only tortured its victim in endless agony, was their tails.

For each held the stinger of a scorpion.

Thus began the plague of demon locusts that was the fifth judgment.

CHAPTER 18
PASSAGE TO FLORENCE

Revelation 9:4–5 (NLT): *They were told not to harm the grass or plants or trees, but only the people who did not have the seal of God on their foreheads. They were told not to kill them but to torture them for five months with pain like the pain of a scorpion sting.*

On the Train to Florence – December, Year 5

Early morning in the third week of December, the train from Vernazza squealed into La Spezia Centrale. Among the handful of passengers stepping onto the platform were Chelsea, Enzo, and Fabio. As their feet echoed in the empty passageway, they descended stairs to the bypass tunnel, emerging next to Track 1 and the ticket hall.

"Wait here." Already dressed as a CSA agent, Fabio waved toward the WC. "I need to use the restroom."

Enzo faced Chelsea, shuffled his feet, and nodded toward the exit. "I guess this is goodbye. If I can't find an abandoned vehicle in the parking lot, I'll hitch a ride to Lucca and try there."

She'd been in good spirits all morning. But Enzo's departure was a cloud blocking the sunshine. She bit her lip and drew a hand through her hair. "We've been through a lot together, haven't we?"

"We have, but now we must go our separate ways. I to my home. You to your brother. I will never forget you, Chelsea."

"You've been a good companion and friend." Then she hugged him.

"May the Lord go with you, Chelsea Turner." He tried on a smile, but it faded.

Fighting back tears, she nodded.

He threw his rucksack over one shoulder and began to walk away. But he hadn't taken two steps before he whirled. "Don't trust him, Chelsea. You can't believe anything he says."

"I know." She wiped moisture from her cheeks, shot a glance toward the WC, and faced Enzo again. "If he can get me past Florence, I'll ditch him."

Enzo stepped forward, they hugged again, and he strolled toward the exit.

Long moments later, Fabio returned. "Is he gone?"

Still stunned by Fabio's fearsome appearance in the CSA uniform, all she could do was nod. It was as if the skull-and-crossbones patches and the green-and-white uniform was made for him. In a holster on his leather belt, he'd stuck his own pistol. But when he lifted his right wrist, she gasped. There, he'd drawn a reasonable facsimile of the mark of the beast.

"I used a fine ink pen." He tilted his hand to the light, smiled, and turned it again. "I should have been an artist, no?"

It was so expertly drawn, it could have been the official tattoo. "You outdid yourself."

Making sure no one was about, he fished in his bag and brought out a pair of handcuffs. He jingled them and motioned for her to approach. "He had these in his pocket. If you are my prisoner, you must wear these. Beyond La Spezia, officialdom won't be as lax."

She stared at the cuffs, at Fabio, then again at the cuffs. "I–I guess so." She presented her wrists, and he cuffed her. The cold metal bit into her hands and chaffed.

"I've bought tickets for Florence." He waved two pieces of paper toward the stairwell. "The train leaves in half an hour. Track 2. Let's cross over."

After reentering the subway bypass, they mounted the steps to the next track.

They hadn't waited ten minutes before other passengers joined them. Among them was a group of six CSA men and women. When they glanced her way, Chelsea sucked in breath and turned her head. Would their ruse hold up to scrutiny?

97

The train whooshed into the station on time, Fabio pushed her up the steps into the cabin, and they took seats in the premium section. He threw her bag in the rack above, and she sat by the window. The ceiling monitor announced it would take two and a half hours to reach their destination, an hour longer than normal. After the quakes, they had to replace the tracks in a few spots with substandard rails, forcing the high-speed train to slow its journey.

Before they started, the six CSA agents entered the car and walked down the aisle from the far end. They took seats beside and in front of Fabio and Chelsea.

Across the aisle, a tall, thin-faced man with a scar on his cheek leaned toward Fabio. Above the skull-and-crossbones emblem on his shoulder was a second patch with three wavy lines, indicating he must be a captain. "Where are you taking your prisoner?"

"Florence." Fabio faced forward, avoiding the other's gaze.

The man pointed at Chelsea. "Directive 42 says you should cuff her to yourself."

"Oh, of course." Fabio fumbled for the keys in his pocket.

"Sometimes, we get a bit lax with all these regulations." The man gave Fabio a knowing smile. "But you wouldn't want her to get away, now, would you?"

"No, sir." Fabio uncuffed her left wrist and locked the cuffs around his left wrist.

Moments later, the train started away from the station, picked up speed, and rushed through the countryside.

A woman in uniform, pushing a cart with drinks and snacks, appeared at the aisle's far end. When it reached Fabio, he ordered a beer for himself but nothing for her.

Chelsea rested her head against the seat back. They would be in Florence before noon. If Fabio could commandeer a car, she could pass the checkpoints, leave the city, and be at the villa this afternoon. Her heart sped up. Was it possible? Could she be in touch with Dylan today?

She closed her eyes and slept. When next she opened her eyes, they were only thirty minutes from their destination. Again, she relaxed back on the headrest and closed her eyes.

Then the car filled with the sound of buzzing insects.

Fabio jerked her right hand, and when she opened her eyes, she gasped.

A horror of a creature flew between Fabio and the seat back ahead. With a human head, a tiny breastplate, a crown of gold, and a mouthful of teeth, it hovered at eye level. Fabio squirmed in his seat, tried to knock it away, but every time his hand approached, it jumped aside. Its tail, ending in a long stinger, was curved up and over its back like a scorpion.

Someone screamed, and from seats all around came cries of pain, curses, and shouts. She glanced aside, and the CSA captain was beating at another of the creatures. One of his men was running down the aisle trying to escape with two creatures close behind him.

Beside her, Fabio beat frantically at the air, but none of his efforts stopped the tiny locustlike monster from hovering. Its tiny face leered and mocked him.

On Fabio's next swipe, instead of jumping aside, the creature flicked its tail forward, and its stinger plunged deep into Fabio's right hand above the mark.

He screamed.

Staring at his arm, he gasped for breath and rocked his head from side to side. When she briefly caught his glance, his eyes were wide, his forehead scrunched, and his jaw muscles rigid.

Everywhere in the car, it was the same. All the CSA agents were writhing in pain or beating the air as the demons—and yes, now she remembered the passage in Revelation that predicted this!—attacked.

All the CSA agents had the mark. That's why the demons struck them and not her. But what about Fabio? He'd drawn the mark on his wrist, but it wasn't real. Or was it?

"It's because you have the mark that they attacked you," she finally said to him.

"W–what?" As if concentrating was an effort, he tried to focus on her.

"They only strike people with the mark of the beast. And you placed the mark on yourself."

He stared at his wrist below an ugly red welt. He jerked his left hand toward the mark, pulling hers along with it. Spitting into his palm, he tried to rub off his artwork.

"It won't come off." He rubbed faster, harder. "It's burnt into my skin!"

Then he smashed both hands onto his forehead and shook his head from side to side. "It's horrible. The pain won't quit."

"Release me," she said. "You need both hands now."

He fumbled in his pocket, brought out the key, and passed it to her. She removed the cuffs and handed them back.

Screams and shouts filled the remainder of the trip. A woman was crying now. Another man was rolling in the aisle. Others, like the captain in the aisle beside them, sat rigid in their seats, faces twisted with pain, neck and arm muscles taut and bulging. But the creatures had departed. The first wave was over.

When the train pulled into Firenze Santa Maria Novella, no one exited. So preoccupied with pain were they, that everyone just sat or lay where they were, breathing heavily, fighting off the agony.

Finally, the captain rose, an ugly red circle marring his forehead. "We must get off. Whatever this is, we must endure it and carry on." He began to walk down the aisle, shaking his men, urging them to stand and bear it.

As the CSA leader was doing this, Fabio turned to Chelsea. "They didn't attack you. And I can't remove the mark. I must be one of them now. That's why they attacked me."

"It appears so."

"This changes everything." He stood and waved to the captain.

The thin-faced CSA leader turned at Fabio's approach. "What do you want?"

"I'm here to report that I have the fugitive, Chelsea Turner, in my possession." Fabio shot a glance in her direction. "I captured her in La Spezia and want to claim my reward."

A chill started in her shoulders and rippled down her spine. She should never have trusted him, even for one second. She knew it all along. Enzo had even warned her.

And now he was turning her over to the CSA and to what?

A return to Jerusalem? For torture and a public execution?

CHAPTER 19
CHELSEA'S ESCAPE

Florence, Italy — December, Year 5

Chelsea shot a glance toward the exit, but the captain blocked the aisle.

His eyes widened, and he focused on her. "This is Chelsea Turner, the traitor?"

"It is," answered Fabio.

The captain stared down at her. He was about to say something when his hands began to shake, his eyes rolled back in his head, and he wrapped his arms around his chest. When the pain passed, he resumed his inspection.

"I am Captain Bartolo Calabrese, and this will bring great honor to our unit. Possibly a reward." He turned to Fabio. "Agent, what is your name?"

"Ferro Bellini."

"Well, Agent Ferro, I will be glad to escort you and your prisoner to—" But again, a ripple of pain gripped him, and for a moment, he couldn't speak. Finally, he regained his composure. "I will escort you both to regional headquarters where you and I will collect a reward."

As sweat dripped off his forehead, Fabio nodded.

Before they left the cabin, Calabrese took her bag, opened it, and pawed through its contents. Then the captain cuffed her to himself and herded his shattered crew, Fabio, and Chelsea off the train.

On the platform, bedlam ruled. A few creatures were chasing passengers down the concrete. But most of the first wave seemed to have passed, and all who remained were dealing with pain.

Handcuffed to the captain, Chelsea could only follow where her captor led. At the end of the platform was a security checkpoint, now unmanned. Outside the station, cabs were waiting, and the CSA men jumped to the head of a ragged line. But the line was in disarray. Some of the waiting passengers writhed in agony on the sidewalk. Here and there, demon locusts still pursued their victims, and men, women, and nonbinaries were running into the street, back into the station, or far down the sidewalk ahead of their torturers.

"CSA Regional Headquarters," said Bartolo Calabrese to the driver. But the man behind the wheel was shivering, his eyes were closed, and his hands shook.

"Driver!" said Calabrese again. "Can you drive us or not?"

The man opened his eyes, saw who had slipped into the seat, and nodded. Behind them, the rest of Calabrese's unit had commandeered a second cab.

The headquarters was only a few blocks away, and when they arrived, they stepped out without paying—perks of working for the Unitum Imperium. The captain waited for the rest of his crew to assemble then started down the narrow walk toward the entrance.

The station was an old fortress, surrounded by a high brick wall, and as they approached the massive brick-lined gate, Chelsea's heart sped up. How could she ever escape a place like that?

They stopped at the entrance where two guards, both shivering in pain, manned a booth and asked for IDs.

Frowning, Calabrese reached into his pocket and pulled out his ID card.

Then he looked up.

Above them, the air filled with the buzzing of demon locusts. As if out of thin air, dozens of the horrid creatures hovered above the six agents, Fabio, and Chelsea.

The guards abandoned their posts and fled.

Calabrese's men and Fabio scattered in all directions, each pursued by one or more of the demon creatures.

But Calabrese was chained to Chelsea. While her right arm hindered

103

his left, he batted his hands at three of the monsters as they played a game of Whac-A-Mole. Each time he tried to knock them away, they jumped aside, their little faces mocking and leering.

Then, just as they had toyed with Fabio back in the train car, one of the demons didn't jump away, but hovered in place. When Calabrese's right hand reached out to knock it aside, the creature's stinger arced down and plunged deep into the man's wrist.

At the same instant, two other demons rushed in and stung him on each arm.

The demons backed away, hovered, then were gone.

They left the captain shivering with pain. His face was white, covered with sweat, and his eyes bulged. His knees buckled, and he slipped to the pavement where some kind of seizure wracked his body.

Chelsea knelt and rifled through his pockets until she retrieved the key to unlock the cuffs. As she did, only once did he look up at her, but his eyes were unseeing.

Free again, she ran down the street, looking inside each parked car.

The second wave of demons plunged the city into chaos, and people abandoned whatever they'd been doing in an effort to escape the terror. She hadn't walked far when she found an unoccupied VW sedan with the door open and the engine running. Slipping behind the wheel, she followed side streets to the A1 and then drove north.

She encountered few vehicles, and the roads were empty.

On the city's north side, the CSA had blocked the highway with barrels, funneling traffic into a single lane and a checkpoint. But as she drove to the makeshift gate, again no one manned it. She left the car, lifted the gate, and drove on.

It was only an hour's drive to the villa. She kept glancing in the rearview mirror. But she had the road mostly to herself, and no one followed. The demon attacks couldn't have come at a better time.

Soon, she'd see Bettino, eat his pasta, drink the villa's wine, and get in touch with Dylan.

CHAPTER 20
DYLAN'S DECISION

In the Tuscan Countryside – December, Year 5

When Victor's alarm sounded, Dylan was at the bishop's villa in the downstairs kitchen, eating a lunch of penne pasta and pesto. His plan to escape notice at the bishop's place wasn't as good as at the family villa. Grabbing the backpack he kept at his side at all times, he left his meal and ran through the house to the back door.

The alarm meant that some vehicle had crossed the drive and was nearing the house. At the bishop's place, it barely gave him enough time to exit the back door onto the hillside and into the vineyard. Sprinting across the lawn, he gained the third row of vines, dropped down to his belly, and faced the house.

Below, a black van pulled into the lot beside the villa. CSA men exited and headed for the entrance. He drew a hand through his hair. This was their third inspection trip this week. Once at the family villa. Twice at the bishop's.

He rolled onto his back and shut his eyes.

It was becoming too dangerous to stay. One of these times, he'd be too slow getting out, and they'd catch him. They might not know it was the same person, but they knew someone was living in both places, and they seemed intent on finding whoever it was.

For the next hour, he watched the villa until the men left the house, returned to their vehicle, and departed.

When his pocket alarm sounded again, they'd passed the sensor, and it was safe to leave again. But not at the bishop's place.

He climbed the hill toward the family villa. At the top, before he

105

started down, his phone played Beethoven's Fifth, and he answered.

"Dylan, how are you doing?" René asked. "It's been two months since you left. When are you coming back?"

That was the question, wasn't it? He'd waited in Tuscany for over eight weeks based on a feeling that Chelsea would soon arrive. But each day, the danger increased. "Soon, René."

"What if she's been captured? What if she's in some prison back in Jerusalem or New Babylon? Even if she escaped, the odds of her returning to Italy are, well . . ."

"Yes. I know. Nearly impossible."

"We need you back here, Dylan. Margot needs you."

For a time, silence filled the speaker. Then René spoke again. "Last time we spoke, you said the CSA had been checking the villa every week. Is that still happening?"

"Unfortunately, they're coming every other day now."

"Then what are you doing there? Come back."

He sat on a log and released his breath. "Okay. You're right. I'll leave her a note and start on my way."

"Great! When?"

"This afternoon."

"Good. We'll expect you tonight?"

"Probably tomorrow. The trip here was problematic."

"Of course."

After they hung up, he descended the hill and entered the family villa. In the kitchen, he tore up the cryptic note advising Chelsea to check the other place. Then he sat at the table and tried to devise a new message only Chelsea would understand. He didn't want to leave his phone number where the CSA could find it. What he was writing couldn't make sense to anyone but her.

He wrote:

> Once upon a time, a man saved you from the apple tree. And every evening thereafter, his wife found solace in quiet action. There is where you will find your way home.

Was it too cryptic? Would Chelsea remember that Allegra Pisano, Bettino's wife, always sat in her favorite chair after supper to knit? Of course, she'd remember. Who wouldn't?

Upstairs in Bettino's bedroom, he wrote his number on a piece of paper, along with a warning and some directions, then stuffed it down a crack in the chair's cushion. In the kitchen, he planted his first cryptic note on the refrigerator door.

Taking a last glance around the place, he headed for the garage. It was now midafternoon. The trip to Kronberg Mountain was normally eight hours. But with crevasses to avoid in these troubled times, who knew how long such a journey might take?

CHAPTER 21
A LONG-AWAITED ARRIVAL

In the Tuscan Countryside – December, Year 5

It was midafternoon, and Chelsea's heart raced with anticipation as her tires bounced over cracks in the long drive leading up to the family villa. The cypresses bore only brown needles now, and the grapes hanging on the vines were half as big as they should be. But it was the closest thing to home she had left. She parked the car in the lot and raced up the steps to the second-floor living room.

Inside, a light was on, and her heart pounded.

"Bettino?" she called but received no answer. "It's Chelsea."

Walking through the living room, she cried out for him, again and again. But all that returned to her was silence. Faster, she ran through each room, checking if someone, anyone, was here.

Then, in the kitchen, the refrigerator held a note that could only have been written by her brother. It was his way of saying he'd left a message either in Allegra's knitting basket or in the chair where she spent each evening with needle and yarn. Or it could be under the portcullis on the patio where she sometimes sat in the evenings.

Chelsea started with the patio but found no clues. She raced to the top-floor sitting room overlooking the pasture where horses once grazed. The knitting basket was on the dresser. She riffled through its contents but again—nothing.

Then she went to Allegra's favorite chair and pulled out the cushion. There, she unearthed a small device with a speaker and, as expected, another note. Her heart pounding, she took it to the window and read:

Chelsea,

If you're reading this, beware that the CSA is checking our villa and the bishop's place most every day now. I waited for you. But it's become too dangerous, and I had to leave for our base in Switzerland where it's safer. The alarm I left with this note will warn you if a car is coming up the entrance road. Keep it with you and, if it sounds, flee. If you need transportation, there's a car in the bishop's garage filled with gas and ready to go. If you're looking for Bettino, I have sad news to report. I found his body when I arrived and buried him in the woods. Call me after reading this.

Dylan

On the back of the note, he'd left his number.

Breathing deeply, she walked to the couch and slumped against the cushions, both sad and joyful. Bettino was dead, but Dylan had left a way to contact him. Fumbling for her phone, she brought it out and began to punch numbers when the alarm rang.

Startled, she crumpled the note, shoved it in her pocket, and raced for the stairs. If someone was coming down the drive, she had to get to her car and grab her backpack—fast! She flew down the steps to the second floor and descended to the walk leading downhill to the parking lot.

A glance down the drive revealed no vehicle. How long did it take to drive a kilometer?

She yanked open the car door, grabbed her backpack, and raced toward the back of the house. If she could cross the field to the woods, the CSA would never find her. She knew those woods, its trails, and how to lose them.

When she turned the corner around the back of the villa, she peered toward the drive just as a black van pulled beside her VW and two men got out.

They bore the unmistakable features of Fabio Caruso and Captain

Calabrese. How was this possible?

Breathing heavily, she lurched from the corner and sprinted uphill through dry, knee-high grass. Only after she'd crossed the pasture and entered the woods did she dare to look back.

No one pursued. They'd seen her car and must be inside the house, searching for her.

But how did they follow her here? It wasn't through her phone. On a hunch, she took off her backpack and rummaged through it. Inside, she discovered a black foreign device no bigger than a cigarette lighter. A tracking device?

The captain must have dropped it into her backpack before they left the train. She pulled off the back, laid it on a rock, and smashed it to pieces with another rock. That should foil further attempts at tracking her.

She followed the forest until it topped the hill. On the far side, she hiked west through the trees then south until she arrived at the top where the bishop's and the family's vineyards met.

Lying flat on the ground, she peered over the edge toward the bishop's villa. The sun was setting, and she could barely make out Fabio and the CSA leader standing in the yard, apparently arguing. With them were two other agents.

Suddenly, the men began beating at the air, running in different directions, crying out in pain. The demons had struck again! Soon, they were on the ground, writhing and rolling in agony. Then it became too dark to see.

Breathing easier, she walked a few meters down the trail over the ridge. With another demon attack, they would give up the search for her today. They had no idea about the bishop's place, and she'd destroyed their ability to track her.

She brought out her phone and dialed Dylan's number. As she waited, her heart raced faster.

"Hello?" answered the voice she so longed to hear.

"Dylan? It's Chelsea."

"Chelsea! Is that really you?" The joy in his voice nearly brought her to tears.

"Of course it's me, silly." She'd said in jest, but now tears were running down her face. "I'm at the family villa, and I'm about to head over the hill to the bishop's place."

"Really? I left there only hours ago. I can't believe you're here. I waited there two months for you."

"I've been trying to get here for years. A moment ago, your alarm warned me about some CSA agents who tracked me all the way from Florence, but they won't be tracking me anymore. Where are you?"

Then he gave her directions to meet him at a park in Parma, only 160 kilometers to the north.

Happier than she'd been in months, she hiked down the hill in the dark toward the bishop's villa and the car Dylan had left there.

* * *

AN HOUR AND A HALF LATER, Chelsea pulled into a dark parking lot, occupied only by a blue Opal sedan. She parked, left her car, and approached.

A man opened the door, switched on his phone's flashlight, and stood before her. "Chelsea!" Dylan opened his arms, and she melted into them.

They hugged, and when they parted, tears were again rolling down her cheeks. "How long has it been since we last met? Was it three years ago in the Paris restaurant?"

"Far too long. And too much has happened since then. It's so good to see you." He switched off his light, and they hugged again. He motioned for her to get in. "But why didn't you call?"

Now in the passenger seat, she explained how, when she'd switched to a new solar phone in Jerusalem, she'd lost all her contacts.

"But, Chelsea, where have you been all this time?" He turned on the overhead light.

Then she told the story of her destitute wandering in Tel Aviv, how she met Ariel Geller, how she ended up on a freezer trawler captained by Fabio Caruso and journeyed across the Mediterranean, how they escaped a tsunami, and how she ended up in Italy.

After she finished, Dylan shook his head and grasped her hand.

"That's quite a story. But let's start for home." He gave her hand a comforting squeeze. "We might have trouble getting around the checkpoints, and I'd rather do it at night."

"But haven't you heard? The demon locusts from the fifth trumpet have been loosed. They've been attacking the CSA and Truth Squads everywhere. For the next five months, most of them will be incapacitated."

"Then it's happened!" A smile broadened his lips. "I read about it, but you've actually seen this?"

"Yes. They attacked everyone with the mark on the train and in the city. For months to come, all the goons working for Davato will barely be able to function."

"The timing couldn't be better. In two hours, we can cross the Swiss border at Lugano. Border security might still be tighter than at the random checkpoints. After Lugano, we can find a place to pull off and sleep in the car."

"Where are we going?"

"We've taken over a resort at Kronberg Mountain, Switzerland. As soon as I fill the tank from your car, we'll leave. Margot is there with all that's left of the Nazarene Friends. They're like family now. And, Chelsea"—he smiled at her—"soon they'll be your family too."

He left the car, took a siphon hose and gas can from the trunk, and headed for her vehicle.

She rested her head against the seat back and breathed out. For the first time in a very long time, she felt safe. She was finally with Dylan, and soon she would join his circle of friends.

CHAPTER 22
THE TEMPLE CEREMONY

Amos 18b–19 (HCSB): *What will the Day of the Lord be for you? It will be darkness and not light. It will be like a man who flees from a lion only to have a bear confront him. He goes home and rests his hand against the wall only to have a snake bite him.*

New Babylon, Iraq – December, Year 5

Along with thousands of other worshipers, Grady Wilson entered the remodeled, renamed Temple of Davato and looked for Marcia, the black-haired beauty with whom he had a sharing thing going. Unable to find her, he wove through the milling crowd and found a seat halfway from the front.

After the remodel, the jade image of Gaia had been replaced with a white marble statue of Davato. It stood forty feet tall, its right hand lifting a marble globe, and its left holding a marble lightning bolt. It wasn't the moveable giant in the central park, but the statue was still impressive. Hanging from the sixty-foot ceiling, on the right and left, screens showed a closeup view of the Prophet. He stood now on an elevated platform beneath Davato's image.

"There you are!" came a female voice from behind.

Grady turned to find Marcia giving him a knowing grin and slipping her hand into his. He gripped her fingers and returned a lecherous smile. He couldn't wait to get the Prophet's words behind them and get her upstairs into a private room.

How many women had he been with this week? He'd lost track. After a while, they all merged into one continuous memory of sweaty bodies joined together in lusty heat. Strangely, he felt no particular attraction for any of them. And sadly, the feeling left him empty and soiled. Yet he couldn't stop.

"Praise and glory to the Imperator!" The Prophet's voice echoed through the microphone and off the high ceiling.

His audience repeated the refrain, and the green-eyed Sebastien glanced from side to side. "Yes, praise to our divine ruler, he who came back from the dead, he who united the world, and he who will lead us into the next century. Praise to the one who ended the shackles of moralist, prudish dogma, who brought us the freedom to be whatever we want, to lie with whomever we wish, in whatever manner we desire. Praise and glory to the Imperator!"

His audience clapped and shouted their agreement.

"But today, my message is about the Dragon and how he, above all others, is the great and beneficent force behind the universe. He is all-powerful, all-knowing, and it was he who brought our Imperator back from the dead. Yes, my friends, the Dragon is behind everything that I and Davato the Divine have done, and for that, he deserves our praise and honor and worship. Abaddon is also one of his names, and now I ask that you get down on your knees, bow to the Dragon, and—"

But a loud buzzing from somewhere inside the temple drowned him out, and he looked up.

Grady, too, looked up.

Above them, appearing out of nowhere, was a growing cloud of insects. But no, they weren't insects. One of the things lowered to a few meters above Grady's head. Its face bore the caricature of a human face, and its mouth was filled with a carnivore's teeth.

He shuddered and backed away.

Beside him, Marcia looked up, ripped her hand from his, and covered her mouth.

The insect cloud thickened. So many tiny wings now beat the air, it was like someone had started a chain saw in the building.

He shot a glance toward the exit, now clogged with people trying to escape. The creatures were multiplying, and the cloud was descending.

Grady's heart beat wildly, and he searched frantically for a way out.

But he was trapped.

Up on the podium, the Prophet beat at the air then fled toward a side door.

Someone screamed, and the cloud buzzed and whirred and began to drop down.

Now, he had a closer look at the things. Gold crowns topped their heads, women's hair fell down onto tiny breastplates, and long tails curved up and over their heads, ending in scorpion stingers.

As Grady stared, disbelieving, a word popped into his head—demons.

Yes, what hovered before him was surely a demon, and as it approached, he batted the air. But it jumped aside. Was that a mocking smile? Was the thing leering at him?

As he backed away, it followed. He glanced again at the crush of people crowding and blocking the exits. No way out.

He turned toward the demon creature, but now it hovered half a meter before his face. Bringing up his right hand, he tried to swat it away. But it jumped aside, flew straight at him, and plunged its stinger into his forehead.

Molten lead pumped into his skin, burning its way down his neck and into his shoulders.

His eyes watered, his torso shook, and he staggered. For a moment, he was blind.

From somewhere close by came more buzzing wings, and he lurched away from the sound, ricocheting off another body.

He couldn't see, but as he struggled to remain upright, another demon creature thrust a stinger through his shirt, plunging a needle of prickling, burning fire into his right arm.

Grady slumped to his knees, rivers of pain shivering through every nerve of his body. He brought both hands to the top of his head, and tears rolled down his cheeks.

What was happening? Where did these things come from? When would it end?

His eyes cleared, and everywhere around him, others were rolling on the floor. The demon creatures dropped down, struck, then rose, then struck again. And their horrible little faces mocked and sneered and laughed at their victims.

Rivers of pain roared through him. Tears ran down his cheeks. He curled into a ball, and he prayed to the Dragon for it to end.

Finally, the buzzing chain saw silenced, and the cloud of tiny monsters departed. But they left behind a temple filled with moaning, crying, shuddering worshipers, most of whom lay prone and helpless on the floor.

He tried to stand, staggered, and remained upright. The exits were clear now, and he stepped over bodies toward the door. It helped to move, and he pushed through into the foyer then to the doors leading outside.

A handful of creatures were there, chasing others down the walkway.

Another wave of pain rolled over him, and he stopped, shivering, until it passed. Only a few blocks east was the Devil's Brew, his favorite bar, and he started for it. Whiskey was what he needed now. Lots and lots of whiskey.

But would the buzzing monsters return? Could he make it that far? Down the walkway, demon creatures still pursued victims. He picked up the pace.

The pain began to subside, but it rose again in waves, forcing him to stop, breathe deeply, and wait for it to pass.

The bar was ahead, but the entrance was crowded. He wove through desperate customers until he neared the bartender doling out triple shots at a furious pace.

The buzzing sound began again.

A cluster of demons now hovered above the bar crowd and began their descent. He shot a glance behind him, but again, he was trapped in a crush of bodies.

The people in back were running now, heading for the open walkway. But the demons flew after them.

Grady riveted his gaze on a buzzing, scorpion-tailed creature with a mocking face that dropped down even with his eyes. He tried to knock it away, but it flitted from side to side. Then, faster than he thought possible, it flew straight at his chest.

Its stinger curved, plunged, and thrust its needle deep into a nipple.

Molten metal spread out from his chest. A river of fire burned a swath to his shoulder, out into his arms, and down into his thighs and feet.

And at that moment, Grady wished for nothing more than death.

CHAPTER 23
A CHRISTMAS EVE DINNER

Sela Rock City, Jordan – December, Year 5

A struggling, pale-yellow sun dipped low in the western sky as Ariel Geller slammed the truck gears into park with a screech of metal. When he returned to Tel Aviv, he must have his mechanics look into that noise.

He turned to Noah Blum, aka Kishke, the runner he'd chosen to take with him on this trip. Kishke was a lanky, black-haired, twenty-one-year-old, who had lived his entire adult life in the Tribulation. "This is As Sela." Ariel waved at the shadowy mount on his right. "We're here."

Kishke peered out the window beyond the cliff shadows to the red rock mountain stronghold. "The Refuge, Big Matza?"

"Yes. Now come with me." As they left the vehicle, Ariel wondered what it would be like to live all of your adult life at the end of time? Would you view the strange events in the sky and earth as normal? Or would you fear the air and land as unreliable? Ariel had chosen Noah for the trip because he seemed to handle most situations with good sense. You didn't find that in everyone nowadays. Even so, he was glad he wasn't in Noah's position, glad he'd grown up before the craziness now gripping the world.

In the back of the truck, Ariel lifted the pin, turned the bar, and opened the back doors. He pulled out the ramp, and two dozen refugees jumped down onto the sand, stretching, gaping, and smiling.

It was the easiest trip they'd had yet. Most of the checkpoints had been unmanned. Either the guards were stuck in their barracks, trying to ward off the pain with whiskey, brandy, barbiturates, and fentanyl. Or they were outside in a vain attempt to outrun the demon locusts. Or they no longer cared and waved everyone through, unchecked.

He grinned. It was just what they deserved. Before he left Tel Aviv, he'd ordered his staff to begin raids on every CSA warehouse and headquarters from Haifa to Jerusalem. For the next five months, the Unitum Imperium's storehouses would provide whatever the Jewish and Christian refugees needed to survive and escape Davato's reign of terror.

It was difficult, but he told himself he was doing it out of love for those he was helping, not revenge. He was, after all, now a Christian. At the same time, he couldn't help but grin at the damage he was doing to the CSA and the Antichrist's organization.

Behind them, the rest of his caravan—twenty buses, trucks, and vans—pulled off the road, and people poured out, assembled on the sand, and waited for directions.

Ariel pointed at two men emerging from the cliff shadows. "Here come our hosts—Baruch Abramovich and David Benjamin."

The middle-aged man brushed aside a swath of curly black hair and extended a hand. "Welcome, Ariel. I'm so glad you finally came."

Kishke shot Ariel a surprised glance. "Yes, Kishke, Ariel is my real name. While we're here, we can dispense with the code names. But keep it a secret."

He introduced Kishke as Noah Blum then added, "With the demon attacks, I decided my organization could do without me for a few days. I can't wait to see this Refuge you've said so much about."

Baruch introduced David Benjamin then motioned toward the mountain. "My greeters will take care of your people. If you and Noah will follow me, I'll give you a personal tour."

David lit four torches and handed one to each of them. Then Baruch led them across the sand to the foot of the mountain and the eastern entrance. They climbed the rock staircase, passing an ancient stone watchtower. As they ascended between spires of red sandstone, the route twisted and turned. At the top, Ariel stopped to catch his breath and look upon thousands of fires dotting the plain below.

"We didn't know how we'd make space for all the refugees here." Baruch waved over the firelit vista. "But twice now, we've awakened to a different topography. Overnight, without a sound, the mountaintop has expanded to meet our needs."

"Expanded?" Ariel gawked at his host. "The mountain *grew?*"

David Benjamin waved his torch. "Baruch keeps telling me the Lord will provide, and I keep asking how. When two hundred hectares of flat rock appeared that first morning, I didn't believe it either. *And nobody heard a sound!*"

Beside Ariel, Noah's jaw was hanging open.

"But come, you must see our water supply." Then Baruch led them to where four basins, one more than the original three, were constantly being filled from holes in the cliffside.

Again, Ariel was amazed. He'd read about signs and wonders in the Bible—but that was then, and this was now. God was displaying his power and mercy right here in the rock city of Sela.

To keep the campfires burning and the people warm, God had also provided groves of eucalyptus that, again, after they were picked, replenished themselves overnight.

They walked through clusters of tents and campfires. As they went, a few toddlers screamed and chased each other. Since the vanishing, they were the first youngsters Ariel had seen. So many couples had decided that, in these troubled times, they couldn't bring children into Davato's adult, hedonistic world. The Unitum Imperium handed out free birth control to everyone, no questions asked.

And having kids was also dangerous. Davato was waging a war on the nuclear family, and a couple with children screamed "family", making them a target for removal to the death camps.

"I've never seen so many children, Baruch."

"Most of the two-year-olds were born here. A handful of the older ones were smuggled past the checkpoints."

"How can Davato expect to create a world, even an evil one, without children?"

"His hatred of the family and everything good has blinded him."

Ariel nodded. Though he'd never been around children much, it warmed his heart to see them again. Maybe, in this place, the babies and their parents would be safe.

Stopping at a large desert tent, Baruch parted the heavy cloth entrance and led the others inside where tall stands held flickering oil lamps. They passed a carpeted space lined with dozens of pillows for group meetings. On their left was a carpeted bedroom, separated by wall hangings. Then Baruch led them to an intimate outside corner holding six pillows arranged in a circle around a low cedarwood table. The table held a clay pitcher, plates and silverware for four, and four goblets filled with some kind of red liquid.

"This is Christmas Eve, and though our daily fare is water, manna bread, and quail—tasty enough—today, the Lord decided to reward us with a special meal." He clapped his hands, and a blonde-haired woman brought a silver tray with two serving platters, heaped full. "This is Ruth. I tried to dissuade her, but she insists on preparing and serving my meals. Two years ago, the Truth Squads took her husband and their two teenagers to a death camp. She is her family's last survivor."

"I'm so sorry for your loss," said Ariel. "I, too, lost my family to the Antichrist's evil."

She placed her tray on the center table and bowed to each of the newcomers. "Baruch brought me here six months ago from Jerusalem. He's been a godsend to everyone who saw the three angels and the signs in the sky, who heard of the battle of Gog and Magog, and who decided to follow Jesus." Tears came to her eyes, and she brushed them away. "Thank you, again, Baruch."

"You don't have to thank me, Ruth. Please make an extra place and sit with us." He waved toward an empty spot.

"Thank you, no. I will eat later. And you won't believe how it tastes tonight. Besides the manna today, there were several new spice plants to work with." She gave them an impish grin and backed away. "I'll return to my tent. I have other mouths to feed."

They said goodbye, and after she left, Baruch faced his guests. "She's taken in two orphans, two and three years old, both born in the Tribulation. Life goes on. But let us pray."

Then he thanked the Lord for his mercy toward all who had taken sanctuary in the Refuge. He praised Jesus for being born as a babe and for leaving Heaven to live a life as a mortal man on earth. He thanked his Savior for dying on the cross, for pardoning everyone's sins, and especially for forgetting about their previous disbelief. And he thanked the Lord for Ariel, for what he'd done for the refugees, and lastly, for the food God provided each day. "Now, let's eat!"

Ariel dished a mound of red sauce with chunks of meat onto his plate. He took a large slice of what appeared to be white bread. Picking up his goblet, he sipped, and his eyes widened. "Why, this is the tastiest wine I've ever had."

Baruch sipped his and nodded. "It's not alcoholic, but when we poured water in these clay pitchers we were commanded to make, it changed to this. I've never had wine, but this is outstanding."

When Ariel tasted the manna, he was sure it was the best bread he'd ever eaten, and when he lifted a forkful of the spicy red sauce with chunks of succulent quail, he was certain this was what the redeemed would eat in Heaven.

Satisfied after the best meal he'd eaten in years, he settled into the cushions. He sipped the "wine" and regarded his host. "Can I ask a personal question about your faith, Baruch?"

"Of course, Ariel. Anything for our greatest benefactor."

"I've heard you are the leader of the 144,000 mentioned in the Bible, but that before you came to Christ, you were a righteous Jew. How did your conversion take place?"

Baruch smiled, and his gaze drifted to the candles flickering on the low table. "From the very beginning, I knew the Lord had a special task for the Great Assembly, as we called our group. But when I appointed twelve leaders, I had no idea that those who were eventually called under them would end up numbering 144,000. Such a biblical number!"

"Y–you are the leader of the 144,000?" Noah's eyes widened as he looked from Baruch to Ariel.

"I thought you knew," said Ariel.

Noah shook his head.

"But you were saying . . ." Ariel faced Baruch and waved a hand.

"Yes, well . . . as to how I came to Christ, it was after they captured me and sent me down to the catacombs in one of the Antichrist's Roman prisons. There I met a man whose name was Caleb Turner, and he told me an impossible tale of how a demon had tried to stop him from blogging about the truth of the Rapture. He pointed me to Isaiah chapter fifty-three, and when I pondered it, everything he said began to make sense. And then his brother, Dylan, assisted by his sister, Chelsea, helped everyone in the catacombs to—"

"Wait a minute!" Ariel sat upright. "His sister was Chelsea? The same Chelsea Turner who was Davato's personal secretary?"

"The very same, but she disappeared. I fear what might have happened to her."

"No, my friend, she should be just fine." Ariel grinned, whistled, and shook his head. "You aren't going to believe this, but . . ." Then he described how he found a woman, destitute and hungry, in a Tel Aviv park, and how she needed passage to Italy where she could meet her brother. "I gave her money and clothes and put her on a ship bound for Venice. I assume she got there safely and rejoined her brother."

A smiling David Benjamin turned to Baruch. "As you keep saying, 'The Lord will provide.'"

"This cannot be a coincidence." Baruch's eyes lit up. "That both you and I have met this woman and have both assisted her—or at least in my case, I *tried* to assist her—the hand of God is surely behind what has happened here."

"I wonder if she ever connected with her brother?" Now Ariel's gaze settled on the candlelight.

"The Lord is good," said Baruch. "She has already played an important role in God's plan. I just hope she has turned to Jesus. Then, perhaps, he will look after her. If she joins the family of God, perhaps she'll join us here? She knows where to find the directions."

Ariel looked up. "At the Jerusalem travel agency?"

Baruch nodded.

Ariel had too often neglected the travel agency with its cryptic directions to the Refuge. When he returned to Israel, he must ensure that a runner would check in on the building every night. Based on what Baruch said, Chelsea might someday return there, pull out the brick, and—if she was now a Christian—be able to read the Refuge's location.

Baruch was right. It was surely divine coincidence that both men had encountered the same woman. And Chelsea Turner might not be the only one depending on the travel agency for a way to safety.

As he had many times before, Ariel vowed again to do all he could to help every wandering soul—especially Chelsea—to escape the clutches of the Antichrist and his goons.

CHAPTER 24
HOME AT LAST

Kronberg Mountain, Switzerland – December, Year 5

The hum and bounce of tires over broken asphalt was their constant companion as Chelsea and Dylan drove from Parma, Italy, to Kronberg Mountain. The trip took two days, not because of the CSA checkpoints, through which they breezed unmolested, but because of crevasses around which they were forced to detour. By day, a weak, yellow sun shone dimly through an overcast sky. By night, a pallid moon barely lit a sky missing too many stars. On the way, Dylan told Chelsea everything that had happened to him since they parted.

As they started the drive into the Swiss Alps, it began to snow. Somehow, despite the agony of the demon attacks, the UI plow drivers still kept most highways clear. But by the time they parked the car in the hidden spot in the trees below the resort, the fallen snow was almost a meter deep beside the road.

It was midafternoon, nearly dark, when Chelsea and Dylan started up the trail, trudging laboriously through deep drifts already closing behind them. Exhausted and wet, they pushed through the door into the resort where the Nazarene Friends welcomed them with rejoicing, hot coffee, and cookies Danielle had baked that morning.

Chelsea renewed her acquaintance with Margot. Then Dylan introduced her to Pasqual, René, Victor, Danielle, and Jakob and Emma Huber. When they learned Chelsea had been saved, they rejoiced and hugged her anew. They had many questions about her experience. But it was obvious the two travelers were beat, and Pasqual raised a hand.

"You two look like you could use a shower and a nap. Let's save the questions for later." He turned to Chelsea and Dylan. "Did you realize tonight was Christmas Eve?"

"No." Chelsea smiled. "What a pleasant surprise. But you're right. I could use some rest."

* * *

AFTER A SHORT NAP, DYLAN RETURNED to the main room downstairs when his phone rang.

"It's so good to hear your voice!" Dylan laughed upon hearing his brother. "A lot has happened since we last talked. Where are you now?"

"We're staying in Custer, South Dakota, for the winter, but right now, I'm with a group scouting far north of town where we found a cell signal," he said. "We're going to a small church here and have made some friends. This spring, I want to go to Colorado Springs and look for the Sanctuary, but Tanya is ready to put down roots and stay here. Have you heard from Chelsea?"

"She's with me right now."

"She is? That's wonderful news."

After Caleb related all that had happened to her for the last two years, the signal began fading, and their conversation ended. But it left Dylan with a feeling of joy he hadn't felt in months. He mounted the stairs, knocked on Chelsea's door, and told her about his conversation.

When she heard, tears came to her eyes, and she hugged him. "Caleb's safe? That's wonderful news! Somehow, after all that's happened, we all made it through."

"It's as if someone were watching over us, isn't it?"

She smiled and nodded. "And who do you think that might be?"

Feigning ignorance, Dylan shrugged, and she slapped him on the shoulder.

* * *

THAT EVENING, THEY ATE A MEAL of roasted venison, for Jakob had shot a deer earlier that week. Margot had cooked potatoes covered with cheese, and Danielle added homemade bread with butter and jam. After the raid on the CSA headquarters, their larder was stocked for a year.

During the meal, Chelsea told them how she discovered a way to make the solar phones untraceable. When René and Victor heard this, they beamed. Victor couldn't wait to lay his hands on their phones and make the change.

After supper in the common room, they gathered around a pine someone had chopped down and decorated. In Dylan's absence, Victor had procured a guitar. While he played, the rest sang carols that everyone knew.

Then they sat around the woodstove, sipping wine and talking.

Chelsea sat with Dylan, and in a break in the conversation, she turned to him. "Dylan, I've never felt closer to you and to Caleb than when we've been apart. When we were kids and even teenagers, I never felt like that. But you and Caleb—" She cupped her hands on her lap. "You are my family, my only lifeline to what we once had, back in the world we left. And I'm holding onto that with all I've got."

Dylan reached across and gripped both her hands. "I know what you're feeling, sis. I've had this powerful desire to find you and to reunite all three of us."

She smiled, raised his hands to her lips, and kissed them.

Then René asked the travelers about the demon attacks. "You're telling me you were able to bypass every checkpoint without trouble?"

"That's right," answered Chelsea. "I've seen it. The creatures only attack those with the mark."

Pasqual nodded. "If that has started, then from what the Bible says, the CSA, the squaddies, and all the followers of the Antichrist will be nearly incapacitated for the next five months."

René graced them with a rare smile. "But this is wonderful. We should take full advantage of this by making more raids and stocking up on more supplies."

"But there's worse to come, isn't there?" asked Margot.

"There is," said René, "and after the fifth month, we'll again be at risk of discovery. Eventually, we'll have to move again."

"How many safe places can we move to before we're discovered?" Pasqual ran a hand through his hair.

"I know of a place where God has promised to protect everyone," said Chelsea. "Somewhere Davato will never find."

Everyone's gaze fell on her, especially René's. "What do you mean?" he asked. "Where is such a place?"

Then she told them about her meeting with Baruch Abramovich and the Refuge God promised for the Jews and for all who follow Christ. "Baruch left directions to the Refuge on a marked brick at a certain travel agency in Jerusalem. But when I returned there to find them, the words were supernaturally hidden from me. At the time, I wasn't saved. But I am now. If we return, we'll have the directions we need to find it."

René exchanged glances with Pasqual, Dylan, and Margot.

"Then perhaps . . ." René rubbed his chin. "Perhaps while the CSA and the squaddies are preoccupied with demons, we should leave here and travel to this Refuge."

"There will not be a better time," added Dylan. "But what about the snow? We barely made it through. There are only a few plows out now, and if the wind picks up, we could see two- and three-meter drifts."

"We have time." René scratched his chin. "The attacks won't end until late May. We can wait."

"That sounds like a plan," said Pasqual. "Who wants to go to this Refuge?"

All but Victor, Danielle, Jakob, and Emma raised their hands.

"We have our eyes on a farm not far from here," said Jakob. "We don't want to leave Switzerland."

"What about you, Victor and Danielle?" asked Pasqual.

Victor glanced aside at Danielle. She nodded, and then he spoke. "We want to stay at Kronberg Mountain as long as we can."

"But eventually, they may find you," said René. "And you don't have the mark."

"We'll take our chances," answered Danielle. "If it's no longer safe, we'll find another place nearby."

"Okay," said René. "The rest of us will leave as soon as the roads clear. Then we'll head for Jerusalem."

CHAPTER 25
DEMONS

Revelation 9:5–6 (HCSB): *They were not permitted to kill them but were to torment them for five months; their torment is like the torment caused by a scorpion when it strikes a man. In those days people will seek death and will not find it; they will long to die, but death will flee from them.*

New Babylon, Iraq – February, Year 5

Adam Turner couldn't take it any longer, and he feared he was losing his mind. Others around him had already gone that way. The demon attacks and the pain were relentless. Not once in the last three months had he slept more than four hours—the longest interval, ever, between attacks. He feared lack of sleep was making him psychotic. And all of it sent him plunging into a deep well of despair, hopelessness, and drunkenness.

To top it off, for the first time since joining Worldnet and becoming head of Davato's Ministry of Truth, he had serious doubts about the man in charge.

Yesterday, Grady Wilson had confessed to Adam that every morning it was his job to place a liter of whiskey in the secure bombproof box equipped with explosive and poison detection devices leading into the Imperator's apartment. That meant the supposedly divine leader of the Unitum Imperium was suffering like everyone else.

Adam had just come from a "meeting" with the Imperator, and it left him even more shaken. Not since the demon attacks started had Davato once left his penthouse suite in the World Casino. No one had seen him on video or face-to-face.

This afternoon was no exception.

Davato had asked to "meet" with Adam Turner and Gaston Soucy, head of the Ministry of Charity. Both had sat in the conference room with Grady Wilson taking notes. The welts from frequent stings covered the faces and arms of all three attendees. And, as they were most of the time lately, everyone was half drunk with liquor and fearing the next attack.

"I've heard reports," boomed the Imperator's voice from the speakers above, "that some provinces are running out of whiskey, rum, vodka, and brandy? What can you do about this, Soucy?"

Soucy leaned toward the microphone box on the table. "We're going through supplies at a rapid clip, and it's hard to keep up. We're running short of wheat, potatoes, grapes, sugarcane—just about all raw materials. Harvests are far below what they once were. In some places, they have to haul safe water from far away. Also, the distilleries can't get people to show up for work."

"Divert what you need from the food supply. I want the strongest hard stuff you can get into people's hands. I've also heard you're not making enough heroin and fentanyl. Why not?"

"No one is harvesting the poppy fields. And the raw materials for the fentanyl aren't arriving when they should."

From somewhere in the penthouse suite, a fist exploded down beside a microphone, and everyone in the room jumped. "I DON'T CARE! Fix these problems, or I'll find someone who can!"

Across the table, a visibly shaken Soucy nodded. Realizing the Imperator couldn't see him, he spoke. "Yes, yes, my lord. I will attend to it as best I can."

What followed was such a long silence, and Adam wondered if the Imperator had left.

"Adam Turner!"

He jumped again. "Yes, my lord?"

"Am I to understand that since this . . . this demon thing started, the CSA and the Truth Squads have abandoned their posts?"

He swallowed and, repeating Soucy's mistake, nodded.

"WELL? ANSWER ME!"

Never had Adam heard such anger, such loss of control, in Davato's voice.

"My lord, it's true. Mostly. No matter what we do, we cannot keep them manning the checkpoints. Like everyone else, they're drinking, shooting up, and trying to ward off the pain as best they can. Or they're running, willy-nilly, in a vain attempt to escape."

When Davato again spoke, his voice was quiet, controlled, and more like what Adam was used to. "I–I understand. The Enemy and his people, the Jews, will pay for this. The Christians too. We only have two more months to endure this. That's what the Enemy's book says, and for once, I believe it. Just two more months, and we can return to normal. Then I will have my retribution upon all who follow him."

The news left Adam shaking and despairing. Two more months of this torture? How could he endure even one more day? He was glad Davato wasn't in the room with him, because with the Imperator's statement, tears now fell, uncontrollably, down his cheeks.

Another long episode of silence followed, broken not by the Imperator's voice, but by the sound of buzzing wings through the mike, then loud cursing and a click that shut off the overhead microphone.

Adam exchanged glances with Soucy and Grady Wilson. Soucy was shaking his head. "He won't show his face because, like everyone else's, his is covered with the demon's welts and he can't admit that, that . . ."

"That what?" asked Grady.

Soucy pulled on his long Gallic face and uttered words no one in Davato's circle should ever have uttered. "That he's not the divine being he says he is."

Grady's eyes widened, and he shot a fearful look toward the microphone.

Adam wiped at his tears and turned away from the others.

But as the group headed for the door, the demons came again.

Ahead of the others, Adam ran into the hall, trying to flee. He knew it was futile, that there was no escape. But he couldn't just stand there and let them sting him. Not again. This time, one of the laughing, sneering, mocking creatures plunged its needle into his buttocks. As it had ten thousand or more times before, hot lead instantly spread out from the site of the stinger to jangle and pierce and tear at every nerve in his body.

Hours later, back in his room, as the pain began to subside, he took out his Glock 17.

He turned it over. Not since he'd sat in the backyard of his Minneapolis mansion when Turner Enterprises was facing bankruptcy had he contemplated what he was now about to do. He couldn't endure another two months of this. It was impossible. Anything was preferable to this.

After a long swig from the whiskey bottle on the table, he fondled the pistol. Could he do it? There was nothing to live for now, and if he was right, what awaited him was not the Christian hell, but a welcome oblivion.

Davato wasn't the god he claimed to be. He might have risen from the dead, but the Enemy, as Davato called him, was in charge. That was beyond obvious.

Adam shoved the pistol into his belt holster, stood, and left his apartment. The elevator dumped him into the foyer, and he crossed through the revolving doors. Above, a dim sun shed weak rays upon the walkways, empty of all but a few men, women, and nonbinaries huddled on the benches, shivering in pain. He passed the center strip, planted now with the dead sticks of young saplings, so symbolic of what Davato's rule was becoming.

He picked up the pace, eventually arriving at the central park. Ahead loomed the statue that Davato had used to wow the people. Motionless and dark for months now, it was yet another symbol of the Unitum Imperium's decline.

Just as it had done ten thousand times before, a wave of pain from the sting in his buttocks returned. The demon had stuck him over two hours ago, but the pain never really left, did it? It just subsided then came back in waves. He gritted his teeth, found a bench, and sat.

Finally, it passed.

He yanked the pistol from its sheath and hefted it. Just one squeeze on the trigger and it would all end.

The buzzing came again, and he looked up.

Two of the horrid little monsters descended to a meter away then hovered at eye level. There was no mistaking the mocking, leering, sneering expressions on their horrid little faces. He raised the gun, aimed at the one on the right, and pulled the trigger.

The shot exploded in the still air.

But the demon whizzed aside, and the bullet missed.

He sent another bullet exploding from the muzzle, flying off into empty space.

Both demons lurched forward. One stinger dug deep into his left thigh. A second needle plunged into his right nipple.

Adam screamed, and a shivering began in his body that wouldn't quit. Molten metal spread out in all directions, burning a path along every nerve. He fell off the bench onto the ground, rolling and twitching and crying out in pain. How long he did this, he didn't know, but time passed.

When the pain subsided enough, he stood. The Glock 17 was lying on the dead grass. He pulled back on the slide and put a bullet in the chamber. He shoved the barrel into his mouth.

And he pulled the trigger.

But all that followed was an empty click.

He pulled the trigger again.

Again, he heard only a click. Was a bullet stuck in the chamber?

He aimed at the ground and pulled the trigger a third time.

The shot exploded and sent clods of dirt flying.

Sticking the barrel against his forehead, he yanked on the trigger again and again, but it refused to fire.

"No! No! No!" Tears fell down his cheeks. There was no escaping this torture, was there? The Enemy was in charge, and nothing Adam Turner did was going to release him from this unbearable torment.

CHAPTER 26
THE DAVATO YOUTH CORE

Appenzell, Switzerland – May, Year 5

Before they left the mountain, Danielle had painted red blotches on their faces and arms. After Pasqual parked the Volvo on an Appenzell side street and slammed shut the door, Dylan stood beside Margot, and she laughed. "You look like you walked into a mosquito nest."

"You should talk," answered a smiling Dylan. "You look like a pincushion."

It was the first day of May, and tomorrow, they planned to start their journey to Chelsea's Refuge. The plan was to take Fabio Caruso's trawler and sail to Tel Aviv to avoid riskier travel overland. That way, René said they should get there well before the demon attacks ended. But they needed gas credits for the trip south.

Pasqual checked the black-market card in his wallet. "I'll head to the bakery and meet you back here. At the shop, deal only with Oscar. But make sure no one else sees you with the pistols and ammunition."

"Of course," said Dylan. "We've done this before. How much gas credit should we ask for two Heckler and Koch pistols?"

"At least five thousand euros. But get cards with less than two thousand euros credit each. Some pumps are programmed to reject anything carrying more than that unless you've got authorization from the Ministry of Charity Department of Energy."

"Right." Dylan slung the rucksack with the extra weapons over his back. The raid on Kaufbeuren had brought them so many extra weapons, they couldn't use them all. And when they left tomorrow, they'd have to abandon much of what they'd procured.

On the way, they passed two youths from the newly formed Davato Youth Core, strutting down the street as if they owned it. But just like everyone else with the mark, they were covered with welts from the demon attacks. Both were under seventeen, and they wore brown-and-green uniforms with sidearms at their belts. Dylan averted his gaze and continued on. A few steps later, he glanced back. They also were continuing on.

Dylan and Margot easily found the tobacco shop working the black market on the side. But before stepping in, he noticed that the youths had reversed course and were heading back. Once inside, while pretending to examine some crack pipes, he waited until the youths had passed the front before approaching the counter.

The shopkeeper was replenishing cubicles of cigarettes on the wall and had his back to them. Oscar was a short, balding man in his fifties with a white goatee. Much to René's delight, the Unitum Imperium had reestablished a trade route to India, and cigarettes were again available for purchase. Since the Atlantic was filled with blood, ships now refused to cross it, so Europe had lost Brazil as a trading partner for tobacco. Today, Dylan was also supposed to procure a box of cigarettes for their ex-spy.

He approached the counter and cleared his throat. "Oscar?" he whispered. "We've come to trade."

The shopkeeper whirled, recognized the two as previous customers, and nodded. "What do you have for me today?"

Dylan unslung his backpack and laid two Heckler and Koch pistols on the counter, followed by six boxes of ammunition.

Oscar picked up one of the weapons, and his eyes brightened. "I can give you—"

At that moment, the Davato Youth Core members burst through the door bearing pistols. "What have we here?" said the tallest.

Margot gasped, and Dylan froze. They'd been caught in the act, and there was nowhere to hide.

Oscar slid the guns off the counter.

The second, freckle-faced youth, who couldn't be more than sixteen, waved his gun. "Everyone, step away from the counter and put your hands behind your back."

Dylan did as commanded. Margot and Oscar followed.

"Hugo," said the tall one to his younger companion, "cuff them."

The freckle-faced lad put Dylan and Margot in handcuffs, and the tall youth faced the shop owner. "We've had a tip you've been dealing in the black market, and now we have proof."

Oscar's face was white, and his glance bounced from the youths to the door and back. "No, no. I just sell cigarettes, cigars, tobacco, hashish, and opium. Only what is legal."

The older youth stepped behind the counter, cuffed him, and began poking in the drawers beneath. Then he slammed a handful of UI gas ration cards and ID cards on the counter. "Then what is this?"

His eyes wild, Oscar shook his head.

"We've got them, Gustav," said Hugo. "Now what?"

The taller, older leader, now identified as Gustav, smiled. "Now we take them to headquarters."

Gustav headed for the door, but as he laid a hand on the knob, the room filled with the buzzing of demons. He beat at one of them, but it slipped under his arm and stung him on the chest.

Then the demons attacked the shopkeeper and Hugo.

Sensing an advantage, Dylan pulled Margot toward the exit, but though Gustav was shivering with pain, he blocked the door and held a shaking weapon on them. "No!" he managed to say. "Back off, or I'll shoot."

Dylan backed away. Somehow, the youths were better able to withstand the pain.

For what seemed an eternity, Gustav held them inside the shop while the youths' pain subsided. When Oscar was finally able to walk, Gustav led his three prisoners out the door, down the street six blocks, and into the same CSA headquarters from which Dylan and the Nazarene Friends had once freed Jakob and Emma Huber. Since the raid, five agents now manned the building, augmented by the Davato Youth Core.

"What have we here?" asked the desk sergeant.

Gustav explained who he'd captured, and the sergeant congratulated the captors. "Since you youngsters are the least affected by these demons, I'm sending you and Hugo to drive our prisoners to Lucerne this evening."

As Gustav and Hugo beamed and slapped each other on the backs, the sergeant frowned at their enthusiasm.

"Get them behind bars before the demons strike again," ordered the sergeant.

An older CSA man led Dylan and Margot down the back hallway. He opened an iron door, pushed them inside, and removed their handcuffs.

The door banged shut with a metallic clang. A key clicked in the lock, and feet echoed down the hall.

Tears in her eyes, Margot ran into Dylan's open arms. "This can't be happening. Is this leading up to what I painted? Are they going to give us both the mark of the beast?"

He gripped her to his chest and stared at the brick-lined walls. "I don't know. All we can do is put our trust in God and wait to be rescued. What else can we do?"

CHAPTER 27
A CHANGE OF PLANS

To Lucerne, Switzerland – May, Year 5

On the day following Dylan and Margot's capture, René drove Chelsea to a side street to wait while she, alone, went on a mission to the Appenzell CSA headquarters to reconnoiter the situation. Not that long ago, people had seen her face on TV beside Davato, and she feared discovery. As they all did now before going into town, she covered herself with fake welts and wore long sleeves.

Once inside the station, no one asked whether she had the mark. Saying she had a missing brother, she asked if he was in jail for being drunk and disorderly. The answer she received was not what she wanted to hear.

"We don't arrest people for being drunk and disorderly, miss," said the sergeant. "Our jail is empty. All our prisoners were transferred to Lucerne regional HQ last night."

Barely had these words left his mouth than the demons struck the sergeant and his companions. She fled the building before her ruse was discovered.

When René heard what she'd learned, he drove her back to the Kronberg Mountain resort where he, Pasqual, Chelsea, and the others planned what to do next.

"We were going to leave today anyway, but now we have a new destination." René blew out smoke, dropped ashes in a tray, and sat back in his easy chair. "I have a contact in Lucerne who might be able to help us. We'll need a place to hide near their headquarters while we figure out how to free Dylan and Margot. This is as good a time for us to part as any."

René's words calmed her fears. A former spy, a man with contacts and tricks up his sleeve, was in charge. How she could have used guidance like his back in Tel Aviv before she met Ariel Geller!

"We'll be all right here at the resort." Victor glanced at Danielle. "Let us know when you free them."

"We will," answered René.

Jakob Huber stood beside Emma and shuffled his feet. "We might as well leave now for that abandoned farm near our old place. No matter what happens, I can't leave Switzerland."

"We understand," said Pasqual.

"We'll stay here, of course." Victor laid a hand on Danielle's arm, and she nodded in return.

Chelsea, René, and Pasqual said their goodbyes to the others. With some gifts from Victor, they left at sunset in the Opal van, arriving in Lucerne a few hours later. While Chelsea and Pasqual waited in the vehicle in the dark, René left to meet a former spy acquaintance.

A few hours later, he returned. "It's all arranged," he said. "We're staying at the house of a former Muslim who's now a Christian. His place has a view of the Lucerne regional CSA headquarters. It's perfect."

After they parked on the street, the door opened, and Chelsea followed the others into an ancient, three-story house. "Welcome, friends," said a middle-aged man with a gray mustache and thinning gray hair. "I am Ahmet Kaplan, and you will be safe here with me."

Ahmet led them to a top-floor flat. On the apartment's far side, windows overlooked the Reuss River. Only a hundred meters to the west, the river flowed into Lake Lucerne. The top floor had two bedrooms, a tiny bathroom with a shower, a living room, and a staircase leading down to the waterfront on the backside. Restaurants and shops lined the waterfront, but these days, the establishments that were still open serviced a few customers. From the front windows, Chelsea had a clear view of the CSA headquarters.

"Before the Rapture," said Ahmet, "I let out this apartment. But when the Department of Charity required me to register all rentals, I

139

removed it from the rolls." He looked out the front window. "We mustn't leave your vehicle on the street. Some suspicious official might check your plates. I will arrange to park your van a few kilometers away in one of the enclosed single-car garages I own."

"We can't thank you enough for all you're doing," said Pasqual.

"We are all Christians struggling with the Antichrist's reign, are we not? Your spy friend explained your situation to me." Ahmet shook his head. "What little I can do to help my brothers and sisters in need, I will do."

"We appreciate it," added Chelsea.

"But now I will let you wash that makeup off your faces, take showers if you like, and settle in. Meet me downstairs for coffee, and we'll talk more."

An hour later, refreshed and showered, Chelsea joined the others at Ahmet's kitchen table where he served strong espresso in small mugs with lots of sugar.

"Now I know you are curious as to why a Muslim and a Turk came to live in Lucerne. When I was living in Ankara, one night, I, like many other Muslims, had a dream in which Jesus appeared to me. It's difficult to describe, but I knew who he was. And this is what he said to me: 'Ahmet, I know you, but you do not know me. I am the way, the truth, and the life. Follow me, and I will give you eternal life.' That was his message for me, and I can tell you that the vision shattered my faith in Muhammad. The next day, I sought out a Christian pastor and heard the story of Jesus's birth, death, and resurrection. And that began my journey to faith."

"Amazing!" Pasqual slapped his knee. "I'd heard that many Muslims were coming to Christ because of dreams, but yours is the first time I heard the story in person."

"Jesus offers us forgiveness from our sins, once and for all time. Allah, on the other hand, offers only a lifetime of striving to do good. Even then, one never knows if he will let you into Paradise. One can never be good enough, can one? And Allah is known to be capricious."

"Without that forgiveness"—Chelsea lowered her gaze to the table—

"after all I did in the service of the Antichrist, I could never have been saved."

Ahmet's eyes widened. "I thought you looked familiar. Are you the one who once stood beside Davato on television? The one he called a traitor?"

"The very same. But I fled, became a Christian, and was on the run for nearly two years until I joined my brother, Dylan, in Switzerland."

"Ah, yes. He and another woman are the ones in prison across the street, yes?"

"That's right," said René. "Her name is Margot."

"On that subject, you will be pleased to know I have a contact in the CSA headquarters over there."

René's eyes lit up. "A contact? Does he have the mark?"

"Yes, but he regrets it. The demon attacks have made some deeply regret that they ever followed the beast."

René pulled a cigarette from his shirt pocket and raised an eyebrow to Ahmet.

When Ahmet nodded his approval, René lit up. Then he said, "Can you inquire if our friends are still being held here? Can he find out what is the plan for them?"

"Naturally. Like you, I now paint myself with red dots whenever I go out. It has made it much easier to go out in public. With the welts, everyone assumes you have the mark, and they no longer ask. Once the demon attacks end, it will be a different story. But yes. Tomorrow, I will contact my friend and ask."

"You are a dream come true." René was beaming.

"My wife, Ece, will be home soon to prepare dinner. She, too, became a Christian after me."

* * *

THE NEXT AFTERNOON, WHILE PASQUAL was downstairs, Ahmet mounted the steps and reported back to René and Chelsea what his contact had found. And it wasn't good.

Since demons had incapacitated most of the headquarters staff, they'd turned responsibility of the prisoners to a band of Davato Youth Core who appeared to be less affected. Their leader was Gustav, but he was brash and undisciplined.

Unfortunately, Ahmet's contact had no specific information about Dylan and Margot. He could only repeat the general directive for what they normally did with captured Christians and Jews—send them to the German death camp.

"No, this cannot be." Chelsea shook her head. "We cannot let Dylan go to that camp. You rescued Margot from there once. Can you do it a second time?"

"Probably not." René crushed a cigarette under his heel on the tiled floor. "There may be nothing we can do. I checked it out this morning. That headquarters is heavily guarded, and we don't have the mark or the papers to get inside."

Chelsea thanked him, walked to the window, and gazed at the stone and marble façade behind which her brother and Margot were being held.

"Dear Jesus," she whispered, "we need your help now as never before."

CHAPTER 28
DEBAUCHERY'S REPRISE

Revelation 18:4b–5 (NLT): *"Come away from her, my people. Do not take part in her sins, or you will be punished with her. For her sins are piled as high as heaven, and God remembers her evil deeds."*

New Babylon, Iraq – May, Year 5

In the third week of May, the demon locusts left their victims and swarmed back to the glassy shaft near New Babylon that led deep into the bowels of the earth. Behind the last buzzing monster flew the fifth angel, bearing an iron key. At the doorway between the physical and spiritual worlds, he pulled the great iron doors shut with a creaking of hinges. He slipped the key into the door lock and turned it.

The judgment of the fifth trumpet was complete.

* * *

WHEN THE DEMONS LEFT, GRADY was asleep on the couch in his World Casino apartment, still shivering in pain from the last attack. Beside him on the floor, an empty bottle lay in a brown puddle of dried-up whiskey.

For the last five months, he'd slept only a few hours between assaults, staggering through each day in a zombielike haze of drunkenness, misery, and lack of sleep. When the demons stopped coming, he didn't wake. Six hours passed until he again opened his eyes, looked at the clock, and realized how long he'd slept. But so tired was he that he drank a glass of precious water, staggered to his bedroom, slipped under the covers, and slept for another ten hours.

When next he woke, it was evening, and, feeling better than he had in months, he went to the window. On the walkways below, people were milling about, shouting, and rejoicing. The air filled with the whine of electric guitars, the boom of the bass, and the beat of the drums from the clubs, sounds that had been absent for five long months.

He showered, dressed, and hurried to the elevator. He descended to the street where men, women, and nonbinaries were celebrating that the demons had gone.

As usual, the Devil's Brew was serving drinks, and he joined a joyful crowd mobbing the entrance. He found a seat, ordered some wings, a triple whiskey, and a pipe of hashish. Around him, everyone's faces and arms—every area of exposed skin—were covered with welts from the constant stings of the last five months. How long would those take to heal? When would life return to normal?

After gobbling the wings and downing his drink, he lit the pipe.

The usual band took up their instruments. Electric chords, booming bass, and thudding drums reverberated above the crowd's buzz. The band played a wild, rhythmic beat.

Since the demon attacks, something had changed. People seemed desperate to erase the memory of what had happened, crazy for pleasure. A man and a woman in a booth against the wall had stripped off their clothes. The man sat on the bench with the woman above him, and they were coupling. It was the same in the far corner. Others stared and smiled, but he turned his head away.

A woman with braided hair, dressed in black leather, with black mascara shadowing her eye sockets and white makeup covering her face to hide the welts, strolled between revelers. She dropped a card on his table. Shiny gold letters stood out on a black background: "A seance to reach the dead. Guaranteed to resurrect your deceased loved one. Room 5 in back. Two hundred euros. Conjuring guaranteed."

He pushed the card aside as Marcia appeared out of the throng.

"We meet again." Today, Marcia led a red-haired companion. Unbidden, they plopped into seats at his table. "I was hoping you'd be here tonight."

Her tongue played along the edge of her lips. Her eyes were bright with eagerness and lust. "This is Ruby." She laid a hand on Ruby's bare shoulder. "And we need a willing partner."

Stuffing the unfinished pipe into his pocket, he grabbed Marcia's and Ruby's hands and pulled them toward the door. "How long has it been?" he asked her.

"Too long."

Their faces and bodies were a mass of red welts, but nobody cared.

Up in his room, he was ready to make up for lost time.

* * *

WHEN MARCIA AND RUBY HAD LEFT and he was again alone, he slid the bone hash pipe from his pocket and set it on the kitchen table. He didn't light it but stared instead at the pipe and its devil's-head bowl. It was carved from bone—genuine Christian bone, they promised—with black ebony dots for eyes staring out from all the white bone.

After the tryst, why did he feel so drained, so used-up? How many times hadn't he wished for two women at once, and yet, after it was over, it wasn't joy he felt, but emptiness.

It was as if a part of his soul had been sucked out of him. He'd gone from the worst pain imaginable to the heights of passion and pleasure, and yet—

He wasn't happy. There was a hole inside of him, and nothing could fill it, no matter how hard he tried.

With the back of his hand, he knocked the hash pipe across the table and onto the floor.

Tears that wouldn't stop formed at the corners of his eyes. Then he sat at his kitchen table—alone, drained, and empty—and cried.

CHAPTER 29
PLANS FOR REVENGE

New Babylon, Iraq – May, Year 5

Two days after the demons departed, Adam Turner joined the other three ministers to a meeting Davato called. Present were Grady Wilson, Davato's personal secretary; General Eric Hofmann, Minster of Peace; Gaston Soucy, Minister of Charity; and Sebastien Rey, Minister of Virtue. As before, the Imperator refused to attend in person, and all Adam knew of his presence was a voice from the overhead speakers.

"Some of you might suspect why I called you here," he began. "During the last five months, your people have been absent from their posts, and the machinery of the Unitum Imperium has ground to a halt." Then his voice rose to such a volume, it shook even the window behind Adam. "Starting now, that must stop!"

Around him, the others' faces seemed drained of blood, and they exchanged worried glances.

When Davato spoke again, his words were quieter. "You will now put your houses in order, and then I have new instructions for everyone. This includes especially the Davato Youth Core under your command, Adam Turner."

Adam sat higher in his seat. When they'd realized that the younger you were, the less the demon stings affected you, they'd added the youth core in the second month of the demon attacks.

"The Enemy has declared all-out war on us, and now, we will retaliate. You will double, and yes, triple, your attacks on all Jews and Christians. They are in league with the Enemy, and they will pay the price for what we have just endured."

Breathing deeply, Adam nodded. If anyone was responsible, it was the Christians and Jews. In this, he agreed wholeheartedly.

"Wherever they gather, you will seek out those without the mark and capture them. In this, you will not fail."

Across the table, Grady Wilson's fingers clicked over his keyboard.

"Tomorrow, I am calling a video conference with my provincial governors at which I will repeat this order. And that is my only message for you today. You are dismissed." The overhead speaker clicked and was silent.

Adam stood and headed for the door. This was one of the shortest meetings the Imperator had ever called, but Adam's anger toward those who assisted the Enemy was as strong as Davato's.

Instead of returning to his room, he took the elevator to the ground floor, crossed the open plaza, and entered the Temple of Davato. Inside, he took the elevator to the shooting galleries. As one of Davato's elite, he bypassed the line.

Noting the importance of who had entered the gallery, the portly, short-haired game mistress shooed everyone else out of the room, leaving Adam as the only shooter. "What weapon would the Minister of Truth prefer today?"

"A machine gun, I think." He pointed to a rack behind him, and she brought him an AK-47.

Cradling the cold metal in his hands, he smiled. This was what he needed right now—revenge he could feel in his hands.

She spoke into a microphone, and the far end of the aisles filled with naked Christian men and women bearing signs that mocked and belittled their faith.

"Whenever you are ready, Minister," said the game mistress.

Grinning, he laid the gun against his shoulder and aimed. He squeezed the trigger.

The air split with the rat-a-tat-tat of bullets exploding from the barrel. The metal stock rammed back against his shoulder. The air filled with the smell of sulfur. Bodies at the room's far end began dropping.

Remembering how, only two months ago, he was ready to end his life, Adam Turner squeezed the trigger harder and continued firing.

CHAPTER 30
THE MARK OF THE BEAST

Revelation 14:9b–10a (NLT): *"Anyone who worships the beast and his statue or who accepts his mark on the forehead or on the hand must drink the wine of God's anger. It has been poured full strength into God's cup of wrath."*

Lucerne, Switzerland – July, Year 5

Six weeks had passed since their capture, and in the last week of July, Margot lay on her bunk, staring at the chipped paint flaking off the walls. Her cell was two meters by three, with a sink and a toilet. There was barely enough room to pace, which she did for much of the day—back and forth, back and forth. It was something to do. Something to take her mind from her imprisonment. Hugging the ceiling, a single window admitted what passed nowadays for daylight.

Her only consolation was that Dylan's cell was next to hers, and an air vent in the wall above her head allowed them to talk.

Even after the demon attacks stopped, the Davato Youth Core remained in charge of the CSA's prisoners. One guard had just removed the remains of her breakfast gruel, and she waited until his footsteps receded into the distance. Most of the welts covering the faces of those with the mark had receded, putting the guards in a good mood.

"When do you think they'll take us to the camp?" she called through the vent.

"You ask me that every day," said Dylan. "All I know is what the man on the other side has told me. After stopping the transports for five months, they're so backlogged, it may be another month or even longer."

149

"Let's hope it's longer. I cannot imagine going back there."

Then a woman's voice came through the other vent in Margot's cell. "Is anyone there?" she called. "Who are you talking to?"

Margot moved to the opposite wall and spoke to the vent. "Hello. Who are you?"

Her name was Tricia, and she was captured only this morning. "Two of them raped me and beat me in my apartment before bringing me here."

"Oh, that's terrible." Margot cupped a hand to her mouth.

"When they thought I was sleeping in the car, they talked between them. They said there was an acute shortage of guards and they were going to conscript Christians."

"That doesn't make sense. How can they do that? We don't"—a shudder rippled down her back—"have the mark."

"I don't know. It didn't make sense to me either."

"Well, Tricia, all we can do is trust that—"

Footsteps stopped outside her door, and she stopped talking. They'd agreed it was best not to let the guards know they were communicating.

A key clicked in the lock, and Gustav and Hugo entered. "You've got an appointment with the tattoo artist, Margot Durand. And then you're going to be just like us."

"What do you mean?" She recoiled against the bunk. "No, no. You can't do this."

But the two grabbed her arms and forced her out of the cell, down the hall, and into a room where waited a pasty-faced man gripping a tattoo gun. "Sit in the chair," he ordered.

She struggled against her captors, wriggled and fought. But they shoved her down then strapped her arms, torso, and legs. Her eyes wide, she stared as the man brought his pointy smoking needle toward her wrist. "No, no, you can't do this. I don't accept it. I reject your mark."

"Shut her up." The pasty-faced man glanced toward his youthful companions.

Gustav wrapped a cloth around her mouth and tightened it.

The hot needle cut into her wrist, and it burned. The smell of burning flesh rose to her nostrils, but she couldn't move. The man was carving a design, and she stared at it.

This wasn't possible. How could someone else *force* the mark on her?

She raised her glance to the ceiling. *Dear Jesus, save me from what they are doing. I belong only to you.*

CHAPTER 31
THE SIXTH TRUMPET

Revelation 9:13–16 (NLT): *Then the sixth angel blew his trumpet, and I heard a voice speaking from the four horns of the gold altar that stands in the presence of God. And the voice said to the sixth angel who held the trumpet, "Release the four angels who are bound at the great Euphrates River." Then the four angels who had been prepared for this hour and day and month and year were turned loose to kill one-third of all the people on earth. I heard the size of their army, which was 200 million mounted troops.*

Above the Earth – August, Year 6

The sixth angel flew high above the earth. He glanced down through the clouds, past thin streamers of smoke still spewing from the volcanoes and past the snowcapped alpine peaks. And he remembered all that had led up to this moment.

Was it only six years ago that the Ancient of Days had taken his people home? Perhaps 7 percent of mankind went to Heaven that day, and what a great day that was!

When the redeemed were safely home, the God of Hosts then hurled his judgments upon the earth—the seven seals and the first five trumpets.

First, the Lord allowed the man of lawlessness to rise to power.

Then man waged war against man. The United States and China unleashed their electromagnetic pulse and their thermonuclear weapons, effectively destroying each other.

Russia, Iran, and most of the Islamic world attacked Israel, home of God's chosen people. Then the angel of wrath destroyed not only the enemy armies but also the countries that sent them.

Following that came the Black Death, spread by the fleas of a supernaturally exploding rat population. The plague ravaged the human race. And when the Antichrist's corrupt, ineffective government was unable to manufacture the needed antibiotics, they claimed there was no cure.

The angel looked up. There, the Lord had blighted the sun, darkening one-third of the day. He'd diminished the moon and stars by a third. And he'd plunged one-third of the night into a well of inky pitch.

Everywhere, the Lord had caused earthquakes to shake the land, leveling buildings, opening cracks and crevasses.

He'd turned the Atlantic into a foul-smelling sea of rotting blood infested with maggots, ending all maritime commerce there.

His lightning storms and volcanic eruptions burned up one-third of the trees, leaving charred, scarecrow forests everywhere. That incinerated all the green grass. Only now were green shoots struggling again through the charcoal earth, giving hope to a smattering of wild animals.

Of the wild carnivores that remained, he turned even them against mankind.

Then he hurled asteroid debris upon the rivers and freshwater lakes, poisoning one-third of the fresh water. Now the survivors searched constantly for safe water.

Everywhere, the Lord ensured that crops failed and yields plummeted, sending the price of food skyrocketing. Only the wine and liquor still flowed.

But the people had worked hard to plant their harvest of doom. Again and again, they had rejected the Lord of Hosts, blasphemed his name, and denied his existence. They had wallowed in carnal delights and declared that good was evil and evil was good.

And then, worst of all, they accepted the mark of the beast.

After the reaper had left, after all the death and destruction, what was the count of the harvest?

One-fourth of the population.

One-fourth had perished, leaving behind empty houses, abandoned vehicles, and dried-up corpses.

Only the black market kept alive those who came to faith late and who rejected the mark. But the Lord watches over his people.

Wherever the redeemed lived, he gave them fresh water to drink. But their decisions were tardy, and always they struggled to avoid the Central Security Agency and the Truth Squads. For when the Antichrist's minions captured them, they were sent to the death camps, the Colosseum, or the shooting galleries. Yet even in death, they were blessed, for awaiting them was life everlasting and an eternity in the presence of God.

The angel gazed down, past the peaks and clouds to the cities and villages of men, and he spoke. "Woe to you who accepted the mark and worshiped the beast! For what I am about to do will unleash worse terrors than the world has yet seen."

The sixth angel brought the trumpet to his lips. And he blew.

THE SIXTH YEAR

~

DEMONS, DEATH, AND BLOOD

Revelation 14:14–16 (NLT): *Then I saw a white cloud, and seated on the cloud was someone like the Son of Man. He had a gold crown on his head and a sharp sickle in his hand. Then another angel came from the Temple and shouted to the one sitting on the cloud, "Swing the sickle, for the time of harvest has come; the crop on earth is ripe." So the one sitting on the cloud swung his sickle over the earth, and the whole earth was harvested.*

CHAPTER 32
CALEB

Custer, South Dakota – August, Year 6

Out here in the forest, far from town, I clutch my rifle and sit on a favorite log, where I often come to ponder and bring my petitions to God. Above me, a woodpecker machine-guns the trunk of a pine tree that is still with needles.

Constantly, I am gripped with this desire to head south and resume a search for the Sanctuary. But we've found a church in Custer with some good friends, including Marty and Ella Eastwood, and whenever I bring up the Sanctuary, Tanya argues me out of leaving. She is dead set against traveling again. She wants to settle down, and I can't blame her.

But every morning I read Revelation and the prophecies, and knowing what God has in store for this earth in the next year and a half, well—I need to get Tanya, Andy, Brianna, and Nika to a place of permanent safety. And I'm convinced that is *not* in Custer, South Dakota.

Why am I so driven to this goal? Every day, I ponder this question. Is it because I fear for their safety? I do love them so.

Or is it deeper than that? Am I simply insecure? Have I built my life upon such a flimsy foundation of faith that I must defend it behind an impenetrable iron fortress called the Sanctuary?

Or is my desire beyond emotion and even reason itself? Am I driven because of this wisp of a vision that struck me in the dead of night? Has God himself placed this unquenchable need within me?

I keep going back to the morning we left Shetek State Park and my dream of a green mountain valley with log cabins, horses, and happy

157

people. Surely, that was the Sanctuary. In the vision, I *knew*—don't ask me how, but I did—that *this* was where we must go.

I know that sounds crazy, but there it is.

One thing I have pondered yet bothers me. If the Sanctuary is in Cheyenne Mountain, then why did this dream not show that iconic entrance? Everyone's seen it on television, and it's not a green valley with cabins. Still, that's where my desire lures me.

Andy shares my view on leaving, but not with the same conviction. Brianna will go along with anything Tanya and I decide. It's Tanya I must convince.

Two days ago, we had news from a passing stranger of a CSA army, hundreds strong, leaving Rapid City and marching south in our direction. The traveler guessed they'd arrive within days, and it threw the town into an uproar. Everyone began gathering weapons and ammo and preparing for a fight. We even sent a lookout on horseback to the north.

When Tanya heard the news, she changed her mind—finally!—and we packed and made ready to leave. Our bikes were prepped and waiting.

But then a second wayfarer brought a different story: The army's destination, he insisted, was Deadwood and Lead to the north, not Custer. We slowed our preparations, and everyone relaxed. Just in case he was wrong, we didn't recall the lookout.

Since the three of us were ready, I tried to convince Tanya this was the time to go. But she would have none of that. "This is our home now, Caleb," she said. "And if no army is coming for us, I don't want to leave."

So here we stayed.

I did convince her that, for a few days at least, we should leave our gear packed.

My family is always uppermost in my thoughts. I haven't spoken with Dylan in at least nine months. Last I knew, he and Chelsea had just reconnected. Often, they are both in my thoughts.

Father is in so deep with Davato, I recoil at the thought that I am condemned to be his son. How he has changed! And all for the worse. Good grief! The man heads the Ministry of Truth, the CSA, and the Truth

Squads—the same people trying to capture and kill us. I hope never to lay eyes on him again.

Lately, in the evenings, I have been sitting on the porch and spending time with the night sky. Always trapped inside, blinded by electric lights, I never used to care about the moon. But now? Did you know that without it, life on earth could not exist? It's true. Its just-right gravity, its effect on earth's atmosphere, rotation, tides, and climate—so many scientific things to which I could never do justice—our moon is nothing but a miracle for life. And now, this nightly orb, so important for our existence, is shrouded in a pale-yellow gauze, a haze of shadows.

It's a cosmic warning, and it fascinates me.

And I wonder: Does no one else care about the moon and the missing stars? Revelation tells me it's part of God's judgment. Even without that, does no one else look up and see what's been happening in the night sky?

Or are the sheep of earth so focused on themselves, their wild debaucheries, their drunkenness, and their slavish bowing to the latest official decree, that they have no idea what's going on around them?

The world is ending, and every night, God is writing its epitaph in the heavens.

And no one is paying attention.

A branch snaps behind me, and I shoot to my feet, rifle in hand.

I whirl, my heart racing, and I am face-to-face with a bull buffalo. He's a big brute with curved horns, standing only a dozen feet away. How did he get so close? Must have been the woodpecker's rapping.

I click a cartridge into the chamber, raise the barrel, and put him in my sights. He's got enough meat on him to last us for a week or more. But it might take more than one shot. What if he charges and gores me before he falls? Horns like those could rip into my guts so fast that, out here alone in the forest, I could bleed to death in minutes.

He snorts and paws at the ground.

My heart thumps hard in my chest, and my hands are sweating.

Is he going to charge?

But wait! His fur is mottled. His beard is falling out. And he's thin and weak.

159

Like every other wild thing on the planet, he's sickly and dying. Filled with pity, I lower my weapon, and we stare at each other.

What a magnificent animal he once was! And how wretched he is now, just like every other wild creature that's ever crossed my path!

Maybe he senses that the world is ending, that he and I share the same fate on a doomed planet, and that it would be pointless for us to kill each other. Yes, now he stops pawing the dry earth. He shakes his horns and his mane, turns his massive bulk, and ambles a few yards into the pines.

And I let him go.

It's only midafternoon, but the sun is low on the horizon, the conflict is over, and I draw in a deep breath. I should start for home before it gets dark.

A few steps later, I turn back to see what he's doing. The beast has also stopped, and he, like me, is staring. His inscrutable red eyes bore into me. Does he wonder what kind of creature I am?

For a time, we stare at each other.

"Go and live in peace," I say. "This isn't your day to die. Or mine."

As if understanding, he turns away and trots off into the trees.

My heart slows as I begin the long walk home. "Dear Jesus," I begin, "thank you for saving us both this afternoon. And if it be in your will, lead me and my family to the Sanctuary."

CHAPTER 33
THE PRISON

Lucerne, Switzerland – August, Year 6

Dylan sat on his bunk in the narrow cell, stared at the mark on his wrist, and slammed a fist against a knee. How could such a thing happen? He didn't want this, didn't worship the beast, and would never willingly accept the mark. Was it only last week that Gustav and his goons had dragged him off to a room where a tattoo "artist" had burned the hated symbol on his wrist?

Even now, wherever the hot needle had touched, his skin was still red and burning. It was as if his body was rejecting what they had done.

He'd spoken with Margot, of course, and the CSA had forced both her and the woman in the cell beside her to take the mark. But how could they force it on you if you didn't want it?

Footsteps echoed down the hall. A key clicked in the lock. And the iron door squeaked open.

"Here." Gustav threw a CSA uniform onto the bed. But it was green and yellow. "This is a CSA trainee uniform. You are now a trainee."

"*What?*" Dylan stared at the youth. "I will not, cannot, become part of the Antichrist's goon squads."

"Be careful what you say." Gustav yanked a truncheon from his belt and hit it against his palm. Behind him loomed two older men, their arms crossed. "You have the mark. You are now one of us. We are short-staffed, and the decision has been made to conscript the prisoners here in Lucerne. It's a trial run to fill the void. Put on the uniform."

Dylan stood and crossed his arms, imitating the men still in the hall. "No."

"I say you will wear it."

"I will not."

Gustav's truncheon lashed out.

Dylan blocked it with his right arm, but a second blow hit him on the chest.

A third blow struck his forehead, and he staggered. Raising a hand to the wound, he brought it back covered with blood.

"You have no choice." Gustav waved to his companions, who squeezed past and grabbed both of Dylan's arms. "Either put it on, or we'll do it for you."

Another blow to the head like the last one could be fatal. What choice did he have? "All right. But let me clean off this blood."

Gustav allowed him to wash away the blood at the sink and wait until the bleeding stopped.

After Dylan pulled on the uniform, Gustav and his musclemen marched him through hallways until they entered an open courtyard. There, the prisoners were lined up in four rows of ten each. Glancing around, he found Margot in the row behind.

She shot him a quick smile, and he returned it.

Everyone wore the green-and-yellow uniform of a CSA trainee. And everyone bore a new tattoo on their wrists.

Leaning up against the wall behind them, were a dozen guards, each with a truncheon at his or her belt.

"Eyes front, rookies!" shouted an older, shorter Asian man with an Adolf-Hitler mustache. He stood in front with a club in his right hand. "My name is Jonas Lee, and I will be your instructor. We are trying something new with you folks, and you should fall into the dirt and kiss my feet that you were selected. If this facility hadn't been chosen for this trial, you'd already be scheduled for a trip to Weisserwald Camp and certain death."

Gasps came from a few behind Dylan.

The little man, thin of hair and stocky of frame, raised himself to all the height he could muster. "If you don't want to be part of our trial . . ." He slammed the truncheon against his left palm. "We can skip the line and arrange your transport to Weisserwald tomorrow."

He stuck out his chin and glared down the rows, one recruit at a time, until he reached the end. "We will start with the oath every one of you must take. Refuse it, and that will be your ticket to the termination chambers. Now repeat after me, 'I—then state your name—do acknowledge and declare that Davato the Divine, the Imperator who rules the Unitum Imperium, is the one true god.' Now repeat what I just said. 'I—your name—do acknowledge and declare . . .'"

Dylan's heart hammered in his chest as he listened for responses. No way would he ever renounce the Jesus who had ensured his salvation. What did this Jonas expect from them?

"Repeat what I said." Then Jonas began screaming. *"Or you're going to the camp!"*

What followed was a lone voice repeating the oath from a man standing in front of Dylan, a young twenty-something with a mop of black hair.

"That's better. But do the rest of you value your lives so little? Now let me say again—"

But the man's speech stopped, and horror twisted his face.

Before him, appearing out of thin air, sat a demon horseman upon a demon horse. Stringy black hair fell across a pale, jaundiced face. The horseman's eyes pulsed and glowed a ruby red. He wore a breastplate of sulfur yellow. That creature and the appearance of the demon horse upon which he sat stopped the breath in Dylan's mouth and caused him and everyone in the yard to back away.

The demon horse bore a lion's head, not a horse's. From the lion mouth spewed fire and yellow smoke. Its tail whipped back and forth, but it wasn't a horse's tail—it was a snake's—and it ended in three viper heads with open mouths, each bristling with fangs.

A second mounted demon like the first materialized out of nowhere, and the breastplate on that demon rider was hyacinth blue.

The recruits and the guards broke ranks and ran for all sides of the courtyard. Some of the guards disappeared through the open doorway opposite.

When Dylan reached the wall, he turned in time to see one of the demon horses breathe a sulfur-yellow cloud that engulfed Jonas's face. The CSA trainer slumped to the concrete, his chest heaving, his arms thrashing, his body twitching. Then he was still.

Dylan whipped his gaze to the second monster, now standing over the prone body of the lone recruit who'd begun spouting the trainer's oath. His limbs still twitched. But in moments, they stilled, and he, too, lay dead.

The first creature then flew across the yard to Gustav, now cowering in a far corner. The creature's tail lashed out, and three fangs dug into the youth's torso. Gustav convulsed, his body trembled, jerked, and he, too, stopped moving.

His heart pounding, Dylan's gaze flew to the second creature, now finishing up with two more victims. The bodies of two guards lay dead and lifeless beneath its burnished hooves.

Were the demons going to kill them all? Everyone here had the mark. Would the creatures now turn on Dylan, Margot, and the rest of the prisoners?

He shot a glance around the yard. Only the prisoners remained—those who hadn't repeated the oath. Four men, including Jonas Lee and the single recruit, lay dead. The rest of the guards had fled through the door on the opposite wall.

One of the demons approached, and the entire group smashed themselves against the bricks. For where else could they go?

It stopped two meters before Dylan. Glowing red eyes peered down at his wrist then rose to look deep into Dylan's own. And then—

Both monsters vanished.

One moment, they were there.

The next, they weren't.

He stared into the space where they had been. Closing his eyes, he breathed deeply, trying to calm a wildly beating heart.

A hand closed about his and squeezed. He opened his eyes to find Margot standing beside him. "They're gone," she said. "And this is our chance to escape."

The other prisoners still huddled against the wall, still stunned by what had happened. Grabbing her hand, he led her toward the open door. After a few paces, he whirled toward the other prisoners. "Let's get out of here!"

He raced for the door. Behind him came a rush of footsteps. In the hallway beyond, he passed more dead CSA men and women. He continued until he came to the junction of three passages. "Which way?" he called behind him.

"To the right," came a woman's reply.

He turned right and ran until they arrived at the main entrance. No one manned the desk or the turnstile where entrants inserted their badges to gain access. He jumped over the gate and pushed out through the revolving doors into the street. Margot followed.

Up and down the sidewalk, demon creatures were chasing people. Those who weren't running from demon monsters were running for cover.

He faced Margot and hugged her. "We're free."

"Maybe we should find an abandoned car and—"

But Dylan laid a hand on her shoulder and pointed across the street. When she saw what he did, her eyes widened. "How . . . ?"

Running toward them, with smiles on their faces, were Chelsea, René, and Pasqual.

When Chelsea reached them, she wrapped her arms about Dylan's chest and hugged him. Then she hugged Margot.

"How are you here?" Dylan hugged René and Pasqual. "How did you find us?"

René waved a hand. "Through my contacts. After we learned where you were imprisoned, we've been keeping watch from a house across the street. When the demons appeared, we figured you'd find a way out."

But now Pasqual's horrified gaze was fixed on Dylan's wrist. "W– what happened? What did they do to you?"

"And why are you wearing CSA uniforms?" asked René.

"They forced the mark upon us," said Margot. "But the demon creatures didn't bother us and look—" She raised her wrist for all to see.

"I think it's fading."

Dylan lifted his hand and examined it. "Not sure, but . . . I think mine is too."

"But you didn't accept it, did you?" added Pasqual. "You didn't worship the beast?"

"No!" answered Dylan. "So it didn't take."

"And that's why the creatures didn't touch any of us," added Margot.

"What do we do now?" asked Dylan.

"We drive to Vernazza and take Chelsea's boat to Jerusalem." René pointed east. "Our car is in a garage a kilometer away. But these creatures couldn't have come at a better time. Most everyone who could stop us now has the mark. They'll be fleeing for their lives, not manning checkpoints."

"What are we waiting for?" asked Dylan. "Let's go!"

CHAPTER 34
THE ATTACK

Custer, South Dakota – August, Year 6

On the day of the battle, the midday sun shone a dim, jaundiced light, and the air held a chill. A half mile north on US-16A, metal screeched and wheels ground over asphalt as the advancing enemy pushed before them a wall of five-foot-square, wheel-mounted metal shields. To the east and west, on both sides of the two hundred armed CSA troops, was open country.

Caleb clutched his rifle to his chest and hunkered down behind a dirt-filled barrel. Beside him, forty men and women manned the barricade blocking the road. The highway cut through a hill, and on both slopes before the trees and behind makeshift trenches, another twenty-five fighters pointed their weapons north.

Even so, they were outnumbered three to one.

Caleb and Tanya held M16s, Andy clutched his AR-15, and Brianna gripped her Glock 19 pistol. But none of them should be here. They should have left last spring. Or earlier this week after the first wayfarer had brought news of the approaching threat.

Now, they stood with the Custer army, about to battle the forces of the Antichrist.

"You don't have to be here, Caleb." Scratching his beard with a finger still holding his pistol, Marty Eastwood dropped down beside him. "I know how much finding that Sanctuary means to you. You should go. Now. Today. This isn't your fight."

"But you folks have taken us in. We've been going to your church. It's our duty to help you."

"Three more rifles and a pistol aren't going to make much difference."

"You sure about that?" Caleb shot a glance down the highway. The enemy force was now a quarter mile distant. A lot of green-and-white uniforms. And some green-and-brown ones from the new Davato Youth Core.

"I'm sure," continued Marty. "Go home, get your stuff, and leave. I'll tell the others what I'm telling you. They'll understand. You've got the atlas I gave you with the maps. I want you to go."

"You've been a good friend, Marty. Let me think about it."

Marty watched the approaching army then faced him again. "I don't like the looks of this. It may not turn out well." He beckoned to Tanya. "Tell him to get you folks out of here."

Then he returned to his post a few yards away.

Tanya sidled up beside Caleb. "He's right. We should leave. I convinced you to stay because I wanted safety and security, but I admit I was wrong. We should have left two days ago." She ran a hand through her hair. "No place is safe, is it? Maybe the Sanctuary will be better. Let's leave. I don't want my stubbornness to get us killed."

Caleb called over to Andy. "What do you think?"

"This could get ugly. But we owe these folks. We should stay."

Brianna came up beside him. "I'd rather leave. But I'll fight if you want."

Patting her shoulder in appreciation, Caleb turned his glance back to the approaching threat. "The time to leave was earlier. We're here now. We can't abandon our friends."

Tanya nodded, closed her eyes, and returned to a position behind a barrel. Brianna followed.

Ahead on the road, the CSA had closed the gap to a hundred feet. One of them raised a megaphone to his mouth. "Throw down your weapons, surrender, and take the mark. That's the only way you're going to leave here alive."

Arnie Brinker, the self-appointed leader of the Custer group, shouted back. "We'll never take your mark. Go back to the hole you crawled out of."

The CSA man shook his head and said something to those beside him, and the enemy throng resumed their slow march toward the barricade. Wheels screeched over concrete, and the metal wall ground closer.

"Pick your targets and shoot!" ordered Arnie.

All along the line, the defenders began firing. A continuous volley of explosions shattered the air. Bullets pinged and slammed and ricocheted off the approaching armor. But their fire didn't penetrate the metal, and the shield wall kept coming.

"We can't stop them." Tanya slid down beneath the barrels. "They're going to overwhelm us."

Caleb swallowed. She was right. None of their shots were breaking through and finding targets.

Then the day descended into chaos.

In the air above, hundreds of impossible creatures appeared—demon horsemen sitting atop demon horses. The riders carried breastplates of ruby red, deep blue, or sulfurous yellow. Fiery red eyes stared out behind stringy hair that fell down over pale, yellow faces.

The heads of the demon horses were lions' heads, breathing fire and sulfur-yellow smoke. Their tails were snakes, ending in viper heads filled with fangs.

The CSA advance stopped, and they looked up.

Then the demon army descended.

The shield wall collapsed, and the enemy scattered in all directions. Behind them came the demon creatures. And when they reached their victims, one of two things happened:

Either the snake tails lashed out, and the viper heads struck. Then their prey writhed and squirmed until they became still and lifeless.

Or the lion heads breathed a fog of sulfur-yellow smoke, engulfing their quarry. Then their victims thrashed and twisted until death left them white-faced and unmoving.

The monsters chased the CSA men, women, and trans persons east and west across the fields, north and south along the highway.

And when it was over, perhaps a third of them lay dead. The rest had abandoned their shields and had fled back the way they had come.

The defenders stood and watched the retreating army in awe.

"It was the sixth trumpet," breathed someone to Caleb's right.

"The creatures attacked only those with the mark," added another.

Caleb turned to Tanya, Andy, and Brianna. "Our bikes are down the road. Let's go home, get our gear and Nika, and start for Cheyenne Mountain. We can make at least twenty miles before dark."

Tanya nodded.

Brianna raised both arms and grinned. "Let's do it!"

CHAPTER 35
THE ADDRESS

Revelation 13:6–8 (HCSB): *A mouth was given to him to speak boasts and blasphemies. He was also given authority to act for 42 months. He began to speak blasphemies against God: to blaspheme His name and His dwelling—those who dwell in heaven. And he was permitted to wage war against the saints and to conquer them. He was also given authority over every tribe, people, language, and nation. All those who live on the earth will worship him, everyone whose name was not written from the foundation of the world in the book of life of the Lamb who was slaughtered.*

New Babylon, Iraq – August, Year 6

Grady Wilson wormed his way to the front of the throng swelling New Babylon's central park. The thousands of voices around him, all talking at once, reminded him of the ocean's roar and its never-ending waves, always rolling up upon the sand. No one had seen Davato since the third week of December, and the announcement of his reappearance through the Giant today had stirred this sea of humanity as never before. They filled the vast space and even spilled into the streets where the city bordered the park.

But Grady was late, and these last weeks, Davato had grown ever more impatient with his staff. When Grady finally took his place on the platform beside Adam Turner, Sebastien Rey, Gaston Soucy, and General Hofmann, he was the last to arrive. But Davato had not yet appeared. Since December, all the Imperator's meetings had been conducted in absentia, via overhead speakers, never via video. Today was the first time Grady would see the man in person.

Everyone's welts were now gone, and as Grady glanced over the ministers and the throng below, he saw clear faces. In the front row below the dignitaries, Marcia smiled up at him. Beside her stood a lithe, grinning Ruby, with whom he and Marcia now shared frequent trysts.

A hush swept over the crowd, and Grady turned to find Davato, clear of face and bright of eye, appearing out of nowhere at the podium's center. Where had he come from?

The Imperator raised both arms in a victory salute, and the crowd cheered. They clapped and shouted their approval, for their leader had returned. The demon stings had gone, and the people—Grady included—had returned to debauchery, drunkenness, and pleasure.

Everything, it seemed, was back to normal.

When the cheering subsided, Davato descended the platform and entered the booth below the statue.

The Prophet stepped to the microphone and lifted green eyes to the crowd. "Welcome, everyone, to this worldwide broadcast. We come to you from New Babylon's central park. Today, our Imperator has an important message for the world. We were all saddened by his absence, but today, we rejoice that our divine Imperator once again addresses his people. Citizens of the world, bow down and worship Davato the Divine." He turned to the console behind him, punched some buttons, and lit up the statue.

Towering ten stories above them, the monstrous image of Davato came to life. Its head stared down at the crowd. Its right hand waved in an arc.

The crowd oohed and aahed. They bowed down to the Giant and shouted their praise.

Then its mouth spoke, and its words were like thunder shaking the park.

"MY PEOPLE, I AM HAPPY TO STAND BEFORE YOU AGAIN, BUT NOW PLEASE STAND AND LISTEN."

Obeying the command, the crowd rose from their knees.

"THE CALAMITY VISITED UPON US BY THE ENEMY IS BEHIND US. I AM HERE TODAY TO TELL YOU THAT THE DEMONS HE SENT TO PLAGUE US

CAME FROM THE PLACE WE ONCE CALLED HEAVEN, FOR THEY
BELONGED TO HIM.

"BUT THEY HAVE DEPARTED, HAVEN'T THEY? NO LONGER DO THEY
ATTACK THE INNOCENT PEOPLE OF THE WORLD. WHY DID THEY STOP?
BECAUSE THE PRAYERS OF THE PROPHET AND YOUR IMPERATOR DROVE
THEM AWAY. WE PRAYED TO THE DRAGON, AND HE, NOT THE ENEMY,
SENT THE DEMONS BACK TO THE HOLE FROM WHICH THEY CAME."

As the crowd roared their applause, Grady shot a glance to Sebastien,
appearing unfazed by that last remark. Grady had no recollection of what
the Imperator had just said. But Davato was continuing. . . .

"NOW LET US CONSIDER WHY THE DEMONS CAME AT ALL. WOULD A
LOVING FATHER INFLICT SUCH TORMENT UPON HIS CHILDREN? NO, OF
COURSE NOT. ONLY A DEMON, HIMSELF, WOULD DO SUCH A THING. A
DEMON IN CHARGE OF A HEAVEN FULL OF DEMONS. YES, ONLY A
MONSTER WOULD TORTURE THOSE HE LOVES FOR MONTHS ON END.
AND THAT IS WHY WE CALL HIM ENEMY."

The Giant lifted a foot and stomped it down, and the platform shook.

"THE ENEMY'S ACTIONS REVEAL A DEEP HATRED FOR THOSE HE
ONCE CALLED HIS CHILDREN. AND SO, TODAY, I CALL UPON EVERYONE
TO RENEW THEIR ATTACKS UPON HIS ALLIES—THOSE AMONG US
WITHOUT THE MARK. THEY ARE IN LEAGUE WITH THE DEMON ENEMY.
EVEN NOW, THESE TRAITORS ARE WORKING TO UNDERMINE MY RULE
AND BRING DOWN THE UNITUM IMPERIUM. I SPEAK, OF COURSE, OF THE
CHRISTIANS AND JEWS WITHOUT THE MARK, THOSE WHO—"

Abruptly, his words ended, and the statue froze. For above the vast
crowd appeared an army of horrors.

Tens of thousands of demon creatures had materialized out of thin
air.

Hovering over the people, demon riders sat upon demon horses.
Long women's hair fell down over pasty-white faces bearing ruby-red
eyes. Breastplates of fiery red, hyacinth blue, or sulfur yellow covered
their chests.

The demon riders sat upon demon horses that bore the heads of
lions. From the lion mouths issued fire and sulfur-yellow smoke. Their

tails were snakes, ending in viper heads with fangs bared.

And they descended.

Screams and shouts shattered the air as the crowd rushed from the center, fleeing in all directions. Davato's ministers headed for the stairs.

Behind the ministers and fearing the rush might trample hundreds, Grady cowered at the platform's edge, not knowing where to go, his heart beating wildly.

Gaston Soucy was last to reach the steps, and one of the monsters landed between him and a frantic Adam Turner, now descending from the platform. The Minister of Charity backed away, toward Grady. But the demon horseman spurred his mount and closed the gap.

The lion mouth opened, and a cloud of sulfur-yellow smoke engulfed Soucy's head.

At the edge of the dais, with nowhere to go, Grady shrank from the demon and tried to roll into a ball.

The minister fell to the wood, his body writhing, his arms twitching, his mouth open and gasping. Moments later, lifeless eyes stared out from a snow-white face.

The drop from the platform to the ground was six feet, and Grady jumped, landing on his feet. He glanced past Marcia and Ruby toward the crowd, but the crush of bodies blocked his escape in all directions.

Another demon creature landed between him and the women. Ruby's frantic glance searched everywhere, but she was trapped. The demon horse pranced toward her, and she screamed. Its snake tail whipped around. Three viper heads opened their mouths. And three fangs dug deep into a shoulder.

Ruby dropped to the ground. She rolled and jerked and squirmed. Then she froze, her body unmoving, her face pale in death.

Marcia whirled, forced herself into the mass of bodies, and disappeared.

Grady raced around the platform, found a narrow opening in back, and crawled underneath. As his eyes adjusted to the dark, he discovered he was not alone. His companions under the platform were Adam Turner, Eric Hofmann, Sebastien Rey, and one other.

Hiding in the far corner, covering his eyes with his hands, was the great leader of the Unitum Imperium—Davato the Divine.

Outside, the screams went on for half an hour as the mob slowly fled from the park, probably to seek hiding places in the city. When quiet had descended, the ministers, who'd not said a word since crawling under the platform, left. Grady departed after Davato and, with the ministers beside him, gazed upon the torchlit scene.

Across the open park lay thousands of lifeless bodies, too many to count. Davato glared at the aftermath, his face red with rage, his eyes bulging. Then a whisper escaped his mouth, so quiet and low Grady could barely hear. And this is what the Imperator said:

"They will pay for this."

CHAPTER 36
BANDITS

As the tires hummed over asphalt, Dylan calculated that their trip from Appenzell, Switzerland, to Vernazza, Italy, should take two days. Normally, it was a seven-hour drive, but with crevasses to avoid, he added extra time. René was driving the van, and Dylan sat in front. Margot, Chelsea, and Pasqual occupied the back.

His sister sat beside Margot, and it warmed his heart to see the two women becoming fast friends. After her experience with Davato and her conversion, Chelsea had changed. Whenever Margot would ask Chelsea about her time with the Antichrist, she seemed vulnerable, unsure of herself. Gone was her former, often unshakable certainty of views. Where before, Chelsea had been skeptical of all things spiritual, now she couldn't ask enough questions about Margot's visions and her paintings. And whenever Pasqual chimed in with something to say about the faith, she listened intently and asked penetrating questions.

Most of the checkpoints in the Swiss countryside were abandoned, and René was ecstatic. "This should be the easiest travel we've ever had," he said. "The guards are running for their lives from the demons."

Near Bellinzona, as Dylan expected, they detoured far into the countryside to avoid a deep crevasse. Back on the main highway, they slept the night in the van on an isolated, dark road outside Lugano.

The next day, early, they drove through the city and crossed an abandoned border checkpoint into Italy without trouble. On their trip south toward Milano, they encountered no CSA presence.

René's prediction about smooth travel seemed prescient, almost too good to be true.

But on the A50 as they circled Milano, two cars parked sideways blocked the highway. René stopped the van behind a black VW van and a Volvo sedan.

"What's going on?" asked Pasqual.

"It's some kind of checkpoint," answered René. "But it's not CSA. I don't like this."

"What is it then?"

"Maybe bandits."

Beside Dylan, the ex-spy slid his Glock 17 onto the seat beside him, out of sight, and asked Dylan to do the same. Swallowing, Dylan complied.

"Can we bypass them?" asked Pasqual from the back seat.

René shot a glance behind and shook his head. Another car had pulled behind them so they couldn't back up.

Ahead, four youths rushed the Volvo sedan. Surrounding it, they pointed handguns inside and gave orders to the passengers.

Two car doors opened, and a middle-aged couple stepped out. The youths ordered the man and woman to lie on the ground then rifled through their pockets. When the man raised his head to object, the tall youth kicked his head, three times, and the man went limp. The bandits entered the vehicle, appearing to search the front and back seats.

They removed two boxes from the back and transferred them to a Peugeot van. When they had finished looting, they shoved the unconscious man into the back seat, pushed the woman into the front, and opened a hole in the barrels to unblock the way. One of the youths drove the looted vehicle through, closed the barricade, and returned.

Tensing, René sat straighter in the seat. "When they pull the VW through, we'll make our move. Get ready!"

The youths waved their pistols, and the black van drove up to the barricade. As before, the youths stood on all sides, knocking on the windows, probably ordering the occupants out.

At first, Dylan couldn't determine what was happening. The opaque windows rolled down, but then the youths backed away, appearing confused.

"It's a CSA van," whispered René. "Let's see what they do."

After conferring among themselves, the taller youth went to the barricade, opened a path, and waved the vehicle through, unmolested.

The van drove on through the opening.

"Roll down your windows and get your weapons ready!" said René.

Dylan grabbed his pistol, opened his window, and wiped sweat from his forehead. What was René doing?

Before the tall youth rolled the barrel to close the gap, René slammed his foot on the accelerator.

The van leaped forward, and the force rocked Dylan against the seat back.

"Stop!" Running beside Dylan, a red-haired youth waved his pistol.

His hands shaking, Dylan pointed his Glock.

The man's gun exploded through the window. Gun smoke and the smell of cordite washed Dylan's face. Before their assailant released another shot, Dylan had no choice but to squeeze the trigger. His gun fired, kicked back, and the youth crumpled to the ground.

Ahead, the tall leader jumped out of the way only seconds before René shot the van through the opening. Another shot rang out from behind, and Dylan heard a bullet ricocheting off the left-side metal door.

"We're through!" exclaimed Pasqual.

"We made it!" But as Dylan glanced aside at René, he gasped. "You're hit!"

René drove on but didn't respond. Blood soaked his right arm, and he was leaning to one side, gritting his teeth.

"You need attention," said Margot. "Pull over."

"N—not yet," answered the ex-spy.

When they were kilometers from the barricade and the CSA vehicle was out of sight, René pulled into a turnoff. Then his head dropped onto the steering wheel.

While Pasqual helped him to the back seat, Margot grabbed the medical kit from the back and ran to his side. "It got him in the right arm. But . . . I think it shattered the bone." By the expression on her face—

Was she close to tears? "This is serious. Not good."

"Can you stop the bleeding?" asked Chelsea.

"I don't know. But this is beyond my skills to tend. He needs a hospital."

"N–no hospital." René's voice was weak. "Teofilo Delucci. Doctor in Porta Romana. Maybe Piazzala Libia. I can't remember."

"In Milano?" asked Pasqual.

"Oui." And then he passed out.

Dylan stood on the concrete, watching Margot's efforts at staunching the bleeding.

Pasqual lifted a worried glance to him. "I'll find the doctor's address. You drive."

Nodding, Dylan slipped behind the wheel and drove.

Pasqual searched René's pockets for his phone. Moments later, after poring through his contacts, he exclaimed from the back seat. "Found it! It's cryptic, but this entry must be the doctor's. I've got the address."

"But how do we know this man won't turn us in?" asked Dylan.

"We don't," said Margot. "But René said he was okay. What else can we do? René needs more skills than I can offer."

Dylan drove on. Their plans to reach the Refuge without incident were in shambles. But they needed to do whatever it took to save René's life.

CHAPTER 37
THE NIGHT VISITOR

Between Custer and Colorado Springs – September, Year 6

As their bike tires thrummed and bounced over uneven asphalt, Caleb estimated that the trip to Colorado Springs would take only two weeks. But it took far longer than planned. Although they carried five-gallon water jugs in the bike carriers, filling them was a problem. Several times a day, they checked for wells, usually clear of poison. Tainted water announced itself on one's tongue with an unusual taste. But finding a well with a hand pump was difficult. Without power, towns and villages relied on hand pumps and untainted streams.

As they crossed Nebraska, a dust tornado ripped through the Oglala National Grassland only a mile from US 25 South. They found a depression, hid, and prayed. But the twister spared them and went on, leaving behind an ominous yellow sky.

A second dust storm hit south of Scottsbluff, much smaller than the first, and they hunkered down in their tents for the afternoon until it passed. It left only a quarter inch of dust on the road.

Three weeks out from Custer, they encountered few people on the highway. Then, late in the day, mere miles east of Fort Collins, they passed houses with candles in the windows and armed men patrolling the streets.

If the Denver area had been hit with a nuclear blast, Dylan wondered what they would find there and how to get around it. He tried to ask one of the armed patrols about this, but the men refused to talk and ordered the travelers to move on. Some miles beyond, they pitched camp in a vacant field.

Andy made a fire, they sat in a circle around the flames, and they ate a supper of smoked deer meat and beans.

While he ate, Caleb pulled out his solar phone. Realizing he had a signal, he called Dylan.

They hadn't talked in months, and both were happy to hear that the other was alive and well. Caleb told Dylan where he was and about their plans to head south to Cheyenne Mountain and the Sanctuary.

Then Dylan related how the CSA had captured him and Margot and how demons on demon horses helped them escape from prison. Then on their way south, René, the ex-spy who'd become their unofficial leader, had been seriously wounded, and the group now hid in a doctor's apartment in Milan, Italy. René wasn't doing well, and they'd run out of antibiotics. The doctor wanted to amputate René's right arm, but René said he'd rather die first.

"I'm sorry, Dylan. It doesn't sound good for him."

"So we're just waiting and praying for healing. René's situation is grim. If we ever leave here, Chelsea knows of a boat we can use in Italy. If René's situation improves, we'll sail to Israel. In Jerusalem, she knows how to find directions to a place where we'll be safe from the squaddies and the CSA. The place is called the Refuge."

"Where is it?" Caleb asked.

"She doesn't know, and she's rather mysterious about details. But she's quite certain it exists."

"So we're both heading for places to hide from the squaddies?"

"It appears so. Oh, and here's another piece of news that can help you. Chelsea discovered a way to avoid all tracking on the solar phones."

"What? That's great!"

"I'll send you a picture of the dip switches you have to set. I just hope no one is tracking you and listening in."

"We just got a signal a minute ago. I doubt anyone would have time yet."

They talked longer before they hung up.

Tanya, especially, was happy that Chelsea and Dylan were safe, and Andy gave him congratulations. But then the conversation turned to their current situation.

"We're running low on meat, beans, and rice." Andy shook a water jug. "And this is only half-full."

"Do we have enough to get us to the Sanctuary?" Caleb asked.

"I think so," answered Andy.

"But what if there's nothing there?" Tanya raised crinkled brows. "What if we get to Cheyenne Mountain, and it's all just a myth?"

"We can only pray that it isn't." Caleb finished the last of his meal and set down his plate. "We have to trust that God will—"

Nika growled, and a surprise visitor, a red-haired teenager, wandered in out of the dark. "Hi, folks. Name's Mat. What's happening?"

Startled, Caleb reached for the rifle beside him. But after giving the boy a once-over and seeing no mark on his wrist, he let it go. "Hi, Mat. Have a seat."

"Don't mind if I do." His glance focused first on everyone's wrist then on Nika who approached warily. When she was within reach, he knelt to pet her, and she lifted her neck to his probing fingers. He smiled at Brianna and sat beside her. "What's your name?"

She told him, blushed, and faced away.

Caleb cleared his throat to gain Mat's attention. "We've been trying to get information about the area south of here. Can you help us?"

"If I can." Mat's smile was infectious. "What do you want to know? That's where we came from."

"Do you know about conditions around Denver? We heard that nukes hit the city."

Frowning, Mat nodded. "We came from Lakewood. East of there, toward the Denver city center—well, you don't want to go there. Everything's fried."

"What about radiation?" asked Andy. "Is it safe if we bypass the city?"

"Who knows? The half-life of Strontium 90 is twenty-nine years. It's going to be a long time before anyone can live there again, if ever. But if you're traveling through, you could go west on US 70 and south on Colorado 470. No blast damage there. That's the route we took to get here."

"Half-life?" asked Brianna. "What's that?"

He cocked his head as if surprised she didn't know. "The time it takes for a nuclear isotope to fall to half its value."

"Oh." She gave him a puzzled glance. "Not something I learned. I was homeschooled in the Northwoods after the vanishing."

Again, Caleb cleared his throat to turn Mat's attention from his adopted daughter. "What's the squaddie situation—I mean the Truth Squad situation—around here?"

"Squaddies?" Mat slapped his knee. "What a great name for those weasels. They're about forty miles south of here in Lafayette. So be careful passing that way. Sometimes, they come up here with an armed force, but we've got patrols out to warn us. When they're heading our way, we collect our little army and make a stand. So far, they've decided not to fight. But who knows?"

"What about Colorado Springs." Andy leaned toward the fire. "That's where we're going."

"Colorado Springs?" Mat cocked his head. "You don't want to go there either. They also got nuked."

"*What?*" Caleb jerked his head toward the newcomer. "That's the first we heard about *that!*"

"Yeah, direct hit on the city. Not much left, I understand. You'd be advised to steer clear. Is that meat I see?" The half-eaten venison on Brianna's plate drew his eager glance. "We haven't seen meat in weeks."

"Can he have some?" Before anyone could reply, Brianna grabbed an extra plate, a fork, and a knife, and gave him what she hadn't eaten.

"Hey, thanks." Smiling, he accepted the plate. "You're great."

When he patted her knee, Brianna blushed again, and Tanya frowned.

While crickets broke the silence, Mat devoured the meat, and Caleb tried to digest the news about Colorado Springs.

Then their visitor raised his glance to Brianna. "We're having a dance tomorrow night. A guitar, an accordion, and a fiddle player. They're pretty good. Wanna come?"

"What's an accordion?" she asked.

Mat's brows wrinkled as if that were the stupidest question he'd ever heard. "It's a musical instrument. You don't know much, do you?"

"I do too." She scrunched her face and jerked her head away.

"Thanks for the offer," said Tanya. "But we're moving on in the morning."

"No problemo. Just thought I'd ask. We don't see many new girls around here."

From somewhere out in the dark, a man's voice called Mat's name. "What are you doing, boy? Get back to camp. You know the policy on strangers."

Mat wolfed down the last of the venison, rose, and shook his head. "They think everyone's out to get you. But it's good to make new friends. I'd better go." He thanked them again, everyone said goodbye, and he headed out into the dark.

"He thought he was pretty smart, didn't he?" Her gaze still on Mat's retreating back, Brianna frowned. "Even though he was a smarty-pants, I would have gone with him to that dance."

Andy tried to cover his mirth with a hand, but Caleb and Tanya were frowning.

When he'd gone, Tanya faced Caleb. "Our destination is in a nuclear blast zone?"

"It appears so. But Cheyenne Mountain is well protected. It may be okay."

"I don't like this." She shook her head.

"We've come this far. We're not turning back now."

CHAPTER 38
ADAM'S SECOND CURSE

Isaiah 5:20–21, 24, 25b (NLT): *What sorrow for those who say that evil is good and good is evil, that dark is light and light is dark, that bitter is sweet and sweet is bitter. What sorrow for those who are wise in their own eyes and think themselves so clever. . . . Therefore, just as fire licks up stubble and dry grass shrivels in the flame, so their roots will rot and their flowers wither. For they have rejected the law of the LORD of Heaven's Armies; they have despised the word of the Holy One of Israel. . . . The mountains tremble, and the corpses of his people litter the streets like garbage.*

New Babylon, Iraq – September, Year 6

The bulldozer engines roared in the trench below as Adam Turner stepped from the edge and, for the hundredth time that morning, shot a nervous glance in both directions. Would the demons return again today? Next time, would they come for him as they had for so many of the workers in his charge?

But it was foolish to keep watch, wasn't it? They materialized out of nowhere, in front of you, and there was nothing anyone could do to outrun them. You couldn't hide or escape. Still, he couldn't help himself, and he completed his survey, convinced that, for the moment, he was safe.

He shivered and wrapped the handkerchief closer about his nose. The stench from the pit was overwhelming. Once again, Davato had charged Adam with a task he loathed with every fiber of his being. He'd ordered bulldozers to excavate the trough. Two hundred meters long, twenty meters wide, and ten meters deep—he'd hoped it would be enough. Yet, by the end of the week, two of his foremen had warned it would be full.

He asked the engineers about building a crematorium, but the time to complete the task was months, and Davato wanted the corpses removed as soon as possible. And so here Adam was, out in the desert, kilometers from the city, again overseeing the disposal of the dead. At the trench's far end, smoke from burning bodies mixed with the odor of rotting flesh, and he gagged.

Every half hour, a steady stream of dump trucks arrived. Loaded with bodies, they backed to the edge, deposited their loads, and returned to the city. It was a grisly sight, the emptying of those trucks. And each night, the trucks, the rotting corpses, and the stench haunted his dreams.

In every city district, he'd conscripted citizens to canvass their neighbors, determine who was still alive, and report back who wasn't. Civilian units had been conscripted to bring the dead to collection centers on each block. The sight of the death carts, loaded with carcasses, rolling through apartment foyers and down streets, sent citizens either fleeing to their rooms or crowding into the nearest bar.

After the massive toll from the initial attacks, the demons now came and went at random, picking off a few each day, just enough to feed a constant fear. It was as if they knew how to keep their victims forever on edge. Everyone knew someone whom the demons had killed. And no one knew when or where the monsters would strike next.

In the trench below, a skid loader rode over twisted arms, legs, and torsos, trying to level the pile of corpses. Wearing a hazmat suit with a respirator, the driver looked like some kind of alien. Adam turned away from the red ooze left by the caterpillar tracks and wished he were elsewhere.

But it wasn't only fear and disgust that gripped him, was it? It was also doubt. If the Imperator was a god, then why didn't he stop the demons? Why did he allow this Being—Davato called him the Enemy—to continue the killing? Where was the power Davato claimed to have? Or was the Imperator just a man? Were his claims of divinity nothing but lies?

That was the first doubt. The second was even worse. For now, he

186

doubted his own unbelief. From everything that had happened, it was obvious the Christian and Jewish God was real. There had always been the signs in the heavens, the earthquakes, the volcanoes, the blood in the Atlantic, the asteroids. Then came the worldwide pronouncements from the three angels and the eagle. After that, the horrid little demons brought five months of such torture, he was ready to end it all.

Now, this—demons on horseback bringing random death.

Yes, he had to admit it. There was a God, and he had proven himself far more powerful than the Imperator and his Prophet. He was surely the enemy of everyone in New Babylon, everyone who had taken Davato's mark. And what if the three angels spoke the truth? Then God's vengeance against Davato's people would extend into eternity itself.

Adam shuddered and wrapped his arms about his chest. Would he face an eternity of empty loneliness, of time without end tortured by a God with a vendetta against him, personally, all because he'd taken the mark?

Why had he left his whiskey flask back in New Babylon? He slammed a fist against a thigh.

But if ever he voiced such thoughts to anyone, he'd end up in the Colosseum or the shooting galleries.

But wait! After attendance plummeted at the Colosseum, they'd closed the venue. For how could anyone enjoy sitting in the bleachers watching Christians die in the arena below when a demon horseman could materialize beside you and bring death to *you* instead?

It was better to drink, shoot up, or smoke oneself into a mindless stupor. Better not to think. Better not to dwell on life, or death, as one found it in Davato's New Babylon today.

That is what Adam looked forward to now. In midafternoon, when it became too dark for the trucks and dozers and skid loaders to do their work, Adam would flee to his room in the World Casino, wrap his hands around a whiskey bottle, and seek a welcome oblivion.

CHAPTER 39
BLAST ZONES

South of Fort Collins, Colorado – September, Year 6

After they left the Fort Collins area, Caleb kept checking the map to keep track of how far they must go to reach their goal. On the second day out, as they neared Lafayette, Andy spied a checkpoint ahead, the first they'd seen on US 25.

"Quick!" Caleb veered onto the next side street. "We'll detour through the neighborhoods."

But as they made the turn, Tanya looked back. "They saw us. Three of them. And they've also got bikes."

"Then let's ride!" Brianna raced ahead of Caleb and the others.

They cycled west, but minutes later, a glance back revealed their three pursuers had closed the gap by half.

"Stop or we'll shoot!" came a faint cry from behind.

"Ignore them." Caleb pedaled faster. "We've been riding for weeks, we're stronger, and we can outrun them."

A shot rang out, but he didn't even hear a ricochet. It must have gone wild.

At the next intersection, they turned east. When next he glanced back, their pursuers had fallen far behind.

Pumping hard, they rode until they reached the interstate, and they had pulled even further ahead. Finally, no one was behind them. Breathing hard, he brought everyone to a stop. "Let's hope we don't have to go that way again."

"But we outran them, didn't we?" Brianna clapped.

"That we did, and now I'm beat." Andy stepped off his bike and rubbed his rump.

Before noon, they reached the junction of US 25 South and US 70 West. They climbed an overpass and glanced toward Denver.

They'd reached the edge of the blast area. To the south, houses had lost their roofs. Cars were overturned or piled in heaps. Apartment buildings were missing most of their windows and some walls. Everywhere, debris littered the ground, and not a person was in sight.

"If anyone had lived next to this," said Tanya, "no wonder they left."

Caleb rubbed his beard and gazed at the devastation wrought by a Chinese thermonuclear bomb. How many lives had been lost in this attack? How many people had died later of radiation? How many had packed up and left? And this was only on the outskirts. He shook his head, got back on his bike, and pedaled.

* * *

FOR THE NEXT THREE DAYS, THEY followed US 70 back to US 25 and then south, skirting the Denver blast zone. Beyond the area of devastation, they passed occasional occupied settlements, identified by candles in the windows and patrols bearing rifles. They entered open country, and on the third night, after making a record sixty miles, they camped in a field ten miles north of Colorado Springs.

The next morning, they rose in semidarkness under a heavy cloud cover.

They ate their breakfast, packed their tents, and mounted their bikes. Caleb looked back from his position in the lead. "Today is the day we've been waiting for. If all goes well, we should reach Cheyenne Mountain and the Sanctuary by noon."

Tanya smiled, and Andy gave him a thumbs-up.

"Let's do it!" Brianna hopped on her bike and began pedaling, and Caleb started out.

Before noon, they entered the outskirts of the Colorado Springs blast zone. As in Denver, houses beside the highway had lost their roofs, cars were overturned, and debris cluttered the way. Caleb brought everyone to a halt and peered ahead. "What should we do?"

"Let's keep going and see how bad it gets," said Andy.

"No." Tanya looked behind them. "We should find another route."

Ignoring her scowl, Caleb started forward. "Let's go a bit farther."

A half mile later, debris blocked the highway. On all sides, rubble replaced most of the buildings. Many had burned to cinders. Before them was a moonscape of charred walls, tumbled bricks, twisted steel, and skeleton tree trunks.

"This can't be safe." Tanya turned her bike back the way they came and began pedaling. "I'm not going any further."

"Yeah." Caleb followed her. "We'll find another route."

When they'd returned to the area outside the blast zone, Caleb found an alternate route in the atlas Marty Eastwood had given him. They backtracked to Chase Bluffs Parkway and headed east. Weaving in and out of abandoned, rusted cars, they pedaled to North Powers Boulevard then south to Colorado 21. Although he saw no evidence of the blast, the entire area was eerily vacant. How bad was the radiation here?

Beside Peterson Space Force Base, Andy stopped them. Here, there was no blast damage, but the trees were leafless, the grass was brown, and the bodies of dead birds littered the yards. Andy pointed to a dozen moldering human remains beside the road. "Radiation poisoning?"

"Maybe fallout from the day of the attack." Caleb waved them on. "We should be safe if we keep moving."

The Milton East Proby Parkway led them west, and as darkness descended, they passed the Cheyenne Mountain Zoo and began climbing a dirt road through green pines under an anemic moon.

But only two miles from the entrance a rusted jeep, parked sideways, blocked the way. Caleb dismounted and approached. Two desiccated corpses occupied the front seats.

"How long has this been here?" Tanya glanced up and down the deserted road. "Has anyone been on this road recently?"

"I don't know, but we're going on." Trying to suppress his doubts, Caleb exchanged a worried glance with Andy.

They walked their bikes around the jeep and pedaled up the mountain. But a mile later, he brought them to a halt. "It's too dark to go on. We'll camp here and go up tomorrow."

Between the pines and under a sickly, pallid moon, they huddled around a campfire and ate the last of their meat and beans in silence. Caleb shook his water container. It held only inches at the bottom. "Our destination is a few miles ahead," he said. "Tomorrow, we should find the Sanctuary."

"You keep saying that, but . . ." Tanya shook her head. "But that vehicle back there tells me no one has been on this road for a long time."

"She's right, Caleb." Andy's face was long. "That jeep doesn't bode well."

"I know." The night was chill, and a shiver raced down Caleb's back. "But we must have faith. We've come this far. We have to see this through to the end."

"We'd better find something," said Tanya. "If there's nothing at Cheyenne Mountain, we're out of food, out of water, and . . ." She wiped a tear from her cheek. "And we have nowhere else to go."

Caleb left his seat, sat beside her, and wrapped an arm about her shoulders. "It will be all right. You'll see."

"Why is everyone so gloomy?" Brianna's voice rose into the night. "I believe Caleb, and I don't care about that jeep. Tomorrow, we're going to find the Sanctuary."

He shot her a smile and pulled a shivering Tanya closer.

If only he had as much confidence in his own words as Brianna.

Later, as he laid down in the tent and tried to sleep, a nagging thought kept him awake, one he'd mulled ever since they left Custer. What about the vision he'd had nearly a year ago? At the time, he'd been convinced that the green valley—with log cabins and horses in a pasture—was the Sanctuary.

Now their goal was Cheyenne Mountain. People they'd met had said it was so. But he'd seen pictures of the site's iconic entrance. Where were the log cabins, the horses in a pasture? He rolled onto his back, cupped his hands behind his head, and stared at the moon shadows on the tent ceiling.

If they didn't find the Sanctuary tomorrow, Tanya was right—they were short on everything and where then could they go?

CHAPTER 40
THE SANCTUARY

Cheyenne Mountain, Colorado — September, Year 6

Caleb woke to a gloomy Tanya and a downcast Andy. The others' moods had even subdued Brianna's normally bright disposition. Having eaten the last of their food yesterday, they packed their gear, hopped on their bikes, and ascended the winding dirt road. But a few miles later, Andy called out, "Look there!"

At a sign announcing the trailhead for the Rock Creek Trail, Caleb pulled into a gravel parking lot. Beside a sign pointing to the trail, someone had cleared a swath of ground wide enough to contain dozens upon dozens of wooden crosses.

"It's a cemetery." Tanya raised a hand to her mouth. "And it's recent."

"I count over eighty graves, maybe more." Andy waved toward the crosses. "A lot of people died here recently."

"Let's go on." Trying to suppress his growing doubts, Caleb pedaled back to the road.

A hundred yards later, they passed through what had once been some kind of checkpoint. But the gate was raised, the guard booth was empty, and the coiled barbed wire had been pushed aside.

They kept going, and a mile later, they passed through a second abandoned checkpoint. A quarter mile after that, they reached the iconic, semicircular tunnel leading into Cheyenne Mountain, supposedly the most secure facility in North America. Chain-link fencing and barbed wire bordered both sides of a parking lot.

192

A single red sedan was parked there, but muddy circles of rain spots dotted its windows, and weeds had grown up through the front bumpers.

Caleb and the others dismounted, and they approached the tunnel entrance. Brianna released Nika from the carrier and led her by the leash.

Under the rock overhang, tumbleweeds were piled up. The dust covering the floor revealed only small animal footprints. And the fluorescent ceiling lights were dark. He took a deep breath. The place looked abandoned.

Andy walked to a phone on the wall. Picking it up and listening, he turned to the others. "Dead. Nothing."

Caleb peered into the dark shaft. "Well, let's start in. Maybe we'll find something."

They began walking. Several yards in, they switched on their phone flashlights. Their feet echoed ahead of them, and Nika barked after the rats scampering out of their way. The air turned colder, and the tunnel went on and on. The light from the opening, already dim, narrowed to a pinpoint.

They must have walked a mile when the shaft made a ninety-degree turn. In pitch-black, they came to a closed metal door. Caleb examined a wall of steel. It was a blast door, and another phone hung on the wall beside it. Taking a deep breath, he lifted the mouthpiece. But just like at the entrance, this one, too, was silent. He tried to turn the door's metal wheel, but it was locked and wouldn't budge. He knocked on the door, but the metal was thick. Even if someone was inside, could they hear his feeble pounding?

Something inside him—was it hope?—seemed to shrivel and dry up, and he wrapped his arms about his chest and shivered.

Tanya glanced back the way they'd come then at him. She put her hands to her mouth. "It was all a myth, wasn't it? There hasn't been anyone here in a very long time. The place is abandoned."

Tears were in her eyes, and he took a step toward her. But she tore her glance from his and shook her head. "I'm going back."

Nodding, he followed her and the others in silence back to the entrance.

193

When they again stepped into the faded light of a midday sun, he eyed his companions. If the day had started out in poor spirits, their expressions now sent the blood draining from his face. They'd trekked across half a continent and endured months of arduous travel. They were out of food and water. They'd put all their hopes on the Sanctuary. Now, it appeared their journey had been for nothing.

"It doesn't look good, does it?" asked Andy.

Shaking his head, Caleb drew a hand through his hair. No, it didn't look good, and he had no idea what to do next.

"Now what?" Tanya waved from Caleb to Andy to Brianna. "Now where do we go?"

"What's this?" Brianna pulled a piece of faded, yellowed paper from under one of the tumbleweeds. She read it then handed it to Caleb. Half covered with muddy rain spots, it was a message:

Julia,

We have moved. Follow the Rock Creek Trail across 369 and continue south. Turn right at the trail junction.

Daniel

"What does it mean?" Brianna asked.

"I don't know." Caleb passed it along to Andy. "What do you think?"

"Maybe whoever was living at the mountain decided to abandon the place?" Andy scratched his beard. "Maybe conditions inside became too difficult? After all, it's been six years since V-Day. That cemetery we passed must have been where they buried their dead. Maybe their supplies ran out? Maybe the plague got them?"

"That would make sense." Caleb raised a questioning glance to the others. "What if we follow these directions and see where it leads?"

"I'm all for it." Brianna's eyes lit up. "Let's do it!"

Caleb faced his wife. "Are you up for a hike?"

"Do we have any other options?"

He shook his head. "Let's go to the trailhead, put everything we need into our backpacks, and start out on foot."

So, they hid their bikes in the trees far from the trailhead then began their hike. The Rock Creek Trail ascended and descended a tortuous mountain path. Brianna let Nika off the leash, and the dog, her tail wagging, ran ahead and behind them, sniffing animal scents and returning often to her human companions before again racing on ahead.

Several miles later, they crossed the dirt road labeled Colorado 369 just as the cryptic directions indicated and plunged into deep pine woods. For the next three miles, the forest had burned, holding only charred trunks.

Then they entered a piney greenwood.

Filled with roots and rocks, the trail followed the streams of mountain valleys. Just as the sun was setting, they topped yet another rise and looked down into a green valley.

"A village!" cried Brianna. "With log houses, horses in a pasture, and—what do I smell?"

"It's meat cooking over a fire!" Andy grinned. "Is this what we've been looking for?"

Caleb peered down at the valley, and his heart raced. It was what he saw in his dream before they left Shetek State Park. "Let's go down and find out."

Tanya beamed, and Brianna clapped.

Fifteen minutes later, they emerged at the beginning of a wide field. The creek ran down the valley's center, and to Caleb's right, plowed fields and a garden. But the tomato plants were yellow, barely a foot tall, and the cornstalks were short and shriveled. On his left, in a log-fenced pasture, two sickly horses grazed on green grass. Three log cabins surrounded a central square where a man and a woman were chopping wood. Smoke from a rock chimney wafted the smell of cooking meat.

Caleb felt like shouting for joy.

Beside him, Tanya's smile matched Brianna's.

His spirits buoyed, he strode beside the stream while the others followed. When they turned the corner around the first house, they came face-to-face with a black-haired, middle-aged man carrying a heavy sack.

"Wh–what?" He stared at the pistols on their belts and the rifles over their shoulders then shot a glance behind him as if deciding whether or not to run. Instead, he dropped his bag and laid a hand on the pistol at his belt. "What are y'all doing here?"

"We mean you no harm." Caleb raised both hands. "We're looking for the Sanctuary. Is this it? Have we found it?"

Frowning, the man closed his fingers about his weapon. "Where did you come from?"

"From the Minnesota Northwoods, and we've been traveling for— what?—two years, to get here."

"From a forest land in the far north?" His eyes widened, and his hand slipped from the gun.

"You could say that, yes."

The man took a closer look at the four travelers. His next words came with a distinct southern accent. "How did y'all hear of us?"

"Everywhere we've been, we heard rumors, and . . ." Should Caleb tell this man about his vision? He'd never mentioned it to the others. He swallowed. Something whispered to him that he should. "And about a year ago, I had a dream—a vision, actually—where I saw this valley."

"You had a–a vision about our valley?"

"I did."

Both Tanya and Andy shot him puzzled glances.

"Are y'all Christians?"

"We are."

"Then, welcome!" The man beamed, and his demeanor morphed from wary suspicion to eager camaraderie. "Yes, welcome. Welcome, indeed. And yes, the Sanctuary is what we call our little settlement, although we've moved twice now. We've been expecting—no, praying— for you, Caleb, to come. My name is Daniel Price."

A bit puzzled, Caleb stepped forward to take Daniel's welcoming hand. Then he introduced his traveling companions.

The man grabbed his sack and waved them toward the central square where a couple was splitting logs.

As they followed in his wake, Tanya whispered to Caleb. "They've

196

been expecting us?"

"Apparently. I don't understand this either."

Daniel whirled to face the travelers with a smile. "I heard that, so I'll say this. You, Caleb Turner, are the man we all have been waiting for."

"Me?" Startled, he stopped walking. "Why do you say that?"

"Because two of us have seen it. We are in constant danger from the CSA here. We've also read the Scriptures, and we know what's coming. Ever since we arrived, we've been waiting for you to come, because it is you, Caleb Turner, who will lead us to a place where our crops won't grow stunted, where our animals won't die unexpectedly, and where the Unitum Imperium will stop searching for us. It's only by the grace of God that the CSA hasn't found us again."

"But why do you say that *I* will lead you?" Caleb shook his head. "I'm not your guy."

"But you *are*, Caleb." Daniel laid a hand on his shoulder. "Two of us had the same dream, more like a vision. Yes, Caleb, believe it or not, Amber Bright and I had the same dream! It was almost a year ago that an angel of God, shining like the sun, gave me the message first. He told me that a man was coming from a forest land in the north. And this man— that's you, Caleb Turner—had been traveling for years to find us. And when he arrived, he would show us the way to a place of safety, somewhere where the forces of the Unitum Imperium couldn't harm us, and where Jesus, the Son of God, is greatly honored."

Caleb's mouth dropped open, for Daniel was mistaken. Caleb was no such savior. And hadn't they just journeyed across half a continent, hoping that the Sanctuary was the very place Daniel was seeking?

CHAPTER 41
South Camp

Somewhere in the Colorado Mountains – September, Year 6

"I know of no such place as you describe." Caleb shifted his feet. "I am not the savior you are waiting for."

"But you are, Caleb Turner. The angel also told us that you, yourself, might not yet know your true destiny and that we might have to wait for it to be revealed. But come." The man waved them toward the couple now approaching. "You must meet the others."

Then he introduced them to Chase Cooper and Amber Bright, both about thirty years of age. Chase wore wire-rim glasses and stood a head shorter than Daniel. Amber's baseball cap covered brunette hair that she tied in a ponytail. With her clear skin, pleasing face, and smiling eyes, he'd never seen a more beautiful woman.

Daniel walked to a bell yoked to a pole, grabbed the rope, and shook the clapper. His ringing brought three more folks into the central yard. They clustered about with quizzical expressions. When all had gathered, Daniel raised his hands for silence. "I am happy to announce the arrival of the man we have long awaited—Caleb Turner. He comes from the Minnesota Northwoods. He and his companions have been traveling for two years to get here. And one year ago, he saw our valley in a dream."

Daniel's announcement caused gasps, claps of joy, and excited conversation. Overwhelmed, Caleb accepted their handshakes, welcomes, and joyful smiles. The three who'd joined them were Lena Chang, Robert Williams, and Sam Smith, all around thirty years of age. Lena was of Asian descent, and Robert was black. Their welcoming went on until Daniel spoke above the throng. "This calls for a community feast

198

tonight in the dining hall." He lowered his glance to Caleb's group. "Are you folks hungry?"

"Yes!" answered Brianna.

* * *

THE SIX SURVIVING MEMBERS OF what they called South Camp filled one long table. For some reason, they were convinced that Caleb was the man God had prophesied to lead them. He and Tanya sat beside Daniel, apparently the leader, and across from Lena Chang, another pilot with whom Caleb gleaned Daniel had a special relationship.

Perhaps it was the monotony of their diet on the road or his hunger, but Caleb thought he'd never eaten a more satisfying meal than what the Sanctuary served that evening: deer meat roasted with potatoes and carrots, ears of corn slathered with butter, wheat bread with more butter, and a kind of ale with a hint of berries. A few seats away, Andy and Brianna wolfed down their meals. Beside him, Tanya sighed with contentment.

When he'd finished, Caleb sat back, happy and satisfied, but burning with questions. He turned to his host. "We found you after reading a message at the Cheyenne Mountain entrance. Many people on our travels told us Cheyenne Mountain was the Sanctuary. So how did you come to be here?"

Daniel turned in his seat. "It's a long story, and you folks need to hear it."

The conversation quieted. While Brianna slipped pieces of bread and venison to Nika under the table, Andy asked for more ale. Beside Caleb, a smiling Tanya finished her meal and faced their host.

Daniel cleared his throat. "Everyone here was once part of the US Space Force stationed at Cheyenne Mountain. When the Chinese EMP attack took out the country's power and communications, we lost our early warning system. After the EMP strike, a few Chinese nukes hit Denver and the country's main cities. Another nuke hit Colorado Springs when half of our coworkers were sleeping in the city. None of them ever came back. After that, we began calling Cheyenne Mountain the Sanctuary." He lowered his gaze to the tabletop and shook his head.

"We'd lost the war—I'm not sure there was a winner—and Colorado Springs was destroyed. The area around Peterson Space Force Base was radioactive. We pleaded for instructions, but President Harper couldn't decide what to do with us. Our mission of defending the nation from attack was gone. Even so, Camp David ordered us to remain where we were. Then the US joined the Unitum Imperium, and our supplies stopped. So did most communications from the top brass back East."

Down the table, Chase pushed his wire-rim glasses further onto his nose. "They either abandoned or forgot about us. We asked them repeatedly. The new command said we should stay put, but they gave us no new mission. The only time they remembered us was when a group came to confiscate our antibiotics."

"And that," added Amber Bright, "left us vulnerable to the plague. We lost about half our number to the Black Death. It was bizarre how the rats appeared everywhere, overnight. We couldn't stop them."

"That explains the cemetery at the Rock Creek Trail trailhead," said Andy.

"Yes," answered Daniel. "We were isolated inside the mountain, confined to five underground rooms, and the disease spread rapidly. Still, we were loyal. We waited for a mission that never came. We had long arguments among ourselves. Since the top brass couldn't make up its mind about what to do with us, some of us thought we should abandon the place. But Colonel Scott insisted the facility was too important to abandon, so we stayed."

Lena nodded. "By then, some of us figured out that the Bible had prophesied everything that had happened. Before the vanishing, Caleb, none of us were Christians, or we'd have been taken."

"What fools we were then!" Daniel patted the tabletop. "We began reading the Bibles our fellow Christians left behind on V-Day. Then, on the day the three angels flew overhead, something drew everyone outside. We saw them, and we heard their warnings. That convinced me and twenty others. We couldn't deny God's hand in what was happening. That's when we divided into two camps—Christians on one side, atheists on the other. It finally came to a head when the North American government ordered us to join a command in New Mexico. But when they demanded that we take the mark, that's when we split from the others and went our own way."

"But this is amazing!" Tanya looked to Daniel with eager eyes. "For the last two years, Caleb has insisted we find the Sanctuary, and all along, you've been waiting for us. It's almost as if . . . as if . . . "

"As if everyone was divinely guided?" Daniel grinned.

"Yes!" She beamed.

"But why do you want to leave here now?" asked Caleb.

"Two reasons. When we first left Cheyenne Mountain, we settled about fifteen miles north of the complex. Twenty souls comprised our group then. But the CSA tracked us, probably using our phones. The army swooped down on us, there was a firefight, and that day, we lost thirteen good men and women. We started a search for a new location and sent Julia on a trip north for reconnaissance. While she was gone, we found this valley, southwest of the mountain. As arranged, I left her a note at the mountain telling her where we'd moved. This place is far better, but still, the CSA won't rest until they find and destroy us.

"That's the first reason. The second is that we've read the Scriptures, and we know no place will be safe when the bowl judgments hit the earth."

"But when you arrived here, you had seven. Now you are six. What happened?"

"Julia was mauled by a grizzly bear, and she died later from her wounds. Now, whenever anyone leaves the camp looking for berries— or anything, for that matter—we always take a rifle with us."

"Oh, I'm sorry," said Tanya.

"But I have some good news for you." Caleb set down his glass of beer. "My sister gave me a way to defeat the tracking on the solar phones."

"She did?" Chase's smile was wide. "That's great!"

"But you're wrong about one thing—I don't know anything about this place of safety that I'm supposed to lead you to."

"You will, Caleb." Daniel smiled. "Someday you will lead us to the

Refuge."

"*What!* What did you call it?" Caleb's heart began racing.

"In our dreams, the angel called it the Refuge." Daniel lifted an eyebrow. "Why?"

"Because my sister, Chelsea's group is heading to Jerusalem where she says there are directions to a place called the Refuge."

His eyes wide, Daniel gasped. "Then our visions were true, and you *did* know! So the Refuge God promised us is in Israel?"

"We're not sure. All we know is that the *directions* to it are in Jerusalem."

"Still, this is confirmation. It must be somewhere *near* Israel."

Lena frowned at Daniel. "That's a continent and an ocean away. We have no way to get there."

"Maybe we do," said Chase. "There's a rumor about a special hangar at Peterson where they kept an old Convair B-36 for the top brass. Supposedly, they hardened the hangar against radiation and nuclear attack. But it was only a rumor."

"Chase, are you sure it's not in their Air and Space Museum?" Daniel shook his head. "That was a prop plane. Even if the rumor is true, the plane would be so old, how do you know it's airworthy?"

"I don't. But you and Lena are pilots. Amber and I are mechanics. We were both trained as civilian pilots years ago, so we know something about prop planes. Of course, we don't know what shape that plane is in. And finding enough aviation fuel could be a problem. But a B-36 could easily fly nonstop to Israel. Maybe we should check it out?"

As Daniel rubbed his beard, a grin spread across his face. "Yes! Let us mount an expedition to Peterson and break into this hangar. We have nothing to lose."

CHAPTER 42
GRADY'S FALL

The demon assaults ended without an announcement. Everyone was still on edge, peering around every corner, fearing the next attack. But when two days passed without a single demon rider on a single demon horse appearing anywhere in the city, the streets of New Babylon exploded with shouts of rejoicing.

Like moths at midnight, every soul flew straight to the flames of intemperance and debauchery. They flooded the bars lining the thoroughfares. They mobbed the flesh rooms in the Temple of Davato. And they jammed the numerous drug dens serving hashish, heroin, methamphetamine, fentanyl, and mescaline. Pounding music again blasted the day and throbbed long into the night.

With wild and eager abandon, Grady Wilson, the personal secretary to the Imperator of the Unitum Imperium, joined in.

When he found Marcia, their bodies became reacquainted. "You've changed," she said after one such assignation. "You're wilder. And sometimes, Grady, you scare me."

He nodded, left the bed, and donned his pants and shirt. He strode to the kitchen where waited another bottle of whiskey. After pouring a half glass and downing it in one gulp, he filled another for lithe, black-haired Marcia. "I'm leaving now for the poker tables. Want to come?"

"No." She pulled a blouse over her bare chest. "Gambling doesn't interest me."

Dressed now, he started for the door but changed his mind and went to a top drawer by the refrigerator. He took the Ruger Max 9 he'd bought in one of the gun shops on the strip. Heavy and cold, it was strangely comforting in his hand. Strapping the holster to his waist, he slipped the gun into the leather. Increasingly, the news warned of random, unprovoked attacks after dusk and spontaneous bar fights leaving a trail of bodies. He'd witnessed too many of those lately, and lots of folks were now carrying firearms wherever they went.

He took the elevator to the third floor and wended his way through the World Casino's array of baccarat tables, roulette wheels, crap tables, and its endless rows of slot machines. As one of Davato's favorites, Grady's salary was greater than most. Yet, for some reason, money just seemed to leak out of his account. The city had too many pleasures for sale, and his goal lately was to sample them all.

At a kiosk, he slipped in his card and bought thirty thousand euros worth of poker chips then strolled through acres of tables until he claimed an empty seat. The casino decided long ago to abandon credit slips and revert to something you could hold in your hand.

He sat across from a black-bearded giant of a man with Neanderthal features and a permanent scowl. When the current deal ended—five-card draw was the game—the dealer dealt him a hand. He examined his cards, discarded three, and found himself holding three kings. He tossed a five-hundred-euro chip in the center pile and called. The Asian man beside him added his five hundred and called. The Neanderthal frowned and threw seven hundred into the center, raising the pot by two hundred.

Grady eyed the black-bearded giant. No one was going to read that permanent frown, but he felt lucky today. He raised the bid by another two hundred.

The Asian man folded, but the Neanderthal met his bid.

They laid down their cards, and Grady's three kings beat the Neanderthal's three queens. Grady raked in the pot.

The game went on for another hour, and, scarcely believing his luck, Grady lost only once. The Asian man dropped out, and two more people joined the party. But as Grady's pile of chips grew, those belonging to the Neanderthal dwindled to a handful, and the man's expression turned a darker shade of sour.

At the end of the next deal, the black-bearded man lost again, and he slammed a fist on the table and stood. The chips bounced, and the other players shot him a wary glance. The dealer's face warned he expected trouble. He left his post and backed away.

"I don't like the way you're playing, and I don't like your face." Neanderthal's hand slapped the pistol at his belt. "I think you're cheating."

"It's not possible to cheat," called the dealer from a few meters away. "Not at the World Casino tables."

"Stay out of this, little man." The Neanderthal glared at the dealer, and everyone but Grady retreated to a safe distance. "Hand over your winnings, and we can both walk away from this alive."

Grady shook his head.

"I said I want what you stole from me, and—"

And something inside Grady snapped. He was here to play, not be bullied by some loudmouth giant with rocks for brains. An odd calm settled over him, and he smiled. "I won't give you what you want, but I will give you what you deserve." His fingers yanked the Ruger Max 9 from its holster, raised the barrel, and fired—once, twice, three times—at the center of the big man's chest.

As red sprouted from his chest, Neanderthal Man toppled to the floor.

Grady stared at the empty space where his opponent had stood. A strange elation buoyed him. He turned the pistol over, admiring its gleaming black metal. It held the power of life and death, and it was Grady Wilson who controlled it. No one was going to push him around anymore. Now he understood, at some deeply profound level, what it was like to wield raw, unimpeded power.

The dealer and the other players now standing nearby stared at him with frightened eyes. Their fear only increased his elation.

But the feeling passed as quickly as it had come, and a moment later, he was shaking. What had he done?

His heart thumping hard, sweat dripping from his brows, he returned the gun to its holster. He gathered his chips into the winner's bag and, with a quiet voice, apologized to the dealer and said he was finished. He walked away in a daze.

Such incidents happened several times a day, and as security men headed toward the body, the players at the other tables shot Grady wary glances before resuming their play.

At the service window, he turned in his chips, adding them to his account. Still shaking, he took the elevator to the ground floor and the street.

Outside, a dim sun burned in a hazy sky, and the air had cooled. He found a bench, plopped into it, and dropped his head in his hands. What was happening to him? He'd just killed a man, and his immediate reaction was joy, a sense of power, and wild elation.

Raising his glance, he stared at the fingers that pulled the trigger. As if the murdering appendages held more conscience than the mind that ordered it, the hand shook.

He was a murderer, but in Davato's realm, what the authorities were most concerned about was removing the bodies, keeping a clean floor, and restoring a semblance of order.

Still staring at the offending hand, he focused on the tattoo blackening his wrist.

Chelsea's words when she first saw the mark came back to him: "I like you, Grady. But now I'm sorry for you. . . ."

The words from the third angel, etched forever in his mind, also rose again to haunt him: "The smoke of their torment will rise forever and ever, and they will have no relief day or night, for they have worshiped the beast and his statue and have accepted the mark of his name."

His eyes clouded with moisture. His heart raced, and his chest constricted. He clutched his head into his hands and sobbed.

"What has happened to me?" he spoke to the concrete. "What have I become?"

CHAPTER 43
THE CONVAIR
B-36 PEACEMAKER

Colorado Springs, Colorado — October, Year 6

Two weeks after Caleb's arrival, the expedition to investigate the mystery hangar at Peterson Space Force Base left the Sanctuary at what passed for dawn. Comprising the group were Daniel Price, pilot; Amber Bright, mechanic; Chase Cooper, mechanic and electrician; and Caleb, who knew where to find the bicycles. They carried pistols, rifles, four days' worth of food, and tools to break into the hangar. Retracing the route Caleb had taken, they followed him to the hidden bikes. Then they pedaled down the mountain and skirted the blast zone around Colorado Springs.

When they reached a main highway, Amber Bright rode up beside Caleb and shot him a smile. Wearing tight jeans and a baseball cap, she'd tied her long brunette hair in a ponytail. "When we left the base and became civilians again, I decided to drop the military cut and grow it long again. A woman should look like a woman, don't you think?"

Caleb nodded, for she was the most beautiful mechanic he'd ever seen.

Before the blast zone, she measured the radiation level and pronounced it safe enough. But soon, they passed a number of corpses, some of which had been picked clean by the crows whose dead bodies littered the nearby pavement. And when they turned north into the area near Peterson, the trees had turned into lifeless trunks, the grass and bushes were brown and dead, and Amber's Geiger counter ticked wildly. She glanced up beneath her cap. "I hope this hangar we're heading for is radiation-hardened, because this area is still active. We don't want to hang around outside for long."

Daniel glanced at the sky. "It's already past noon. If we can't get into the hangar in the next three hours, we'll have to find safer ground and camp before dark."

The base security gate was open, and Daniel led them inside and through a warren of streets. They cycled onto the asphalt apron and began inspecting the hangars bordering the runways.

"We're looking for one that's hardened," said Chase, "with thick concrete walls."

Halfway down the apron, they came to the only building meeting that description. With concrete walls and roof, it was more a bunker than an airplane hangar. And it was wider than anything else on the strip. They dismounted, and Daniel approached the metal overhang where two massive concrete portals met. "These walls are probably three feet thick. How are we ever going to open this?"

"From inside," said Chase. "There must be another entrance."

Amber poked her head from around the corner. "Over here."

They walked their bikes to where she beckoned, parked them, and entered a six-foot concrete tunnel leading to a smaller door faced with steel.

Chase brought a sack from his saddlebags and approached the front panel. "There's no way we could ever open this with force. It's operated by electronics. Let's just hope there's enough battery power left."

He took a drill from his bag and drilled through the one-way screws, revealing a circuit board and wires. With an electrical probe, he found what he was looking for then used a battery-powered solder gun to attach a few wires. When he crossed the final wire between two points, two feet of concrete moaned and ground over the floor. It rolled outward, revealing a dark interior.

"Who's first?" asked Daniel.

"Ladies, of course." Amber Bright turned on a flashlight and entered.

Inside, Caleb shone his flashlight into a vast interior, illuminating a bit of hull attached to a monstrous airplane extending off into the dark.

He gasped. "It's enormous!"

"The B-36 had the widest wingspan of any US bomber," said Daniel.

"Why did they call it the Peacemaker?"

"Before 1959 when it was removed from service, it was the Strategic Air Command's only long-range bomber capable of delivering a nuclear warhead to Russia. It held a crew of fifteen."

"That would be perfect for us." Amber then took out her Geiger counter and pronounced the interior safe.

Breathing the hangar's stale air, they explored by flashlight and found repair bays with tools, storage bins stocked with dried and canned food, rows of full water canisters, and a separate room with sixteen bunks, tables and chairs, and computer and television monitors.

"Someone planned to hole up here in case of nuclear war," said Daniel. "And this plane was their escape route to somewhere."

"What do you think happened?" asked Caleb.

"Who knows?" Chase approached two giant metal barrels. "Maybe when the nuke hit the city without warning, it took out whoever was planning to use this place."

"Probably top brass," said Amber.

"No doubt. And then the prevailing winds dropped fallout across the base." Chase was looking at an indicator on one of the barrels. "These should have been filled with aviation fuel, but they're almost empty."

"What?" Daniel went to his side, saw what Chase saw, and shook his head.

"I'll check out the plane's tanks." Amber climbed into the hatch, already open under the front wheel well, then waved to them from the flight deck's window.

As Caleb shone his light on an airplane pushback tug in one corner, Chase walked to the far end of the building occupied by an even larger tank. A pipe led from the tank through a wall into a corner room. "This holds diesel fuel. It must be for the generator providing the hangar's electricity. But the tank is only a tenth full."

Amber popped her head out of the plane's entry door. "The plane's tanks are empty too. And I think I just drained the last of the batteries.

But I have some good news. The plane's been upgraded with JAFF. For you, Caleb, that means if we detect an incoming missile, we can release chaff with a corresponding jamming signal that matches our Doppler."

"That's good news," said Chase. "Maybe it's got other improvements as well." He then opened the door to the corner room and entered. Moments later, a roar followed him out, and the overhead lights came on. He closed the door on the noise. "At least the generator works. The exhaust is piped to the outside. No doubt the air intake is heavily filtered. This should soon give us some fresh air."

The lights were now on, and as Chase walked to the building's front, Caleb gasped while he took in the scale of the B-36. Each enormous wing carried three props and two jet engines to help with takeoff.

"It has a wingspan of two hundred thirty feet," said Daniel, and Caleb craned his neck to take it all in. "They were the longest wings the air force ever built. The plane has a range of ten thousand miles, more than enough to reach Israel."

"Impressive." As Caleb circled it, Daniel reached the hangar's front.

Daniel pushed some buttons on another panel. "Now that we have power, let's see what this does."

The massive front doors lifted half an inch and began sliding out on hidden rollers. Metal screeched and ground over concrete, and the floor shimmied. The doors crept outward, opening to both sides. Five minutes later, the hangar was open to the dying light of a setting sun.

"Well, that works." Chase punched the panel again, and the doors began their return journey until they closed.

"So now what?" asked Caleb.

"We find fuel and bring it here," answered Daniel. "That seems to be what's missing."

"Yeah," said Chase. "Aviation fuel and plenty of diesel. The generator powering the air filter and lights will empty that tank in a few days. The tug that moves the plane in and out of the hangar also uses diesel. We can't work in the dark, and without electricity, we can't check out this plane and determine if it's airworthy."

"But not today." Daniel ran a hand through his hair. "It will be dark soon. Let's bring our bikes inside and shut the door on the radiation. Tomorrow, we can begin our search for fuel."

"We can check what's here at Peterson first," said Chase.

"How are we going to haul the fuel back here?" asked Amber.

"We can use the tug." Chase scratched his chin. "But we'll need a baggage cart that's not irradiated, and that won't be here at Peterson. And if this base doesn't have the fuel we need, we can try Fort Carson. There's also the Air Force Academy to the north, but it's further away. Since the attack, both have been abandoned."

They brought their bikes inside, closed the door, and sat at the table where they ate their dried venison and cornmeal bread.

After the meal, Daniel faced his two mechanics. "It's going to take time to do all this. This plane needs an incredible amount of fuel. We could be at this for weeks. Maybe months. We should abandon South Camp and bring the others here to help."

Amber nodded. "And we need to check out everything on the plane. We've had training on prop planes, of course, but neither of us have ever worked on a B-36. It's old, and if we need parts—then what?"

"There might be a parts inventory in one of these maintenance bays. The top brass must have been planning on using this plane as their backup escape route." Daniel caught each of their glances. "This plane is a complicated baby, but we have to get it airworthy. The CSA has been getting closer to South Camp each week."

"We'll get it working," said Amber. "You and I had the same vision, didn't we? If God is leading us to the Refuge, why would he not give us a way to get there?"

CHAPTER 44
THE SEVENTH TRUMPET

In the Great Throne Room – February, Year 6

Revelation 11:15 (NLT): *Then the seventh angel blew his trumpet, and there were loud voices shouting in heaven: "The world has now become the Kingdom of our Lord and of his Christ, and he will reign forever and ever."*

Revelation 15:1–3a (HCSB): *Then I saw another great and awe-inspiring sign in heaven: seven angels with the seven last plagues, for with them, God's wrath will be completed. I also saw something like a sea of glass mixed with fire, and those who had won the victory over the beast, his image, and the number of his name, were standing on the sea of glass with harps from God. They sang the song of God's servant Moses and the song of the Lamb.*

For this greatest of all events, Blake was privileged to stand with the millions gathered in the vast throne room of the Lord of Hosts. He stood in back, miles from the Ancient of Days himself, and yet, with his heavenly vision, he could see every detail of what was happening miles away. In front, each of the martyrs who had turned from the beast during the Tribulation held harps.

Adding to the gravity of the moment, the glassy floor beneath his feet shimmered with flame and fire.

In the room's center, the God who was, who is, and who is to come, sat upon his high throne, shining with a light brighter than a thousand suns. Thunder, lightning, and smoke issued from behind the great seat, and the train of his robe extended to the Temple's farthest reaches. The

212

redeemed and the angels, filling the room for miles in all directions, bowed and murmured their praises.

Ever since Jesus had pulled Blake off the slopes of Mt. Hood in the Rapture, his every moment in Heaven had been filled with awe, wonder, and thankfulness that he'd trusted his life to the Son of God. Time flowed by in moments he could stretch out or speed up at will. Each day brought a new understanding of who God was and of his love for his people. And each day he encountered new wonders keeping him in perpetual amazement.

But today, events were approaching a climax. By earth time, the long-awaited rule of Christ was less than a year and a half away. And Blake was privileged to be present for what was coming.

Sometimes, his thoughts turned to that day, six years ago, when he'd left Caleb on Mt. Hood's slopes and was caught up in the Rapture. But Jesus had assured Blake that his friend was saved. So he had no need to worry about Caleb.

But something was happening toward the front, and he craned his neck to see. The martyrs who'd been killed during the Tribulation had lifted their harps and begun to sing.

"Who will not fear you, Lord, and glorify your name?" they sang. "For you alone are holy. All nations will come and worship before you, for your righteous deeds have been revealed."

Blake and the rest of the assembled joined in, raising a glorious hymn of praise to the Lord.

As they sang, the fearsome and mighty seraphim, each with six wings, continued to hover at the throne's base. Lightning and thunder flashed between them.

When the song concluded, the seraphim's voices broke the silence, echoing to the farthest reaches of the hall, shaking the floor's foundations. "Holy, holy, holy, is the Lord of Heaven's Armies! The whole earth is filled with his glory!"

Blake joined a mighty chorus and echoed back the refrain.

Now, the seventh angel, one and a half times taller than a man, stepped out of the crowd. He folded his wings and bowed before a throne bristling with multicolored gems. Surrounded by an ethereal glow, he faced the gathered multitudes. The trumpet in his hands gleamed bright and golden by the throne's heavenly light.

He raised the massive trumpet to his lips.

Then the angel blew. And the sound reverberated off the ceiling and walls.

Now the twenty-four elders beneath the Lord rose from their seats, faced the mighty God, and fell to the ground. Then they spoke as one: "We give thanks to you, Lord God, the Almighty, the one who is and who always was, for now you have assumed your great power and have begun to reign. The nations were filled with wrath, but now the time of your wrath has come. It is time to judge the dead and reward your servants the prophets, as well as your holy people, and all who fear your name, from the least to the greatest. It is time to destroy all who have caused destruction on the earth."

A collective gasp issued from the millions filling the vast hall. Blake fell to his knees, gripped with awe at what the seventh trumpet was about to usher in. . . .

The seven angels would pour the seven bowls upon the earth.

The rebellion and iniquity of Christ's enemies would end.

The rescue of God's remaining people on earth would begin.

And Jesus would reign for a thousand years.

CHAPTER 45
THE FIRST BOWL JUDGMENT

Revelation 16:1–2 (HCSB): *Then I heard a loud voice from the sanctuary saying to the seven angels, "Go and pour out the seven bowls of God's wrath on the earth." The first went and poured out his bowl on the earth, and severely painful sores broke out on the people who had the mark of the beast and who worshiped his image.*

New Babylon, Iraq – February, Year 6

To the buzz of conversation from the thousands already crowded into New Babylon's central park, Grady joined the elite group at the dais. The night was pleasantly cool, and he wore only a thin sweater. Any moment now, Davato would enter the control booth, and the Giant would light up with his image. It had been five months since the last of the demon assaults, life had returned to normal, and people speculated that the worst was over.

Despite the loneliness and emptiness always gnawing at his insides, Grady had spent the last months in wild debauchery, each night visiting the drug dens, the bars, and the brothels. He'd acquired a fondness for gambling, and now he spent much of his free time at the poker and craps tables. As he looked back on it, his winnings were fewer than his losses. But soon, he was certain, his luck would change.

The meetings Davato now held were full of plans for revenge against the Christians and especially the Jews. News had reached New Babylon of a revolt brewing in several Israeli cities. When the CSA and Truth Squads had been decimated by the demon attacks, some of the Jews had organized into a group calling themselves the Jericho Faction. Already, they'd attacked CSA outposts in Tel Aviv, Haifa, Jerusalem, and Hebron.

Following the path of many he knew, Grady never left the apartment without his Ruger Max 9 strapped to his belt.

Beside him on the dais, Adam Turner whispered. "Nice weapon, Grady. I've heard you had a chance to use it."

"He had it coming." Had the news of how he shot his Neanderthal opponent at the poker table reached even Davato's staff?

"I'm sure he did. Perhaps someday, the Imperator will have use of your newfound courage."

Not knowing how to respond, Grady nodded. "However I can serve, Minister."

But Davato had stepped inside the booth, and the Giant came to life, morphing into the image of Davato the Divine.

"Welcome, friends and citizens, to this worldwide broadcast."

The Giant's words throbbed in Grady's chest and thundered across the park.

"We rejoice that the threat from the Enemy has passed and life has returned to normal. He has shown his disregard and hatred for us in so many ways, I can no longer count them. What more can he do to prove he is the monster we know him to be?"

Agreements rose from everywhere among the crowd.

"So today, I begin the first step toward our revenge against the Enemy and his allies. I've mentioned before how the Jews and Christians have worked tirelessly against you, me, and everything the Unitum Imperium stands for. They are true opponents of peace and prosperity, and they are in league with the Enemy himself.

"But lately, they have even attacked agents of the Unitum Imperium. And for such rebellion, we cannot stand!"

When Davato stomped one foot down on the pedestal, the ground and the dais shook.

"AND SO, CITIZENS OF THE WORLD, I ASK YOU TO LOOK AROUND YOU ONCE AGAIN. DO YOU SUSPECT A NEIGHBOR, A SHOPKEEPER, OR A PASSERBY OF BEING A JEW OR A CHRISTIAN? DOES SOMEONE HOLD SECRET MEETINGS IN A HOUSE OR APARTMENT NEAR YOU? IF SO, THEN I URGE YOU TO REPORT THEM TO THE NEAREST CSA OFFICE IN EXCHANGE FOR A HANDSOME REWARD. YES, YOUR DILIGENCE IN SERVICE TO THE UNITUM IMPERIUM WILL NOT GO UNREWARDED. IT WILL—"

But before the sentence was finished, Grady and everyone around him cried out in pain. He gasped, so great was the pain that had burst out in a dozen places all over his body. He pulled back his sweater and stared at a suppurating boil that, as if by magic, had broken through his skin. Shuddering, he glanced up at the Giant.

An open sore had appeared on the Giant's forehead, and when Davato raised a hand to his face, another was visible on his left wrist. The Prophet killed the image, and the pixels bringing the Giant to life darkened. The motors ceased, the arms dropped to its sides, and the life went out of it.

Around Grady now arose a great moaning for the open sores had afflicted everyone gathered in New Babylon's central park. It was just like during Davato's last big address when demons on horseback had come and killed a third of all present. It was as if the Enemy had waited for the worst possible moment to publicly humiliate the Imperator.

Grimacing from the pain, Grady pulled a whiskey flask from his front pocket and drank deeply.

The Imperator was right. The Christians and Jews in league with the Enemy who'd done this must pay.

But right now, he needed to end the pain, whatever it took. If he hurried, he could get to the Devil's Brew before the rest of the mob. But as he took his first steps, he winced.

Boils had sprouted even on the soles of his feet.

CHAPTER 46
SAYING GOODBYE

Milan, Italy – April, Year 6

Dylan clutched the leather saddlebags and pushed through the revolving doors of the doctor's apartment building. He glanced both ways on the sidewalk, but no one was about. As he headed for the bike rack around the corner, his steps echoed across the concrete.

The anemic sun had just set, and it was safe to leave. He'd put on the makeup to create the illusion of boils on his hands and face. Still, they only went out when darkness kept curious passersby from seeing their wrists. He didn't want to meet a nosy Truth Squad on his way to tonight's rendezvous.

He found his bicycle, dialed the combination to unlock it, hopped on, and started pedaling. In the city, a bicycle was less likely to attract the CSA's attention and easier to maneuver through back alleys and byways.

Half the streetlights were out, which suited him just fine. When he picked up speed, a chill breeze bit even through his sweatshirt. He should have dressed warmer.

Dr. Delucci was seriously concerned that René would not recover. He'd run out of antibiotics, and gangrene was spreading up René's arm. The doctor wanted to amputate, but René was adamant that he would never give up his arm. When Dylan had left the apartment, his friend's breathing was shallow, and he had no strength left in him.

"If he hadn't smoked so much, he would have had a better chance," the good doctor kept saying. "But without amputating, I fear nothing can help him now." It bothered Dylan that the doctor sometimes spoke about René in the past tense.

218

"Go on without me," René had urged them more than once. "It's long past time that you left."

But the group wouldn't hear of it. And they stayed.

Now all they could do was pray for a man who, time and again, had saved them and led them through many dangers.

Delucci had been more than generous with his surprise visitors. After a couple from the doctor's former patients had been raptured, he'd taken over their luxurious flat on the top floor of a nearly empty apartment building. Like everyone else, he'd come to Christ too late.

"Only by the grace of God has the CSA not found me," he said after they arrived. "I moved here five years ago, and it's fortuitous that René and I exchanged texts about the move. You are welcome to use my extra rooms. I only serve patients from the underground network now. Their gifts of food and bootleg identity cards keep me going."

But with the extra mouths, the doctor's food stores were running out, and it was to an underground cell that Dylan was now headed.

His destination was only a few kilometers away, but as he turned the next corner, a black van, probably CSA, passed in the opposite lane. He shot a glance behind to see what it would do.

The vehicle slowed, and he pedaled faster. Sometimes, even though he appeared to bear the boils on his face, they checked IDs and wrists.

On his right, an alley—too narrow for a car—beckoned, and he swerved into it.

Behind him, the van backed up. Back on the street, doors opened and slammed shut. *Oh no, not again.* Flashlights played on his back, and someone shouted, "Stop!"

He pedaled on.

The alley connected to the next street over, and as shouting followed, he bolted across the thoroughfare. He found yet another alley and dove into its dark recesses. Rats scampered ahead, but he outran them.

The passage dumped into the service drive of an abandoned factory. He pulled behind a rusting truck missing its tires and dismounted. Would the CSA now put out an alert for a man on a bicycle? Good thing he hadn't taken the van. They would surely have taken him then.

He slumped cross-legged to the concrete beside crumbling bricks from a collapsed wall. Everywhere, the quakes had left their mark. Wrapping his arms about his chest, he again regretted not wearing a jacket.

Pulling out his phone, he tried to call Caleb but received no answer. Wherever his brother was, there was probably still no signal.

He waited thirty minutes before again mounting his bike and pedaling back to the main street. The CSA van was gone, so he made his way to a bakery where he gave the secret knock.

A red-haired woman opened the door a crack and peered out. "Who is knocking at this hour?" That was her request for the pass phrase.

"Morning, evening, noon, or night—a friend is always welcome."

It was the proper response, and she let him in. "We expected you earlier. Did you have trouble?"

"Yes, a CSA van. But I lost them in the alleys. Do you have the supplies?"

"We do." She led him into the next room where two men and a woman sat at a table playing cards. She waved at a pile of paper-wrapped goods burdening a chest in the corner. "Today, we have sausage, rice, beans, canned peaches and pears. And a twenty-liter jug of water."

"Sounds good. What do I owe you?"

"Dr. Delucci has been such a godsend for us, whatever you can pay we'll accept."

Pulling out his wallet, he counted out five hundred euros, currency no one except the black market would accept these days. "Will this do?"

"It's more than enough." The woman smiled and filled her arms with packages.

Dylan took as much as he could, and she helped carry it to the street where they stuffed the packages into his saddlebags and tied the bottle on top.

The return to the apartment was uneventful, but as he carried a load up the stairs, Margot met him with tears in her eyes. "He's gone, Dylan. Shortly after you left, René passed away."

He dropped his load on the table, closed his eyes, and gripped his head with both hands.

How could René, of all people, die? He'd been the strongest among them, always leading, always knowing what to do in the face of danger. More than once he'd saved them from death.

How could he be gone?

Margot fell into his arms, and they hugged. Then she pulled away. "Can you guess what he said to me this morning when he was still awake? His last words?"

"No. What?"

"As best I can remember, this is what he said: 'That bullet gave me an incredible gift, Margot. I don't have to struggle anymore. My fight against the madness is over. Instead, I see a glorious future in the presence of Christ. Yes, Margot, this is me, René, the one who shoots people, saying this. But I did it all to save you and the others, to further the cause of Christ. Maybe that wasn't the best way, but it was the only way I knew. I haven't been the best of Christians, I admit. But I have repented, and Jesus has forgiven me. And now, I am going home.'"

She wiped a tear from her cheek. "Yes, Dylan, I know it's hard to believe, but that's what René said."

Across the room, Pasqual, sitting in an easy chair, raised a head from his hands. "He said that, did he?"

"As best I can recall."

Pasqual smiled. "That rascal. He was hiding it all along."

Sitting beside Pasqual, Chelsea wiped tears from her eyes and looked up. "God bless him. He helped us all."

Dr. Delucci emerged from the bedroom that, for the last eight months, had become René's sick room. "There was nothing more I could do. Once a person gets gangrene, if we don't amputate, the infection will enter the bloodstream."

"You did everything you could, doctor," said Margot. "We appreciate all you have done for us."

All the rest of that day, they mourned. Morbid though it was, they had to dispose of the body. Dr. Delucci suggested they wrap him in a sheet and drop him near the center where they were still collecting the bodies of those killed by the horseback demons. So many had died that the city was transporting the dead en masse to trenches in the countryside for burial.

With no other options, early the next morning, they dropped René's corpse at the collection center and returned to the apartment.

"It's becoming more dangerous to stay here all the time." Dylan peered out the window at four members of a Truth Squad strutting down the sidewalk. "It's time we leave. Doctor, maybe you should consider coming with us?"

"Thank you, but no. I will never leave Milan."

Nodding, Dylan turned to his companions. "Then it's time we leave."

"I agree." Pasqual came up beside him.

"Then tonight, we pack, and tomorrow, we head for Vernazza."

CHAPTER 47
ARIEL'S MISSION

Joel 3:15–16 (NLT): *The sun and moon will grow dark, and the stars will no longer shine. The LORD's voice will roar from Zion and thunder from Jerusalem, and the heavens and the earth will shake. But the LORD will be a refuge for his people, a strong fortress for the people of Israel.*

Haifa, Israel – April, Year 6

As the midafternoon sun dropped its pallid disk over the horizon, Ariel Geller, aka Big Matza, and Yitzhak, aka Latke, slammed shut the van door and exited to the street. Then, to be safe, Ariel walked his runner around the run-down building holding this last group of refugees.

Continuing his penchant for Jewish food names that he hoped would irritate any listening UI goons, he'd christened Yitzhak with *Latke*, a type of Jewish pancake on top of which one poured sour cream or even applesauce. The other runners in Ariel's employ were also out seeking converted Jews and Christians needing a way to the Refuge.

"Big Matza, how long can we keep this up?" The shorter, plumper Latke walked a pace slower, and he took a few steps to catch up. "We're finding fewer people each time. Even Baruch warned that in a few months, we need to head to Sela before the last of the bowl judgments hit."

"We have time yet. As long as there are Jews and Christians in need of rescue, we must be there for them. And now the UI goons are all covered with"—a wide grin split his face, and he slapped a hand on his thigh—"boils!"

"A wonderful thing, that. It makes our job so much easier. But when will we leave for the Refuge?"

Ariel simply grinned and kept walking.

Graffiti covered the building's outside walls. Empty bottles and trash littered the sidewalk. And all the windows were dark. At the entrance, he pushed into an unlit hallway with more graffiti, discarded needles, and the faint smell of urine. At the first floor, he knocked on the door to number 10 and waited.

Receiving no answer, he knocked again. After his third try, the door opened a crack, and a middle-aged man with wire-rim glasses and a long beard peered out. "Who is it?"

Ariel said the password: "When the light shines down upon the trees, sometimes the snow melts only from a few."

"Yes, yes. Come in, come in. My name is Elisha Cohen." He pointed to a ragged group of ten others huddling in a dark and dirty apartment lit only by two candles. "We've been waiting weeks for someone to get us to safety. I apologize for this place. We had to leave the last apartment in a hurry and find something else fast. This building has been abandoned for some time."

After Ariel introduced himself and Latke using their code names, he glanced over the six women, two youths, and two men sitting on chairs, a couch, and cross-legged on the floor. All were thin, and two had a yellow pallor. "When was the last time you folks ate?"

"Two days ago." Elisha hung his head. "We've had nothing to drink since yesterday."

Ariel frowned. "Before we leave, you must have water and a good meal. We'll return to the van and bring it in."

Elisha's eyes lit up. "That would be most appreciated."

As Ariel led Latke outside, his companion hurried to catch up. "The van barely has room for eight." Latke frowned. "How can we fit them all in back?"

"We won't leave anyone behind. These folks are in bad shape."

"How about this?" He stopped. "If one of us picked up Kishke in Tel Aviv, we'd have his car. Then the other could drive these folks back to Sela. That way, we could put one more up front and make some space."

"Good idea." Ariel patted Latke on the shoulder then kept going. "I'll go with Kishke, and you can take the van to Jordan from Tel Aviv. You're right about one thing. It's time for everyone working for me to wrap up operations. But there's one last couple asking for help in Ramallah. I'll get Kishke in Tel Aviv, and we will get the last couple, leaving you to drive these folks to Sela."

"Sounds like a plan."

"And yet . . ." As Ariel opened the back of the van, he stopped. "I should call Falafel. He's a new Jerusalem runner and a new convert. He may not know how to get to Sela. Someone was supposed to brief him, but with everyone leaving, he might have fallen through the cracks. And then there's the issue of the Jerusalem travel agency."

"What about it?" The light from the van door lit up the worry in Latke's face. "No one has used that drop in months."

"Still, I have a nagging feeling someone is going to show up there and need a ride."

"That's crazy, Big Matza. You don't know when or if there's anyone left to pick up or even if that's where they'll go."

"Still, Baruch has told folks about it, and so have I. Who knows how many will go there looking for a way out? Baruch said we might have six months before things get really bad with the next bowl judgments. That's plenty of time. Even Baruch isn't leaving Israel yet. The travel agency is the only lifeline to safety some will have. I'll hang around Jerusalem a few months longer. Just in case."

"You should get out while you can—now!"

"I can get out whenever I want. I've got safe houses all over Jerusalem with cars, vans, guns, food—you name it. Don't worry about me."

Latke shook his head. "I'll say it again, Big Matza: You're crazy."

Ariel just grinned and grabbed the bag with cumin, sweet paprika, and fixings for Israeli beans and rice. Simple, tasty, and nourishing. Latke loaded his arms with liter bottles of safe water.

Back in the apartment, the women cooked the rice and beans while everyone satisfied their thirst with cups of water.

Breathing in the smell of unwashed bodies and stale air, Ariel sat with Elisha. "If I may ask, how did you hear of our group?"

"Through a friend of a friend. Unfortunately, one was taken, but one of your men drove the other to safety. We are all latecomers here. Late to become Christians, that is."

"As are we all." Ariel grinned.

"We are so thankful for your mission, Big Matza." Elisha returned the smile. "I suppose that name is for the Unitum Imperium's benefit?"

"Of course. They hate Jewish food." Ariel's grin faded. "Do you know of anyone else needing rescue?"

"No. When we heard you were coming, I gathered every Christian I could find to wait for you. We're probably the last converts in Haifa. And I'll tell you this: Some of us haven't had a decent meal in weeks."

Ariel's lips returned to their usual grin. "Where you're going, Elisha, God will provide everything you need. Including food and water."

The women called out from the kitchen that the food was ready. If the refugees' eyes were formerly dark wells of despair, they now became bright beams of sunlight breaking through the clouds. Ariel's heart warmed as they wolfed down their first meal in days.

When everyone had eaten their fill, they led the group outside. It was pitch-dark as the ten men, women, and youths crowded into the back of the van. With Ariel at the wheel, they left Haifa's outskirts, driving through a dark countryside.

"For some time, Latke, I've had this feeling whenever we leave a place."

"What's that?"

"The next time we return to any of the cities we've just left—be it Haifa, Tel Aviv, or Jerusalem—when we go back, that city will have changed beyond all recognition."

Latke just stared at him, and they drove on in silence.

They'd be in Tel Aviv in less than an hour.

CHAPTER 48
FAMILY NEWS

Proverbs 30:11–15 (HCSB): *There is a generation that curses its father and does not bless its mother. There is a generation that is pure in its own eyes, yet is not washed from its filth. There is a generation—how haughty its eyes and pretentious its looks. There is a generation whose teeth are swords, whose fangs are knives, devouring the oppressed from the land and the needy from among mankind.*

Vernazza, Italy – April, Year 6

As Dylan drove the van south, Chelsea sat beside him in the front seat. She welcomed the familiar hum of tires over asphalt. They'd been through so much lately, and René's death had cast a shadow on their journey. But moving again was somehow . . . reassuring. Was it because the act of traveling gave the illusion of leaving the past behind and starting over?

They passed few vehicles in the dark. An hour after they started, Dylan turned on the radio to a Unitum Imperium official blaring more government propaganda. He was about to shut it off when, from the back, Pasqual asked him to leave it on. "Even if we disagree, we should keep abreast of what's happening."

Nodding, Dylan kept driving, and Chelsea listened.

Yes, fellow citizens, the family is a concept straight from the Enemy. It is long past time we move beyond such outdated notions as mother, father, son, and daughter. The idea of a monogamous marriage between one man and one woman should be abhorrent to all enlightened individuals.

Chelsea scrunched her face. "I heard this kind of thing before V-Day."

The announcer continued:

In previous broadcasts, we have urged you to abandon the concepts of male and female. Indeed, it is your right and privilege to embrace whatever gender your inner spirit desires. We must not let the Enemy's morality dictate how we live. And know this: Those who still cling to such outdated concepts are suspect. They might well be Christians or Jews. So, if you observe a household that still follows this ancient model of human behavior or who are holding secret meetings in their home or who have children, it is your solemn duty to report them to the nearest CSA office. Waiting for anyone who turns in a Christian or Jew is a handsome—

Dylan switched off the radio and shook his head. "I've heard enough."

"Back before the vanishing," said Chelsea, "I heard the same sort of thing from every liberal organization to which I ever belonged."

"Man and woman," said Dylan, "are supposed to join, make a family, and be fruitful. The Unitum Imperium wants to destroy all that."

"The Antichrist's goal is complete moral chaos," added Pasqual from the back. "He cannot abide an institution ordained by God that's supposed to form the backbone of society."

A smile broadened Chelsea's face as she turned to Dylan. "If you believe as you do about the importance of family, why don't you start one with Margot? Then the two of you can be fruitful. You seem rather close."

From the seat behind them, Margot cleared her throat. "Interesting suggestion, Chelsea."

From the seat beside her, Dylan only smiled.

They drove until nine o'clock, four hours after leaving Milan, and Dylan parked in the La Spezia station lot. "We have to leave the van here," said Chelsea. "Take what you need as we can't come back."

Before they left, Pasqual checked that everyone's makeup was good enough to pass for someone with the sores. "This might be the most dangerous part of the trip," he said. "So far, the makeup seems to assure the officials that we have the mark."

"Security is lax in the Cinque Terra," added Chelsea. "We'll be all right."

Though it was late, the trains were still running. But as they boarded for the twenty-minute trip to Vernazza, her heart sped up. Would the trawler still be there? Or had Fabio returned for it?

The train wound through dark tunnels cut into rocky hillsides, stopping at Riomaggiore, Manarola, and Corniglia before they exited at Vernazza. Under a sickly half-moon, she led them down to the sheltered harbor, their roller bags bumping over the cobbles.

"I hope it's still there," she whispered to Dylan. "It's been a year and a half since I left. What if Fabio returned and took the ship?"

He shot her a worried look then raised his gaze to the tiny port and a trawler anchored beside small fishing boats. "Is that it?"

"Yes!"

They followed her onto the deck. Using her phone's flashlight, she went to a winch on the aft deck, lifted a hidden plate, and brought out a set of keys. "They're still here."

She opened the crew cabins, the engine room, and the pantry. Someone had cracked the glass on the wheelhouse door, but since nothing of value was visible inside, the thieves must have given up, deciding it wasn't worth the effort. Two of the four crew cabins had been broken into, but again, nothing was taken. Counting the cabin behind the wheelhouse, everyone would have their own bed.

But when she checked the galley, all the food had been stolen.

Just after ten thirty, Dylan gathered everyone in the galley. "Before we turn in," he said, "we should decide on a plan for tomorrow. Chelsea, how much diesel is in the tanks?"

"Only about a tenth of what we need."

"Naturally." He drew a hand through his hair. "So where can we get diesel fuel and food?"

"La Spezia is probably our best bet," she answered. "If we can find someone who will take cash, we can sail from there."

* * *

THE NEXT MORNING, DYLAN AND the others gathered in the wheelhouse as Chelsea punched in the remembered combination to unlock the motor. When the Mercedes-Benz 484 kilowatt diesel engine began throbbing belowdecks, they cheered and clapped.

Pasqual untied the moorings and pushed them away.

Chelsea maneuvered the ship out of the harbor. She revved the motor, and once at sea, the bow crashed through the waves.

After she gave Dylan and the others lessons on how to run the ship, she handed the controls to Pasqual. When he was comfortable at the helm, Dylan followed her from the pilothouse to the bow.

The ship hugged the rocky shores and cliffs of the Cinque Terra. As she grabbed the rail, lifted her head to the wind, and breathed deeply of the salt sea air, Dylan smiled.

"When I left this tug," she said, "I was so sick of it. But now I'm glad to be back at sea."

"You look like a real sailor. How long were you on this ship?"

"Over three years. But for most of that time, I was a prisoner."

Dylan's phone began playing Tchaikovsky's fourth symphony, and he pulled it out. "It's Caleb!" He answered the call to hear a voice he hadn't heard in six months.

"Where are you?" asked Caleb. "Last I heard you were stuck in Milan."

"We're on a ship at sea, heading for La Spezia where we hope to find fuel and food. After that, we'll be on our way to Israel. But I have some bad news. Our friend René passed away."

"Oh, I'm sorry."

"He fought the infection for months. But it was gangrenous, and he wouldn't let Dr. Delucci amputate. He was our leader, and we're going to miss him."

Silence filled the speaker until Dylan spoke again. "But Chelsea is here with me now."

"Chelsea! Can I talk with her?"

"I'll put it on speaker so we can all hear."

"Hey, brother." Chelsea was beaming. "It's so good to hear your voice."

"I heard about all you went through, Chelsea, and I'm so glad you're with Dylan now. But now I have good news for you both. We found the Sanctuary, but they moved, and you won't believe this, but . . ."

Then he explained how the military abandoned Cheyenne Mountain and how the Christian personnel separated and created their own hidden base in the mountains. Then he told them how two people had the same vision—that Caleb would come and lead them to a place of permanent safety called the Refuge.

"Seriously?" Chelsea raised a startled expression to Dylan. "They dreamed that *you* would lead them to the Refuge? Amazing!"

"Yeah, and two different people had the same dream."

"More than amazing," added Dylan. "God is leading us all in different ways, isn't he?"

"He is."

Dylan exchanged puzzled looks with his sister. "But how are you going to get to Israel from Colorado?"

"That's my next bit of news. The folks I'm with were once part of the US Space Force, and we found a hardened hangar at Peterson Space Force Base where—guess what we found?—a Convair B-36 Peacemaker!"

"What's that?" asked Chelsea.

"It's a bomber the Strategic Air Command once used in the Cold War. It's a prop plane—quite a relic—but it has a range of ten thousand miles, more than enough to get us to Israel."

Dylan caught Chelsea's amazed expression. "If it was a relic," he asked, "can it still fly?"

"We think so. We found a maintenance log that tells us they kept the plane airworthy. The hangar also has an inventory of B-36 parts. Apparently, they kept the plane as a last resort to ferry top brass or even the President's surviving staff from Cheyenne Mountain to a safe location either in the US or overseas. But either they changed their plans or something unexpected happened because they never used it."

"So it can fly?"

"Like I said, we think so. Our real problem is fuel. They must have had some warning here at Peterson because all but two planes were gone, and we found only a thousand gallons in the base fuel tanks. After some exploring, we found full tanks at the Air Force Base north of Colorado Springs. That's where we are now. But we have to veer far around the city to get here. And oh, did I mention that the Chinese nuked the city? So most of the equipment outside the hangar is radioactive, and we can't use it."

"So how are you getting fuel?"

"Every day, we take a circuitous route around the blast zone. In the hangar, they left us an airplane tug. And we found one cart at the Air Force Academy that's safe. But the carburetors and fuel lines in all the tug engines here at the Academy are hopelessly fouled, so we only have one tug. The process of bringing fuel back to the hangar is slow, laboriously slow. We can only make one trip per day. We load the cart with ten stainless-steel milk cans we found at a nearby dairy. The cart can't take more than that. Between hand pumping the fuel out of the air force tanks into the cans, driving back to the hangar, and then pumping the fuel into the plane—that takes all day. And that only gets us three hundred and eighty gallons. But we need thirty thousand gallons to fill the plane. And three or four times a week, we have to make side trips to bring back diesel fuel just to keep the tug running and the hangar lights and air filtration going. We've been at this since early November when we figured out this system."

"Why didn't you call sooner?"

"That's another problem. We only had a cell signal today. And that has us worried. We're guessing the CSA has put up a new base somewhere nearby with a cell tower. We just hope they don't come our way anytime soon."

"So when do you think you can leave?"

"Maybe in another few months. But there's another problem: The mechanics are trying to get one of the six Pratt and Whitney engines working. It sputters after a few minutes and doesn't sound good. At least, that's my technical analysis."

"So can you fly to Israel?"

"If we solve all these problems. So tell me: Where is this Refuge?"

Dylan waved to Chelsea.

"Caleb," she said. "I won't know the location until we get to Jerusalem. All I know is that there's a certain travel agency"—she gave him the street name and number—"and that directions to the Refuge are there, under a marked brick. We'll probably beat you to Jerusalem. Maybe you should call us after you land. Tell you what: When you get as far as a highway leading into the city, I will meet you and lead you past the checkpoints."

"Sounds good, but about the landing." He paused. "They wanted me to ask you where we should do that?"

Chelsea scowled. "You can't use any of the Unitum Imperium airports. The CSA would be all over you in minutes. Instead, you should try landing on a highway somewhere between Tel Aviv and Jerusalem."

"*On a highway?* Did I mention that this plane is huge? Well, I'll tell Daniel, our pilot, what you said and let him figure it out. Anyways, at least you know what we're doing, and now we have a plan of sorts."

They talked for a while longer until Caleb's group had finished filling the cans and was ready to leave. Then he hung up.

Dylan faced his sister. "Can you believe this? It never seemed possible, but we might be together again."

"For so many years," she said, "I thought Caleb was dead. Now there's hope we'll reunite."

"Still, there are a lot of obstacles standing in the way of a reunion."

"Not least of which is what happens after we arrive in Jerusalem. Davato and his goons control the city." She shivered. "Last time, I barely escaped."

CHAPTER 49
THE REVOLT

Jerusalem, Israel — April, Year 6

Fifty meters behind Amos Bernstein, the tank's engine roared, and its metal tracks clanked over asphalt. His heart racing, he ducked into the shadows of a storefront. Beside him ran the youthful Han. Both had been the bait to lure the mechanized monster into this lane where he and a dozen soldiers of the Jericho Faction hoped to kill it. Across the street where his companions hid, weaponry glinted in the shadows. Shifting the Uzi to his left hand, Amos raised the walkie-talkie to his mouth. With his right, he spoke to Sheba. "Is it below you yet?"

On the other end of the device, looking down on the target from her two-story window, Sheba was a spitfire of a woman dedicated to the UI's destruction. He could hear the eagerness in her reply. "It's right below me now. Should I do it?"

"Yes! And try to hit the air intake."

"Of course."

Amos waited a few seconds then stuck his head out. Fire had engulfed the rear of the Israeli Merkava tank, now part of the Unitum Imperium arsenal. As he watched, Sheba dropped a second glass bottle of gasoline mixed with soap, their homemade version of napalm, and it exploded in sticky flames.

The hatch opened. Out poured smoke, followed by the torso of a uniformed CSA soldier. Amos knelt, aimed his Uzi, and released a volley. Half in and half out, the man's corpse slumped against the top of the turret, hopefully blocking his companion inside.

Behind the tank, a squad of twelve soldiers in green-and-brown camouflage hunkered down, and Amos ducked back. The enemy soldiers were suffering from their sores, fighting well below their ability. He couldn't believe their good fortune.

He waved a signal to the shadowy recesses across the street that said to wait.

Seconds passed, and Sheba should have found a safer position. Any moment now, he expected Emanuel Horowitz, his sniper on the roof across the street, to give him the signal. Emanuel was ex-IDF, a crack shot, trained as a sniper in the Israeli army.

Waiting was the most difficult part. The CSA squad would now continue, warily and wincing with pain from their sores, down the street toward them. Amos and his soldiers couldn't show themselves until all the enemy were within range.

The walkie-talkie crackled with Emanuel's signal. "Now!"

Amos waved to the shadows opposite.

As one, seven men jumped into the street, knelt, and began firing their Uzis. With his IWI Dan sniper rifle on the roof, Emanuel also began picking off the enemy, one by one.

The CSA troops didn't know what hit them. Half were down before they could return a single shot. Three tried to hide behind the tank's flaming wreckage, but Emanuel's fire brought down two. Only one out of the twelve-member squad remained, and he turned and ran.

A beaming Amos shouted to the fighters beside him, "Time to retreat." He relayed the same message to Emanuel and Sheba.

Until their next mission, his attack squad would melt into the shadows and merge with civilians. In the last five engagements, he'd not lost a single man, and for that, he thanked not only his planning and leadership skills, but the God of Abraham, Isaac, and Jacob.

Amos and Han ran to the end of the street, hid their weapons beneath their jackets, then dropped to a walking pace. He hadn't known if he'd be able to make the meeting with Baruch Abramovich, but now it appeared he would. He pulled out his phone, typed a text to Baruch, and hit send.

He'd already had one conversation with the man, and now Baruch wanted a second.

But just as he had with the first meeting, he doubted another face-to-face would amount to anything.

"A great success, huh?" said Han beside him, and Amos nodded. Only twenty years old, Han had lived all his adult life in the Tribulation, as the Christian book called it.

Amos, like his companions, still clung to the Jewish faith, surviving because of a deep-seated hatred of Davato and the Unitum Imperium, helped by Rabbi Ehud Efron and Big Matza's black market. Whoever Big Matza was, Amos owed him a huge debt of gratitude.

For the last year, their travel and bogus ID cards had allowed Amos to go to Tel Aviv, Haifa, Ashdod, Be'er Sheva, and Jerusalem. There, he'd sought like-minded Jews, creating the Jericho Faction, his network of resistance cells.

The most difficult part of the last year had been the demon attacks. Amos had read the Christians' book of Revelation. Even after the flying monsters with mocking faces had tortured his people for five months, Amos held onto his faith. Some of his carefully selected men had converted, but many more were like him—lifelong Jews clinging to the religion they'd been born with, grown up with, and dedicated their lives to. But then, after the demons on horseback had killed a third of his followers, even more left the faith and converted.

Amos himself was on the verge of belief. But tradition, lifelong patterns of thought, and a deep, unfulfilled desire for revenge held him back.

Then, two months ago, the Christians' first bowl judgment inflicted debilitating sores upon the enemy, but not on the Jews, and his time had come. With one-third of the CSA dead and every enemy soldier suffering and in pain—but not Amos's people—the Jericho Faction emerged from the shadows.

In a little less than two months, they'd brought the CSA in Israel to its knees. Rumor had it that Davato would soon begin a grand counteroffensive, flying in more men to bolster his decimated troops. But for now, Amos and his followers had the upper hand, and they would make the most of it.

Around the corner in an alley, they found their two hidden motorcycles. They mounted and drove toward Amos's rendezvous with the man some were calling a Christian prophet.

* * *

BARUCH OPENED THE DOOR TO A short, black-bearded man bearing a stern, unforgiving expression. Beside him was a black-haired, beardless youth in his early twenties, tall and thin. No one ate well these days.

"Shalom, Amos Bernstein, and welcome!" He extended a hand. "I am so glad you could make it today." Amos introduced Han, but without a last name. Then Baruch bid them to take one of the four folding chairs he'd placed at the front of the room. But as the two passed, Baruch caught a whiff of sulfur. Had they just come from another battle with the CSA?

Today, they were meeting in one of the empty apartments Baruch often used as a temporary venue for his secret gatherings, and thirty folding chairs filled the room. David Benjamin offered their guests coffee, but they declined, and everyone took a seat.

Amos cleared his throat. "I am happy to meet with you, Baruch Abramovich, but it's no use. I am not ready to convert. I am first and foremost—and, for now, at least—still a Jew."

"As am I. But sitting before you is a Jew who has discovered new information that has convinced me this Jesus of Nazareth whom our ancestors rejected was the true Messiah."

"Maybe he was." Amos frowned. "But maybe I have things to do before I become one of your followers."

"It is not I whom you must follow, Amos, but the risen Christ. Last time, you told me you'd read the book of Revelation. How, after reading that, can you deny the reality of Christianity?"

"I don't deny it." Amos leaned forward in the chair and speared him with dark, intense eyes.

"I'll tell you a secret, Baruch, one I haven't shared with anyone, even with my men. But I'm guessing they probably think the same as I. Someday soon, I will become a Christian."

Beside him, Han gasped and shot him a startled expression.

Baruch sat back in his chair. This was unexpected. He realized now that his goal for this meeting was nigh onto impossible. "Then, pray tell, why wait?"

"Because I have things to do first. The time for revenge against the Unitum Imperium and Davato is now. If I convert to your faith, I must give up everything I need to do battle."

Baruch shook his head. "Your heart is not right, Amos Bernstein. But believe it or not, that's not why I asked you here today."

"If not to hear another plea to become a Christian, then why am I here?"

Baruch rubbed his temples and sighed. "I requested this meeting to ask you to hold back from further attacks. You know what the Torah says about hate and revenge. If you claim to be a Jew, you know that what you are doing is not right. Your attacks are only inflaming Davato's hatred of both Christians and Jews, making it even more difficult to rescue those who wish to escape his persecutions. God, not you, will wreak revenge upon the Antichrist and all those who follow the Adversary."

"You know I can't do that." Amos crossed his arms. "I will not give up the fight until the last CSA goon is lying dead at my feet. We are of two minds about this, and that's just the way it's going to be."

"That is unfortunate. I see your mind is made up, but I will not give up on you."

Amos Bernstein stood, and Han followed his lead. "I respect you, Baruch Abramovich," said Amos. "You are helping Christians and Jews in the way given to you. But I am helping the Jewish people in the way given to me—with Uzis, grenades, and rifles."

"Then I will pray for you. May God go with you both."

After they left, David unplugged the coffeepot, turned off the lights, and faced his friend. "We've done what we could to warn Amos Bernstein and his Jericho Faction. He is misguided. We can only pray Jesus will open his eyes and turn him from his path of hate, revenge, and murder."

"I agree."

Then David laid a hand on Baruch's shoulder. "I've said it before, and I'll say it again. We need to leave for Sela and abandon Israel before it's too late."

Baruch shook his head. "There are people who still need our help escaping the Antichrist's net. They're still looking for a way out. We can't let them down."

"But we are finding fewer of those folks each week. How long do you plan to stay here?"

"I don't know. But we have time yet."

David released his friend and shook his head. "I fear we are cutting it too close. When the fourth bowl judgment hits, we may be stuck here for months."

CHAPTER 50
THE SECOND BOWL JUDGMENT

Revelation 16:3 (HCSB): *The second [angel] poured out his bowl into the sea. It turned to blood like a dead man's, and all life in the sea died.*

Revelation 11:3, 6b (HCSB): *I will empower my two witnesses, and they will prophesy. . . . They also have power over the waters to turn them into blood.*

High above the Pacific – April, Year 6

The second angel had flown from the Temple of God in the heavenly realm. Spotless white linen, crossed with a gold sash, draped his body. His hands bore the second bowl of God's wrath, a judgment that would kill every living thing in the world's oceans.

High above the earth, he soared until he was over the Pacific. Down he flew. He hovered over the rolling swells and tipped his bowl, pouring out some of its contents. The sea churned and roiled, and where it emerged again from below, the water had turned to blood.

Traveling at sixteen and a half kilometers per hour, the toxic red tide spread out in a circle. And wherever it passed, the waters would bob with the corpses of bluefish, cod, flounder, halibut, krill, porpoises, tarpon, tuna, and whales—every living thing.

His first task completed, he flew higher then paused. With tears in his eyes, he looked back.

"Mourn for the denizens of the deep!" he cried. "Grieve for the last of the ocean creatures! Sing a lament for all that live beneath the briny waters! God's final judgments upon his creation has begun."

He wiped his eyes and flew higher, heading for the Indian Ocean. After that, he would visit the Arctic, the Antarctic, the Black Sea, the Caspian Sea, the Red Sea, the Aral Sea, and the Baltic Sea. Lastly, he would pour what remained of his bowl into the western Mediterranean. From there, the blood would spread until it reached the shores of the country occupied by the Antichrist.

As he flew, he wept for the fish and fauna under the briny deep—the undersea masterworks of God's hand. Then he wept for the people who had rebelled and rejected a God who wanted only to love them, to be their God, and for them to be his people. But their hearts were stubborn, proud, and disdainful. Given every opportunity to believe in and follow the Son of the Most High, they scoffed at the very mention of his name. They turned their backs on him. They engaged in grievous sins. And they followed the Adversary.

Now they must endure God's judgment against the planet itself.

But the end had been decreed from the beginning.

And the one who had molded the pot, fired it in the oven, and set it on the shelf had every right to lift it high and smash it to bits upon the stone.

* * *

Jerusalem, Israel

THE TWO WITNESSES HAD STOOD in Temple Square for thirty-nine months. They had prophesied, warned, and cajoled the people. But their time of prophesy was nearing an end.

The white-haired prophet, garbed in camel's hair, spread his feet and slammed his staff onto the cobbles. Much louder than usual, his voice echoed across the square. And everyone crossing before him stopped what they were doing, turned toward the old man, and listened. "The second judgment has come. The second bowl has been poured." His voice thundered and roared. "The earth itself now mourns and laments."

The gray-bearded prophet beside him also struck his staff. The sound reverberated off the Temple walls. And when he spoke, his voice was like a dark sky heavy-laden with clouds, warning of a thunderstorm. "The seas of the world are turning to blood. Every living thing in all the oceans will soon be dead. You are running out of time to avoid eternal judgment, you who follow the son of destruction, the man of lawlessness, the one called the beast."

The white-haired old man again struck his staff and spoke. "If you have not taken the mark of the beast, now is the time to repent."

The gray-bearded prophet's staff thundered onto the stone. "Turn from eternal death to eternal life. Believe in Jesus, Lord of Lords and King of Kings. Before it's too late."

Then the white-haired prophet added this: "Woe to you upon the earth, for the third judgment is coming!"

CHAPTER 51
THE BLOOD-RED SEA

In the Mediterranean – April, Year 6

It took a week to find enough fuel to top off the trawler's tank and buy enough food and water for the journey. With everyone taking a turn at the wheel, the new and surviving members of the Nazarene Friends—Chelsea, Dylan, Margot, and Pasqual—chugged out of La Spezia harbor and headed south along the Italian coast. Two days later, they passed through the Strait of Messina. But the instant they rounded the tip of Italy, they entered blood-red waters, and everyone gathered in the wheelhouse while Pasqual piloted.

"What's happening to the sea?" Margot gripped the top of her head. "Why is it so dark and red?"

"Whatever it is"—Pasqual waved through the window—"it's spreading east in front of us."

"And look!" Chelsea whirled to look back. "The waves back there are covered with dead fish."

"I know that smell." Dylan crinkled his nose. "It's blood! The sea is turning to blood."

"This is the second bowl judgment," said Pasqual. "The oceans are turning to blood."

Above them, large flocks of gulls flew east. But their cries were quick and shrill, reflecting alarm that something in the world was terribly amiss. Dylan wondered how long until they, too, would die. "But look!" He pointed east. "The waters there aren't affected."

Perhaps a hundred meters ahead, the spreading blood met the blue-green waters, and the sea foamed and churned. Dylan gripped the railing and sucked in the metallic smell of blood. "Can we outrun it?"

The instant he asked the question, the engine began to sputter. He shot a glance to the control panels, where Pasqual's alarmed glance was buried.

"The engine is struggling," he whispered. "It can't cool itself."

"Oh no." Margot covered her mouth with her hands. "What if we stall out here?"

"We're gaining on it." Pasqual's eyes were fixed on the dials in front of him. "But our speed is dropping."

"Can you give it more power?" asked Dylan. "We're almost at the boundary."

"I've given it all I can." Pasqual shrugged. "But the engine's overheating."

The normal, steady chugging of the engine now came intermittently, and Dylan strained to peer ahead. They were only meters from the border between normal water and blood. Just a bit more, and they'd be clear.

Minutes passed, and they inched closer to the border. The engine sputtered, slowed, then resumed its normal pace, and Dylan gripped the railing so hard his knuckles ached.

"I'm letting up on the power." Pasqual eased back on the throttle, and the engine recovered. But at the cost of slowing progress.

Perhaps half an hour after they'd sighted the boundary, the bow inched into the blue-green water. Just a few meters more.

Dylan left the wheelhouse, descended the ladder, and leaned over the side. Where the blood met the salt sea, the waters roiled and bubbled.

Long minutes passed as the ship crept across the writhing, seething boundary. What was taking so long?

The stern followed the bow and broke through into the blue-green sea, and the engine returned to its normal rhythmic pulsing. They pulled away from the blood-red sea.

Margot came up beside him, relief on her face. "We're free, but now we can't stop until we get to Israel."

"No." Dylan stared at another flock of screaming gulls heading east. "If we stopped, that would be the end of us."

CHAPTER 52
TROUBLE IN RAMALLAH

Ramallah, Israel – April, Year 6

Ariel passed the two black vans and kept going. "I don't like the looks of this. I'm going to go around the block."

Kishke, aka Noah Blum, slumped down in the seat as they neared the suspicious vehicles. "We're only a block away. The address is one street over. And we're late."

"Still, I'm going to circle. You can't take too many precautions." Ariel turned right at the end of the street, drove past the address where the two refugees were waiting, then cruised onto the next street over.

But another black van was parked along that street. Ariel shook his head and kept on. "Too many coincidences. Three black vans within a short distance of our destination."

At the end of the block, his phone rang. He grabbed it with one hand, answered, and pulled over.

"Big Matza, it's Falafel. I haven't heard from anyone in a while, and I–I was wondering—"

"Yes, Falafel. I know you're on your own, and I haven't forgotten about you." Ariel glanced up, checking the street ahead and behind them. All clear. "Right now, I'm in Ramallah with Kishke. After we pick up our last two refugees, we'll swing by Jerusalem."

"Great! I'm a bit worried. CSA troops are fighting the rebellion everywhere here. What if the UI sends in more troops? What if they blockade the city?"

247

Ariel paused. Was it getting *that* bad? "No one's talking about that yet. Just hold on. We'll be there this afternoon. Then you can take my place in the car and go with Kishke to the Refuge."

"I don't know where it is. No one's ever told me."

"I'm sorry about that, but it doesn't matter. We'll be there later, and Kishke will drive you in my stead. I'm planning to stay in Jerusalem for a bit in case anyone shows up at the travel agency."

"The travel agency? It's nothing but rubble now."

Ariel frowned. "In that case, go there now and leave a note for anyone who might show up. Put it on a marked brick in plain sight. Tell them to check back every night at twenty-two hundred hours. Watch from a distance at that time but be wary. If whoever shows up looks okay, take them to the safe house and wait for us."

"I'll do that."

"Good. We'll be there later to relieve you. Whatever happens, don't leave until I come."

"Thanks. I was getting worried."

When he hung up, Kishke turned a worried face toward him. "That doesn't sound good."

"No. We have to pick up this new man, Falafel. Tonight, we can all stay in the safe house. Tomorrow morning, you can take him to the Refuge with the refugees."

"You're crazy to stay behind. What do you think you'll accomplish?"

"I just have this weird feeling we have more people to rescue."

Kishke shook his head, and Ariel pulled away.

"It's getting late. We're going to risk it." He turned the corner onto the rendezvous street. "I've never seen vans parked so far from a target. It's probably all right."

"Good. Let's get this over with."

Ariel parked, and they approached the ground-floor apartment of the last couple needing a ride out of the country. He knocked on the door and waited. Receiving no answer, he knocked again.

An elderly man with a stubbled beard answered. "W–we've been expecting you. Come in." The man waved a shaking hand and bid the visitors to enter. But his eyes darted from side to side, and a warning bell rang inside Ariel's head. Before entering, he peered into the dark room. Only the old man and his wife.

With one hand on the Glock 17 at his hip, he entered. Kishke was right behind him.

"We must leave quickly. Get your bags and—"

Three men in green-and-white uniforms, pistols out, burst from four corners of the room. Another came from behind the door. The scars of boils marred every face.

Ariel whirled back to the entrance, but another four men were racing around the sides of the building, and four others had already crossed the street to his car.

"Hands up!" shouted someone behind him. "Or we'll shoot."

Back in the room, they'd already taken Kishke's weapon. And they were putting cuffs on the elderly couple.

"It's over, Big Matza." The short, balding captain held a pistol in one hand and a cane in the other. "Get your hands off that piece on your hip."

Ariel began to comply when someone from behind removed his weapon, yanked his hands behind his back, and cuffed him.

As twelve CSA agents converged on the room, a middle-aged woman with a tight bun appeared in the doorway. She regarded the elderly couple, and a grin split a face marred with boils. "I knew something was wrong here. After you two weren't affected by the sores, I slipped a bug in your apartment. They give them out for free, you know. Then I heard you praying out loud and reading the Enemy's book to each other. And when I learned about today's rendezvous with these two traitors, I made sure the CSA was here to welcome them."

"I would ask the Lord to forgive you, Emma," said the elderly woman. "But for anyone who's taken the mark, there is no forgiveness, is there?"

One of the soldiers slapped her cheek so hard, she staggered back.

"I wouldn't pay a single euro for the Enemy's forgiveness." Smiling at the soldier's rebuke of her neighbor, the quisling named Emma whirled toward the captain. "When can I receive my reward?"

"Take this receipt." The balding captain handed her a piece of paper. "After we secure these prisoners, someone will contact you with payment. Meanwhile, the Unitum Imperium gives you its undying thanks."

Before the agents shoved Ariel, Noah, and the elderly couple into the rear of a black van, Ariel faced the CSA leader. "Where are you taking us?"

"Jerusalem. Mish'ol HaGvura Prison."

A shudder rippled down his back. After the Unitum Imperium came to power, they refurbished and resurrected the prison where they once kept Jewish rebels protesting British rule. With triple-fenced walls, guard dogs, and electronic surveillance, it was reputedly impossible to break out of.

And the guards had a reputation for being the worst of the worst.

* * *

CAPTAIN DARIO LOMBARDO OF THE Central Security Agency was able to shove aside the pain from the ever-present sores long enough to break into a wide smile. His men had just locked his personal conquest behind iron walls and an iron door. For years, Ariel Geller, aka Big Matza, had mocked and flouted the CSA at every turn. To find and capture the elusive rebel and his accomplices, the CSA created special units like Dario's. Of all those assigned to capture Big Matza himself, Dario Lombardo and his men had accomplished what no other unit had ever done.

To cover his region, CSA HQ had stationed Dario at Mish'ol HaGvura Prison, and when the tip arrived from Ramallah dropping the name of Big Matza, Dario had rushed his men north. He pushed aside the local CSA unit—four inexperienced, incompetent agents—and took charge.

Now, after years of attempts by the entirety of the Israeli CSA, Dario had imprisoned Ariel Geller. He anticipated a big reward and possible promotion. His joy was only marred by the boils afflicting his rear, his arms, his legs, and the sole of one foot.

Limping back to his office—a bullet wound from one of the rebels last year—he picked up his cell phone. He punched the numbers for the man at the top—Adam Turner, the Minister of Truth, below which was the CSA, the Truth Squads, and a legion of enforcement and administrative staff. As the minister himself answered, sweat formed on Dario's forehead.

* * *

WHEN ADAM'S PHONE RANG, HE was sitting in his custom-built ergonomic chair in his upper-floor office of New Babylon's World Casino. As usual these days, he'd been drinking heavily, and he was in a foul mood. Only drink dulled the pain from the nagging, pestering sores that had burst out in a dozen places all over his body. It wasn't quite as bad as the attacks of the mocking demon creatures, but it came close. What was especially annoying about the call was that his aide had just set before him a specially-prepared supper—American hamburgers, french fries, and beer. Every once in a while, Adam pined for the food he'd had back home in Minnesota before rising to the precipice of world power. "Yes, what is it?"

"Minister Turner?"

"Yes, yes, what do you want?"

"This is Captain Dario Lombardo from the Mish'ol HaGvura Prison in Jerusalem."

Adam took a deep breath. Was this yet another squabble from these backwater Israeli hicks that the local CSA HQ couldn't resolve? What was wrong with these people? Couldn't they make the simplest of decisions on their own? "This had better be good, Captain Lombardo. Get to the point."

"I was told to call you personally if we ever captured Big Matza. Well, we just did."

The news took time to filter past the half liter of whiskey he'd consumed.

Then slowly, oh so slowly, a smile spread across his face. They'd been after Big Matza for years. He was a high-level target, one of the biggest thorns in the CSA's side, especially after the demons had killed so many agents. But caution returned, and Adam said, "Are you sure about this, Captain? We've had false alarms before."

"I'm absolutely certain."

"If true, you will be amply rewarded. Hold the prisoner under maximum guard. I will be on a plane to come there in person to oversee his interrogation." He glanced at his watch. "Tomorrow. I'll be there tomorrow."

"Very good, sir, I mean, Minister."

Adam hung up, sat back in his chair, and beamed. But the movement sent a needle of pain jolting up from his buttocks, and he reached for the half-empty bottle on the desk. He took one—no, two—deep swallows.

Then he leaned forward and bit into the American burger. After his flight to Israel, he would personally oversee this interrogation. If Ariel Geller's capture, interrogation, and torture was all the revenge he could wreak upon the Enemy—well, he'd take whatever he could get.

CHAPTER 53
RETURN TO JERUSALEM

In the Mediterranean near Tel Aviv, Israel – May, Year 6

The engine room was hot and stifling, and Chelsea scrunched her face at the clinking, clanking sounds coming from the motor. For the last twenty-four hours, the trawler's speed had been dropping, and now, the engine might quit.

"Do any of you have any mechanical expertise?" Margot stepped off the ladder to join Chelsea and Dylan in the cramped space, but both shook their heads.

"How far to Tel Aviv?" Dylan drew a hand through his hair and faced her.

"Pasqual said about fifteen kilometers." Margot frowned and brought hands to her ears. "We should see the coastline within the hour."

Chelsea was about to utter some words of hope that they'd make it when Pasqual shouted down the open hatch. "Everyone, come up on deck!"

They climbed the ladder and followed him aft where he pointed to the sea behind them. "It's gaining on us."

Indeed, the trawler had slowed so much and for so long that the blood-red waters were closing in on the ship. Chelsea shot a glance to the east, but she couldn't see the coast. Maybe it was visible from the wheelhouse? She climbed the ladder after Pasqual, returning to pilot the ship.

"I'm giving it everything it's got." He wiped sweat from his brow. "But we're still losing speed."

A thin band of black—a shoreline?—rose on the horizon, and she squinted. "How long until we reach the harbor?"

"At this rate, two hours. But look at the temperature gauge. I'm cutting back on the power."

As Pasqual pulled back on the throttle, the temperature dial on the control panel hovered inside the red mark. When it climbed even higher, he cut the power further. For long minutes, the needle wavered in the danger zone, and Chelsea held her breath. Then it inched back into the green.

She whirled to face aft. From the pilothouse, the western sea appeared as a swath of deep purple, and it shook her. This was so abnormal, so "not right", that she crossed her arms about her chest and shivered.

"What's wrong?" he asked.

"It's the sea. That's what's wrong. I'm going back down."

While Pasqual stayed behind the wheel, she joined Margot and Dylan on the aft deck. As the blood crept closer, they stood watch. With each meter the red tide gained, she prayed that the engine would work long enough to bring them into port.

Then the crimson waters swarmed the propellers, edged along the port and starboard hull, engulfed the bow, and crawled west before them.

The engine worked harder now. The clinking, clanking noises increased. And the ship slowed even more.

Dylan caught Chelsea's gaze and shook his head. "All we can do is wait and hope. But we don't have far to go."

Now she could make out houses on the Israeli shoreline.

Hours later, they were within five kilometers of their goal.

Time itself slowed as the engine groaned and complained. Metal parts clanged and banged. And the ship slogged through the blood-red sea. The bloody tide now covered every meter of sea—north, south, east, and west. Its metallic odor overwhelmed the ever-present smell of fish, salt sea, and diesel exhaust. Rising everywhere to the surface now came the white corpses of krill, mackerel, octopi, porpoises, and tuna.

254

The jaundiced orb of the sun sank below the horizon, and Chelsea remained on deck in twilight, pacing, staring, waiting. The sickly-pale imitation of the moon rose into a star-starved sky.

Were they moving at all? After so many hours listening to a struggling, complaining engine, was the coastline any closer? She paced. She exchanged worried glances with Dylan and Margot.

The night descended into pitch darkness, and she waited.

Then the ashen light of dawn illuminated the Tel Aviv docks only a few hundred meters away. The engines had been working all along!

It was seven o'clock in the morning when the pier loomed close enough to hit with a stone, and Dylan called down from the pilothouse. "Prepare to leave and put on your makeup."

She breathed out a breath she didn't remember holding and ran to her cabin. Earlier, they'd shoved everything they needed for an overland journey into their backpacks, and hers was ready.

Before the mirror, she dotted her face, arms, and hands with red paint so no one would suspect she didn't have the mark. As she joined the others on deck, Pasqual eased the ship into a slot beside the quay, and everyone cheered. Pasqual gathered his gear and put on makeup, and Dylan and Margot tied the ship to pilings.

They stepped onto the concrete jetty. Dylan opened his hands in a question, and everyone faced her. "You know this country better than anyone, Chelsea. The harbormaster will surely come and ask how we got here, demanding our IDs and travel passes, so we need to leave now. How do we get to Jerusalem?"

Stunned that everyone was now relying on her, she closed her gaping mouth and glanced from Dylan, to Margot, to Pasqual.

They were thirty-three miles from Jerusalem, and that was good. But they didn't have travel passes for Israel, and if they took a bus or a train, they would surely be discovered. On foot, they had Victor's IDs, and those might work if they were stopped. But everyone was carrying backpacks—not good for claiming they were locals. She knew the back alleys and parks and how to get through the city. But the real problem was that, because of the rebellion, the Unitum Imperium was putting up checkpoints on every city outskirt. It would be the same in Jerusalem. They'd heard that on the radio.

She placed hands on hips. "I can lead you to the edge of Tel Aviv on foot. We can walk around the checkpoints. Once outside the city, we can find an abandoned car. Hopefully, we won't encounter a checkpoint on the highway. Before we enter Jerusalem, we'll abandon the vehicle and enter the city on foot, again bypassing the checkpoint."

For a moment, her traveling companions only stared at her. Then Dylan broke the silence. "Good plan, Chelsea. Let's go!"

Thus, did she lead them into the back ways of Tel Aviv. Somehow, they'd make it to Jerusalem, the city she'd last fled in fear of her life. But that was years ago. It was fortunate that with all the deaths among their ranks, the CSA had never got their face-recognition system up and running.

But would anyone still remember the face of the woman who once stood beside Davato on every television appearance—the traitor who was once the most wanted woman in the land?

Saying a silent prayer, she swallowed and led them on familiar pathways she hoped never to have walked again.

CHAPTER 54
MISH'OL HAGVURA PRISON

Jerusalem, Israel – May, Year 6

When Adam Turner's jet landed at the Tel Aviv airport, it was after nine in the morning, and he expected the usual limousine and motorcycle escort. The motorcycles were there, but what substituted for a limousine was an armored car and two armored troop carriers. That alone shook his confidence in the Israeli situation. And when they entered Jerusalem, they waited an hour while CSA troops battled Jewish rebels on the street ahead. How things had deteriorated since his last visit!

After the guards admitted the armored car into the prison courtyard, Adam had to open his own door—no chauffeur on this trip. Then a short, balding man with a limp and a cane rushed forward with an outstretched hand. "I am so happy you came, Minister."

Suppressing a frown, Adam glanced at the sweaty, welcoming fingers. Hesitating, he took them. "If this man is who you say it is, you have done well, Lieutenant Lombardy."

"Excuse, Minister, but it's Captain Lombardo."

"Of course, Lombardo. Is your interrogator here? Get him, get some muscle, and get me to the prisoner."

"You want to begin now?"

"Yes."

The captain motioned to the side where stood a burly, six-foot muscleman and a short, middle-aged man with wire-rim glasses. "This is Ernst Bauer." Lombardo pointed to the shorter man. "He is German, but he has been living in Israel for the last ten years. He is good at his work."

257

Adam nodded and let Lombardo lead them through a series of key-card-protected gates, down dark hallways, then to an interior cell with the number six. "Bring out the prisoner," he ordered.

Captain Lombardo removed a set of keys from his pocket and shoved one into the lock. Pausing, he turned to his guest. "This was an old prison that we repurposed. Otherwise, we'd have installed modern electronic locks on every cell."

Adam waved him on, the captain turned the key, and the door creaked open.

The man the entire CSA in Israel had sought for so long turned a rough-hewn face Adam's way and grinned. "And I suppose you are the head of the Ministry of Truth they promised me?"

Scowling, Adam waved to his two companions who entered, took the prisoner by the arms, handcuffed him behind his back, and hustled him out. Lombardo led, Adam followed, and the muscleman and the interrogator brought up the rear with the prisoner. The procession wended its way to a basement room without windows where Bauer sat the prisoner on a metal chair. Then he snapped ankle chains to Geller's ankles and to the chair legs.

Adam faced the prisoner. He hadn't done much interrogation, but Davato had ordered him to oversee this affair personally. After pacing once around a grinning Geller, Adam stopped to face him. "Tell us where you've taken all your refugees, Ariel Geller, Big Matza, or whatever you call yourself, and you'll spare yourself a lot of pain."

Geller continued grinning. "Never!"

Adam rolled his eyes and waved to Ernst Bauer who walked behind the man. With the burly guard's help, he lifted both chair and prisoner and turned him 180 degrees to face a tub of water, sunken into the floor.

"I find the oldest, simplest techniques are often the best." Then, with the muscleman's help, Bauer grabbed his prisoner, ripped him off the chair, and forced him onto his knees. In one quick motion, the two men dunked the prisoner's head under the water.

Bauer held it there for perhaps twenty seconds. Then they lifted him out.

Geller emerged, dripping and soaked.

"You will tell us where you have been taking the refugees." Bauer's manner was calm, cold, and professional—as if he'd done this a hundred times. "We can do this all day, Geller. Everyone breaks. It's only a matter of time. Save us the trouble. Save yourself from what we are about to do. Where are they hiding?"

Ariel lifted his gaze to Bauer, to Lombardo, and to Adam, and that annoying grin returned. "No."

Bauer jerked the head down toward the tub, and Adam heard a short intake of breath.

Geller went under, this time for thirty seconds. When Geller began struggling, Bauer pulled his prisoner back out.

Sputtering and coughing, Geller shook his head side to side, spraying his interrogators with water. Much to Adam's annoyance, the grin returned.

"Where are the refugees?" asked Bauer.

"I won't tell you that." Geller spat to the side. "But I will tell you something else."

Adam nodded. If they got one piece of information at a time out of this man, maybe the interrogation was working.

"What is that?" Bauer sneered.

"All of you have taken the mark of the beast—you, Dario, Adam, Ernst, and you, whatever your name is." He nodded toward the muscleman. "I don't know if it's possible, but I will pray for you. I will pray that, on your journey through an eternity in the lake of fire, God will grant you mercy."

His response seemed to have caught everyone by surprise—even Bauer, whose face registered shock. For long moments, the only sounds came from water dripping off Geller's clothes.

For Adam, Geller's statement resurrected the pronouncements from the three demons, the ones the Christians called angels, who'd flown over New Babylon so long ago. He shuddered. Twice recently, the demons' words had returned to haunt him. Why, he didn't know. He'd tried to shove that incident to the furthest recesses of his mind and forget he'd ever seen or heard them. Still, their words, like some familiar song rising up unbidden in his head, had returned to plague him.

"The smoke of their torment will rise forever and ever . . ." Forever and ever. That's what they'd said. His shaking began again. ". . . and they will have no relief day or night, for they have worshiped the beast and his statue and have accepted the mark of his name."

Just as before, it left him shaking and filled with doubt. Did an eternity of fire await everyone with the mark? Would the Enemy prevail over Davato, the Prophet, and the Dragon? He'd had doubts about Davato's divinity and power. The events of the last year had surely done that. He shuddered.

Captain Lombardo broke the spell by announcing he had duties to attend to and must leave. "Call me if you have a need."

Adam waved, and the captain departed.

His jaw tensing, Bauer jerked his prisoner's head back under. This time, he held the man under for well over thirty seconds, and when he pulled his prisoner out of the water, Geller coughed and wretched.

"Now what is your answer?" Bauer's calm, professional manner was shattered. He was clenching his jaw and speaking through clenched teeth. "And I don't want to see another grin."

"My answer, Ernst?" Geller breathed in deeply, coughed, and spat water. "Here is my answer: *Never!*" Then he grinned.

Again, Bauer dunked the man's head under.

Time passed as Bauer dunked, Geller grinned, and Adam waited.

Once, as Bauer and his burly assistant paused to rest, Adam asked a question of the German. "Have you ever drowned a prisoner during these interrogations?"

Adam's question brought a fleeting smile to Bauer's lips. "Unfortunately, it has happened. Twice. The trick is to take them up to the point of drowning and then bring them back before they take in too much water. Otherwise, if the prisoner drowns, one doesn't get the answer one desires, does one?"

Marveling at the coldness of the answer, Adam nodded, and the dunking continued.

After three hours of this, when both interrogators and prisoner were soaked, shivering, and exhausted, Bauer ended the session in apparent defeat. They returned Geller to his cell, and Adam found quarters in a nearby upscale hotel.

For the next three days, they continued the interrogation without success. Then he decided to leave Geller in his cell and work on the accomplice, a man named Noah Blum.

But after only two hours of Bauer's ministrations, Blum cracked.

Inwardly rejoicing, Adam took the answer he'd received to Ariel Geller.

* * *

WHEN ARIEL HEARD A KEY CLANKING in his cell door lock, he steeled himself for another round of water torture. This time, he hoped they would simply drown him and get it over with. He would never tell them the location of Baruch's Refuge where tens of thousands of refugees were hiding.

He was expecting the German to enter, but the one opening the door was Adam Turner, the Minister of Truth. Two guards with machine guns stood in the hall beyond. But why was Turner smiling?

"Well, well, Big Matza, it appears you underwent all that pain for nothing because now we know where your Jews and Christians are hiding."

A shiver rippled down Ariel's back. Yet, it could be a trick. "I don't believe you."

"But your smug little grin is gone, isn't it? And that tells me you do believe me. When we started working on your accomplice, Noah Blum, he broke rather quickly. He spilled his guts."

To that, Ariel had no reply. Had Noah really broken? Knowing the consequences, could Noah give up all those people to the Unitum Imperium? "I won't believe you until you tell me where they are."

"They're in the Refuge, in a place called Sela. I've already forwarded the information to the Imperator."

Ariel sucked in breath, and he closed his eyes. Everyone was different, and some people didn't have the fortitude, the stamina, or the inner strength to withstand the kind of suffering Ernst Bauer administered. But then he remembered something Baruch had told him.

He opened his eyes and faced this man who had ordered the capture, imprisonment, and execution of so many, and his grin returned. "Knowing the location of the Refuge won't do you any good, you know."

"And why is that?"

"Because even if you know its location and you approach it, God will hide it. And even if God chooses not to hide it, he will protect everyone there. Your fate, Adam Turner, and the fate of everyone working for the Antichrist is sealed. It's inevitable. There will be only one victor in this struggle, and it is the Son whom God sent into the world, the one whose name is Jesus."

For a moment, Ariel's answer left his visitor speechless. Then Turner narrowed his eyes and straightened to his full height. "We'll see who wins this battle, Geller. You seem to forget you are the one in prison and I am the one holding the key to your life. Or your death."

Then Turner spun on his heels and left.

CHAPTER 55
THE TRAVEL AGENCY

Revelation 12:1–2 (HCSB): *A great sign appeared in heaven: a woman clothed with the sun, with the moon under her feet and a crown of 12 stars on her head. She was pregnant and cried out in labor and agony as she was about to give birth.*

Jerusalem, Israel – May, Year 6

When the white houses of Jerusalem topped the ridge on the valley's opposite side, Chelsea asked Dylan to stop their stolen VW. Tires crunched over gravel as the car parked on the side of Highway 1 near Harei Yehuda.

The only scare they'd had on the trip from Tel Aviv was when flashing lights appeared in the rearview mirror, and Dylan pulled over. "Let's hope they pass us," he'd said. "But just in case, have your weapons ready."

Then Margot added, "That's something René would have said."

With a wildly beating heart, Chelsea had gripped the Ruger LCP Max at her belt and prayed they wouldn't be stopped. Moments later, her prayers were answered when the procession rushed past. With sirens blaring, two motorcycles led an armored troop carrier, followed by an armored car, followed by a second troop carrier.

But what shook her was the flag fluttering from the armored car in the center. It bore the pen and pistol on a green-and-white background, the symbol of the head of the Ministry of Truth. Was her father, Adam Turner, inside that vehicle, heading into the city? She shuddered.

Although it had been hours ago, she was still shaking from the episode.

Now they left the car and trekked down into a valley, then up through a dry pine forest to the city's outskirts. After they'd had so little exercise on the ship, the hike through brush and over stone walls left her sweating and puffing. As expected, there were no checkpoints on the side streets. But inside the city, the familiar lanes that should have led to the travel agency had changed for the worse.

Earthquakes had shaken many buildings into rubble, and some streets were still clogged with debris. Twice, bands of Jewish rebels blocked the intersections. At first, the armed men behind the barricades were suspicious of the group. But when they discovered the travelers bore no marks, they let them pass. Somewhere in the distance, a gun battle raged, and even here, in Davato's second city, anarchy reigned.

Though it was midmorning, no one was about as she led them into the Christian quarter of the Old City. The Church of the Holy Sepulcher still stood, but its dome had fallen in.

After twice missing the turn, she guided them down the cobbled lane belonging to the travel agency. Halfway from the corner, only a few structures were still intact. She stopped, confused. Many buildings were nothing but tumbled piles of stone, and nothing was familiar. Where was the travel agency?

She walked back and forth along the lane's eastern edge, searching the rubble.

Part of a cracked wooden sign appeared under a pile of bricks. There—a picture beneath the dust. Was it a woman? Kneeling, she cleared away rocks and debris.

Yes! The sign of a pregnant woman wrapped in a bright garment with a crown of twelve stars on her head and the moon at her feet.

Her heart beating faster, she picked her way past the jumbled stones at the entrance. Not a wall was standing, and her quest seemed hopeless. But someone had been here recently because, four meters from the entrance, one brick stood out among all others.

Would this show the way to the Refuge? She was now a Christian, and she should be able to read whatever it said. Reaching down, she picked it up.

White string tied a piece of leather around the brick. Her hands shaking, she undid the tie and removed the parchment. On the underside, something was written in black ink. She read:

This is for all whose hearts belong to the one above, looking for a way out. Return here each night at twenty-two hundred hours and wait. The password is what King David wrote in the first chapter, the sixth verse, of the Bible's longest book.

She stared at the words and tried to swallow her disappointment. She expected directions, not some cryptic request for a rendezvous. Did Baruch write this? If not, then who? What if it was a trap?

"What did you find?" Dylan and the others came up beside her.

"This." She handed him the parchment, and he read.

"It isn't what you were hoping for, is it?" He raised a worried glance.

"No. Let's search for the brick with directions. Maybe it's still here." She pointed. "It should be over where the north wall used to be."

Pasqual read the note then joined them as they poked through the debris. For half an hour, they searched but found nothing.

"Someone must have taken it." She gripped the top of her head with both hands. "Or else it's buried so deep we'll never find it."

Pasqual returned to the note. "Whoever wrote this is pointing to Psalm one, verse six. But even a CSA agent could have come up with it."

Dylan took the parchment again and cocked his head. "It could be a trap."

"But what can we do?" She drew a hand through her hair. "This is our only link to someone who can lead us to the Refuge."

"We'll return tonight." He pointed toward the end of the block. "We can hole up in that building down the street. It looks abandoned, and it still has walls."

She nodded. She'd done what she could. Now they'd have to wait until tonight.

* * *

CHELSEA SPENT THE DAY TAKING naps inside what must have been a pastry shop, one of the few buildings still standing. But looters had long ago taken everything of value, and the ground-floor structure was now a home for rats that Margot and Dylan kept shooing away. They took turns standing watch, and when, in midafternoon, a CSA patrol wandered down the street, Dylan hurried everyone into the shadows in back.

The squaddies entered the building, shone their lights in the dark, heard rats, then moved on.

Fifteen minutes before twenty-two hundred hours, the moon shed a chalky glow onto the bricks, and they followed Dylan's plan for the rendezvous. Chelsea and Pasqual would wait in the travel agency ruins for whoever might show up. Margot and Dylan would hide in the ruins next door with guns ready. "I'll be able to hear what you say," said Dylan. "If things go south, I'll be René and back you up."

She sat on bricks beside Pasqual, occasionally checking her watch. At twenty-two hundred hours, she scanned the street. "Look! Someone is coming."

He followed her gaze, and the two stood up. A man approached, and Chelsea whispered, "It's not Baruch. I don't know him."

Beside her, Pasqual dropped a hand to his pistol.

Whoever it was, the man approached warily. He stopped on the street, checked both ways, then peered into the ruins. One hand went to his hip where he, too, carried a pistol. "What is the password?"

She swallowed and said what she'd memorized this afternoon. "The Lord watches over the path of the godly, but the path of the wicked leads to destruction."

"That's right." The man took a few steps closer. "Who told you about this place?"

"Baruch Abramovich."

"Yes, yes." He took his hand off the gun. Smiling, he approached them with an outstretched hand. "My name is Falafel, and—"

"Falafel!" She clapped. "Let me guess. You work for Ariel—I mean Big Matza!"

"Yes, yes. I wasn't sure who you might be, but . . . if you know Big Matza's real name, then you must have known him well."

"I did. He rescued me several years ago, and now I and my friends need passage to the Refuge." She turned to the ruins beside them. "It's all right. Come out."

Dylan and Margot left their hiding place in the dark and joined them.

"All four of you need passage?" Falafel glanced over the group and placed hands on top of his head.

"Is that a problem?" asked Chelsea.

"No, it's just that . . . I didn't know what to expect. Ariel hasn't contacted me in days, and he doesn't answer his phone. He was on his way here to relieve me and take me to the Refuge—I'm rather new at this and don't know the way. He was supposed to meet me here only hours after we talked, but he never showed up. I fear something has happened to him."

"You don't know the way to the Refuge?" asked Dylan.

"I'm sorry, but no, I don't."

After Chelsea introduced everyone, Falafel told them he was dropping his code name. "We're among friends here. My real name is Menachem."

"Glad to meet you, Menachem," she said.

He shot a glance up and down the street. "We should leave. They sometimes patrol here. But first, I need to show you something." He took them to the street and pointed to a hammer painted on a brick. Then he explained how that sign identified this location as a safe house for this month. "We used to change the sign at the first of every month and rotate it among two others so that only one-third of the signs point to a valid location. If any UI goon suspects it means something, he'll only be right one-third of the time. Now follow me."

Following a circuitous route, he led them many blocks away to the ruins of a house with only its back wall still standing.

"How can we live in *this*?" asked Margot.

"It's the perfect cover. You'll see. Follow me." Then he descended stairs. At the bottom, he opened a door into a carpeted basement room lined with pillows and intact walls. Overhead ceiling lights were on. "I'm glad to have company. I've been here all alone in Jerusalem."

"All alone?" she asked. "Isn't anyone in Ariel's organization still around?"

"Maybe a few in isolated safe houses who haven't left. But I haven't found anyone yet."

Now Dylan joined the conversation. "We appreciate what you've done for us in bringing us here, Menachem, but we have traveled far for one purpose. You said you don't know the way to the Refuge. Do you have any idea how to find it?"

He closed his eyes and shook his head.

"Then what do we do now?" Dylan exchanged glances with Chelsea, Pasqual, and Margot before his gaze settled on their host.

"Without Ariel or someone who knows how to get there"—Menachem shrugged—"all we can do is hunker down and wait."

"Wait for what?" Dylan grimaced.

"For Ariel to return. He said he would." As he glanced about the room, Menachem's brows wrinkled. "What else can we do?"

CHAPTER 56
THE THIRD BOWL JUDGMENT

Revelation 16:4–7 (HCSB): *The third [angel] poured out his bowl into the rivers and the springs of water, and they became blood. I heard the angel of the waters say: You are righteous, who is and who was, the Holy One, for You have decided these things. Because they poured out the blood of the saints and the prophets, You also gave them blood to drink; they deserve it! Then I heard someone from the altar say: Yes, Lord God, the Almighty, true and righteous are Your judgments.*

New Babylon, Iraq – July, Year 6

In the basement of the World Casino, a miserable Grady Wilson, barely able to see for the sweat dripping into his eyes, threw another clump of desert brush into a crackling fire beneath a massive boiler. Elsewhere in the room, dozens of others worked to bring in fuel from the trucks outside, to feed the fires, fill the jugs and bottles, and carry out the pallets of the finished product. For two hours today, as it would be for two days a week hence, he manned the distilling operation that would provide potable water for everyone in his city district.

The distilleries belonged to PetroSol, owned by Sam Wainwright, one of the world's richest men, and only his vast network of utilities could do what Davato had ordered. Two weeks ago, after the Two Witnesses had declared the next plague upon the world, Grady had been assigned this odious task. Even his status as a member of Davato's staff couldn't keep him from this token duty—Davato had insisted on that.

Too many people were drinking blood and getting sick.

Whenever he looked back on that day two weeks ago when it all started, his own blood boiled as hot as what bubbled in the tanks before him. And he vowed that if he ever saw another Jew or Christian—well, his Ruger Max 9 held twelve rounds, didn't it?

When they'd heard the news about the plague, he'd been sitting beside Davato in a World Casino conference room. Likely realizing that the sores weren't going away and that his long absences were causing dissension and loss of control, the Imperator had finally emerged from hiding.

An aide had run in, and the television broadcast of the Two Witnesses in Temple Square interrupted a meeting on liquor production. Even before the broadcast, Davato was snapping at people, shifting uncomfortably in his seat, probably vexed, like everyone else, with boils on his legs and rear.

"The third angel has poured his bowl." The white-haired ancient's words thundered through the set as his staff struck the cobbles. "And the rivers and streams will turn to blood."

"The third judgment has come," shouted the gray-bearded prophet, "and now you who have shed the blood of the righteous will have to drink blood."

At the table's head, Davato's face had tensed with rage, and when the cowering aide shut off the set, Grady feared the Imperator might strike out at someone in the room.

Barely had the set gone blank when the calls came in. Both the Tigris and Euphrates Rivers had turned to blood. Since two years ago in May, New Babylon had been hauling all their water from the Tigris, for the Euphrates was poisoned. Now both rivers were fouled.

His face turning purple, his eyes as black as ink, Davato pounded the table with a fist. "The Enemy and all his people will pay for this. Wherever they are, we will root them out and destroy them. Especially the Jews with their troublesome rebellion."

Then the Imperator had ended the meeting, and the staff had fled to their rooms. No one wanted to be within range of Davato when he fell into one of his increasingly frequent rages.

That was two weeks ago. Now, everywhere across the globe, PetroSol manufacturing plants were turning out giant stainless-steel tanks and kilometers of piping for the distillation of blood. Now every citizen of the Unitum Imperium was assigned a time to bring fuel, feed the fires, man the boilers, fill the plastic jugs and bottles, and distribute the water necessary for life. Overnight, bottled water became as precious as gold, and many activities once taken for granted became impossibly expensive luxuries—hot baths; long, cool showers; swimming in a pool or stream; even putting ice in one's cocktail.

What made Grady's stint in the distilling rooms all the more unbearable were the dozen or more suppurating sores on his legs, arms, face, chest, and even on the soles of his feet. Heat only aggravated the itch and the pain.

Along with the distilling operations, the Unitum Imperium had drastically increased the production of hard liquor. To dull the pain, everyone was consuming far more liquor than they ever had. In the entire world, was there a single person who didn't start and end his day with two, three, or four shots of whiskey, vodka, or rum?

At the room's far end, a bell clanged. He dropped the prickly bush, grabbed his bag with his change of clothes and his pistol, and started for the exit. Around him, everyone on his shift also left their posts as the next group descended the steel staircase.

At the top of the stairs, women waited with two shot glasses of water for each worker—paltry wages for two hours of sweating before a fire.

Outside, even the heat of an Iraqi desert was preferable to a stint at the stills. What he needed right now was a cool shower, and forty seconds once a day under cool running water was one perk, at least, to which each member of Davato's staff was entitled.

That's where he was headed now—to the shower mart. Were he not part of the elite, a forty-second shower would set him back two thousand euros. And four minutes under a delicious stream of cool, flowing water? Twelve thousand euros.

At the end of the street, the water distribution line stretched, as usual, around the block. Even now, CSA soldiers were escorting four bloodied men and two battered women in handcuffs toward the prison vans. It happened every time, didn't it? Fights over one's place in line. Arguments over how many bottles this person received versus that one. Almost every day, some fool died when he tried to barge ahead of others in line.

Grady shook his head. It wasn't the people in line who deserved to die. It was the Jews and Christians working for the Enemy. Maybe when Davato and his staff headed back to Jerusalem tomorrow, Grady'd get a chance to help with that.

He smiled. Once in Jerusalem, he'd be excused from his token duty manning the distilleries.

He stepped inside the shower mart entrance, glad for the air-conditioning.

CHAPTER 57
STALKING THE ENEMY

Jerusalem, Israel – July, Year 6

For an hour, Grady had waited in the shadows of a back alley in Old Town, his Ruger Max 9 at his hip. Only yesterday, he'd arrived in Jerusalem with Davato's entourage.

Above, a sallow half-moon bounced an ashen light off the cobbles. In the distance, gunshots echoed. The rebellion never ceased.

For some time, his hate and desire for revenge had been building, fed by the lack of fresh water and the nagging pain and itch of the boils plaguing his body. Tonight, he would fulfill his vow to strike back at the first person he found in league with the Enemy.

He was almost ready to find a new location when footsteps echoed down the dark lane. Dropping a hand to his weapon, he drew a deep breath. From around the corner, a CSA patrol led five prisoners chained together.

Stepping out of the shadows, he held up his ID. "Stop!" he ordered. "Who are these prisoners, and where are you taking them?"

The officer was young, thin, probably in his twenties. At first, his hand went to the pistol at his belt. But after he peered at Grady's badge announcing him as a member of Davato's inner staff, his face registered shock. "Th–these are Jews, sir. We caught them in the act of rebellion. We're taking them to Mish'ol HaGvura Prison."

Grady's glance went down the line of five prisoners and settled on a middle-aged man with a stubbled chin and defiant eyes. "Pull that one out of line. Have him stand over there." He pointed to a spot against the alley wall.

After a moment's hesitation, the lieutenant slipped a key into a chain about the man's waist and released him from the group. Then he shoved the prisoner against the wall.

"Now stand back." Grady waved the lieutenant away.

"What are you doing?" asked the young man.

"I'm following the Imperator's directive to strike back at all those responsible for the demon attacks, the nagging sores, and the water turned to blood."

The lieutenant's mouth opened. He exchanged puzzled glances with the other four members of his patrol. But he did nothing to stop what was about to happen.

Grady yanked the pistol from his belt. He pulled back on the slide and put a bullet in the chamber. He raised the barrel and pointed it at the prisoner's head.

The man's face, formerly filled with defiance, now scrunched with surprise and shock—or was it fear?—and he shook his head, back and forth.

Grady's hand began to tremble. He'd been planning this for some time, and now it was time to carry it out. Only once before had he killed—in the World Casino when the Neanderthal across the table had accused him of cheating. But that was in self-defense. And the man had been ready to shoot him.

This was different. This was an act of revenge. But could he take someone's life in cold blood just because he was a Jew? Was this man really responsible for all that had happened to the earth and to those following Davato?

His finger slipped from the trigger. He returned the pistol to its holster. And he walked away.

CHAPTER 58
TAKEOFF

The Air Force Academy, Colorado Springs – July, Year 6

With each downward plunge, the pump squished fuel as Caleb put his back into it. They only needed four thousand gallons to top off the B-36's tanks. After Amber Bright and Chase Cooper had fixed the malfunctioning engine number 3, Chase said they had enough fuel to get to Israel. But Daniel disagreed. He wanted full tanks. So here they were, still making daily trips to the Air Force Academy north of Colorado Springs, just as they'd done for the last nine months. Today, Andy joined them.

But when Andy laid a hand on Caleb's shoulder and pointed north, Caleb stopped pumping. Daniel had been in the control tower, keeping watch, and now he was running down the apron. Months ago, they'd begun getting a cell signal at the Academy, and they feared there was a new CSA base somewhere nearby. Now with every visit here, they kept watch for threats from the north. If Daniel was running, it wasn't a good sign.

Caleb wiped sweat from his brow as Daniel reached the tug.

"We have to leave. Now!" he said.

"What did you see?" asked Andy.

"About fifty CSA troops heading this way. They'll be here within minutes."

Caleb yanked the hose from the larger tank. As Daniel and Andy found seats up front, he twisted the caps back on the milk cans. Daniel started the engine, and they drove off, pulling the cart behind them. But a few yards later, Daniel stopped and released the cart. "We won't have time to empty these, and the cart will only slow us up."

By the time they reached US 25 and turned south, the CSA army was only a quarter mile north and within view.

"They've seen us!" Andy stared back.

"They're on foot, but the tug is faster." Daniel pressed the accelerator to the floor, but they were already doing the vehicle's top speed of twenty miles per hour. "This changes everything. We'll have to take off today."

Caleb turned a worried look his way. "Are we ready for that?"

"Everyone's living at the hangar. Number 3 is working now. We've been practicing preflights. And Chase says we have enough fuel. I wanted full tanks, just in case, but we'll have to go with what we have. We can't fight fifty armed soldiers of the Unitum Imperium."

Caleb swallowed. In a few minutes, the squaddies would be out of sight. But seeing the cart back there loaded with fuel, the enemy would guess that the tug's destination was Peterson Space Force Base. Someone would know their vehicle was an airplane tug heading for an airfield. And they would surely take the same route around the blast zone and follow them.

It would be a race against time—

Before the enemy found the hangar.

Before they loaded everything they needed into the plane.

And before they completed the complicated steps needed to get the B-36 off the ground.

* * *

AFTER CALEB, ANDY, AND DANIEL stopped the tug outside the hangar, Daniel informed everyone of the approaching threat. He concluded with this warning: "We need to take off—now!"

All agreed, and Chase started the motors that slowly cranked open the massive hangar bay doors. He backed up the pushback tug to the B-36 and hooked it to the plane. Then everyone began loading the gear and food they'd prepared into the access hatch beneath the front landing wheel.

Brianna carried Nika up the steel ladder. Caleb, Tanya, and Andy, wearing their backpacks, followed.

Occupying the top level of the flight deck were the two pilots, Daniel and Lena, and the two engineers, Chase and Amber. Below on the lower deck and facing forward were seats for six more—Caleb, Tanya, Brianna, and Andy took four of these. Robert would man the radar, and he took a fifth seat. Andy was trained to run the two front cannons, but everyone hoped that would not be necessary. Sam disappeared into the tunnel connecting the flight deck to the aft crew quarters. He would man one of the tail guns. In flight, the tunnel was pressurized. To go aft, you laid on a cart on your back, pulling yourself along a track with a rope.

After everyone boarded, Chase started the tug and pulled the plane out of the hangar onto the apron. He parked the vehicle out of the way. Then he climbed into the forward hatch and locked the door. Once on the top level, he took his seat at the engineer's station beside Lena, facing toward the back of the plane.

Caleb had always marveled at the complicated bank of engineering dials, levers, and knobs. How could anyone manage it all?

Then Daniel began pressurizing the plane, and Caleb's ears popped.

Everyone now donned headphones, and Daniel spoke through his mike. "We've been practicing preflight checks, and to do this right, we should do one today before takeoff. This baby is way too complicated. Anything could go wrong."

Daniel gave instructions to his engineers, and the six reciprocating engines began to turn, one after another. Amber and Chase, taking the role of in-flight engineers, reported that each engine had sufficient power for takeoff.

"Finish the preflight checks," Daniel ordered, and the mechanics began rattling off the aircraft's systems, one by one. To Caleb's relief, everything was okay.

But then Lena startled everyone with the words they feared to hear. "Look north. They're on the apron."

Caleb peered through the windows. A mob of green-and-white uniformed soldiers were running down the row of hangars, heading for the plane.

"We haven't finished our preflight," said Amber. "We're not ready."

"Doesn't matter." Daniel's voice crackled through the headphones. "We've got to go. Now!"

Daniel gave the order, the engineers throttled the engines, and they increased in pitch. The plane crept across the apron onto the parallel runway. At the end, the aircraft made a U-turn onto the takeoff runway. The fuselage rattled, and the engines increased in pitch as they struggled against the brakes. Months earlier, to reduce complexity, they'd decided not to use the jet engines on takeoff. "We won't be carrying a bomb load," Chase had said. "So we don't need the extra horsepower."

Out the window, the enemy army was running on a course to intersect them.

The engineers released the brakes. The plane lunged forward.

"Number 2 engine is sick," came Daniel's voice over the headphones. "Idle it."

"Can we still take off?" asked Caleb.

"Cross your fingers," came Chase's worried voice.

The cabin vibrated. They ate up tarmac. Caleb prayed they could leave the ground and enemy fire wouldn't hit the plane.

As the grass in the median flew by on the right, they passed the CSA and the flash of rifle and machine-gun fire on the left.

The end of the runway approached.

Beside him, Brianna gripped her seat and clutched Nika to her chest. Caleb patted her knee and smiled. But terror widened her eyes, and Nika was shivering. Brianna had never been in a plane, had she? How strange this must be for her!

Even for Caleb, to be in the air again after six years of living such a primitive lifestyle in the wild brought memories flooding back of a world gone forever.

The front wheels left the ground, then the back wheels. Then they were in the air and climbing.

"I'm feathering number 2," said Daniel. "We'll have to reach Israel with only five engines."

"Engine 5 is smoking," said Amber. "They must have hit it."

"Feather it," ordered Daniel. "Correction: We're going to Israel with only four engines."

"Is that possible?" Caleb asked again through his mike.

"Yes." Daniel's voice crackled through the headphones. "I think."

The landing gear clanked into the fuselage, and they climbed higher yet.

"Our cruising altitude will be twenty-five thousand feet," said Lena. "You folks on the lower deck can either sit where you are or go back to the crew quarters. Everyone but Andy and Robert. That's where the head is, but it's just as cramped back there as it is up here, and you'll have a better view where you are."

Tanya laid a hand on his shoulder and nodded. They'd stay where they were.

Caleb asked, and Daniel informed them that the flight to Israel would take twenty-two hours.

Beside him, Brianna quickly got over her initial panic. She leaned forward and stared at the ground. "Everything's so small," came her awestruck voice over the mike. "The houses, the trees, even the hills."

"We used to fly across the country all the time," he said. "What do you think of your first time in the air?"

"Awesome!"

At her feet, Nika curled into a ball.

Soon, they climbed above the cloud ceiling. They'd worked hard to get in the air, and they'd done it. But could they reach their destination with only four engines?

CHAPTER 59
THE TWO WITNESSES

Revelation 11:7–10 (NLT): *When they complete their testimony, the beast that comes up out of the bottomless pit will declare war against them, and he will conquer them and kill them. And their bodies will lie in the main street of Jerusalem, the city that is figuratively called "Sodom" and "Egypt," the city where their Lord was crucified. And for three and a half days, all peoples, tribes, languages, and nations will stare at their bodies. No one will be allowed to bury them. All the people who belong to this world will gloat over them and give presents to each other to celebrate the death of the two prophets who had tormented them.*

Jerusalem, Israel – July, Year 6

It was midmorning when Grady followed the others—nearly all of Davato's staff—down the Clal Center elevators to the four waiting buses, their engines purring. Accompanying the buses were tanks and armored personnel carriers filled with troops.

Before they left, Davato had hinted that something special would happen today but wouldn't say what. What was he up to?

After the short trip to Old Town, Grady left the carrier reserved for the inner staff. The ministers, ambassadors, and workers who'd recently flown from New Babylon filed out of the other buses.

At the bottom of the steps leading up to the square, Davato met him and laid a hand on his shoulder. "I've heard reports of your nighttime activities, Grady, and I am well pleased. You hold the Jews and Christians responsible for what's been happening to us, don't you?"

Startled that the Imperator knew of his attempt to shoot a Jew, he nodded.

"You are a valued member of my staff, and today, I am giving you an opportunity to prove your loyalty to me." Davato narrowed his eyes. "Do not let me down."

"I will never let you down, my lord."

"See that you don't."

At the top of the steps, the square was unusually full. Normally, it held only a sparse crowd, especially with the ever-present, annoying pronouncements from the Two Witnesses. But as the two walked, the giant monitors high on every corner of the square had zeroed in on Davato and Grady, and his mouth opened in surprise.

"I have gathered this crowd for today's event." Davato was smiling. "It's also being broadcast across the world. And, Grady?"

"Yes?" He faced the Imperator.

"This is an event in which you will play the biggest role."

His heart beat faster now, for he couldn't imagine what the Imperator had in mind, why the monitors showed just him and the Imperator, or why there'd be a worldwide broadcast.

"You will understand. Follow me."

Davato led him to the two ancients standing in the center. They were uttering their usual judgments on the world, just as they'd done for the last three and a half years. Normally, the crowds ignored the two old men. But today, the people had formed a circle around them.

"You have followed the beast," shouted the white-haired prophet at the people. "And you will burn in fire for all eternity."

The second ancient rammed his staff onto the cobbles and stared at Davato. "You are the son of Satan, the man of lawlessness. You and all who follow you are doomed."

Davato crossed his arms and shook his head. "Your time is up, you old fools. For today, it is you who are doomed."

The Imperator speared Grady with a chilling stare. "Take the pistol from your belt and shoot the one with the gray beard."

Grady's heart became a wild animal trying to escape his chest, and he shook his head. He'd seen what happened to anyone who threatened these two. Fire shot from their mouths, instantly incinerating any threat.

"I say you will do this." Davato's voice rose, and his eyes darkened. "It will be all right. You won't die today. Now take your weapon and kill these men. Do it!"

Grady slowly removed the Ruger Max 9 from his belt. But what rose up before his eyes was what had happened to the CSA men who had also raised their weapons so many years ago—how fire had come like a flamethrower from the mouths of the two prophets and how those men, also following Davato's orders, had burned with supernatural intensity. Instead of raising his pistol, he began to shake.

"Shoot them. *Now!*" The anger in Davato's voice was a storm greater than the memory of the dead CSA men. "Do it, or it is you who will die here today!"

His arm shaking, Grady pulled back on the slide, put a bullet in the chamber, and raised his arm. Would they strike him now? Would flames now shoot forth from their mouths?

But nothing happened.

He aimed at the gray-bearded prophet's head. And he pulled the trigger.

The shot thundered across the square.

And the man dropped to the cobbles.

His heart beating wildly, Grady couldn't believe he'd done it. They hadn't fought back.

"Now kill the other one!" Davato ordered.

Grady put the white-haired old man in his sights and squeezed the trigger.

This one, too, fell! Both prophets now lay lifeless and unmoving at his feet.

"Congratulations, Grady Wilson." Davato patted him on the back. "You have struck a blow for all of us."

Everywhere around him, the crowd began to clap. Then a great cheer arose. People rushed forward, lifted him onto their shoulders, and paraded him around the square. For half an hour, they cheered, carried him high, and, when they learned his name, shouted it out in praise.

Finally, they set him down beside Davato, still standing over Grady's victims.

"Let's bury them," came a man's voice from the back.

"No, let's burn them," said a woman. "Just like they burned the others."

"No!" said Davato. "We will leave them here in the square. We'll put a rope around them and watch them rot. This day, Grady Wilson, my personal secretary, has struck a mighty blow against the Enemy, and I want all the world to see them rot." He raised his arms high. "Let all the world rejoice!"

The crowd responded with more cheers, praise for Grady, and joyous clapping.

CHAPTER 60
FLIGHT OF THE B-36

Approaching Israel from the Sea – July, Year 6

Once in the air, the B-36's four reciprocating engines sent a steady hum and vibration through the cabin. Caleb and his companions took turns using the chute to visit the aft crew quarters where they could sleep in the six bunk beds. And wherever Brianna went, Nika went too. After their naps, everyone returned to their seats on the lower front flight deck. Nowhere was comfortable, but at least getting up and moving about stretched their legs.

Over the Atlantic, the clouds dissipated, and they stared down at the strange violet sea. Nothing was right anymore, and the blood-red ocean only drove home how much the world had changed for the worse.

After a long day, they crossed the crimson Mediterranean, and Daniel began their descent into Israel.

Robert operated the radar up front, but when they were a half hour from their destination, Amber left her engineer's post and replaced him on the radar. Robert then joined Sam aft to man the second tail gun. And Andy moved to a seat before the two front cannons on which he'd been trained. But everyone hoped that their gunners wouldn't be needed.

When they came within range of a Unitum Imperium cell tower, Caleb called Chelsea to tell her they'd be landing soon. But then she relayed some bad news. "We lost our guide, Menachem."

"What do you mean?"

"A few days ago, he left us, saying he was going to check out some other safe houses. He hoped to find someone who could show us the way to the Refuge. But he never came back."

"So you're on your own?"

"It appears that way."

She gave him directions on where to meet her outside Jerusalem when they got that far. She would then lead them on foot to the safe house. Before they hung up, she also promised she had a surprise waiting for them.

The coast appeared below, and Tanya gripped Caleb's hand and scrunched her brows. This was the most dangerous part of the journey.

Months ago, when Caleb had informed Daniel they couldn't land at any official airport and that a highway was their best bet, Daniel had thrown his hands in the air. "Madness!" he'd said. "Utter madness!"

"What other choice do we have?" Chase had asked.

Then Daniel had delved into the hangar's extensive library of maps, researching Israeli geography. He came up with a plan to land in an open field beside part of the Israeli National Trail paralleling Highway 1, about halfway between Tel Aviv and Jerusalem.

But when they were on their approach path for landing, Amber gave a warning from the radar station. "Behind us—two bogies at ten o'clock!"

"I see them." From his position aft, Sam's voice crackled over the intercom. "Two Unitum Imperium jets."

After a period of silence, punctuated by Caleb's thumping heart, Daniel reported that he'd received a stern warning over the radio to land at Ben Gurion Airport in Tel Aviv or be shot down.

"What did you tell him?" asked Andy.

"Nothing," said Daniel. "Tail gunners, take them out!"

The sound of the cannons roared even above the engine noise.

Caleb stiffened. How could they land with enemy jets on their tail?

"Two missiles released!" came Amber's tense voice.

"Jamming and releasing chaff," said Chase over the mike. Earlier, he'd explained to Caleb that, besides the chaff to confuse the missiles, the plane was equipped with a highly sophisticated jamming signal.

Beside Caleb, Tanya grabbed his right knee and squeezed.

"Both missiles destroyed!" said Amber.

"Tail gunners, keep firing!" ordered Daniel.

The booming of the cannons thundered again.

"Cross off one UI jet!" came Robert's excited voice over the intercom.

Below, the Israeli countryside loomed closer. The plane dropped, and its nose rose. The ground was only two hundred feet beneath them now, and the landing gear clanked out of the wings.

"Another missile released," announced Amber.

"Release chaff!" said Daniel.

"It's stuck," came Chase's frantic reply. "Not releasing."

Caleb pushed back against the seat and gripped the chair arms. Would the missile take them out before they landed?

"Chaff finally released," said Chase. But the words barely left his mouth when the plane shook with the sound of an explosion.

Yet they were still flying.

"Engine 1 is on fire, trailing heavy smoke," said Chase. "Only three props left."

The plane tilted left, but Daniel righted it. "Doesn't matter," said Daniel. "Brace yourselves. We're landing."

A quarter mile ahead, a grove of trees was approaching—not good!

The back wheels slammed into the dirt. The plane bounced, rose into the air, then rocked down again. The front wheels rammed the ground. The aircraft shimmied and vibrated over the uneven ground.

They were going too fast.

The brakes screeched. The B-36 shook and rattled. But the plane was slowing.

A grove of maples raced toward them. Caleb gripped Tanya's hands as the nose passed between two trunks. A sickening crunch of metal, and both wings sheared off. Then the nose lurched down, and he was jerked forward against the seat belt. They were plowing up the ground, throwing up dirt. Had the front wheel broken off?

The fuselage kept going. Toward a clearing ahead.

Then they slid to a stop.

But the bottom door was now blocked, forcing them to use the narrower escape hatch beside the flight deck. Amber opened it and let down a rope ladder. "Everyone, out!" She threw her backpack out the hole first then descended.

From inside the fuselage came the roar of crackling flames. Fire was racing through the midsection.

Caleb, Tanya, Brianna, and Andy threw their backpacks out after Amber's. Caleb helped Tanya step onto the ladder. Brianna was next, dropping Nika out the hole into Tanya's waiting arms before she followed. Andy descended and then Caleb.

As Caleb's feet touched the ground, Daniel began his descent but stopped to shout back inside the cabin. "What are y'all doing? Get out!"

"Go on." Lena called back. "My pack is in the sextant stowage. Chase is still looking for his."

Once on the ground, Caleb fixed his glance on the fuselage. Flames surrounded the ragged stubs of wings, the entire tail section, and, behind the aircraft, most of the maple trees.

Daniel reached the ground then shouted back toward the hole. "Forget your packs! The plane is on fire."

Two backpacks flew out the escape hatch and hit the ground.

"Go!" came Chase's muffled voice. "We're coming."

Lena's feet touched the top rung of the rope ladder.

"Run!" Amber was already breaking into a sprint. "It could blow at any moment."

Caleb whirled away from the plane and followed.

Behind Caleb, Daniel's feet pounded the earth.

They'd gone barely ten yards when the explosion hit.

A blast of air knocked Caleb forward. Shards of metal and glass ripped into the earth. He stopped his fall with his hands. For long seconds, he lay on his stomach, head spinning, ears roaring. Finally, he rose and turned back.

Flames and smoke engulfed the plane's nose and fuselage and the trees on all sides. Barely visible beyond a wall of fire, Lena's unmoving body lay on the ground.

"No, no, no!" Amber cupped both hands over her mouth. "Sam, Robert, Chase, Lena—they're gone!"

"Lena, my Lena!" Daniel took a few steps toward the blazing inferno, stopped, tried to go further, then backed up. He gripped his head. "She's . . . gone."

"I am so sorry." Tanya returned and laid a hand on his shoulder. "You were close, weren't you?"

Daniel wiped tears from his eyes and nodded.

The heat was so intense it forced them to back up another thirty yards.

Amber turned to Daniel and hugged him. Tears ran down both their cheeks.

For long minutes, Caleb and the survivors stared at the raging inferno consuming the B-36 and the forest.

A jet screamed overhead, interrupting their mourning.

"Those are UI jets," said Andy. "We need to get out of here."

Amber broke from her embrace of Daniel, wiped tears from her eyes, and nodded.

"What's next?" asked Andy.

As the jets circled back, Caleb glanced ahead through the forest. "Chelsea said we should find an abandoned car in some village away from the highway and drive to the GPS coordinates she gave me."

"Then let's go!" Andy waved them on. "The CSA will soon be swarming all over this place."

But when Daniel didn't want to leave, Amber took an arm, whispered to him, and led him away.

CHAPTER 61
REUNION

Caleb's group, now numbering six, slunk from tree to tree as they left the crash site with the burning plane and the UI jets screaming overhead. They traveled through a forest of wilting Syrian maples, heading away from the main highway. An hour later, they entered a village. After the demon attacks, every street held abandoned vehicles, and on a back lane, Amber found an Opal Vivaro van with a quarter tank of fuel that she could wire.

After she started it, they piled into the vehicle, and Caleb drove.

In the third row in back, Amber tried to console a devastated Daniel. "There was nothing anyone could do," she said. "They should have left their packs."

"Still, she's gone. Chase is gone. They're all gone." Daniel's voice was drained of his usual aura of command. "We were going to get married one day."

"I'm sorry," said Tanya, sitting beside him.

They drove from the village back to Highway 1 and followed it east to the location where Chelsea said they should park. Leaving the van, they trekked down a slope into a valley through a small forest to the GPS coordinates she'd given him—a rock pile surrounded by terebinth trees. It had taken three hours to reach the rendezvous point, and the midafternoon shadows of the ten-meter-tall terebinths crept across the clearing.

"Are you sure this is the place?" asked Tanya. "She's not here."

"Look there." Caleb pointed. "Someone's hiking along the slope."

Indeed, as a woman neared, his heart sped up, and a smile broadened his lips. It was Chelsea, and she raced into his arms.

When they separated, tears ran down her cheeks. "It's been so long. So much has happened. I can't believe you're here."

He pulled her close again and kissed her wet face. "It's a miracle, isn't it? Everything that had to happen for us to meet again."

"It *was* a miracle." She eased away then hugged Tanya. "It's so good to see you, Tanya. And Nika. You brought Nika!" She bent down to pet the dog whose wagging tail thumped against Tanya's leg.

"We could never leave Nika," added Brianna.

Then Caleb introduced Chelsea to Brianna, Andy, Daniel, and Amber.

"What happened to the others?" Chelsea glanced around the clearing.

When Caleb explained what happened, she expressed her sympathy. "It seems we've all lost folks dear to us. We're still mourning René's death." She glanced at the sky. "In a few minutes, it will be dark, safe enough to lead such a big group into the city. But have you heard what happened three days ago in Temple Square?"

"No, what?" asked Caleb.

"Someone killed the Two Witnesses in front of a large crowd. They broadcast it worldwide, and I saw the whole thing. The thing is, I know the man who shot them."

"You do?" asked Tanya.

"It was Grady Wilson, the former ambassador from the Province of North America, the man who took my place as personal secretary to Davato. I worked with him."

"You're kidding!" Caleb's jaw opened.

"I wish I were." Her face scrunched in a frown. "He's not the same person he was. The longer you walk with Davato, the deeper you fall."

"It's the same with Father, isn't it?"

"Unfortunately, yes."

A few minutes later, she guided them along the slope in the dark then up to an opening in the wall where they entered a Jerusalem side street.

From there, she led them through shadowy alleys and across deserted main streets until they stood before a house missing three of its four walls.

"This is where you're hiding?" asked Andy. "In ruins?"

"It looks like ruins, doesn't it?" she said. "Christians used to gather here before the CSA took them away. Now follow me."

Before descending stone steps, Caleb caught a whiff of burning rubber but decided to ask about that later. The stairs led to a door and a large carpeted room lined with stuffed pillows.

Dylan rose from a pillow, ran to Caleb and Tanya, and embraced them. "We're all together again. This is wonderful!"

At the room's far end, two tables held six chairs each.

As Pasqual rose from his seat, Chelsea introduced everybody, and they shook hands.

"What a happy day!" Margot descended steps from a door beyond the tables and embraced Caleb. When they parted, she said to everyone, "We've been waiting for this for so long, so when we heard you were on your way, we decided to throw a feast to celebrate."

"For some time," added Chelsea, "we've been stockpiling water and food, but for a celebration feast, we needed something special. When I saw the text that you were on your way, we began cooking some ribs we'd been saving. We are still hooked to the electric grid and have a refrigerator. We also found some Texas barbecue sauce on the black market. The Israelis didn't know what to do with it. It's old but still good."

"And," added Margot with a smile, "we've made potato latkes, spicy shakshuka, and for dessert, jelly-filled sufganiyot."

"My mouth is already watering." Brianna clapped. "When do we eat?"

"Not for another three hours, at least." Chelsea waved to the newcomers. "Now let me show you our kitchen."

They followed her up steps and through another door. They passed through a storage room burdened with rows of food boxes and twenty-liter plastic water bottles. This led to a second level with an outside kitchen and a fire-burning stove. Rafters supported a ceiling of flat stones covering half the room. They'd left piles of rubble at the exposed end for camouflage.

"From above"—Chelsea pointed—"our kitchen looks like a crater with rubble and no way in or out. If you smelled burning rubber when you came in, that's from the fire up there. We burn it to mask the smell of meat when we're cooking. But the ribs have much longer to cook, so let's go back inside, take a glass of wine, and catch up on everything since we parted."

Sitting at one table, Chelsea, Dylan, Caleb, Margot, Tanya, and Brianna gathered, while, at the far end of the room, the other four became acquainted.

After all that had happened, Caleb couldn't imagine anything that could bring him down from the heights of joy now threatening to carry him up into the clouds.

CHAPTER 62
RESURRECTION!

Revelation 11:11–13 (NLT): *But after three and a half days, God breathed life into them, and they stood up! Terror struck all who were staring at them. Then a loud voice from heaven called to the two prophets, "Come up here!" And they rose to heaven in a cloud as their enemies watched. At the same time there was a terrible earthquake that destroyed a tenth of the city. Seven thousand people died in that earthquake, and everyone else was terrified and gave glory to the God of heaven.*

Jerusalem, Israel – July, Year 6

Floodlights illuminated the square as Grady's feet clopped over the cobbles. As he'd done for the last three days, he'd come again to gloat over what was turning out to be his life's greatest accomplishment. After killing the two prophets, he'd been feted, celebrated, and cheered wherever he went. Even now, a middle-aged man he didn't know called out his name and shouted congratulations.

Every hour, television screens all over the world flashed his name and picture and replayed the video of him shooting the two men who'd been such a thorn in everyone's side. Davato had publicly congratulated him, and Adam Turner had sent a case of whiskey to his room in the Clal Center.

Looking back on it, Grady marveled that he, above all others, had been destined to kill the two men. Now, whenever he entered a bar for yet another round of whiskey to dull the incessant pain from the boils, people he didn't know stood, clapped, and pounded him on the back.

If it weren't for the sores covering his torso, arms, legs, feet, and forehead, he could have had any woman in any bar in Jerusalem. But, of course, the women all suffered the same fate as he, and these days, no one was interested in sex anymore. What people needed now was brandy, vodka, whiskey, fentanyl, or heroin. Anything to dull the constant, nagging pain of the ever-present, oozing sores.

As he approached the ropes around the bodies, he smiled for the cameras broadcasting the progress of the rotting corpses. In years past, he might have thought this scene gruesome and barbaric. But now, after all these men had put the world through—it seemed only just.

A small crowd gawked at the results of his work, and he walked toward them. He tried to slow his pace so as not to appear he was strutting.

"Congratulations, Grady Wilson!" If it weren't for the sores on both cheeks, the young woman stretching out a hand to him would have been beautiful. "How can we ever thank you?"

"It's nothing, really." He smiled. Before the sores, he would have asked her back to his room this minute. "But thank you."

"We cannot thank you enough," said a nonbinary of indeterminate sex. She or he patted him on the back, and Grady winced. For the arm had landed on a particularly painful sore.

"No need, really. I—"

The onlookers surrounding the moldering corpses gasped and jumped away from the ropes.

Grady ripped his glance toward what startled them.

The Two Witnesses were moving.

It was impossible. This couldn't be happening.

But both men were standing up. They were whole and alive again!

The white-haired old man and the gray-bearded prophet were now glancing around the square. They picked up the staffs at their feet.

Grady's heart tried to escape his chest. He staggered, not believing what was happening. Such things just couldn't be.

Then a voice thundered down onto the square from above, a sound like roaring waterfalls that vibrated in his chest. "Come up here!" it commanded.

Grady snapped his gaze to the heavens where a cloud of glowing, churning light had gathered. Fingers of blazing light reached down and engulfed the two men. Slowly, they rose into the sky. The cloud followed and was gone.

Then the ground began to shake.

The earth heaved. It threw Grady off his feet, onto his knees. He grasped at the cobbles but found no purchase. He was in the air. Then his knees rammed the cobbles, and he cried out in pain.

All around him, the city groaned with a deep, primeval moan. Stones from the Temple tumbled and fell, crushing bystanders nearest the Temple walls. Cracks opened in the square and closed again.

From the city beyond came the sound of crashing stones and falling walls.

And when it was over, he glanced aside to find the Imperator racing across the square toward him, cursing the Enemy and vowing revenge.

CHAPTER 63
A DEADLY VOW

Zechariah 13:8–9 (HCSB): *"In the whole land—this is the LORD's declaration—two-thirds will be cut off and die, but a third will be left in it. I will put this third through the fire; I will refine them as silver is refined and test them as gold is tested. They will call on My name, and I will answer them. I will say: They are My people, and they will say: Yahweh is our God."*

Jerusalem, Israel – July, Year 6

Davato was fortunate that he and his staff had been in Temple Square when the quake hit. After he returned to the Clal Center, he found the building demolished. Bystanders had reported that the roof collapsed first then floor after floor pancaked down on top of the floors below. When the dust and smoke cleared, all that was left of the center was broken bricks, dust, and twisted steel.

Reports came in of thousands dead. At least a tenth of the city had been destroyed.

But he had prepared for this. He'd read the Enemy's book, and though he didn't believe all of it, he was ready for most eventualities. He'd already stocked what he needed in nearby Sacher Park, only three kilometers away.

Within ninety minutes, his people had erected a command tent. It had no electricity, computers, or communications, of course. But workers were erecting a separate room with a cot where he would sleep tonight. Others were preparing food and drink. Already, they'd set up a conference table, chairs, and candles in the tent's main room. That was enough to gather whom he needed to plot his revenge.

Around the table sat Grady Wilson, his personal secretary; Sebastien Rey, heading the Ministry of Virtue; Adam Turner, heading the Ministry of Truth; and General Hofmann, heading the Ministry of Peace. Open sores marred the exposed skin of each, belying Davato's claim to divinity.

He'd seen the reports on what the people whispered when they thought no one was listening: "Why doesn't the Imperator stop this agony? The sores affect even him, don't they? If he's a god, why didn't he stop the demon attacks, the earthquakes, and the seas and rivers turning to blood?"

Lately, he fought a constant state of rage. Reports like that and the attacks of the Enemy like what had just happened in Temple Square fueled his anger. But there was still time to prevail. Nothing written in the Enemy's book was preordained.

Today, General Hofmann would be the target of his ire. But he would start with Adam Turner, someone, at least, who'd brought good news. "Turner, you have done well by capturing the leader of the black-market operation here in Israel. At least someone is doing their job. Not only that, the man has told us where the Jews and Christians are hiding."

"It was his accomplice who broke, my lord. We are holding both men with the other rebel leaders."

Davato smiled. "Excellent. But we'll go after their hideout later."

Then he faced General Hofmann, his eyes narrowed to slits, and his jaw muscles tensed. "Before we deal with their so-called Refuge, we must deal with these rebels. General, I hold you responsible for what's happening in the streets of this country. You let it fester. You should have crushed this opposition long ago."

Hofmann's eyes sought the tabletop. "I'm sorry, my lord. I had confidence in my troops, but I only arrived here two weeks ago, and I—"

"That is no excuse." Davato's fist pounded the tabletop. "Months ago, we had reports of this rebellion. Why wasn't it crushed in its infancy?"

"I–I'm sorry. Everyone has been distracted by what's been going on with the water, the nagging sores, and the—"

"Enough! In spite of the difficulties, we have work to do." His gaze drilled into the general. "Since you can't seem to handle the situation, I will now give you my plan to quell this rebellion and strike back against the Enemy."

His gaze swept the table, and every face wilted before him.

"We will start with Jerusalem. If we cut off the head and crush it, the rest will fall afterward. We will fly in thirty thousand troops and erect an ironclad cordon around the city. That will take time, but once it's in place, we'll allow no one in or out of the city without new, secure passes. Then we'll crush these rebels in the streets with overwhelming force. If necessary, we'll go house to house and root them out. Then we'll repeat the process for every city where Jews are fighting the Unitum Imperium. That's the first step."

"Excellent, my lord," said Hofmann. "I agree wholeheartedly."

"Of course you do." Davato would not be swayed by the general's tardy agreement. "After we have secured the country, we will begin a plan to exterminate each and every Christian and Jew wherever they're hiding, including an assault on their Refuge. We will wreak our revenge upon the Enemy by destroying every one of his followers."

He raised himself in the chair and slammed both palms down on the table.

"Tomorrow, I am returning to New Babylon. But everyone at this table will remain here and carry out my plan to eliminate every Jew and Christian in the land. But there's one more thing."

He stood then glared down at the men before him.

"If possible, I want you to capture the rebellion's ringleaders and send them to Mish'ol HaGvura Prison. When that prison's cells are bursting with their stinking bodies, we will execute them, one by one, in the public squares. And the first person whose head will roll away from the guillotines before the cameras will be"—he grinned—"Ariel Geller."

CHAPTER 64
A FEAST OF CELEBRATION

Jerusalem, Israel — July, Year 6

When the quake hit, Caleb had been climbing the steps to the kitchen, and it threw him forward onto the stairs. A deep, primordial rumbling rolled beneath him. Would the basement ceiling and walls now collapse and crush everyone? Unnerved and with chills racing down his back, he crawled back into the room.

The hideout swayed back and forth. The ceiling lights flickered. The glasses on the table trembled toward the edge. He tried to head for the outside staircase, but with every step, he found himself on the floor.

When it was over, he glanced around the room. Everyone had come through unharmed.

"It's a miracle!" Amber examined the wall. "There are only a few cracks."

Dylan ran outside. As Tanya put the glasses back where they belonged, he returned down the steps. "Our ruins are just as they were before," he said. "But there are fires in the distance, and more buildings on the street have collapsed. How we came through this without any damage is amazing."

Margot and Chelsea descended the steps from the storage room. "The kitchen is okay." Margot was beaming. "The roof is intact, and the ribs are still cooking."

"It seems God is protecting us," added Pasqual with a smile.

"So we can still hold our feast?" Brianna clapped.

299

"Yes!" Chelsea waved them toward the tables. "We won't let a little earthquake interrupt our feast. The ribs are ready, so everyone take a seat."

As the group found their places, Chelsea, Margot, and Amber brought dishes to the table. Dylan poured wine for anyone who wanted it, water for the rest.

When all were seated, Pasqual prayed. "Lord God, we thank you and praise you. Some of our comrades have fallen, and we know they are with you now. But you saved the rest of us from disaster, and you brought us together from far-flung parts of the earth. So today, we express our gratitude for your mercy, grace, and majesty. We thank you for bringing every one of us together. We thank you for the food we are about to eat, and we ask for your guiding hand as we seek a way to the Refuge. In Jesus's name, we pray."

As Caleb dove into the ribs and the tasty Jewish dishes, he couldn't remember a more satisfying meal. But it wasn't just the food. It was the knowledge that he'd reunited with Dylan, Chelsea, Margot, and the others. Joy swelled his heart, lifting him, and he floated on air. As he sat back and glanced around both tables, he saw smiles, contented faces. The only exceptions were Daniel and Amber. But they sat beside each other, and occasionally, Amber would whisper something to Daniel that elicited a nod or a weak smile.

They ate, they conversed, and they sipped their wine.

At one point, Margot beamed at Caleb and Tanya. "So you two are now married. We never had a chance to congratulate you. So I'm doing it now."

"Thanks." Tanya smiled back at Dylan and Margot. "But you two have been rather close. When will *you* tie the knot?"

Blushing, Margot shot a sideways glance to Dylan.

Before answering, he buried his gaze in the plate then lifted his head. "Someday maybe. When things settle down."

Sitting beside him, Margot laid a hand on his. Then he leaned toward her and planted a kiss on her cheek. That elicited a roomful of cheers, and Caleb grinned.

About halfway through the meal, Dylan stood up and tapped his fork against his glass until he had everyone's attention. "It's been years ago now since René asked Margot and me to join a group of believers fighting against the Antichrist. We followed him to a villa in the south of France where we joined a group calling themselves the Nazarene Friends dedicated to helping Christians and thwarting the Antichrist wherever we could. Much has happened since then. We lost some good friends, including René, and we dwindled to a handful. We added Chelsea, but Pasqual, Margot, and I are all that's left of that original group. Today, I believe I speak for the three of us as we welcome Caleb, Tanya, Andy, Brianna, Daniel, and Amber to the group, for we are now ten." He raised his glass high. "Here's to the new members of the Nazarene Friends!"

Everyone cheered, even Daniel and Amber, and they drank to his toast.

When the meal was over and after more wine was poured, Caleb sat back and faced his siblings. "Now that we're all here, how are we going to get to the Refuge?"

"That's a problem," said Chelsea. "Here's why: A man named Ariel Geller bought my passage on a trawler so I could escape Tel Aviv. He's a good man who has helped many. Weeks ago, he was supposed to meet Menachem and tell us the way to the Refuge. But Ariel never showed up, and he stopped answering his phone. So something must have happened to him." She opened both hands and raised them. "Without Ariel, we have no idea how to find the Refuge."

"So what do we do?" asked Amber. "We hoped you would lead us to this place of safety. Daniel and I had visions that Caleb would lead us here. Caleb, himself, had a vision that led him to us. If this was all divinely inspired, how could we now find ourselves at a dead end?"

"Good question," added Dylan.

"Without question, your visions and Caleb's were divinely inspired." Pasqual glanced around the room. "So our next step must also be of divine origin."

Suddenly, everyone's phones began buzzing with an alarm. Caleb pulled his out and laid it on the table. It was a Unitum Imperium general news flash. "Oh no!"

"What does it say?" asked Margot. "My phone is in my pack."

Before Caleb began to read, their phones began speaking the broadcast out loud:

Attention! As of tonight, the Unitum Imperium announces that the city has been cordoned off. Troops will soon arrive to surround Jerusalem and crush the rebellion. Until the army secures the city, helicopter gunships with infrared sights will patrol a one-hundred-meter border on the outskirts. Anyone entering this new death zone marked by red flags will be machine-gunned on sight. In addition, a curfew has been ordered from nineteen hundred hours until dawn. Anyone caught on the streets violating curfew will be shot on sight. All praise and glory to the Imperator, the Prophet, the Dragon, and the Unitum Imperium!

Andy glanced around the room. "We're trapped."

"Can we get out tonight?" asked Tanya. "Before they mark off this new death zone?"

"Even if we did," said Dylan, "where would we go? We don't know how to get to the Refuge."

"Then what do we do?" Tanya faced Caleb.

In the silence that followed, Pasqual stood up.

"The answer, my friends, is what I was about to say before the broadcast interrupted me." Pulling out his Bible, he flipped to the middle. "Our answer is in Isaiah, chapter thirty, verse eighteen." Then he read: "'Therefore the LORD is waiting to show you mercy, and is rising up to show you compassion, for the LORD is a just God. All who wait patiently for Him are happy.'"

Breaking the silence, helicopter blades whirred overhead before retreating into the distance. When everyone's startled glances returned from the ceiling and the copters had passed, Pasqual sat, and Brianna stood up, taking his place.

All other members of the Nazarene Friends turned in their seats toward her. "I'm the youngest one here." She placed hands on her hips. "And you might not want to hear what I have to say. But it's clear to me what we must do now."

"What's that?" asked Dylan.

"We must wait on the Lord."

Caleb beamed ear to ear. And after she sat, he placed a kiss on her cheek.

AUTHOR'S NOTES

A SPIRITUAL BATTLE IS WAGING AROUND US

The Bible, God's revelation to mankind, declares these truths: The spiritual worlds are real. Heaven and Hell exist. And spiritual beings called angels inhabit those realms. In their rebellion against God, the angels who followed Lucifer were driven out of Heaven. They are now called demons. And Satan has sent those demons to wage war—now, here, today, as you read this—against the people of God.

Believe it. If the God who created the universe declares it to be so, then it is so.

Yes, an unseen spiritual battle is being waged against all who follow Jesus. It's happening every day in our cities and towns. It's happening to me, to you who declare Christ, and to the leaders who control our lives.

This novel's second chapter opens with the following quote from Ephesians 6:12 (HCSB):

> For our battle is not against flesh and blood, but against the rulers, against the authorities, against the world powers of this darkness, against the spiritual forces of evil in the heavens.

Jonathan Cahn, in his book, *The Return of the Gods*, makes a compelling case that when a people abandons God, it leaves a vacuum that does not remain empty. Just as a person can be possessed by evil spirits, so can a nation. When God is banished from the heart of a nation, the "gods" of the ancient world—demons, really—will move in to take his place. And from all appearances, Satan's minions now control the atheistic elites running this country and the world.

In our world today, God has been banished from every aspect of public life. Entire governments and political parties now urgently endorse the killing of the unborn in the womb. They not only promote the idea that a man can become a woman and a woman can become a man, they endorse surgery and drugs to accomplish it—even in children too young to understand the ramifications. Some have even made it unlawful to speak against their insane ideology. In the public schools, they teach gender confusion, sexual immorality, and hatred of our ancestry. The list of their affronts against God and mankind mount daily.

In their zeal to advance their sinful ideologies, they have become enemies of God.

They are begging for both earthly and eternal judgment. Surely, God will soon accommodate their request.

It's all preparing the world for a coming Tribulation and the rule of the man of lawlessness.

Some want to ignore the signs, plug their ears, and turn their eyes from what is happening. That's understandable. If we are to keep our eyes on Jesus, how are we to dwell on all that is good, right, and worthy?

On the other hand, who then will be the watchmen on the wall, warning others of the approaching danger? Who will point to what they call good and declare, instead, that the God of the universe calls it evil? And if the unredeemed are not warned and invited into God's kingdom, what then will be their fate?

The apostle John tells us that love is inextricably bound with truth. One cannot love one's neighbors, or even one's enemies, without speaking love in truth.

Thus, this author writes of what is to come, of what God has in store for those who have put their faith not in Jesus, the redeemer, but in the twisted, sinful ideologies of the world that will send their followers on the path to eternal destruction.

HOW DO WE PREPARE FOR THE END?

We've said it before, but it bears repeating. The only way to avoid the coming judgment is to repent and turn to the Son whom God sent to save a sinful human race from eternal destruction.

What does it mean to repent?

First, it's to acknowledge one's sins. But far more than that, it means to turn from old ways of thinking by the renewal one's mind, through Christ. It means repudiating the sinful, destructive ideologies of the world for a new way of thinking. It means restructuring one's thoughts, allegiances, and actions by being born again into a new life, one based on biblical truth and grounded thoroughly in Christ.

But don't believe what I have written. Believe the words of the apostle John in verses 3:16–19 (NLT) [emphasis added]:

> For God loved the world so much that he gave his one and only Son, so that everyone who believes in him will not perish but have eternal life. God sent his Son into the world not to judge the world, but to save the world through him. There is no judgment against anyone who believes in him. But anyone who does not believe in him has already been judged for not believing in God's one and only Son. And the judgment is based on this fact: God's light came into the world, *but people loved the darkness more than the light, for their actions were evil.*

That is how we prepare for the end, whether it comes through God's judgment on the entire planet through the Tribulation. Or through the natural course of life and death destined for every person ever born on earth.

NEWSLETTER INVITATION #2

Subscribe to Mark's Newsletter.

Keep abreast of new releases & book news.

The shadow of the Tribulation already darkens our world. Know what's to come, stay true to the faith, and seek refuge in Christ.

Subscribe to Mark's newsletter and receive two free gifts:

1. 10 Reasons Why the End Times Could Come Tomorrow.
2. How the Green Agenda Prepares the Way for Earth Worship and the Antichrist.

Go to: www.MarkFisherAuthor.com/newsletter

SCRIPTURE REFERENCES

* Preface:
    - Woe to those who say evil is good and good is evil. Isaiah 5:18 &20 (NLT)
    - Jesus's warning about the signs of the end: Matthew 24:6–8 (HCSB)
    - Paul's description of the Rapture: 1 Thessalonians 4:16–18 (NLT)
    - A warning for those who don't warn of the coming danger: Ezekiel 33:6 (HCSB)
    - Jesus warns of the Tribulation and promises that believers will escape it: Matthew 24:21–22 (HCSB)
* Chapter 1: Daniel's description of the Tribulation: Daniel 12:1b (HCSB)
* Chapter 2: Paul warns we are in a spiritual battle against demonic forces: Ephesians 6:12 (HCSB)
* Chapter 3: A description of Babylon, the great prostitute: Revelation: 17:3b–6 (NLT)
* Chapter 5: A description of the earth after the trumpet judgments: Joel 2:10–11 (HCSB)
* Chapter 6: Jesus's warning that the world will hate his followers: John 15:18 (NLT)
* Chapter 8: Another description of the earth after God's judgment: Ezekiel 32:7–8 (HCSB)
* Chapter 10: A promise that in the end times, some will see

visions: Joel 2:28–31 (NLT)

* Chapter 12: Another description of the earth after God's judgments: Joel 2:1b–2a (NLT)

* Chapter 14: A prophecy of the Antichrist and the ten kingdoms he will create: Daniel 7:23–25a (NLT)

* Chapter 17:
    – Announcing the fifth trumpet and the demons with scorpion tails: Revelation 91–2 (NLT)
    – God threw the rebellious angels, now demons, into the bottomless pit: 2 Peter 2:4 (NLT)

* Chapter 18: The scorpion demons would torture their victims for five months: Revelation 9:4–5 (NLT)

* Chapter 22: In the Tribulation, the enemies of God cannot flee Amos 18b–19 (HCSB)

* Chapter 25: Unbelievers trying to escape the scorpion demons would seek death but not find it: Revelation 9:5–6 (HCSB)

* Chapter 28: A warning not to take part in Babylon's sins: Revelation 18:4b–5 (NLT)

* Chapter 30: A warning for those who take the mark of the beast: Revelation 14:9b–10a (NLT)

* Chapter 31: Announcing the sixth trumpet and the horseback demons who kill: Revelation 9:13–16 (NLT)

* Chapter 35: A prophecy that the Antichrist will blaspheme God and rule over the earth: Revelation 13:6–8 (HCSB)

* Chapter 38: For those who say evil is good and good is evil, woe awaits, and the corpses of his people will litter the streets. Isaiah 5:20–21, 24, 25b (NLT)

* Chapter 44:
    – Announcing the seventh trumpet, and the coming of Christ's reign on earth: Revelation 11:15 (NLT)
    –Seven angels carry the seven bowl judgments as the saints from the Tribulation sing a song before God: Revelation 15:1–3a (HCSB)

* Chapter 45: Announcing the first bowl judgment—severely

painful sores on those who accepted the mark: Revelation 16:1–2 (HCSB)

* Chapter 47: In the Tribulation, the Lord will be a refuge for new believers: Joel 3:15–16 (NLT)

* Chapter 48: There is a generation that will curse father, mother, and the family: Proverbs 30:11–15 (HCSB)

* Chapter 50:
    – Announcing the second bowl judgment—the sea turns to blood: Revelation 16:3 (HCSB)

    –The Two Witnesses have the power to turn water to blood: Revelation 11:3, 6b (HCSB)

* Chapter 55: The sign of Israel giving birth to the Messiah: Revelation 12:1–2 (HCSB)

* Chapter 56: Announcing the third bowl judgment—the springs and rivers turn to blood: Revelation 16:4–7 (HCSB)

* Chapter 59: After 1,260 days, God will allow the Two Witnesses to be killed. Their bodies will rot for three-and-one-half days: Revelation 11:7–10 (NLT)

* Chapter 62: After three and a half days, the Two Witnesses will be resurrected and taken up to Heaven: Revelation 11:11–13 (NLT)

* Chapter 63: Two-thirds of Jews will die in the Tribulation: Zechariah 13:8–9 (HCSB)

* Chapter 64: Blessed are those who wait upon the Lord: Isaiah 30:18 (HCSB)

* Author's Notes: God's promise of salvation for those who believe in Jesus, and a promise of judgment for those who reject him: John 3:16–19 (NLT)

Mark's Books

Christian Historical Fiction:
* Book 1: The Bonfires of Beltane: Following St. Patrick Across Ancient, Celtic Ireland
* Book 2: The Medallion: An Epic Quest in A.D. 486
* The Slaves of Autumn: A Tale of Stolen Love in Ancient, Celtic Ireland (A standalone book)

General Market Historical Fiction:
* Death of the Master Builder: Love, Envy, and the Struggle to Raise the Greatest Cathedral of the Italian Renaissance

Days of the Apocalypse—A Bestselling Series of Christian End-Times Thrillers:
* Book 1: The Day the End Began
* Book 2: Days of War and Famine
* Book 3: Days of Trial and Tribulation
* Book 4: Days of Death and Darkness
* Book 5: Last Days of the End (April 2024)
* Book 6: Days of the Millennium (October 2024)

The Scepter and Tower Trilogy, an epic fantasy for young adults of all ages:
* The Stolen Scroll, a novella prequel (eBook only)
* Book 1: Quest for the Scepter
* Book 2: Into the Druid's Lair
* Book 3: Return to the Tower

Visit MarkFisherAuthor.com to learn more about Mark's books.

ABOUT THE AUTHOR

Mark E. Fisher wrote his first twelve pages at the age of ten, complete with drawings of a prairie fire, Indians, and a stampede. Since then, he's authored novels of epic fantasy and historical fiction for the Christian and the general market. But his current project is Days of the Apocalypse, a bestselling series of Christian end-times thrillers closely based on the biblical prophecies in the books of Revelation, Matthew, Joel, Ezekiel, Daniel, and others.

At various times, Mark has helped to weld rails for the railroad, inspected glass in a glass factory, given aid checks to welfare clients, and programmed microcode for IBM. He has a bachelor's degree in anthropology/sociology, and Masters' degrees in both computer science and ministry. He once helped plant a church. Once a month, he plays acoustic and electric guitar in the church band. He is also the treasurer for New Gospel Frontiers, a 501(c)(3) organization dedicated to funding missions opportunities for the unreached peoples of Central Asia and Africa.

If not traveling, he's at his desk writing, eating out, or walking his miniature Australian shepherd around the neighborhood. He and his wife enjoy traveling with recent trips to Mexico, Japan, the Dominican Republic, Ireland, France, Italy, and Switzerland.

Made in United States
Orlando, FL
03 October 2023

37539923R00183